Pandora's Gardener

David C Mason

II

Published by Wen-Chang Books
ISBN 978-0-9561805-2-0

Cover design and typesetting by D Charles Mason Photography
www.dcharlesmason.co.uk

III

For
Mum and Dad.

IV

The Titan Prometheus steals the heavenly fire from
Mount Olympus, and brings it down to man.

Zeus looks down upon the Earth, and in revenge pledges to bring
misery upon humanity for the theft of fire. He orders Hephaestus,
the god of smiths and master of crafts, to create the first woman, a
creature so beautiful that she will be irresistible to either god or man.

The Olympian gods endow her with various gifts,
and so she is called Pandora, the "all gifted". Among
these gifts are curiosity, and an intricately carved box
which Pandora is told must never be opened.

Hermes offers Pandora to Epithemus, (brother of Prometheus), to be his wife. Despite the warnings of Prometheus to never
accept anything from the gods, Epithemus is smitten, and marries
Pandora, believing the box to be a wedding gift from Zeus.

Over time, curiosity gets the better of Pandora,
and as she opens the box, all the evils placed within
it by Zeus, sickness, death, turmoil, strife, jealousy,
hatred, famine, escape and spread over the Earth.

The only thing left trapped in the box as
Pandora slams the lid shut is Hope...

VI

Contents

VIII

1 / The Generation Game

The streetlights reflected in the wet pavement and tarmac road, mixing with the oil spills to create a multi-coloured urban scape so beloved of photographers and film directors; distracting from the ruination and neglect of the back streets. Even here, London was wearing its party face.

A lean gentleman, of at least pensionable age, stood tall and erect in the shadows of the derelict municipal swimming baths. He checked his watch again.

It was time.

He adjusted his grip on the briefcase and climbed the steps to the steel shutters that covered the entrance. He rapped on the door with his walking stick; he didn't need it but the deception had stood him in good stead in the past. As it opened, he stooped slightly and a young man in sunglasses with a prominent golden tooth looked him up and down, the gun in his shoulder holster on display.

'Wha' do ya want Grandad?' sneered the golden toothed stooge.

'Good evening. A mutual friend advised that these are the offices of Mr Kingpin. I'm here to make a purchase. I believe I'm here at the appointed time.' He held up the briefcase, inferring that it contained cash.

Goldtooth invited him in with a wave of his gun. 'Face the wall Grandad, arms up and legs spread. Come on, I ain't got all day.'

'There really is no need, but if you must. Could you hold this for me?' asked the old man as he handed over the walking stick. 'That would be most awfully kind.'

Goldtooth dropped it to the floor and waited impatiently while the old man struggled to raise his arms above his head. Tired of waiting he did a cursory search, not believing that this relic could pose any threat, but rules were rules, and one thing Kingpin would not tolerate was people not following his edicts.

'That'll do. Move,' said Goldtooth gesturing at the elegant enamelled arrow to the Turkish bath. 'The boss-man don't like waiting.'

'Would you mind?' asked the old man, pointing at the walking stick. 'It's the arthritis; it's not good in this weather.'

Goldtooth rolled his eyes and shoved the stick into the waiting hand. To emphasise the urgency he pushed his gun into the small of the old man's back, who slowly and deliberately moved forward, maintaining the pretence of frailty.

There had been multiple opportunities for the old man to hurt Goldtooth, but for the moment he would bide his time while he took an inventory of how many thugs there were skulking in this abandoned building. If he could complete the deal without violence that would be preferable, experience had replaced the hot- headed anger of years ago. The jibes about his age were nothing; mere observations by the ignorant of a persona he temporarily wore.

Shuffling along the terrazzo floor, much to the annoyance of Goldtooth, they passed through the changing rooms into the baths themselves. It sounded like they were the only two on the move. They entered what would have been the main steam room, which retained much of its brick sized bevelled tiles, so distinctive of an early twentieth century utilitarian architecture.

In the centre of the room was a table large enough to hold a conference of fifteen people. At its head, an immaculately dressed man with a regal air sat in a lavish chair, surrounded by gold plated electronic devices. His hand rested on a pistol with a diamond-encrusted grip. To this man's left, on a tiled bench tier by the wall, was a rotund ogre, at least twenty stone in weight, devouring a huge double burger and fries. Standing to the right, was a broad thickset bulldog of a man, his neck covered in gold chains.

The old man did a quick tally, Goldtooth, Kingpin, Ogre Man, and Bulldog. Four to one, it could be worse.

'Mr Kingpin?' the old man asked with false innocence.

Kingpin turned his attention to Goldtooth. 'Who's this? I'm expecting some top men any minute now and you go and let this old fart in.'

'But Boss,' Goldtooth protested, 'he's got the money.'

'He's having you on, look at him.   Get back to the door you berk.'

As Goldtooth was leaving, the old man sneezed violently. Taking out his handkerchief, unnoticed he dropped a small twisted paper package onto the floor and placed his foot over it, hiding it between the heel and sole of his shoe.

'Sorry about that,' said the old man, 'terrible trouble with my sinus in this weather. Mr Kingpin, I'm here on behalf of my employer, Mr Jones, who I believe you've had some discussions with.'

'You're Smith? Bleedin' 'ell your lot must be desperate. Come on then, show me the money; otherwise these boys will give you a good kicking for wasting my time.'

The old man slid the briefcase across the table. Kingpin opened it, examined the bundles of notes, closed it and put it on the floor beside his chair.

'Is this what you want?' asked Kingpin. He held up a square plastic case, not much larger than his thumbnail, inside of which was a data storage card. He played with it, moving it between his forefinger and thumb, taunting the old man, who he could tell from his reaction, recognised it, wanted it.

'The briefcase contains the agreed amount, you're welcome to check. If I could take a closer look,' continued the old man, holding his hand out for the card, 'then we can conclude our business and I'll be on my way.'

Kingpin put the card into the top pocket of his jacket.

'There's been a change of plan. I don't give a monkey's what this has on it,' Kingpin said patting his chest, 'but what I do know is that you're not the only one who wants it. The thing is my other buyer is going to pay a lot more if he finds you dead when he gets here.'

'If your other buyers are who I think they are, I would strongly recommend that you take my offer. They're not gentlemen.'

'Smith,' said Kingpin picking up the diamond embellished gun, 'you're priceless, you know that? "Not gentlemen",' he said mocking the old man's accent. 'Business is business, and you've been outbid.'

'You want me to sort him out Boss?' asked Bulldog.

'Yeah, but outside, I just had this floor polished.'

'Last chance,' said the old man.

'Will you take him outside and put him down,' said Kingpin, becoming visibly annoyed that the pensioner hadn't at least pleaded with him to reconsider.

The old man knew exactly where everyone was in the room. Kingpin was at the head of the table; gun in hand, and out of reach. Ogre Man was on the tiled bench, still stuffing his face. With his bulk, he couldn't cover any distance quickly. Assuming he hadn't eaten his gun, he was probably armed. Bulldog was to his right, gun drawn ready to take him outside for the planned execution. If he fought back now, the only casualty he could claim would be Bulldog before the others shot him down. What was needed now was the advantage of the element of surprise.

He stepped back, bringing the sole of his shoe down onto the small twisted package that he had dropped earlier. There was a loud snap as the contents detonated.

As Bulldog looked round, the old man placed the crook of his walking stick over the wrist of Bulldog's gun hand and dropped onto his good knee while holding onto the stick. His weight dragged Bulldog's wrist down onto the top of the table where it collided with a loud crack, forcing him to drop his weapon.

A gunshot went past the old man's head, the act of ducking

down having dodged that fatal bullet. In that split second, the old man grabbed Bulldog's pistol and let off three shots in quick succession into Kingpin's chest. At the same he hurled his walking stick at Ogre Man who brushed it aside, but the moment it took to take that action enabled the old man to let off a further three shots. Ogre Man collapsed to the floor, burying his face into a jumbo milkshake.

Bulldog threw himself onto the old man, knocking the gun out of his hand. With his remaining good hand he grasped the old man's throat in a steel grip, choking him in a last ditch attempt for survival.

He grabbed Bulldog's broken wrist, and with a scream of pain, the choke hold was loosened. He then took hold of Bulldog's chains, twisting them and wrapping them around his throat, throttling him until he lapsed into unconsciousness.

The old man breathed heavily, his pulse racing. Three down. Damn! Where was Goldtooth? He heard steps behind him. Rolling forward, he grabbed a pistol, and lying prostrate on the floor, levelled his weapon. If this was the end, Goldtooth was coming with him.

'Will you watch where you're pointing that thing! Jee-sus; is that all the thanks I get?'

Standing in the doorway, over the prone body of Goldtooth, was a tall athletic man in a tailored three-piece suit, briefcase in hand. The old man relaxed. Placing the weapon on the floor, and supporting himself on the table, he got to his feet, fastidiously brushing himself off, there now being no trace of the stoop.

'Sorry old chap,' replied the old man. 'I thought you were that rude doorman fellow.'

'The Man with the Golden Mouth you mean? Honestly, do I look like the sort of guy who would shoot you in the back?'

'No, only a cad would do that.'

'I see you started without me,' said the well-dressed man surveying the carnage.

'I didn't have much choice, business discussions broke down.'

'Let me guess, the harmless knackered old codger act. How

many times do I have to tell you, it doesn't work. The only thing these people respect is power. We should have come in here mob handed and just taken the thing.'

'Coming in "mob-handed" would have been difficult on my own. You were late.'

'Yeah, well, I would have been earlier, but I was stuck in a last minute meeting with a client. Sorry about that.'

The old man frowned.

'Some of us have a day job you know,' said the well-dressed man in his defence.

Ignoring the protest the old man stepped over Bulldog and recovered the data card from Kingpin's jacket.

'Do you think they used it?' asked the well-dressed man.

'No, they didn't have a clue. They were only interested in selling it on for profit.' The old man checked the card with a device the size of a slim cigarette case and nodded his approval. 'We need to go; Erikson's men are on the way.'

'What – again! How do they do it?'

'If I knew that, it wouldn't be a problem.'

'After you,' gestured the well-dressed man courteously.

The old man picked up the cash laden briefcase and headed towards the doorway. Why did his colleague have a briefcase as well? No wonder he was always busy if he took his work home; bloody part-timers.

Well-dressed man put his right hand into his pocket, threading his fingers through a set of brass knuckles and aimed a punch at the base of the old man's head.

Some say it is intuition, others a sixth sense; or maybe it's the accumulation of years of experience, but whatever it was, the old man turned just in time for a glancing blow to hit him below the cheek. Despite his age, normally he would have been able to withstand the attack of a straight punch, but the metal protrusions caused him to falter and he could feel the room spinning as he fell to his knees. With the briefcase still in his hand he swung it in an accelerating arc at his attacker's knees, trying to gain the vital seconds that he could use to escape. A further metalled punch landed squarely on his temple as his assailant neatly sidestepped. Everything faded to black.

Well-dressed man took the data-card. 'Sorry, but I've got plans for this, you know how it is.'

Exchanging his brief case for the one the old man had, he made his way to the basement. Following the corridors of pipe-work and innards, he arrived at a flight of stairs that led him out to the rear of the property via a door that he had earlier forced.

He strode out along the back streets until he exited onto the Mile End road. Satisfied that he had put sufficient distance between himself and the baths, he hailed a black cab. Settling back into the sumptuous rear bench seat he touched the screen on his smartphone, and then once again to confirm his request.

The conflagration that engulfed the municipal baths illumi-nated the London skyline.

2 / *Parasite Lost*

There are autumn days when the sun rises above dew covered landscapes and casts a halo of rim light around tree branches, highlighting the leaves as they start the slow transformation to copper glory, before falling and revealing their intricate autumn fretwork. There are September days when to witness the marvel and magic of Nature's beauty makes it incapable for even the most churlish and miserable of souls not to give thanks for being alive.

This wasn't one of those days.

John Cranston wasn't in the best of moods. He was running late. He hated being late. His thoughts spun in a forlorn search for an inspired explanation for his anticipated untimely arrival. Freud would probably say his Id was panicking, but what did he know? Oedipus didn't even know it was his mother.

Hoping that he could make up the lost time he finally turned off the sluggish M25 orbital road only to find himself on a single lane road stuck behind a slow wheel drive. Its owner obviously thought that the National speed limit was aspirational.

A length of dual carriageway interrupted just as John had mentally engaged the virtual rocket launcher on the roof of his Citroen BX. His target lived to drive another day, and as he overtook, the tension slowly seeped from his shoulders. The road ahead was clear; there was a good chance he could make up the time, legally, arrive punctually, and win the contract. From what Alice had told him this could be a chance for him to channel his inner Capability Brown.

He tuned the radio to a random station. A risky business, but that was the sort of guy he was he told himself. An auto-tuned voice warbled a version of the Eagles 'Desperado'. John's mood lifted as he sang along with all the self-belief, volume and gusto that characterises the tonally challenged, oblivious to the risk that any Robins within earshot might spontaneously explode.

The house address was simply 'The Oaks, Sussex'. To John this signified money. Only the historic landed gentry and rich had no need of a postal address. Everyone that mattered would have known where the Lord of the Manor lived, back in the day.

He knew he was close as the road followed a wall that stretched for miles before he finally came to a gated entrance. The drive to the manor house was at least another half mile; flanked either side by poplar trees. He was now only fifteen minutes behind the appointed time, which he could in all good conscience put down to traffic.

The gravel chippings scrunched under his tyres as he pulled up at the grand palladian frontage. As he gathered his paperwork up from the passenger seat, there an insistent tapping on the window by a young lady in dungarees and wellingtons.

'Excuse me. Hello? Are you Mr Cranston?' she said, her voice muffled by the glass.

He wound the window down.

'Mr Cranston?'

'Yes. That's me. I'm here to see Mr Pargetter about some gardening work. I'm running a bit late. Sorry about that.'

'Oh don't worry,' said the young lady reassuringly. 'We had someone down last week about a golf course and he was a day late. His satnav took him through France and then he got stuck on the ferry back. I'm Molly by the way, general handy-lady come Personal Assistant.' She held out her soiled hand in greeting.

'John. John Cranston,' he reciprocated. 'Glad to meet you. Is he around?'

'He's down by the temple; follow the path to the right and keep the lake on your left. You can't miss him. He's the large gentleman. He'll probably want to talk to you about the oak.' Her smile turned downcast at the mention of the tree.

John didn't remember Alice saying anything about oak trees. There was only one way to find out. He thanked Molly for her help and set off at a brisk stroll along the garden trail. He anticipated grand gardens, the palladian frontage hinted as much. As he walked through the hedge doorway, the expanse and beauty of the manufactured views of the grounds tickled his gardening taste buds. It was typical of the English landscape movement; inspired by the wealthy and their grand tours through Europe, collecting a new visual vocabulary that they then brought back with them. This was nature enhanced with constructed viewpoints and visual surprises, with nothing left to chance. It was grand, ambitious, and breath taking.

Mr Pargetter was seated in an electric golf cart outside the temple, a scaled down version of the Pantheon in Rome. He had the kind of flesh corrupted by too much good food and wine. His neck consisted of a series of stacked chins. Molly was right, he couldn't be missed.

'Mr Pargetter?' John enquired as he approached.

'Yes, and who are you?'

'John Cranston, Cranston Gardening Services' he replied, refusing to be intimidated by the brusque response. 'You made an appointment with my office.'

'You're late.'

'Sorry about that, got stuck behind a Ferrari.'

Pargetter scowled. 'I like Ferrari's, got two of them in the garage.'

'Always good to have a spare,' muttered John under his breath, as he smiled falsely and acknowledged the boast.

Pargetter shifted himself in the seat of the buggy; the suspension groaned. 'You're here now, so let's get on with it. Follow me,' he said, it not even occurring to him to offer John a ride.

They proceeded further into the gardens. With the lake to their left, John could see through the opening in the next hedge an artistically obscured view of a distant bridge. It would no doubt reveal itself in total as they moved into the next garden room. John surmised that there would probably be a carefully manicured slope with a winding path leading down to the lake edge. He was wrong.

Cut into the slope was a lagoon-sized swimming pool. Steam rose from its surface, softening the black polished granite of the pool edge. Laid out at regular intervals, sun loungers, each with their own industrial patio heater, rippled the air with butane heat as silicon enhanced girls exposed their orange bikini clad bodies to the low autumn rays. Had he stumbled into an alternate Hugh Hefner universe John asked himself? One of the nubiles bounced past him towards Pargetter.

'Chummykin! Where have you been? You're missing the party!'

'I've been busy Babe,' replied Pargetter like a lecherous school-boy. 'You run along and I'll see you later,' and he patted her on the behind. 'That's my wife, Shazira. Bit of alright isn't she?'

Pargetter's guard had dropped and he reinforced his chauvinist credentials by nudging John gently in the ribs. John thought it would only be polite to return the gesture, a wink, a hard friendly nudge in the face. He resisted.

'Lovely girl, nice eyes...' John ventured.

Pargetter resumed his arrogant, superior demeanour. 'You see that big tree over there, to the left of the karaoke bar?'

'The oak,' confirmed John.

'Whatever. I want you to take it down, soon as possible.'

'What's the rush?'

'It's spoiling the view, I want it down. I'm having the whole pool side extended to there with decking.'

'Any plants?' John enquired in forlorn hope.

'No, just decking.'

'I assume that taking the tree down is part of the landscaping work you wanted to talk about?'

'Landscaping work? Don't know where you got that idea. That'll get done when they put the golf course in, but they can't start for a month and I want that tree taken down now.'

'But your office said "landscaping".'

'Okay, I admit it was a bit of an exaggeration, but I wanted to keep my options open. No harm done eh?' said Pargetter without the smallest indication of remorse of the false premise he had used.

John's first inclination was to refuse the job and leave. He had nothing to gain from dealing with this rich lout, but as he looked across at the majestic tree, he knew that if he didn't chop it down, someone else would. Pargetter obviously had money to indulge himself, and if he was as fickle as John perceived him to be, maybe he could engineer a reprieve for the oak. What had he to lose?

'Fair enough,' said John. 'I'm here now and...' He made a show of looking at the tree. 'You know, something's not right. I'll just go and have a look, won't be a minute.'

With its leaves starting to turn into golden reds, the colours enhanced by the autumn suns fading light, it looked magnificent. John now understood Molly's despondency when talking about the great tree. By his estimation, it was at least one hundred feet tall, so probably over one hundred and fifty years old, maybe more. If it could talk what tales it would tell. Now it was at the mercy of a wealthy boor and a vacuous girl with a pneumatic chest. He placed his hand on the trunk. 'Don't worry old man. I'll think of something.'

From where Pargetter was parked John looked like a character from a shadow play as the waning sun backlit him and the oak tree. Pargetter watched as the silhouetted figure paced from one side of the tree canopy to the other, scratched his head, paced again, placed his face close to the trunk and then stood, his chin resting on his hand. After this performance the figure returned as promised, running his hand across his head.

'How much?' Pargetter enquired.

'To be honest Mr Pargetter, I can't take that tree down, it's infested with a rare parasite. It's a specialist job, and I'm not equipped for it I'm afraid. Thing is, it's on the increase, so now I've seen it I'm professionally obliged to report it to the Department of Environment. Nothing to worry about - it's standard practice for something this nasty.'

'Eh! What's the idea of getting some government wonks involved? You said you couldn't do the job, so this is none of your business now. Besides, if it's infested shouldn't it be taken down anyway?'

'Its not that straightforward, you see these particular parasites prefer the tree alive, and without proper precautions, the moment someone takes a chainsaw to it, they'll spread like wildfire. Even though I can't do the job, I'm sure they'll be plenty of experts that'll know what to do, so I'll leave you to it.'

Pargetter's tone became more conciliatory. 'Now Mr Cranston, maybe I was a bit hasty. There's no need to involve inspectors and the like, surely? Maybe we could come to some arrangement?'

'I'm not sure about that, it could be a bit tricky, unless...'

'Unless?'

'If the oak stayed up, then the parasites will stay put. With the right precautions, it wouldn't be such a problem. I could treat this as an advisory, for a small consultancy fee you understand.'

'Fine, but if I'm paying for advice, I want to receive it.'

'Okay, I think that oak has an infestation of...arthropoda mortus vivens.'

'Arthur what?'

'You've never heard of them?' John sucked through his teeth. 'They're about the size of a pinhead; most people call them crabs, although technically they're mites. Normally you'd find them in more exotic areas, but with climate change we're seeing a lot more of them in Europe, and they've become quite partial to oak trees. Normally they move around by infesting monkeys. If a tree's dying, they bore under a monkey's skin and when they move on, the mites crawl out and start over. At the moment, even with the mite, that tree will live for years, and you'd never know they were there, but chop it down though,' he shook his head. 'With no monkeys around, they'll go for the next best thing, people. That's why I can't do the job. I haven't got the licences or the full body bio suit.'

Pargetter's skin started to involuntarily itch. 'Bio suit?'

'Can't do the job without one. When they burrow in they have this kind of anaesthetic. You don't know you've been infected until it's too late.'

'Too late?' asked Pargetter, intrigued.

'Yeah, by the time you show any symptoms, you'll be mad as a hatter.' John circled his finger at his temple. 'I don't know why but it's especially bad for women, and sometimes incurable. You know those lost tribes in the Amazon? They're not lost, they're in quarantine. Most of the men are being held prisoner by a bunch of bunny boilers a bun short of a baker's dozen.'

'What? Isn't there a law against it, or something?' said Pargetter, a slight hint of concern in his voice.

John pressed home the advantage. 'If for the sake of argument someone was to notify the authorities, it might mean a full quarantine, you can never tell with these inspectors. That would be a half mile exclusion zone around that tree for about six months, at least, and you can forget the golf course while they're at it. Also to be on the safe side they might insist your wife move out as well.'

John cast his gaze deliberately towards Shazira and her friends as they cavorted around the pools edge. 'If you want to have any more pool parties, personally I'd leave well enough alone.'

Pargetter stared at the tree and then at the cavorting nymphs by the pool. He looked like a man whose fish and chip supper had been stolen by a seagull, which had then followed up by leaving a present on the dessert.

'Mr Cranston, you've been very helpful. In light of this new information, what if I was to reconsider my proposal for the tree?'

'I seem to have forgotten why I wanted to talk to the environment people, how odd. Providing the circumstances don't change, I'm sure I wouldn't remember, but news of the tree coming down could jog my memory.'

'I see. Good day. I think we're all done here.'

'Thank you for your time, and don't worry, I'll see myself out,' said John making a conscious effort to conceal the sarcasm in his voice.

As he retraced his steps and approached the house he saw Molly and nodded in acknowledgement.

'You're taking the oak down then?' she said disapprovingly.

'If it happens, it won't be me. In my professional opinion there's an infestation of arthropoda mortus vivens. I've advised him to leave it alone.'

'Arthropoda mortus vivens?' Molly concentrated as she did the translation. 'Do you normally tell your customers that their trees have zombie crabs?'

'Zombie crabs? Oh, I see what you mean. To be honest I have to admit my Latin's a bit rusty. It's an easy mistake, what I meant to say was...' he didn't get a chance to finish as Molly spoke across him.

'You know what Mr Cranston? If you've been spinning stories like that I've a mind to have you up for fraud. The only reason I won't is if that's the best you can come up with, it would be unkind. I don't want to be accused of cruelty to gardeners, if that's what you really are.'

'Steady on.' He paused. 'Is it really zombie crabs? Bugger. Okay, it's a fair cop. Look, there's no way I'm taking that oak down and I thought that if I said "No", then he'd find someone who will. I'm sorry I lied, but I'm not apologising for trying to save that tree.'

Molly's aspect softened. 'I have to admit I'm quite partial to that oak. If I know Pargetter he'll want a second opinion, but he'll leave that to me. All I'll do is agree with you, so you've done me a big favour. There is one thing though.'

'And what would that be?' said John suspiciously.

'Don't worry, I can keep a secret, but I think we'll need to discuss the exact details of those crabs of yours, you know, to make sure we're on the same hymn sheet. I was thinking maybe over a few glasses of wine and some good food. There's a fantastic Chinese in the village and I'm due to knock off soon.'

'I'm sorry, I'm on a tight schedule at the moment and it's going to make things really awkward. I can't, I'm sorry.'

Molly looked at him firmly. 'Zombie crabs?'

'I've got a long drive and I'm really behind and…' he was running out of excuses. He couldn't say he had to wash his hair; it was so closely cropped a wet flannel would do the job in seconds.

She looked him in the eyes. 'And?'

'Rain check?' he offered in desperation.

'Okay, I'll hold you to that.' Taking a business card from her dungarees she made a small note and slid it into the breast pocket of John's jacket. 'So you don't forget, and in the meantime I expect an email about those undead arthropoda.'

Walking back to the car he thought as autumn days went, all things considered, this one hadn't turned out that bad. He had blagged a reprieve for an oak tree, could potentially be convicted for fraud, (he'd have to forget the consultancy fee), and had turned down an invitation for a Chinese meal with an attractive young lady. Then again, the last time he shared a Chinese meal with an attractive young lady, it hadn't ended that well, so it was probably for the best.

Maybe tomorrow someone would ask him to mow something.

3 / *Another Day In The Office*

The offices of Cranston Gardening Services were a modest affair, despite having a postcode off the Farringdon Road that estate agents would have sold their own mother for, and given the chance, leased out the mothers of all known acquaintances.

Before the property boom and the ubiquity of plastic packaging, it had been a working factory specialising in adding designs to plain glass bottles. Progress however has no respect for the way things 'have always been done' and inevitably, bankruptcy followed. One by one, after a token payoff, the workforce, the family that had been the lifeblood of that factory, had to fend for themselves as the circling creditors thought nothing of stripping out the industrial guts to get their due.

Jack Armstrong, an enterprising businessman who made his money through various activities, some of which were borderline legal, bought the factory shell at auction. The way he figured it, no one was making any more land, so in a couple of years he could sell up at a substantial profit. In the meantime, it would be a useful addition to his network of places to store the more exotic items of his trade. All he needed was to install a small innocuous business for the requisite front of legitimacy, and he would be good to go.

It just so happened that on his weekly visit to his mum, where she would berate him about finding a proper job and to pay more attention to Alice, that she went off piste and started waxing lyrical about her new gardener.

Jack's people made the gardener, 'a lovely boy called John', an offer he couldn't refuse, but he turned it down.

Several weeks later John Cranston's lock-up exploded, owing to an unlucky gas leak. Jack Armstrong, ever the champion of small local business came to the rescue, and so it was that John Cranston Gardening Services was ensconced in prime London real estate.

There was one catch though. In return for a peppercorn rent, John Cranston had to employ Jack's wife, Alice. Jack didn't care in what capacity, but as Alice had been nosing around his business affairs, this way she got her wish to be a part of his empire, at a distance that suited him.

Alice Armstrong turned out to be a natural for administration, and with her assistance, J. Cranston Gardening services grew steadily into a vibrant business. The success of the venture didn't go unnoticed by Jack, but before he could capitalise on this new extortion stream, he died after falling into the Lea Navigation. The coroner ruled a verdict of accidental death, concluding that the impalement on an old pram wheel is what did for him.

Alice Armstrong hunkered down in the gardening venture while the succession of Jack's empire played out around her. She had no interest.

She had found that she quite liked gardening.

*****

'Mornin' Alice,' greeted John as he flung his overcoat towards the stand as it narrowly avoided landing in a crumpled heap. 'How's things been while I've been out pounding the streets?'

'Not bad. How'd it go with the Pargetter job?'

'Bit of a mixed bag really. No landscaping work I'm afraid, but I might have saved an oak tree though.'

'Any money?'

'Nah, he was a wind-up artist. It was never going to work.'

'Lucky for you your landlord is fairly relaxed about the rent.'

'I'll get the money, promise. It's just taking a while to get things back to where they were.'

'Don't worry, it'll keep. What about that quote for a new lawn?'

'No good. All he wanted was astroturf. From his point of view, it's all grass. I had to turn it down, I don't have a clue how it works. So I said to him, if the grass isn't real, what did he need a real gardener for?'

'Never mind, by the way, talking of the Pargetter job, we got an email from a Ms Molly Mackintosh, she seems quite taken with you. Says here she's looking forward to discussing your,' Alice shivered, 'crabs. Not that I'm an expert or anything, but I thought men were supposed to invite girls to look at their etchings, or do I need to get Rentokil in?'

'Its business, and they're mites by the way.'

'Business? It sounds pretty personal to me. Honestly, what am I going to do with you? A woman could stand right in front of you wearing a T-shirt saying, "I fancy you rotten" and you'd still look over your shoulder. Ever since the divorce, you've been like a monk. It's been ages. It's not healthy.'

'Come on, you know we don't talk about that. I'm putting the kettle on, tea or coffee?'

'Tea please,' she replied while looking down at the screen of her new computing tablet, diligently swiping left and right.

It was an uneventful morning, the only thing of interest was Eric, the one legged feral pigeon that regularly landed on the windowsill of John's office, and then slowly fell over. John wondered if there was a market for bespoke pigeon undercarriage. As Alice had often pointed out, diversification was the key to business success.

It was nearly eleven, that time when they reviewed up and coming business opportunities over tea and a biscuit. Typically, the refreshments lasted longer. The heady days of individual landscape projects had evaporated as people hunkered down with their money, redirecting it at sixty-inch televisions and worldwide cruises.

He carried the tray of freshly brewed beverage to Alice's desk.

'Here you go; finest builders tea,' John proffered. 'Help yourself to a biscuit, so what's on the go this week?'

'Lovely. Be with you in a minute,' and Alice continued to swipe and tap her tablet with the occasional *'Mmm'*, and *'Not bad'* before putting it to one side. 'Malcolm rang to check that you were still going rowing Sunday. I said yes, I assumed you wouldn't have anything else on, unless of course you'll be talking pest control with your new girlfriend.'

John ignored the jibe.

Alice continued. 'Martin called. He wondered if you were available for lunch tomorrow. He's got a "proposition".'

'Martin. Martin Ashcombe?'

'Yes, that Martin.'

'He wasn't trying to sell anything was he? I don't see him in ages and then he's up for lunch at a moment's notice. Sounds a bit dodgy to me, what do you reckon?'

'Maybe you're being a bit hard on him. You never know, he might have something this time, but you won't find out if you don't meet him.'

'True. God knows I could do with a big win at the moment, as long as he doesn't try to rope me into one of his rebadged Ponzi schemes. Okay, I'll give him a ring.'

'No need. I've already booked a table at the Nun and Three Ferrets for half past twelve.'

'Alice, one of these days.'

'Promises, promises.'

John cleared his throat. He wasn't going there. 'It's not one of those poncey gastro pubs is it? Last time I went to one it was, what was it called?' He clicked his fingers. 'The Frog and Blowtorch! That's it. Run by that celeb chef Herring Bloomingmad. I can't forget the menu though. Porcine fingers in collagen casings served with obliterated potato covered in a carnivore jus.'

Alice looked confused.

'Sausage and mash to you and me,' John elaborated. 'I wouldn't have minded but it was served up on an old school jumper while some poor sod on work experience floated around the restaurant spraying "Eau de Abattoir" Eau de bloody night-mare more like.'

'Don't worry,' assured Alice. 'I've heard lots of good things about the Nun, very hip and trendy apparently.'

'Hip and trendy? This is me we're talking about.'

'It's about time you started making more of an impression. You can't spend all your time in that tweed jacket of yours hanging around in greasy spoons.'

'Harris tweed' he corrected, 'and I'll have you know many a bed has been double dug on the back of a full English.'

'I'm sure the food will be fine. In fact, I heard that if you pay extra they'll serve the main course on an iPad so you can move your food around and check emails at the same time. How good is that?'

He made a mental note to have a large breakfast before tomor-row's lunch. 'You win. Anything else?'

'That's it,' and she turned her head back down to the tablet to resume her swiping.

He sipped his tea. He could go back to his office and check on Eric, but normally he would have righted himself by now, even if he had fallen off and came in for another landing. Alice was engrossed. What to do now?

'Is that your new tablet computing thing?' he asked.

'Hm- hmm.'

'Any good?'

'Wonderful,' and she remained glued to the screen. 'I found this new dating app, Fumblr. It's not bad, *no, naughty nurse, bloody cheek*. You should try it.' Alice focused on the tablet, swiping left and right. 'The only problem with this app thing is that the profiling is a bit basic. I thought I'd try someone a bit older, more sophisticated, and all I get is beer guts, pink trousers and comb overs.'

John paused, a biscuit hovering at his mouth.

Alice continued. 'So I thought I'd go a bit younger, but they all look the same, sort of a polished six packed tailor's dummy with white tombstone teeth and arms covered in dodgy Celtic tattoos, and they've got absolutely no stamina.'

She heard John clearing his throat and thought nothing of it, pausing only to take a draft of her tea, her attention still glued to the tablet. 'I mean, after a museum and art gallery the poor things are worn out.'

John relaxed.

Alice was in full flow now. 'All they want to do is go back to their hotel room and lie down. They must think I was born yesterday, all they want is sex. They might as well tell me their room number up front; it'd save a lot of messing about...'

John coughed involuntarily, thumping his chest.

'Then I could ignore the randy little gits,' continued Alice, warming to the theme, 'and enjoy the gallery on my own without having to put up with them dropping their hints all the time. Honestly, we're all adults. All they've got to do is ask...'

John's tea went down the wrong hole and he's cheeks swelled as he struggled not to spurt hot brew over the paperwork.

'And I'll say "No". Think of the time I could save, and if they're lucky, I won't knee them in the nuts.'

John, having managed to recover his composure, and confident that normal service had been resumed, reached for another biscuit.

'Mind you though,' said Alice, her lips curling into a knowing smile, 'if they looked like Sean Connery, Picasso could wait.'

Alice's fantasy diversion was abruptly halted by a guttural gargling sound, like a drowning parrot with tonsillitis.

She looked up to see John choking on a custard cream.

As she reached over and slapped him hard on the back, she told herself that she must remember not to mention sex over tea.

4 / *Men Who Do Lunch*

Martin Ashcombe left his Mercedes SL 500 Cabriolet in the local multi- storey car park off the Whitechapel Road. That there was a carpark here at all surprised him. In his day, no one would have left a luxury saloon around there for fear of it not being in one piece on their return, but that was then, and if everything went to plan, it would be the least of his concerns.

It had been a long time since his last visit to the old stomping ground and now, here he was, in a saville row suit with matching bespoke shirt and shoes, but he didn't feel out of place. The surroundings were different, but familiar. The Nun was a short walk past the London Hospital and he surveyed the area, noting the changes. Like him, London had moved on. There was the local sweet shop which now sold mobile phones, and the baker, now a discount shop where everything cost one pound. Over there, the coffee bar, that used to be the Newt's Gasket, where he, John and Pete Chandler would drink themselves into oblivion on a Friday night all those years ago.

A gang of youths were walking in his direction. He slid his fingers into the knuckle-duster in his overcoat pocket as a precaution. They passed him by without incident.

A double life in city banking and as a freelance for the Society, while financially lucrative, was coming to a natural end. When he had first been recruited, his tasks were mainly peddling lies as truth and negotiating underhand deals, while taking any opportunity to divert money into his own private fund. It came easily to him, a clandestine world that traded in intrigue and deception, yet still relied on a trust between colleagues. That was easy enough to fake, but over time the stakes had raised and he now walked a tightrope between success and deadly jeopardy. He knew he had crossed the line with the arson at the baths.

With the Midas device now in his possession he had easily diverted money to a swiss bank account. At the age of thirty-five it was a fair exchange for the dangers he had faced over past years for unsung service to queen and country.

Midas was aptly named, it had made him rich, but once word got out, as it inevitably would, that he had it, the wealth he had gained would be academic. It couldn't be enjoyed by a dead man. People had killed to possess Midas and would do so again, but his greed was an irrational master, tempered only by a sense of self-preservation. The Society was welcome to it, for a reasonable payment of course.

An amateur would have gone to ground by now, raising a red flag to any interested parties that they had something to hide, however in his day-to-day business dealings, a lucrative opportunity had presented itself. It was rich pickings and a man could never have enough easy money he told himself, besides, life would be boring without the cut and thrust of the deal. All he had to do was find a gardener. The rendezvous for the delivery of Midas to the Society would simply follow his lunch with John; it gave him a good reason to be in the area. A truth hidden in a lie, wrapped in a bluff.

The Nun and Three Ferrets stood on the site of an old London bank near the Mile End gate. In years past, it had been a turnpike for travellers heading towards the Alders gate of the City, but now it was considered to be *the* on trend social hostelry of the east end. To Martin Ashcombe it had the décor of a public house from those Saturday nights of memory, complete with dartboard, wonky pool table, one armed bandit, and a gassy lager of a colour that would look more at home in the pathology department of the London Hospital. He looked around the bar and spotted John sitting at a table poring over a crossword. In spite of the now close-cropped hair, the eternal Harris tweed jacket was all the confirmation that he needed. He ordered a tonic from the bar and went to join him.

'John! Mate! How's it going?'

'Martin! Good to see you, it's been a while. I wasn't sure if you were turning up, what with your high flying lifestyle and all,' John said as he pumped Martin's hand in a vice like handshake.

'Sorry it's been so long but things keep happening. Before you know it, where's all the time gone?' said Martin with fake bonhomie.

'Tell me about it. I'm sure someone's winding my watch forward while I'm not looking. What are you drinking?' offered John.

Martin held up his glass. 'Driving…'

'Between me and you, it's probably for the best,' said John peering through the cloudy liquid in his glass. 'I'm in the wrong business. They told me it's because it's an artisan beer, looks like home brew gone wrong to me. I don't know. So what are you up to? Still working for that lot in Canary Wharf?'

'No. I knocked all that on the head months ago. Bunch of crooks, making me look bad. I've gone freelance now. I'm a one man business development venture capitalist facilitator.'

'Come again?'

'It's a kind of business dating agency for the filthy rich. When I was working in high finance, you wouldn't believe the money slushing around. It became pretty obvious that in this line of work there are two types of people, those with lots of money and no sense, and those with lots of sense and no money. It's only by sheer luck that some of them meet up, and even then, it's a business disaster before they even start. All I do is stack the odds. I make sure the right people get together, for a modest fee of course. Everyone makes money, especially me.'

'That sounds…interesting,' said John. Martin's world of money was always a mystery to him.

When old friends meet up after a long absence, conversation can flow as if time is irrelevant. Sometimes however, divergent experiences means that there is no recent common ground.

The only options after the initial niceties are either to attend to the business at hand, coldly but politely, as if dealing with an acquaintance, or to fan the embers of friendship by temporarily looking to the past for shared references.

Rather than getting straight to business, Martin preferred to engage in small talk. Sometimes it was better to be approached than chase, and with his and John's chequered history, he didn't want him to be spooked. He headed off the oncoming pregnant pause with an opening left field gambit.

'How's Lorraine?' enquired Martin, as if he didn't already know.

'Search me. Haven't seen her since the divorce - been years.'

'Oh I'm so sorry,' said Martin wearing his sincerest understanding face. 'Last time I saw you I thought it was all going so well.'

'No, it was already a bit tense, and then it all went downhill after that. We had one of those trial separations. Reckoned she had to go and find herself, or some old tosh. Next thing I know she's shacked up with some clown.'

'What - like that tool of a mayor of ours?'

'No, no, nothing as bad as that. She joined a circus.'

'That's a shame, sorry to hear that. Mind you, thinking about it, I'm not surprised. I knew that Lorraine was trouble, she always had a thing about big feet.'

'Thanks. It would have helped if you'd told me that when you asked her to join us that night for a Chinese.'

'How was I to know you'd hook up? I just thought it'd be a laugh. Personally I could never work out why you didn't take up with Alice.'

'Don't be daft. Me and Alice are strictly business, 'sides, I'd be out of my league.'

'If you say so. How's the gardening world at the moment?' asked Martin, slowly reeling him in.

'It was going great until that mess with your lot in the banks.'

'Steady mate, they're not my banks. I got stung as well.'

'I couldn't believe it, most of the contracts dried up overnight, and I had to lay the team off. Lucky Alice was around. Without her, the whole thing would have gone belly up by now. It's been bloody hard, but it's slowly coming back together. So what's this mysterious proposition you've got for me?'

'That's what I like about you mate. No messing about, straight down to business. Look, I reckon this is right up your street. I've got this client, stacked with money, who's got it into his head that he's going to launch a new internet TV channel. Sport, drama, lifestyle, the works. He's asked me if I knew anyone who could act as a consultant for his new gardening talent competition, so I put your name in the frame as a possible maybe.'

'Go on.'

'All you've got to do is meet up with me and this guy's team and see where it goes.'

'This isn't one of your wind-ups is it?'

'Come on mate, that was years ago, and besides, I seem to remember you gave as good as you got. This is straight up.'

'What's in it for you?'

'Not much, a small introduction fee to be getting on with,' (small would be a five figure sum). 'I reckon it could be big though, so I'm getting in early. Trust me; if you get this for a couple of months, you'll make a mint. What do you say?'

John considered for a moment. Martin hadn't actually asked for any money, so the only thing he stood to lose was his time, which he had an abundance of at the moment. 'Okay, I'm in. Put me down for it. Nothing ventured, nothing gained as they say.'

'Nice one. Let's drink to it. What'll you have?'

John drained his glass, screwing his eyes up as he swallowed and placed his hand over the empty.

'Not for me thanks. I had a couple before you got here. I thought it would improve after the first bottle, it didn't. If I have any more I'll have the mother of all hangovers tomorrow. What's the food like in this place? I could do with something to eat.'

'Never tried it,' said Martin checking the menu. 'Here we go; chef's special is lichen fingers with a slug coulis served on a bed of virgin kelp.'

'Ploughman's?' John suggested.

'Definitely.'

The waiter was disdainful on taking their order, and his attitude didn't improve when they passed on the opportunity for the upgrade to deluxe presentation. After twenty minutes or so, the food was brought to the table, wrapped in newspaper, complete with plastic fork.

Martin unfolded his parcel and out of curiosity scraped the pickle sauce to one side. 'I think mine's been served in a copy of the Daily Mile.'

'How can you tell?'

'It says that Britain is heading for a second Ice Age, and an independent expert has confirmed that Princess Diana is still dead. What about yours?'

'I've got Samantha, twenty one, astrophysicist from Chopping Anger who likes to watch the stars naked from her hot tub. I have to say the chef has done a cracking job laying out the pickled onions.'

'What now? Hold on a minute,' said Martin, irritated at the interruption as he reached into his jacket pocket and retrieved his vibrating phone. 'Sorry, I've got to check this. That's the problem with my sort of work, always on the go. Don't mind me, you tuck in.'

The number was known only to a select few for critical communications. The message was from an unknown caller. Immediately Martin was suspicious and as he read the text, his heart skipped a beat.

Unknown Number: *Cover blown ☹ Operation Prometheus*

Nothing he had done this afternoon or in the past should have raised suspicion, which could only mean that someone, maybe from the Society, had been passing on information to the enemy. He scanned the bar, looking for a type. If asked he wouldn't have been able to describe them, they could be anyone, but there was a bearing that he could instinctively recognise. Nothing. If they were here, they were good. He assumed he was being watched and casually put the phone down on the table as if the message had been routine. A reaction otherwise would confirm that he was a person of interest, especially if it had been sent from inside the bar.

'Anything exciting?' asked John, chasing the remaining pickled onion past Samantha's navel.

'Not really. It's a message from the office. A client of mine needs to see me urgently this afternoon. I bet you when I get there it'll all be for nothing, but I can't really ignore it. We'll have to skip dessert.'

'I think I'll manage,' said John tapping the bread roll onto the side of the table. 'I could put nails in with this. God knows what I could do with their ice-cream'. He looked at the empty beer bottles, 'One for the road?'

'Okay, but it'll have to be a quick one. Make it an orange juice, and then I'd better be off.'

Martin looked at his phone as if having second thoughts. 'Tell you what I'll do, before I forget. I'll put an appointment in my diary for next week to meet-up with this TV guy, and I'll synch it to your phone.'

'You'll do what to my phone?'

'Give it here,' gestured Martin. 'You go and get the drinks in.'

'Right, two orange juices it is,' and John went to the bar, the itinerant waiter having left their table off his wanderings.

With the dexterity and speed of a master illusionist, Martin swapped the small data card from John's phone for the Midas device. He updated the diaries, making exaggerated swipes on the screens, a classic misdirection for the benefit of any onlookers, and John, as he returned with the drinks.

'There you go. All done,' Martin declared. 'The appointment's downloaded into your phones calendar, so now you've got no excuse not to turn up.'

'Don't worry, I'll be there. I'll write it in my diary when I get back to the office.'

'I don't get it. You're the only person I know who only uses his phone for telephone calls. It's no good following technology, try catching it up.'

'I'm not a great fan of having all my eggs in one basket, and as for always being connected, don't get me started.'

They continued with their strained small talk until it was time to part ways. Ever the gentleman, or so he would have people believe, Martin picked up the empties, helpfully placing them on the waitress's tray as she was clearing the tables. He secretly dropped each half of a broken card into separate beer bottles, where they were obscured by the semi-opaque glass.

Walking back along the Whitechapel Road to the carpark, Martin resisted the temptation to look over his shoulder. Nothing about his attitude let on that he had received that text message. If he were confronted, they wouldn't find any trace of Midas on him. He gambled on a slim chance that whoever had leaked the information would be discredited. With that benefit of doubt, he could maintain the deception until he retrieved Midas from John at the meeting next week, using the same sleight of hand and misdirection.

His short journey was uneventful. Only the boldest or most stupid would make a move in the hustle and bustle of Whitechapel market where the sheer number of people would make it difficult for a clean capture. If they were to make a move, it would be in the multi-storey car park. He took the stairs, not wanting to risk an intervention in the close quarters of the lift, his fist clenched around the brass knuckles in his pocket.

Looking through the small window of the entry door to the parking level, he could see his Mercedes SL500. Close by was an elderly man, puffing and wheezing as he lowered himself into his car. A young mother was placing her child into a protective car seat. A couple were loading shopping into the boot of their aging Volvo. Nothing seemed out of place. He heard the lift doors open behind him, and after politely holding the swing door open to the parking level, he tailgated the pedestrians, using them as unwitting cover until he peeled off and got into the relative safety of the Mercedes.

Leaning over and opening the glove compartment he

inspected the magazine of the semi-automatic pistol and pulled back the slide to place a bullet into the barrel. It was a short drive to his meeting with the Society's contact and he intended to get some answers. He wasn't being hung out to dry, not now. Satisfied, he replaced the pistol and put the key in the ignition.

It was then that he felt the cold steel of a gun muzzle pressed against his face.

5 / *Brief Encounters*

'Is it your meeting with Martin and those TV people today?' asked Alice.

'Why else would I be wearing a suit?' replied John.

'I thought you were going to a funeral, mind you, I'm not sure if it's the suit that needs cremating – look at it.'

'Cheek, I've just got it back from the dry cleaners. It may be old but it still fits. I'll have you know that I can still get into a thirty-four. What's wrong with it?'

'Oh I'm sorry, I can't go through it all now, it'd make you late for your meeting. It'll have to do for the moment, but not with that tie though, I don't think black is right.'

'It's not black; it's a dark greeny grey called "liquorice".'

'Trust me, for normal people who haven't got your amazing colour sense, its black. Here, try this on,' and she pulled out a bright yellow tie from her desk drawer.

'Is there anything that isn't in that drawer of yours?' he asked, working the tie into a windsor knot.

'They taught us to be prepared in the Girl Guides. I had to leave after six months though when I got my fire-starter badge by accidentally burning down the clubhouse.'

'Taa Daa! What do you reckon?' asked John as he did a stilted twirl.

Alice looked at him lasciviously. 'You'll do.' She could see him feeling uncomfortable, which was always his reaction to the look. She knew it was cruel, but it was so sweet.

'Right then, I better be off,' said John, keen to excuse himself from the discomfort. 'Mustn't be late. I'm not sure how long this will take so I'll see you tomorrow.'

'Aren't you forgetting something?' Alice asked knowingly.

'No, don't think so.'

'Your phone?'

'It's on charge. I can manage without it today,' and with that he was out the door and on his way.

It wasn't, he just didn't want any distractions. Earlier in the week, Martin had sent him a text changing the venue of the meeting, which didn't surprise him, but in his own irrational way, he felt that if he were contacted, it would be tempting fate to make something go wrong.

The meeting was now at an office block near London Bridge. With time in hand, rather than travelling direct to London Bridge station, he decided to cut his journey short at the Monument and cross the River Thames as a pedestrian. This was preferable to being stuck in a metal underground box for longer than necessary, but as the bridge was as congested, it was a close decision.

He stopped halfway across, looking out at the river below, fascinated by the swirls and currents of the tide as it rose against the concrete banks. Again, he checked the thin neatly bound typed resume of his career. Nothing had changed, no gold gilts at the Chelsea Flower show, no major commissions, he was just a steady jobbing gardener. At least there was nothing in it that he could be caught out on, and besides, what was the worst that could happen at an interview?

With his resolve bolstered, he headed off to the meeting, determined to give it his all.

On reporting to the reception, he was advised that Martin had been unavoidably delayed, but rather than keep him waiting, Mr Black would be delighted to have an informal chat pending Mr Ashcombe's arrival, and so John was given directions to a meeting room on the twenty-third floor.

The elevator was an all glass affair that travelled on the outside of the building providing him with an unparalleled view of London's sprawl below. No wonder, he thought, that it was so full. It was probably the most excitement that people got, away from their desks.

He stood outside the door of the meeting room, took a deep breath, and knocked.

'Come in,' said a voice so English, it could advertise afternoon tea.

A man who John assumed was Mr Black, was sat behind a large executive desk. Two others bordered him, looking out of the floor to ceiling window, only turning their heads slightly in unison to acknowledge John's entrance. He noticed that they were all wearing dark suits; it must be a media thing he told himself. The man stood up from behind the desk and extended his hand in greeting.

'Mr Cranston, a pleasure to meet you. Please, take a seat,' he said gesturing to the chair. 'I'm Mr Black.'

'Thank you,' said John as he sat down. 'Sorry, I didn't catch your friend's names?'

'Excuse their rudeness, Mr Blue and Mr Green are here as impartial observers. It's part of their training.'

John was circumspect. This wasn't how he imagined it. Perhaps they were all like this in the media world, look at Gilbert and George. Maybe slightly weird was the new normal in this industry.

'So, Mr Cranston, you're a gardener,' enquired Mr Black, somewhat disbelievingly.

'Yes, been over ten years now. Look, I'll be honest with you, I haven't got a stack of paper qualifications, but I would like to say up front that with the experience I have, I could be the man you're looking for.'

'You're definitely the man I'm looking for, so let's cut to the chase shall we? The package please.'

'Sorry?'

'The package. Hand it over now.'

'The package. Right. Okaaay.'

John racked his brains as to what were they on about, and then it dawned on him and he handed over his resume. Obviously, they called it something different in media land.

Mr Black examined the bound document, flicking through the several pages and then, holding it by its binding, vigorously shook it before throwing it to the floor with contempt.

'Mr Cranston, while I admire you and your colleague's ability to maintain a cover story, I am finding this tedious.' Mr Black placed a gun on the table top. 'I want it now.'

'Do you know how long it took me to type that?' protested John pointing at the sprawled papers on the floor, deliberately ignoring Mr Black's threat.

Mr Black picked up the gun. Mr Blue was now stood at Mr Black's shoulder and John was aware of Mr Green circling behind him.

'I won't ask again. The package. Now,' Mr Black threatened.

John let out a sigh. 'Okay guys, let's stop it right there. Martin's put you up to this hasn't he? You know, Mr Ashcombe? I'll give you your due; you nearly had me going. You're good. I mean you're really acting the part, but the Tarantino thing and the fake gun, come on, you've been watching too many films. I'm sure it's been fun for you, but I haven't got time for this.'

John stood up and was about to leave, but he hadn't finished. 'And another thing. Next time don't point guns at people, not even toy ones- it's dangerous,' and with that he reached across the table, grabbed the gun by its barrel and wrenched it from Mr Black's grip. He casually hurled it over his shoulder, where by slim chance it hit a surprised Mr Green in the face.

'Owwww!! Dat's by dose!'

John shrugged that particular shrug beloved of snooker players and golfers that says the miraculous fluke shot or hole-in-one was absolutely intended. 'See, I told you it was dangerous.'

In the normal course of events, if the current situation could be called normal, everyone would have seen the lighter side. Concerned colleagues would have rallied around Mr Green and it would have been agreed that some props were best left in the cupboard. John would have apologised for the accident and returned to his office, where Martin would be waiting to gloat over John's naivety and John would fail to see the humour of the set-up. However, as he was about to find out, events were to follow a more abnormal course.

Mr Black's face was deadpan as John felt a sudden sharp blow to the back of his knees which forced his legs to collapse from under him. As he ungracefully sprawled forward and stretched his arms out across the desk in an attempt to save his fall, his wrists were pinned down by Mr Blue and Mr Green. Despite his struggles, he was unable to gain any purchase to escape.

'Bloody hell! Come on guys, the jokes over. Let go!' Then John saw something out of the corner of his eye. 'What the...?'

The joke was becoming darker. Mr Black leant back in the chair and spoke with a calmness that had been missing from his earlier demands. 'I would strongly advise against struggling or making a noise. Mr Blue, oddly enough, has taken up an interest in gardening. He's very keen to try out his latest toy. What do you call them, secateurs? I'm reliably informed that your little finger is the right size. Innovation is so important in our line of work, don't you agree?'

'Wait, I don't know what you're on about. There's some mistake, you can't seriously...'

John was cut short by Mr Black raising his hand and the feeling of the pruning tool blades closing around his finger.

'Did I mention Mr Blue's nerves? Any unexpected noise, loud talk or struggle could trigger a most unfortunate twitch. Do we understand each other?'

John nodded his head rapidly and felt the pressure of the secateurs being relieved from his finger joint. Meanwhile, Mr Green thoroughly searched John's pockets and person.

'Nothing,' said Mr Green.

'Tell me where it is,' demanded Mr Black.

'I told you, I don't know what you want,' replied John. He felt the blades tightening around his finger again and he clenched his eyes in anticipation. 'Wait, wait!' John's words tumbled out in desperation. 'You win. I haven't got it on me. I was meeting Martin today to hand it over, but I don't trust him. I've hidden it somewhere safe. I'll take you to it.'

Mr Black leant forward in his seat. 'I do find it fascinating how people always tell me what I want to hear. I find I get to the absolute truth by the second finger, but I like to think I'm a good judge of character. Tell me where it's hidden, and I'll settle for one.'

'I can't give you an address, I've buried it. I'll take you to it, but I think me spraying blood all over the office carpet on the way out might attract some attention.'

John watched intently as Mr Black sat back, deep into the chair, considering his proposal. Sweat rolled down John's forehead, stinging his eyes.

'Buried, of course, it would be,' Mr Black acknowledged. 'Take us to it, and by the way, if you try to escape, Mr Blue and Mr Green will be more than happy to hurt you with extreme prejudice.' Mr Black nodded and John felt the secateurs being removed from around his finger.

'Gentlemen, I'll see you downstairs in the carpark,' said Mr Black.

John slowly lifted himself off his knees, quickly trying to assess the situation. In an ideal world, the innocent make good their escape in a slick manner. In reality, actions in situations such as the one John found himself in defy rational reasoning after the event, driven as they are by a primal fight or flight urge. He couldn't fight, he was outnumbered. Spending time in hospital, broken, with a sign saying 'You should have seen the other guy' wasn't an option. He was going to run. He knew that, and they knew that. The only advantage he had was that they didn't know when he would make his move. All he knew was that he would have to do something before they got to the carpark, otherwise it would be too late.

'Move it, and don't try any funny business,' said Mr Green shoving John towards the door.

John straightened his tie and exited onto the office floor. He looked around and cursed to himself. Why did people congregate around doorways to have their chats? Didn't they know that at any moment someone might want to escape from a pair of Tarantino psycho groupies?

Mr Green and Mr Blue guided him firmly, but discreetly to

the lift. It was nearly full and before either of them could indicate that they would catch the next one, John had crossed the
threshold and tucked himself into the corner by the lift controls,
pressing as many as he could. Mr Blue put his foot in between
the closing doors, and he and Mr Green squeezed into the now
cramped box. The lift stopped at every floor, some people stepping off, while others joined. John looked at the depleting
columns of illuminated buttons. He wasn't a religious man, but
if there were a higher power, he hoped it was smiling on him
now. This was a gamble that had to pay off. At the next floor, as
the doors were about to close there was a cry.

'Hold the lift please!'

A young office junior with a tray of coffees threaded his way
into the lift with the odd 'Thank you'. As he did so, John hooked
his foot around the junior's ankle and hot coffee spilt over the
other occupants in the lift. In the ensuing pandemonium, John
thrust his elbow into Mr Green's nose and squeezed out onto
the office floor. Mr Blue tried to grab him, but John slipped his
jacket as the lift doors closed behind him.

He ran to the nearest fire escape, pushing his way past the
gossiping managers with an abrupt 'Excuse me!', and part sliding on the banister rails he leapt down each flight of stairs. He
had to be fast, the last thing he needed was to be greeted at the
front entrance by Mr Blue and Green; the distraction in the lift
wouldn't stop them for long. As luck would have it, the fire
escape that he had chosen at random did not lead to the front
reception. Instead, he found himself out on the street at the side
of the building. London Bridge station was nearby.

His instincts were to go there, lose himself in the crowd
and jump on a train to anywhere and put as much distance
as he could between himself and the tower. Reason momentarily prevailed. With the reputation of British trains for
punctuality, he instead joined the pedestrian crowd, briskly
walking across the bridge, impatiently weaving his way between
the aimlessly wandering people, their attention firmly fixed by
their hand-held screens. He was unable to break into a run without barging his way through and drawing attention to himself,
but then the same obstacles would hinder his pursuers. A plan

was forming; he would go to the Monument station and head for the underground walkway that linked it to the Bank station. He could continue his escape without being seen on the street, and catch the first underground train that pulled in. This route also gave him the option of the light railway that linked the City to the Docklands. The last thing he wanted to do was to wait on a platform.

Now clear of London Bridge, as he headed along King William Street, a City of London police car pulled up abruptly at the junction with Monument Street. He slowed his pace to a casual walk. The law-abiding citizen in him was inclined to approach the upholders of the law, explain his predicament, and then that would make everything alright. The realist in him knew that telling such a fantastical story of being tortured in an office block would only delay him while Mr Black and his associates closed in. He continued walking, pretending he didn't have a care in the world.

'Excuse me sir, I'd like to have a word with you,' asked one of the officers as John crossed Monument Street.

'Who, me?' he replied innocently, his shoulders tensing.

'Yes sir. We've had a report of a violent assault on a member of the public in the Imperial Tower, by someone who fits your description.'

'No, really? It's shocking what goes on these days isn't it? Well I hope you find who did it,' and John continued onward only to be stopped by the second policeman, a brute of a man who made a brick outhouse look like flimsy flat-pack furniture.

'Not so fast sir,' said the brute, and he then whispered into John's ear. 'We wouldn't want an accident to happen would we, what with you being in such a rush, if you get my meaning.'

The hairs on the back of John's neck tingled. 'Sorry officer but I don't know what you're on about. I'll tell you what, if I hear anything I'll be straight onto nine-nine-nine and you'll be the first to know. Anyway, I've got to go, train to catch.'

'I'm afraid you'll have to miss that train sir,' said the first officer. 'We need to keep you here for the moment. You see my partner here gets very upset if people don't hang around for his polite questions.'

'Of course' said John holding his hands up in supplication, before bringing the heel of his shoe down hard onto the top of the brute's foot.

John turned and ran back towards London Bridge, then mingled with the throng - hoping to buy himself some time by hiding among the crowd. Ahead of him he caught sight of Mr Black and his lackeys, approaching steadily, without drama.

He looked over his shoulder, hoping for a black cab he could hail and jump into, but instead a car cruised along side the pavement kerb and out limped an angry mini-hulk of a policeman.

Behind John the first policeman was steadily closing in on him.

He was outflanked on all sides.

There was only one option left.

He vaulted the wall of the bridge and hurled himself into the waiting arms of the River Thames.

6 / The Usual Suspect

Detective Inspector Sutherland sat at his desk gazing at the mounting pile of papers that was his caseload. After thirty-nine years on the force, he had been seconded to the City of London police to give his priority attention to a number of missing person cases in the capital. It was a far cry from when he first started his career on the beat, having slowly moved his way up to his current position through vice and the serious crime squad. Those were the days.

Now it was procedure upon procedure upon measurement upon target. Nothing else seemed to matter as long as the pie charts and graphs were the correct profile. At his last quarterly performance review, it had been formally noted that his 'Passion index' had fallen dramatically. Accordingly, he had been offered an 'Exciting opportunity' with which to redeem himself. He knew when he was being sidelined but he hadn't expected his career to end on such a sour note. If he was younger he might have taken more of an interest, but the case of the missing accountants didn't give him that tingling sensation in his gut that said to him there was a bigger picture at play. There were no ransom notes, no bodies, no known enemies of the missing. Nothing untoward, apart from the fact they had simply disappeared.

Up until now, the case had been low priority, but then the Mayor of London reported that his own personal accountant hadn't arrived for work. Sutherland made some enquiries and it turned out that the mayor's bean counter had resigned. The mayor didn't know as the resignation letter had been sent to his secretary, who had also quit. The only crime that had been committed was that of being so unpopular, no one would work for him. Never the less the mayor wasn't going to let facts get in the way. He gave the investigation his full support because he was tough on the loss of accountants, tough on the causes of lost accountants. If there was a potential for votes, they were going to be his. In reality, it amounted to simply cheering from the touchline, rather than anything material such as extra manpower or money. Unfortunately for Sutherland, cursed as he was with professionalism, he was unenthusiastically duty bound to resolve the riddle of the absent accountants before his final year was out.

He picked up the new file that Sergeant Bludgeon had left prominently on his computer keyboard. There was a bright yellow sticky note attached letting him know where and when the suspect would be available for interview. He shook his head. Bludgeon was keen, he'd give him that, but he hadn't yet grasped the nuances and differences between conjecture, hypothesis, evidence and facts.

What had he done, he asked himself, to deserve the most thorough, well-meaning idiot in the police force, and was he really the only one who could see it? In this line of work, thoughts and ideas came and went constantly, like temporary guests riding on a stream of consciousness. With experience you learnt how to ignore the chatter and focus on what was important. In Bludgeon's case however, he reckoned it was less of a stream and more of a stagnant bog. Any guests that he did have, which were infrequent at best, hung around, stuck in the morass that passed for his brain.

It was this innate ability to persist with an idea beyond all reason that must have had Sergeant Bludgeon earmarked for future greatness, his simplistic tenacity being mistaken for endless self-confidence and belief, prime qualities for leadership. It didn't bear consideration. No one, Sutherland thought, realised that a village was missing an idiot, and they didn't want him back.

It was Bludgeon's view that they should be searching for

a serial alphabet kidnapper, who if not caught, would work his way from accountants to zoologists. In a way Sutherland hoped that there was a grain of truth to this, he could then get motivated after the kidnapper had finished with estate agents. Unfortunately Bludgeon's theory had been holed below the waterline by his own latest lead, a gardener. No doubt Bludgeon would insist that this was a good thing, as it would narrow the profile to only those known dyslexic serial alphabet kidnappers.

He looked through the papers, skimming through Bludgeon's report, shaking his head in despair. Through the glass pane of his office he looked at Sergeant Bludgeon, at his desk, staring intently at his computer.

'Bludgeon, a word please.'

'In a moment Sir.'

'Now sergeant.'

Bludgeon sprang to attention and like a young dog eager to please its master, was in Sutherland's office.

'What's the meaning of this?' asked Sutherland holding up the file.

'I think it's the best lead we've had so far on the ABC kidnappings Sir.'

'First things first, we don't know that we're looking for a serial kidnapper, and secondly, what's the idea of telling me when I'm conducting an interview? I thought I was in charge of this investigation, or maybe I'm not going fast enough for you?'

'Sorry about that Sir, but I'm sure this is our man. As you weren't here I had a word with Chief Superintendent Willingdon who said that he'd expect you to give it your priority attention when you got back.'

'Terrific, I'm out of the office for a bit and everyone starts using their bleedin' initiative. We've got a man who jumped off London Bridge. Remind me sergeant, what is it that we do here?'

'Missing persons Sir.'

'Well he's hardly bloody missing if he's downstairs is he! And as for this cock and bull story, is it your secret mission to waste my time?'

'Sir, if I could explain.'

'That'd be a first, go on.'

'It's like this Sir, after he jumped off the bridge, he was picked up by the MPU, Marine Police Unit.'

'I know what MPU stands for.'

'Sorry Sir. Anyway, when they got him on the boat, he kept going on about these people that were trying to abduct him.'

'The Quentin Tarantino tribute band,' Sutherland sneered as he flicked through the file.

'I'm taking that with a pinch of salt Sir; I think that's part of a bigger clever scheme. Anyway the MPU got in touch with me, I was at Hendon with some of them, and they knew I was work-ing on the A,B..., on missing persons, so put me onto it.'

'Get to the point sergeant. I've only got a year left on the force.'

'That's what I'm trying to say Sir. I think he's our man. It's a classic double bluff. He's set this whole thing up to convince us that he's a victim of the kidnapper, when actually he's the kidnapper himself. That way he removes himself as a suspect from the enquiry.'

'And he's doing this now because?'

'He's dead crafty Sir. He knows it's only a matter of time before we get the hang of his modus operandi, so he's getting his excuses in early. I reckon we would have got to him by the time he started on bricklayers.'

'And your evidence for this miraculous insight?'

'It's a gut feeling Sir, like you say, a good copper sometimes has to follow his nose.'

'I have to say,' Sutherland was lost in thought for a second, 'that this is absolutely barking.'

Sergeant Bludgeon puffed out his chest and a grin crept across his face. 'Thank you Sir, that's very kind of you to say so. Shall we go down to the interview room now?'

'I think I can handle this. You get back to work. I'll finish this one off.'

'But Sir, regulations state that you shouldn't be with the prisoner on your own. I'd hate you to get in trouble on my account.'

Sutherland deflated internally. 'Sergeant, how many times do I have to tell you that for someone to be a prisoner they need to be arrested first. I don't see a charge sheet in this file, just a statement. Have you arrested him?'

'Not exactly, it's more of a custodial helping us with our enquiries?'

'Give me strength. I'd better get down there before he decides to sue the arse off us.'

Sergeant Bludgeon's pride of a few moments ago had totally evaporated. 'Could I sit in on the interview Sir? I'd like to learn, and I promise I'll be quiet.'

'Okay, but if I get the slightest whiff of you playing good cop, bad cop, you're out on your ear. Got it?'

'Yes Sir.'

*****

Sutherland looked at Sergeant Bludgeon's suspect through the glass pane of the interview room door. He always liked to take a few seconds, which is all it took after his many years on the force to assess the person he was to talk to.

He checked the file. John Cranston. He looked back through the pane. He reckoned Cranston was about six foot three, twelve stone'ish, cropped hair, with the lean physique that he associated with someone whose occupation was primarily manual labour. Cranston was dressed in regulation paper overalls, his fingers tapping on the desk. For a man who had gone through the drama that he had claimed, he seemed merely agitated. This wouldn't take long he told himself as he entered the room.

'About time, can I go now?' asked John.

'Mr Cranston, I'm Detective Inspector Sutherland and this is Sergeant Bludgeon, who I believe you've met. I've read your statement and there are a few details I'd like to check, and then you're free to go.'

'Okay, fine. Let's get this over with.'

Sutherland opened the file, quickly reviewed the statement again and looked across the table. 'Mr Cranston, you state that you attended a meeting arranged by an old friend of yours and that when you got there, you were instead threatened and assaulted by three men, who you've provided some very colourful descriptions of. Did Mr Ashcombe have any enemies that you know of?'

'I told you, I don't know.'

'Would Mr Ashcombe have any reason for you to come to harm?'

'No. I've known him for years. We went to school together.'

Sutherland referred back to the file. 'You say that the one in charge, this Mr Black, looked like the actor James Mason. Could we narrow that down a bit? Prisoner of Zenda, or North by Northwest?'

'More North by Northwest I would say.'

Sergeant Bludgeon whispered into Sutherland's ear. 'Sorry Sir, is this some kind of code?'

'Not now sergeant.'

Sutherland turned his attention back to John. 'And these other two, Mr Blue has a face like a,' he read directly from the file, "crumpled crisp packet".'

'Yeah, and he was covered in these scars, like he'd had chicken pox or something.'

'And Mr Green looks like a "ferret with a broken nose".'

'That's right, although I think I made it worse when I hit him with the gun.'

Sutherland looked back at the papers. 'This would be the gun that you snatched out of the hand of Mr Black and threw over your shoulder?'

'Yes, but I didn't think it was real at the time.'

Sutherland looked at the clock on the far wall behind Cranston. This was going nowhere. 'I see. Do you have anything else to add to your statement?'

'No.'

He made some notes on his pad. He'd heard enough. He turned the file round and pushed it towards John. 'If you could sign your statement, you'll be free to go.'

'Not dressed like this I'm not.'

'Sergeant?'

'When we brought Mr Cranston in he was still damp and Fletcher didn't want his cell getting wet so we borrowed some overalls from the crime scene boys. I didn't think they'd miss them.'

'Sergeant, get Mr Cranston's clothes.'

Sutherland closed the file jacket with the now signed statement. 'You're in luck. My sergeant picked up your jacket when he went to the Imperial Tower to check out your story. Someone handed it in at the reception. At least that's dry.'

'So you believe me then.'

'Let's just say that we can verify some of your statement and that we'll keep the details on file as part of our enquiries. Of course, if anything else comes to mind you can contact me on this number,' and Sutherland handed over a card with generic contact details. 'One last thing - don't go jumping off any more bridges. You were lucky today - you could have been killed.'

'Thanks - I'll bear that in mind.'

Sergeant Bludgeon returned with John's clothes who changed quickly there and then in the interview room. He was a sorry sight; the trousers were stained and wrinkled, obviously having been dried in a heap near or on a radiator.

With some disappointment, Sergeant Bludgeon led John to the station exit, then as instructed, reported to Sutherland's office.

'Do you think letting him go was a good idea Sir?' Bludgeon asked.

'We can't detain people because we think they might be a paranoid Walter Mitty. We're policemen, not psychiatrists. Anyway, he's not a kidnapping mastermind.'

'Are you sure Sir?'

'Trust me sergeant, I've checked his record and I know the type. All we have to do now is find a James Mason look-alike, someone that could give John Merrick a run for his money, and a short-sighted ferret-man.'

'How do you know he's short-sighted?'

'Elementary my dear Bludgeon,' he'd waited years for this opportunity. 'Anyone who can't see a gun heading for his face obviously needs glasses.'

'Amazing Sir! I'll put out an APB right away.'

'Sergeant.'

'Yes Sir?'

'First things first, don't use those American cop show terms, and secondly, I was being ironic.'

'Oh I see. Like Nelson's column.'

'No, that's iconic.' Count to ten he told himself. 'Get back to what you were doing and leave the Tarantino gang to me.'

Sergeant Bludgeon returned to his desk, only to come back a moment later.

'Don't you ever knock sergeant?'

'Sorry Sir, but I'd thought you'd like to know. Another accountant's been reported missing.'

7 / Gardener On The Run

John's relief after the police rescue was short lived. Sergeant Bludgeon was as thorough and tenacious as a terrier. John reckoned that his only chance of ending the interview quickly was to throw him a bone, and what a bone! A story of intrigue and kidnap which he thought would have had him thrown out on the street for wasting police time, but he didn't count on the sergeant who went over the smallest details, almost as if he believed him. Yet not once was the attack on the policeman mentioned, and he wasn't going to bring it up. The last thing he needed was a charge of assault on an officer of the law.

With his allowed phone call, John had rang the office to tell Alice that she was to close up immediately, and not to argue with him. Instead, he had to leave an ambiguous message on the answer machine.

Whoever these people were, they believed that Martin had given something to him that they wanted. What it was he didn't know, but either by association, or by a deliberate plan, he was up to his eyes in something nasty. It might only be a matter of time before the Tarantino mob visited the office of Cranston Gardening Services, with Alice next on their list. That was why he was running the half-mile or so down the Farringdon Road as fast as his legs would carry him.

The old factory which now housed his base was at the end of a side road leading off from Farringdon Road. A dead end for vehicles, it tapered off into a maze of pedestrian passageways. John ran past this road, doubling back on himself round the back of what was the old piano works, and via the convoluted alleyways made his way to the rear of the factory without being seen from the front entrance.

He raised the shutters on the loading bay, closing them after him and collapsed on the floor to recover his breath. Two minutes, he told himself, two minutes.

At the furthest corner of the loading area, there was a folding scissor gate door with a crude 'Out of Order' sign hanging from the handle. This ancient lift had been in regular use when the factory was operational, on the understanding that no one ever pushed the button for the first floor.

*****

Following the agreement with Jack Armstrong, John was curious as to what he was custodian of, so of course he had taken the lift to the first floor. He found that the way out was blocked by two wooden doors, hinged so that they met in the middle. It was only after Alice investigated a strange banging noise that it turned out the exit was into the original governor's office, which John had taken over. Rather than undergo an extensive conversion to office space, the previous owner had disguised the lift as a built in wardrobe. After sorting through every unlabelled key in a rusting key cabinet, Alice was finally able to open the doors to release John, who had been doing his best Steve McQueen impression, minus the baseball.

*****

He closed the scissor gate behind him and pressed the button for the first floor. The lift shuddered, moved about an inch, and stopped. He opened the gate, and forcefully pushed it closed again, making sure the latch had fully engaged. This was the only concession to safety that this ancient transport had, it wouldn't move if the gate didn't close fully. He tried the button again, the lift shuddered and moved upwards as he watched the concrete of the shaft pass by and it jarred to a halt behind wooden doors. Opening the scissor gate, he peered through the narrow gap where the doors met. He couldn't see Alice at her desk or anyone else in the office.

Pushing the doors outwards he poked his head through

the gap, and as he did so there was a whooshing sound of a cricket bat travelling at speed just as it stopped a fraction of an inch from his head.

'What are you playing at?' exclaimed Alice. 'You nearly frightened the life out of me, what with that message and sneaking around in that lift. I could've killed you! And look at the state of you!'

John stepped out, lowered the venetian blinds, and half looked through the slats. 'I haven't got time to explain. There's a bunch of nutters after me who think I've got something they want, and they're not taking "No" for an answer. I don't know what they've done with Martin, but I'm next.'

'Martin? What's he got to do with this? Who are these people? Can you please slow down.'

'There's no time. You need to get away from here.' John looked out again through the gap of the blinds. A black Range Rover pulled up outside the factory. It was the Tarantino mob. 'Oh for crying out loud. They're here!'

'Who are you talking about?' asked Alice, both exasperated and concerned at John's state.

'Them! The ones that are after me. You need to get out of here now. I'll hide. With a bit of luck they won't find me and they'll move on.'

He took the cricket bat and was about to make a dash for the stairs when Alice stopped him.

'Wait, I've got a better idea,' she ordered. 'Get back in the lift now and don't make a sound.'

'Alice?'

'Quick!', and she shoved him back into the box and closed the wardrobe doors behind him.

Alice went back to her desk and composed herself as she saw a shadow at the half-frosted door. The person who entered wasn't quite what she was expecting. Immaculately dressed in a dark three-piece suit, he reminded her of the actor James Mason.

'Good morning. These are the offices of Cranston Gardening Services, yes?'

John heard that familiar voice, Mr Black. His grip tightened around the bat.

'That's us,' replied Alice. 'What can we help you with today?'

'I was hoping to meet Mr Cranston. He's been recommended to me by a friend as being one of the best gardeners he's used in years.'

'That's good to hear, we always like to have happy customers,' replied Alice in her best receptionist voice, 'but I'm afraid Mr Cranston isn't here at the moment, you've just missed him.'

'Have I really? That's a pity. Never mind, I can always come back later today. Perhaps I could make an appointment?'

John was watching the proceedings through the chink of the doors. Alice was making a show of checking the diary. Meanwhile Mr Black scanned the office, and for one moment, his gaze settled on the wardrobe doors. John held his breath and slowly edged the small inside brass door bolts into place.

Alice diverted Mr Black's attention. 'It looks like the earliest I can do Mr? I'm sorry, I didn't catch your name, it's so rude of me. I got distracted with the diary, sorry.'

'Cooke.'

'Mr Cooke. Is that with or without an 'e'?'

'With.'

'What an interesting name. You know, I had a friend who was into that etymology, you know the sort of thing I mean? Clever what you can learn. Now where was I?'

'The appointment.'

'Oh yes, that's right. Mr Cranston could see you in about four weeks' time. Would that be alright for you Mr Cooke?'

'I'd like to see him earlier if possible. It would be worth his while.'

'Oh dear. I didn't explain things very well, did I? I'm sorry about this. Mr Cranston was only here today to pick up some bits and pieces on his way to the airport.'

'Airport?' said Mr Cooke.

'It's so exciting. He's off to Bahrain. There are loads of English people out there and gardens are the next big thing for them to spend their money on. He's been talking about this for months and then, out of the blue, he gets an email and he's off. I'm so pleased for him.'

'That's a shame. I was hoping to see him before then. Anyway, you've been very helpful Ms?'

'Alice.'

'Alice. What an interesting name, from the Greek for "truth" if I remember rightly.'

'There you go, you learn something new every day,' she replied trying her hardest to maintain her breezy demeanour.

'I'll be in touch in about four weeks. Thank you so much for your time. I'll see myself out.'

John was about to step out of his hiding place when he felt the lift shudder. Slowly the false wardrobe doors appeared to move upwards in front of him and the brick wall of the shaft started rising by his feet. The lift then stopped and shuddered again. Someone was calling the lift, but the scissor gate was open?

He jammed his index finger into where the latch of the scissor gate would normally go and he could feel that the sprung catch hadn't returned to its position. The lift shuddered and moved as he furiously struggled with the catch to bring it back into its place. The lift stopped so that now only two feet of the wardrobe doors were visible. He could hear someone shouting at the bottom of the shaft .

'Bloody things knackered, no-one can hide in there. I'll take the stairs and check the top floor.'

John's makeshift human repair had halted the lift and he clenched his teeth as his index finger increased in pain while he kept the catch in place. 'Not for much longer,' he told himself. Black had left and when the others didn't find anything upstairs, they would move on. Then he heard Alice speak loudly.

'Mr Cooke. Did you forget something?'

'Apologies, I meant to leave my card.'

As he placed it on Alice's desk, she noticed that on his middle left finger were three small tattooed dots, one on each joint.

'Don't be silly. There's no need to apologise. Mr Cranston always says I'd forget my head if it wasn't attached,' replied Alice, disguising her shock with her best smile.

Mr Cooke feigned an expression of amusement at the platitude. 'Give my regards to Mr Cranston next time he's in touch,' and with that he made to leave a second time.

Pretending to mistake the wardrobe doors for the exit, he placed his hand on the door handle and pulled slightly, to no effect.

'Mr Cooke? The door is over there,' said Alice casually pointing at the exit, determined that she would provide no hint of what was on the other side of the false door, or that her heart was in her throat.

'So it is,' he replied, sneakily surveying the office for any changes on his way out.

She listened for the click of the front door closing downstairs, went to the window and watched as an animated Mr Cooke shouted at two others, who from a distance, Alice thought that only a mother could love. They got into a black Range Rover and accelerated away at speed.

She knocked on the wardrobe doors. 'You can come out now.'

John removed his finger and slammed the scissor gate shut. With an insistent jabbing of the first floor button, he coaxed it back to the correct level, and stepped out into the office, rubbing his sore digit, trying to get the blood circulating again.

'They definitely gone?' he asked.

'Three of them took off in a Range Rover, nasty looking bunch,' replied Alice.

'That was close,' he said, relaxing slightly 'You had me going there. What was all that about?'

'Helping you out, that's what it was about. If I'd told him I hadn't seen you, they'd still be parked outside waiting, and if I'd come straight out and said you were at the airport, they'd think I was trying to get rid of them. A little bit of small talk from your scatterbrain receptionist and they're on their way to Heathrow right now. I'm not sure he believed me, but they can't afford to ignore me. For all they know, you're on the next flight out. It'll take all of them to check the terminals if they think they can get to you before you fly out, which should give you a few hours head start at least, but they'll be back. Why didn't you tell me you were in this sort of trouble?'

'I thought I had.'

'Not like this,' she said shaking her head.

'What do you mean, "Not like this"?'

'I think Mr Cooke…'

'Mr Black,' John corrected.

'Whatever he calls himself, I think he might be one of the SPUDS.'

'That doesn't sound right. I don't think he's into gardening.'

'Not potatoes,' Alice spelled it out. 'S.P.U.D.S, they're ex-KGB, Secret Professional Underworld something or other. That's what I mean by trouble.'

'How come you know all this?'

'How long was I married to Jack?'

'Fair point. So what do the D and S in SPUDS stand for then?'

'I don't remember exactly, but we haven't got time to worry about that now.'

'Alice,' said John sternly. 'If there's something I need to know.'

'Forget I mentioned it.'

'Alice, come on. Out with it.'

She lowered her chin and mumbled. 'Death Squad.'

'Sorry?' said John convinced that he must have misheard.

'Special Professional Underworld Death Squad. Jack hated them. He said it was bad enough dealing with gangs south of the river without having some foreigners trying to muscle in. He had a couple of run-ins with them years ago and told me how to recognise them,' said Alice holding up a finger. 'By the tattoo, in case they tried to kidnap me or something.'

John put his face into the palms of his hands, slowly drawing them down to his chin. 'You know what, that's really made my day. Turns out I'm being stalked by a bunch of Russian, Tarantino fan-boy, assassins. I give up.'

'You had to ask, but look on the bright side, it can't get any worse surely?'

'That's what I said to myself this morning. What with being threatened with a lethal manicure, bent coppers, and a swim in the Thames.'

'That explains a lot. Anyway, never mind that, we can't hang around here. I'm off to Spain tonight; Jack had a safe house there. I've got friends in Madrid who'll find you somewhere to lay low until this is all over. Get yourself home, pack light, and meet me at Gatwick.'

John rubbed his forehead with his fingers, trying to relieve the tension above his eyes.

'Alice, I'm sorry, but I can't. I'm not safe to be around at the moment, and the less people that know where I am, the better. I'm going to keep moving until I've found a way out of this mess. I only came back here to make sure you were alright.'

He felt guilty. Alice had done and offered so much, and now here he was throwing back the best offer of help he was likely to get.

She kissed him gently on the cheek.

'What's that for?' he said, slightly taken aback.

'Honestly John Cranston, some days you really are the nicest fool I've ever met.'

'Thanks, I think.'

'Come on, don't just stand there, help me move this desk,' commanded Alice.

The desktop was made from solid oak planks screwed in place onto pedestals the size of tea chests. Its lack of castors required their combined effort to swing it in an arc across the carpet. Where the pedestal had been, Alice lifted up a square of carpet, and removed some cut floorboards to reveal a sunken steel door secured with a combination lock. Inside was a crushed rucksack which she tugged out and heaved onto the desk.

She checked the contents. 'There's twenty-five thousand in small notes. It's yours.'

John's jaw dropped. 'Where did you get all this? I can't take it. I'll never be able to pay it back.'

'Jack never trusted banks; God knows he robbed enough of them. Now listen. If you draw money out of a hole in the wall, or pay for anything on plastic, they'll know where you've been. Pay cash for everything.' She took out a sealed envelope from the holdall. 'Jack said if I was ever in trouble and he wasn't around, all I had to do was to give this to one of the firm and they'd see me right. I know some are in prison; I'm not sure about the rest. If you can find any of them, it might help.'

'What's in it?'

'He wouldn't say, only that if I opened it, "all bets were off".'

Finally Alice opened her desk drawer and took out John's phone.

'Yeah, I meant to explain that,' said John sheepishly.

'Never mind that now. Whatever you do, don't turn this on unless you absolutely have to, they'll track it. And don't lose it.'

'Don't worry. I don't think I'll be using this much. So what counts as "absolutely have to"?'

'If you don't ring me when you're done, the Russians will be the least of your worries. I'm not coming back and running this place on my own.' She meant to say something else next, but the words stuck in her throat. 'And here's my car key, it's parked round the back. Go home, take only what you need, and don't go back. They'll find out where you live soon enough.'

John was at a loss. He'd learnt more about Alice in the past fifteen minutes then he had in years. 'I don't know what to say.'

'Be careful.'

'It's my middle name,' he replied with a false confidence, trying to ignore the pit in his stomach.

The game was afoot.

8 / With a Little Help From Who?

Sutherland entered the station clutching his bacon, sausage and spicy brown sauce sandwich. It was the only way to start the day, sinking his teeth into a glorious bread filled aromatic meat flavour bomb. As he walked to his office he noticed some unfamiliar faces, and ever curious he stopped at Sergeant Bludgeon's desk, who to his credit, always seemed to be the first one in, and the last to leave. He would have to have a word with him about that, there was a time and place for the long haul.

'Mornin' sergeant.'

'Good morning Sir.'

'Sergeant, I'm wondering, who's the new person at the desk over there?'

'Which one Sir?'

'The one over there,' Sutherland gestured with a nod. 'Big bloke with a plaster cast on his foot.'

'That'll be Murray Sir. Normally works on the vehicle response unit but he broke his foot down the gym, a weight slipped off the bar or something. He's been at home resting until they could find him some desk duties. Any reason for asking?'

'I'm being nosey. It's what detectives do.'

'Of course Sir,' said Bludgeon touching the side of his nose and winking. 'Mum's the word.'

'Sergeant.'

'Yes Sir?'

Sutherland could feel his bacon getting cold. It would take too long to explain that his interest in Murray was his inquisitive nature. 'I'll be in the office if anyone wants me.'

He sat down at his desk and cleared a space for his sandwich, carefully removing it from its paper bag and arranging it in his hands for the optimum first bite. It was a morning ritual, having a late breakfast at his desk. It was thinking food; it helped him contemplate the notes and scrawls on his office wall which he would slowly distil down, bit by bit, into a series of connections to reveal the whole picture. He savoured the first bite with his eyes closed, and when ready, he looked upon his current masterpiece in progress.

'Bludgeonnn!!'

Sergeant Bludgeon showed his face around the door. 'Sir?'

'Get in here, and close the door behind you. What's the meaning of this?' demanded Sutherland, pointing at the wall.

'Oh that. It's rather good isn't it? I looked at it after you went home last night. It's very clever the way you stick all the bits of paper up and draw lines between them, so I'd thought I'd take a tip out of your book and arrange my thoughts. Not as good as yours, but as you always say, learn from the best.'

Sutherland was torn. On the one hand, his natural inclination was to give the sergeant a verbal beating such as the like he had never known. Yet on the other hand, Bludgeon's willingness to learn, damn tenacity and work ethic were balancing the scales bit by bit. He was stumped anyway, not that he would admit it in public. The jumble of sticky notes, sketched lines and random thoughts revealed nothing. It was obvious from looking at the board that Bludgeon was persisting with his current theory, so he should be grateful for small mercies at least.

Sherlock Holmes likened his brain to an ordered attic of finite capacity, with which he took great care not to store trivia, for fear of dislodging useful information in his hoard. Sutherland dreaded to think about the size of Bludgeon's mind attic. It was probably more of a matchbox, working solely on a one in, one out principle. What would replace Bludgeon's current thinking if he were distracted? Bludgeon mentally freewheeling would make a visit by the Horsemen of the Apocalypse look like a Sunday afternoon stroll out for a tea and a biscuit.

'Okay sergeant,' asked Sutherland, hoping he wasn't going to regret it. 'Why have you put Mr Black at the centre of our missing accountants puzzle?'

'It's something you said Sir, about the gardener not being the kidnapper, and I have to admit I was struggling, I was sure he was our man. So I thought I'd take my mind of it by watching that film you lent me, North by Northwest, and then it all became obvious.'

'Go on,' said Sutherland, in between taking bites out of his breakfast. This was probably going to take a while.

'It's James Mason Sir, he's the key to all this, I'm sure of it. It's a classic case of mistaken identity. This Tarantino gang really are after the gardener, he's Cary Grant, like in the film. They think he's someone else who knows something about something they're doing which they don't want anyone else to know.'

'Sergeant, has it ever occurred to you that Cranston was lying?'

'Why would he do that?'

'I don't know. I've dealt with some cranks in my time, and there's no reason to most of them. I asked him about James Mason to test him. No-one comes back with an answer to a stupid question like that, that quick, unless it's rehearsed or...'

'It actually happened.'

Sutherland chewed deliberately on his meal, this wasn't right. Sergeant Bludgeon had actually made a point, which on face value seemed to make sense.

'Okay, let's say, for the sake of argument, that Cranston was being chased by some bad people, one of which just happens to look like James Mason from North by Northwest, and his only way of escaping was to jump in the Thames. What has this got to do with the missing accountants?'

'I reckon that this Mr Black, the James Mason...'

Sutherland cut Bludgeon short. 'I know which one looks like James Mason. Get on with it before my breakfast turns into lunch.'

'Jame- Mr Black is hatching an evil plan which obviously needs lots of accountants.'

'Obviously,' said Sutherland, now slowly sinking down in his chair as his life energy, his Chi, debated through which orifice to abandon ship. 'And how do you know Mr Black has an evil plan?'

'He's a villain Sir. A villain without an evil plan is like, is like,' Bludgeon's tongue was slowly crawling out of the side of his mouth, 'is like a bacon and sausage sandwich without brown sauce, and let's not forget Mr Cranston. If the plan weren't that important, why would they go to all that effort to try and trap him? Mr Black is worried that he'll ruin it.'

Sutherland felt a strange itching in his ear, as if something had stirred. Bludgeon's logic was like a Siren's call. He knew there was a risk of mentally crashing onto the rocks of unreason, but he had to go on.

'I still don't understand why this evil plan needs accountants, there's no shortage of people that can count to ten. If I wanted to cause maximum disruption, I'd kidnap, I don't know, all the plumbers. Not everyone needs an accountant, but I bet at some point they'll need a toilet unblocking.'

'Very astute sir, but I'm afraid you've fallen into the trap. If an evil plan relied on plumbers, electricians or bricklayers say, then everyone would be doing it, and then it would be a normal run of the mill villainous scheme. It's the fact that we don't know what they're doing with the accountants that makes it so bad.'

Sutherland cradled his head in his hands, which fortunately for him avoided a catatonic arrest as his Chi, in its weakened condition, seeing that the exit through the ear canal was blocked by a palm, gave up and went home. He had heard enough. At least Odysseus was tied to a mast.

'Okay, let's get this straight. Cranston has somehow been mistaken for someone who could put a spoke in the scheme of this criminal mastermind, Mr Black, which in turn requires an army of accountants. So Mr Black tries to trap Cranston, who manages to escape to the safety of a police station, from which, he- just- walks- free.'

'Yes Sir.'

'Sergeant.'

'Sir?'

'Never in my career have I come across so many false assumptions, conflations and forced correlations. It's truly inspired.'

'Why thank you sir. That's very kind.'

Sergeant Bludgeon returned to his desk feeling quite pleased, having clearly explained what was going on, although he didn't feel that Detective Inspector Sutherland saw it with the same clarity. Time would prove him right though.

Sutherland looked at the dog's dinner that was now his wall-chart. He deserved that, but perversely the walk on the wild side of Sergeant Bludgeon's fantasies had triggered that feeling in his gut, (and it wasn't the sandwich), that he had when things didn't square. If Cranston had been telling the truth, why didn't he protest when escorted from the safety of the station? If he had been lying, what was the point of it all? He doodled on his notepad before turning his attention back to the wall. He was about to take down the pinned notes and sticky papers when the insistent 'bingly-bung' of his phone distracted him. The text message read:

Buckingham

It was a familiar code that meant they, whoever they were, had something for him at last. Over the years, he had been receiving irregular tip-offs from an anonymous source. They were all unsolicited, unscheduled, with an occasional gem, never expected but always welcomed. The only payment requested in exchange was information, any information. The code meant the drop point was at the self-storage facility in Camden. The locker would be empty by the next day; he had learnt that the hard way. He reckoned he could be there and back in time for lunch. It might be a wasted journey, but in the current circumstances, he only stood to gain, and some time away from the station would give him time to think without distractions.

He quickly went through Bludgeon's report on Cranston, deleting anything confidential from the file, and saved it to a memory stick. The convention was that if he didn't leave something in exchange, further intelligence would not be forthcoming for at least six months, and it was scarce enough as it was. This would have to do. He was at their call, but he needed any edge he could get, and a lucky dip tip-off was better than nothing.

'Sergeant, if anyone asks I'm pursuing a line of enquiry. I'll be back by mid-day.'

'Okay Sir,' replied Bludgeon thinking that it was a bit early in the day, even for D.I Sutherland. He was renowned for his ability to hold his drink; obviously it was because he practised.

*****

For a secret exchange, this was about as unexciting as it could get. No rolled up newspapers left on park benches, secret signs left in windows, or rendezvous with mysterious strangers, (preferably a femme fatale) using obscure pass phrases. No, this was dull. He opened the locker, one of many uniform steel boxes, removed a manila envelope and replaced it with the memory stick. As usual he would examine the contents over a pint, without the distractions of the station. There was a pub nearby which had changed names and ownership more often than a politician looking to be re-elected changes their promises, but as long as it served beer, it would do the job.

Taking a seat at a corner table of the Gibbon's Gonads, he removed some photographs from the envelope. He placed each behind the next, like a slow motion flick-book, and as he did so, he could see the fragments of his wallchart coalesce into something in his mind's eye. The first photographs were of a man dressed in black, a dead ringer for James Mason, getting out of a car and obviously waiting for someone. He turned the photograph over to see if there was any explanation. There was a name, Vladimir Orimov. Mr Black was real, and he had a name-Orimov. As he went through the images, there was a second person getting out and taking a package from Mr Black. For the avoidance of doubt, the enlargements were high-resolution. There was no mistaking that second person. It was his superior, Chief Superintendent Willingdon.

He frowned as he fitted the pieces together. He didn't have

the whole jigsaw but now he could see what the missing pieces might look like and where he should concentrate his attention.

If he was to believe Cranston's statement, and it was a leap, it started to make sense. There had been the attempted abduction by Mr Black. Could that be the reason Cranston was uncomfortable at the station, as he knew that the police were in league? Of course he wouldn't know who to trust. However, if Cranston were in the vipers nest, why would he then be allowed to leave? Maybe, while Cranston was in police custody, it was too difficult for Mr Black to get to him, despite having people on the inside.

What if the command to deal with the gardener as a matter of urgency was calculated to set Cranston free, like a fox to the hounds? Sutherland didn't enjoy this train of thought, it meant that someone had played him. By capitalising on his cynicism from years on the force and Sergeant Bludgeons naive handling, Cranston wasn't going to be hanging around for long.

He took another drop of his beer. What did this have to do with the missing persons? He had been looking at occupations as a common strand, but maybe he was looking too close. What if the thread was abduction and the accountants were the highest profile, mostly due to the mayor's grandstanding? He didn't have a reason or a motive, but maybe Cranston had inadvertently given him a glimpse of a method? On that slender supposition he had one prime suspect, Mr Black.

He stopped himself. He was falling into the 'What if?' trap. The problem with 'What if's'?' was that if you slightly indulged them, they would propagate like coat hangers in an empty wardrobe. The next thing you would be onto 'Buts…' and 'However's…' and before you knew it you were back where you started after several hours of head scratching, and the only people to benefit would be those with shares in aspirin.

He weighed up what little actual facts and evidence he had and still kept returning to Mr Black, who to confuse matters was gathering more aliases than a rebranded nutty chocolate bar. There was only one thing for it, if in doubt, test the evidence. All he needed was someone single minded, with sticking power and an uncanny ability for unsubtlety.

He ordered another pint and dialled the station. An audible picture of efficiency answered.

'Sergeant Bludgeon, Snow Hill.'

'Sergeant, its D.I Sutherland here. How do you fancy some overtime?'

'Overtime? I normally work late anyway, I didn't think that counted.'

Sutherland took another swallow of his beer, or Bludgeon juice as he called it. It made dealing with the sergeant easier. He effortlessly sidestepped a discussion as to when overtime started.

'I'll leave it to your discretion sergeant, but I'll consider all claims favourably.'

'Yes Sir.'

'Good. Now I've got a job for you. I want you to check every traffic camera, CCTV, amateur footage on the internet, anything that you can find of London Bridge around the time that Cranston claims he escaped from Mr Black and co. Secondly, I want you to go through all criminal records, mug-shots; everywhere you can, for anything you can find on Mr Black.'

'You mean the James Mason "Mr Black"?' asked Bludgeon, wincing in anticipation of a full volley of verbal abuse down the line.

'That's the one. If anyone asks, you have my full authorisation to request information from anywhere. I don't care, find me something on him, anything. Is that understood?'

'Absolutely Sir. I'll get right onto it.'

'Good man sergeant, and one last thing. You're to report whatever you find to me only.'

'What if the Chief Super asks?'

'Refer him to me and I'll update him.'

'But Sir, if he asks me what's going on, and I haven't told you yet what's going on, then you won't be able to tell him, so I might as well tell him, because once I've told you, you'll tell him anyway.'

Bludgeon juice slipped easily down Sutherland's throat, instilling calmness. He imagined Bludgeon's mental elves frantically rearranging the bungee straps of his mind matchbox in a desperate attempt not to lose vital information, such as the way home.

'Sergeant, I have to admit you've got me there. Okay- I shouldn't, but I'm going to tell you something, but if it gets out, you and me are for the high-jump.'

'Is it a secret Sir?'

'Oh yes. I've been to a meeting this morning with some very important people,' he stressed. 'It seems there's more to this Mr Black than we thought. I had a chat with Chief Superintendent Willingdon and told him that I thought you were the best man for the job, but he was a bit concerned about security.'

'Don't worry Sir, I know all about that. Before I joined the force I had a job interview with Banham's locksmiths, so I've done all the homework.'

'What happened?'

'They said they'd be in touch, but I never heard from them. I think I made an impression though,' Bludgeon said proudly. 'I overheard one of the interviewers say I should be locked up.'

'That's as maybe, but this is going to need something more practical if you're to get the promotion.'

'Promotion?!'

Sutherland could hear Bludgeons ears pricking up. If there was one thing he knew about Sergeant Bludgeon, it was that he was ambitious. There was no chance of this information disturbing his matchbox attic, ambition had pride of place.

'Didn't I mention that? Well don't get ahead of yourself. The Chief Super might test you by asking you what you've found out. If you tell him, any chance of a promotion is out of the window. Remember, you didn't hear that from me.'

'I get it now. Why didn't you say so? Find out as much as I can about Mr Black , however I can, and if anyone asks what I've found out, I'll refer them to you, whether I've updated you or not.'

'That's the ticket sergeant; I knew I could rely on you. And one last thing, be discreet.'

'Don't worry Sir, you can rely on me.'

'I'm counting on it,' thought Sutherland.

He finished the call. With Bludgeon shaking the tree, all he could do was wait and see what, if anything, fell out.

He looked once more at the photographs before putting them away. There was a chance that his last year might become a little bit more interesting.

9 / *At a Secret Location Near Hastings*

It is a common misconception that the Battle of Hastings was actually fought at Hastings, and there is still some discussion amongst academics as to whether King Harold actually said, 'Be careful with that or you'll have someone's eye out.'

Another common misjudgement is that secret organisations are secret, for if they were truly secret, no one would know about them, which would make recruitment a problem. Even if this conundrum is solved, there is then the difficulty of keeping the location of the secret organisation unknown. Any employee of said hidden establishment at some time will be asked, in all innocence and curiosity, 'Where do you work?' to which they will typically use the Battle of Hastings stratagem, and say anywhere that wasn't where they were actually employed.

The downside to this is, if enough people are questioned, unless they all state the same false location, like astronomers finding new cosmic phenomena by looking where they aren't, by process of elimination the actual location of the hidden base can be narrowed down. And so it was that the Brigadier, through years of experience balanced the size of his operation with the need for secrecy.

This had been made more difficult of late by the efforts of the new Human Resources Director, (how the Brigadier hated that title), who believed that by including two questions on the application form of their latest recruitment drive, they had ensured confidentiality.

The Brigadier looked at a copy, reminding him of the near disaster prevented only by his timely intervention.

Q1. *Are you able to work somewhere near Hastings?*
    Yes/No

    If Yes go to Q2

Q2. *Would you have any objection to attending an interview with an opaque paper bag on your head?*

The Brigadier screwed it up and threw it into the waste paper basket. It wasn't an application form; it was a sign of the decay that was setting into the Society. The institutional memory of how to do things properly was being lost as old hands retired or had gone missing in action, until one day all he had left were a handful of experienced staff and a bunch of useless, faceless, bureaucrats.

Like an overgrown garden, if he was to stimulate new growth some brutal pruning and replanting was needed. He had started by summoning his top team to the boardroom, which currently consisted of his right hand man, Sir Arthur Rotherfield and his assistant Jenkins.

A stranger walked in and confidently sat himself down half-way along the table opposite. The Brigadier half-cocked the hammer on the service revolver concealed under the table by his seat.

'Can I help you?' the Brigadier asked.

'No, I don't think so, but I'd make myself scarce if I was you. This is a meeting with the big-wigs, Brigadier Edward Kensington-Smythe the third no less.'

'The Brigadier?' replied the Brigadier looking at the vacant seat at the head of the table. 'On my way out would you like me to let him know you're here?'

'Yes, and while you're at it, get me a coffee. A latte macchiato, heavy on the espresso shot.'

'Of course, and who should I say is waiting in the meeting for him?'

'Simon Tattershall, Director Human Resources. Make sure you don't forget the director bit.'

'At last, a face to a name, I'll shoot him now,' the Brigadier thought.

It was fortunate for Tattershall that at that moment Sir Rotherfield and Jenkins entered the room.

'Good morning Brigadier,' said Sir Rotherfield. 'Apologies for the delay, but I had to deal with an unexpected problem. All clerical support's ground to a halt while everyone was doing a mandatory'; he stressed that word with a sneer, 'three sixty degree peer review and self-evaluation, whatever that is. I've put a stop to it. Normal service will be restored shortly.'

'You're the Brigadier?' said Tattershall looking at the Brigadier, the vacant seat at the end of the table, and then the Brigadier.

'Yes Mr Tattershall, Director Human Resources,' replied the Brigadier, emphasising the job title.

'You're the idiot causing havoc in my operations,' exclaimed Sir Rotherfield.

'Sir, I could shoot him now if you like,' offered Jenkins, who, as Sir Rotherfield's assistant, had been lumbered with sorting out the chaos caused by Tattershall's evaluation.

'Now now gentlemen,' said the Brigadier. 'Settle down. We have some urgent business. I've called you here today -,'he looked across at Tattershall. 'I don't remember asking you.'

'This is a meeting of your top team, and having reviewed and documented your organisational structure,' Tattershall distributed coloured charts, 'you can see that I am part of that team, so I invited myself. I can't add value if I'm not here.'

The Brigadier looked at the chart and put it to one side. 'Mr Tattershall, how long have you worked in the espionage business?'

'About, let me see...' he looked up as if doing mental calculations. 'Three weeks, but driving efficiency and engagement through Employee Value Propositions and Constant Change Alignments via Honest Conversations can be applied to any organisation. I have to say that your Society definitely needs me to help in facilitating a Transformational Evolution Agenda, T.E.A for short.'

'Mr Tattershall, let me be quite clear,' said the Brigadier. 'Your presence here is probationary. The nature of our business is intuitive, but don't mistake any initial latitude for leniency. Screw up and I will have you horsewhipped, and not metaphorically. You'll find that filed under Incentive Motivation Programme.' He looked round the table. 'Now gentlemen, shall we continue?'

Everyone nodded in time. The Brigadier addressed the room.

'Last week we had Midas within our grasp. Today, we have lost two of our key people and we have no information on the whereabouts of Midas. This mission has descended into a bloody shambles and I want to know why. As you know, I am personally accountable for Operation Prometheus, but rest assured, I'm a great believer in sharing. Sir Rotherfield, what have you found out so far?'

'I've reviewed the file Brigadier. If I may quickly recap?'

The Brigadier concurred with a small raise of his index finger.

Sir Rotherfield continued. 'Agents Ashcombe and Gordon tracked Midas to a criminal gang in an abandoned municipal baths in east London. According to Ashcombe's last report, there was an engagement with Erikson's men and he and Gordon were separated. The baths had been rigged with a high yield explosive incendiary, we don't know who by, which was detonated. Ashcombe managed to escape with Midas. We've no intelligence on Gordon. He's missing in action, presumed dead.'

'A trap?' said the Brigadier?

'Possibly,' replied Sir Rotherfield. 'We may have a leak.'

'Damn - go on.'

'In his report Ashcombe advised that he would hand over Midas at the normal scheduled rendezvous. He never showed. We can only assume that this was due to his cover being leaked onto the undernet.'

The Brigadier looked sternly around the table. 'What I want to know is this. The moment that we knew Ashcombe's cover had been compromised, he was sent an urgent message. Why didn't he come in early?'

'The message was delayed,' replied Sir Rotherfield. 'It was only because of a routine check by Jenkins that we found out. We're still getting to the bottom of it.'

The Brigadier looked at Jenkins.

'I found it in the in the comms room pending tray. I know it's not standard procedure,' Jenkins sounded apologetic, 'but all I could think of was to send Ashcombe a text.'

'There's no need to apologise for using your initiative,' said the Brigadier.

Tattershall raised his hand. 'If I may interrupt gentlemen, this goes to show how disorganised you are. I engaged a team of process experts to implement new communication protocols and processes, and Jenkins here, ignores them.'

The Brigadier and Sir Rotherfield exchanged glances, interacting by a nuanced look that could be mistaken for telepathy.

'What new "communication protocols"?' asked Sir Rotherfield.

Tattershall slid identical files of papers across the desk to the Brigadier, Sir Rotherfield and Jenkins. 'Gentlemen, you'll find in these files the new processes that are currently being trialled. I didn't see much point in engaging you initially; this is small beer operational stuff after all. In implementing change as part of the umbrella T.E.A, we may as well start with the low hanging fruit.'

'Tattershall, what exactly have you done? And don't make me read the file,' commanded the Brigadier.

'It's quite simple. Analysis of all outgoing communications showed that ninety per cent were classified as "Urgent", which meant that any labelled as "Normal" were of a lower priority. Of that ninety per cent, following close examination, some were "Normal" priority messages, which to ensure they were sent quicker, had been reclassified as "Urgent". To stop this abuse, we've been trialling a new process whereby all urgent communications are authorised by a newly created Communications Urgency Control Board, which meets once per week.'

'So to be clear,' observed Sir Rotherfield, 'your team of experts read some urgent messages and arbitrarily decided that some of them weren't urgent, and because of that, messages that are urgent will be reviewed once a week to make sure they're not normal.'

'Precisely,' Tattershall said smugly.

'You're a bloody idiot man!' bellowed the Brigadier. 'How the hell are we supposed to get an urgent message out of the door? Do you realise that you've possibly compromised the life of one of our best agents?'

'I don't think so,' replied Tattershall, unfazed by the outburst. 'If this Midas is so important, maybe you should be asking yourself why your man didn't bring it in immediately. I thought I'd throw that out there so we could run it up an open kimono for a helicopter view of the idea shower.'

Sir Rotherfield heard the hammer of a service revolver being moved to full cock; Tattershall was oblivious to it. Everything was going to plan. 'Brigadier, can I suggest that we instead move on to review the Triple A deployment? Now that I've been advised of the new communication arrangements, I can make sure they're operationally fit for purpose.'

The Brigadier returned the hammer to its un-cocked position. Sir Rotherfield was right; they couldn't dwell on the postmortem. The problem had been identified. He would deal with Tattershall later. 'Gentlemen, the Triple A's, as you know are the cream of our field operatives. Working on the assumption that Midas is still out there, I want every available resource on this. Ashcombe is missing and Gordon, I'm not going to write him off yet, but for our purposes, he's unavailable. Let's start with Carlton, operational status.'

'Retired,' said Sir Rotherfield.

'Well un-retire him,' said the Brigadier.

'It's not that easy I'm afraid,' replied Sir Rotherfield. 'Last time we recalled Carlton to active service, Department S turbocharged his mobility scooter. Next thing we knew he was in pursuit of an enemy agent on the M25. Unfortunately, after the second lap he forgot why he was there. We found him several days later barricaded in at Clacket Lane services asking if the war was over. The flesh is willing, but the mind has gone I'm afraid.'

'Damn. What about "Iron Knees" McGinty?'

'He's on long-term sick leave after destroying that secret volcano base in Iceland. I think he inhaled most of that dust cloud, the one that stopped all those air flights,' said Sir Rotherfield.

'What rubbish,' retorted the Brigadier. 'A little bit of dust stopping McGinty? He put down the chartered surveyors insurrection single-handed. He's swinging the lead. Call him in.'

'I've got a letter from his mother. She says he can't come out, he's got a bad chest.'

'Damn.' The Brigadier put a line through his name on the list. 'What about Cooper?'

'Cooper's a strange one.' Sir Rotherfield looked at his sparse notes. 'He really has taken the secret agent thing to heart. In fact, he's so secret, no one knows what he looks like. However he is extremely effective, when we can find him.'

'So where is he now?'

'We're not sure at the moment. The best we have are some conflicting rumours. It's a toss-up between Japan and a tent in Berkshire. He's either setting up a Ninja strike force or competing in the Great British Bake Off. We've activated the Cooper Signal but I don't hold out much hope at the moment.'

'Damn. Blonde?'

'Blonde….Blonde,' Sir Rotherfield muttered to himself as he sorted through the Triple A list. 'Ah, here we go, Jane Blonde. No recent reports on her whereabouts. Normally that's not a problem, we just follow the path of wanton destruction she leaves behind her, but it's been a bit light on that front.'

'What about sex?'

'I'm sorry Brigadier but I must protest. Lady Rotherfield is very particular about that sort of thing being discussed in public.'

'No man, I'm talking about Blonde's habit of extracting information by sleeping with anyone she thinks is useful.'

Jenkins hid a smirk behind his hand.

'Of course, my apologies,' said Sir Rotherfield. 'We've been monitoring police reports for any naked corpses that are either painted gold or covered in crude oil. Nothing I'm afraid.'

Jenkin's went white as a sheet.

Sir Rotherfield continued. 'All we have is an unverified sighting of Blonde in a temple retreat in Cambodia, bothering Buddhists no doubt. I would treat this with some caution, Angkor Wat is still standing.'

The Brigadier tapped one end of the pencil on the desk and then the other end, slowly rotating it while his gaze passed from person to person around the table, daring them to disappoint him further. 'What's the current status of Agent Marsden?' he asked.

Tattershall was diligently making notes and Jenkins was still distracted, thinking of ways to avoid death by rare minerals, leaving Sir Rotherfield to answer.

'Marsden isn't Triple A rated, so they weren't up for discussion. They're currently infiltrating an enemy Three C in the Brighton Pavilion. You can't possibly be considering them?'

'Three C?' asked Tattershall.

'Covert Communication Centre,' said Sir Rotherfield. 'Do pay attention, and don't interrupt.'

The Brigadier continued, 'As our current elite agents are missing, senile, or sick, I don't see that we have much choice. Marsden is a fine asset. They only missed the Triple A rating on a technicality. I want them on this as a matter of urgency.'

'Yes Brigadier- if you insist,' replied Sir Rotherfield, kicking Jenkins under the table to remind him that he was expected to deal with the order.

Ever the pragmatist, the Brigadier decided to move on. He would have preferred more people but Marsden was worth ten slackers, they just needed to be given a chance.

'Gentlemen; one last thing, while not directly relevant to our current crisis, I'll take the opportunity to raise it now as we're all here. It's been brought to my attention that the Department for

Culture and Heritage is concerned about the number of historic sites that are being destroyed, by, from their point of view, an as yet unidentified arsonist.'

'Yes, Windsor Castle was rather unfortunate,' murmured Sir Rotherfield.

The Brigadier continued. 'I know it will prove difficult, but I want all agents, when disabling enemy bases to refrain from blowing up, burning down, or generally demolishing anything. Jenkins, make sure the message gets out, especially to Marsden. I expect the Brighton Pavilion to be in one piece when they're done.'

'What priority would that be?' asked Jenkins, having finally retrieved his wits.

'Today, and if it isn't, I shall hold Mr Tattershall directly responsible. Now, unless anyone has any further pressing business, I'll call this meeting to a close.'

Tattershall raised his hand. 'If I may, I absolutely concur that this is the correct time to close the meeting. I'd like to add that during this session I've made a rough assessment of your team dynamic using a simple Tannenbaum and Schmidt Continuum model. We have a long journey ahead of us, but rest assured I shall be watching every step of the way while you overcome the challenges ahead, together, and I look forward to working you.'

'Deep joy,' muttered Jenkins.

*****

The Brigadier's office lacked the frills and adornment that someone of his status may consider their due, but even though the emphasis was on function, everything was of impeccable quality, down to the smallest detail of his Visconti Limited Edition fountain pens. This wasn't pretentiousness, he valued and enjoyed quality, and each item in the office represented hard-won battles and rewards over many years. Life was too short for hair shirts.

He leaned across from his Hans Wegner Oculus chair, offering a glass of eighteen-year-old Glenmorangie single malt to Sir Arthur Rotherfield. These informal meetings were where the real work was done.

'Thank you Brigadier.'

'Don't mention it, Arthur,' said the Brigadier, signifying that a candid discussion on first name terms was on the cards. 'This Tattershall fellow, you do know that I want him gone.'

'Really – Edward? That's a coincidence; I've just added the final changes to a glowing reference. I believe he'll be head-hunted any time now,' Sir Rotherfield took a satisfying swallow of the malt, 'by one of the big communication utilities. He should fit right in.'

'Excellent. That'll save me having the arrogant swine flogged. How did we end up with him in the first place?'

'He's father-in-law is one of our patrons. They strongly suggested that we find a position for him. When I checked his resume, it was a masterpiece of lies and exaggeration, so I thought he'd be a good candidate for our line of work. I didn't realise he would be, how did Jenkins put it?' He took another taste of the malt. 'Such a "bell end".'

The Brigadier removed an Eiroa Classic Prensado cigar from its custom box, offering one to Sir Rotherfield, who declined. He passed the flame of a long match under the cigar end, drawing in the smoke and savouring the distinct flavour.

'I must admit, it is particularly galling that even a "bell-end", for all his corporate twaddle speak, could see that this organisation isn't working. I'm not sure of the best way to stop the rot. I wondered if you had any fresh perspective.'

'May I speak freely Edward?'

'Of course Arthur, we're all friends here,' said the Brigadier as he topped up Sir Rotherfield's glass.

'This Drake Society, by its nature is disorganised. It's not possible to shoehorn a diverse group of buccaneers and misfits into a strict structure, but that's where our strength has always been, in our flexibility. However, as we've grown, we've been infected with a corporate culture. It's like a cancer, and it feeds on itself.'

The Brigadier took another draw on his cigar. Sir Rotherfield never could hold his liquor. It was interesting how he had omitted that it was he, Sir Rotherfield, who had instigated the changes in good faith, and it was his pride that had doomed him to compound the mistake by repeat efforts to make the original intent work. He could order him to stop, but why force this proud, extremely capable and loyal man to admit to his superior that he was wrong. There was nothing to be gained by fostering resentment. Better to let Sir Rotherfield believe that his current scheme was working.

'So, if I understand correctly Arthur, if we were to go back to our roots, maybe, perhaps going back to S.O.P, we might recover our original... spirit, for want of a better word?'

'Bring back the Standard Operational Procedure? It could work, but it would need a total purge of the Society of anyone, or thing that doesn't, or could never conform to the S.O.P.'

'Is that so? That would require someone of extraordinary tenacity and experience, a rare commodity these days.' The Brigadier drew slowly on his cigar. 'I realise that this is an imposition, but I wondered, if you would be willing ...?'

'I would need total authority, answerable only to you of course, Edward.'

'Of course.'

As the Brigadier and Sir Rotherfield touched glasses, they were interrupted by Jenkins flinging open the door to the office.

'Brigadier, Sir Rotherfield,' said Jenkins quickly acknowledging his seniors. 'Sorry to barge in, but this is just in from the Gossip Network.'

'This better be good Jenkins,' said Sir Rotherfield, furious that his monopolisation of the Brigadier had been interrupted.

'Let the boy speak,' said the Brigadier calmly. 'What is it Jenkins?'

'A report from our Detective Inspector in London. A gardener threw himself off London Bridge.'

'That's hardly news is it Jenkins,' said Sir Rotherfield. 'I often find the desire to jump in a river is preferable to facing Lady Rotherfield, especially after one of her sloe gin tastings.'

'No, that's what got him in the police station. Turns out he went to school with Ashcombe, and this is the clincher, he jumped off to escape from someone who looked like James Mason.'

'Orimov!' exclaimed the Brigadier and Sir Rotherfield in unison.

'Damn.' The Brigadier's brow furrowed as he extinguished his cigar. 'If this gardener knows Ashcombe, then Orimov has made the connection. Are you thinking what I'm thinking?' he asked Sir Rotherfield.

'Ashcombe hid Midas on this gardener chap. He must have been desperate.'

'Why else would Orimov go after him?' said the Brigadier rhetorically. 'That gardener's on borrowed time and I'll wager he doesn't even know why. Gentlemen, I want all eyes, ears, whatever resource we have to focus on one thing only. This is our top priority. Find that gardener before it's too late.'

10 / Underneath The Arches

Beneath a railway arch in east London, punctuated by the sound of the over-ground railway, to the uninitiated it would be easy to mistake the premises for a shoddy workshop of suspect pedigree. But pass through the Judas Gate inset into the two large doors that fill the arch entrance, and you would enter into a bastion of motoring mechanics, where feeler gauges and ninety year old lathes sit alongside electronic diagnostic machines with equal status.

Two men stood either side of the engine of an E-Type Jaguar, one listening intently, hands in the pockets of his worn over-alls, chin on his chest, while his assistant sat in the driver's seat occasionally revving the engine. The other looked on, his hands betraying the lack of any manual labour during his lifetime, pretending to understand what was going on, while remaining absolutely clueless.

'What do you think? A little tune up?'

'You ever heard a V12 on tick-over?'

'Plenty of times,' he lied, not wanting to be thought of as totally ignorant. 'I'm a bit of an aficionado actually. It sounds fine, all it needs is a bit of tweaking, surely? How about you give her a quick once over, oil change and all that, then I can take her out for a spin this weekend.'

'Sounds fine? It's supposed to purr. It's not right, definitely a misfire.'

'Are you sure?'

'Don't take this the wrong way, but to the untrained ear that would probably sound okay. Somethings not right though. Raymond, turn her off for me mate.'

He removed a spark plug from the engine block and placed what looked like a rubber bung into the vacated hole. From the bung protruded a length of metal pipe with a round gauge on the end. He asked Raymond to turn over the engine, looked at the flicking needle on the tool, before repeating the process as he worked his way down the engine. He stopped after four examinations, carefully scrutinised the spark plug, and then removed the oil dipstick, all the while nodding to himself before sucking his breath between his teeth.

'Yeah, thought so. Compressions down on number three, and your oils not looking right. I reckon your head gaskets going home. I'd have to give it a better look over before taking it apart, but I'm normally right about these things.'

'I won't be taking it out this weekend then?'

'If you want, but chances are you'll stuff the engine, but don't take my word for it. If you want to get a second opinion, that's fine by me.'

'Head gasket you say? I had my suspicions but I didn't want to say anything, best left to the professionals these things, and you're definitely on your game. Here's my card. Do whatever you need to do and keep me informed. I'd like to have this beauty top notch for the season next year.'

The clueless man walked out of the workshop and stepped into a black cab conveniently waiting with its For Hire light illuminated. The arches were home to several taxi hire firms as well as repair garages. It was common knowledge that if Pete Chandler had a customer, it would be an easy fare, either back to the City or Canary Wharf.

Pete washed his hands, working the green cleaning gel between his digits. He knew that he should be wearing latex gloves, but he couldn't get on with them, it was like putting his fingers into individual saunas. He opened his plastic lunch box and took a large bite out of his cheese and pickle doorstep sandwich. Out of the corner of his eye, he caught Raymond looking at him.

'What?' Pete protested, defensively patting his well-cultivated paunch. 'It's nearly eleven. Its hungry work doing that sort of surgical diagnosis.'

'Give over,' said Raymond. 'I could tell the head was gone when he drove it up, talk about smokescreen. Then you go through all that palaver, and he says "Fix it" without blinking an eyelid. I don't know how you get away with it.'

'Raymond my son, that's why I'm in charge. People like that lose more money down the back of a sofa then we make in a year. See that Jag,' Pete gestured towards it with his sandwich. 'For the money he's going to spend on that, he expects a bit of showmanship. It'd be daft to disappoint him. I find it lubricates the flow of cash very nicely.'

'And there was me thinking his sort were skint after the bank crisis and all that.'

'Nah, it's the same amount of money slushing around, but owned by less people. If it's rare, classic, or exotic, people like that want it, and they'll pay through the nose for it. Anyway, this won't get the baby bathed, how about you make a start and check out the carbs? I never rated those zenith's, they're probably due for a good clean out. I'm off outside for a fag.'

He'd tried the patches and gum but it wasn't working, from here on in it was going to be sheer willpower. He'd give up tomorrow.

A metallic silver Audi A8 pulled up onto the forecourt. He looked on impassively; it was going to take a lot more than an expensive piece of German engineering to impress him. The face behind the wheel looked familiar though. The person that stepped out looked haggard, in a creased below the knee length coat worn over what looked like a tweed jacket, and a pair of jeans distressed by constant wear, rather than being torn to order in a factory somewhere. There was no mistaking him.

'John me old mucker. I wasn't expecting you today. I see you ditched that old Citroen,' Pete said, nodding at the Audi. 'How's it going?'

John glanced back at the silver car. 'Oh no, no, it's not mine; it's on loan. Look Pete, I need to talk to you about something, now, in private.'

'I'm fine by the way, the missus is good and the kids are doing well thanks.'

'You're not married and you haven't got any kids, not any you know of, unless you've been busy over the last six months.'

'Just making a point. There's ways of asking and ways of asking, if you know what I mean.'

'I need your help and it's urgent.'

'What is it, Citroen packed up again? I told you it was on its last legs.'

'No, this is serious. Can we?' said John nodding towards the workshop.

'It must be gardening then. What is it now, vampire snails? Not really my area of expertise to be honest.'

John was deadpan and didn't reply. Pete knew that look, and he hadn't seen it in a long time. It would have to be dire circumstances to account for John's unusually abrupt attitude. He'd had his bit of fun making the point that he wasn't going to be bossed around, but now it was time to find out what John needed. He didn't need to be reminded of debts owed. He placed his arm around John's shoulder, speaking quietly.

'Okay, you want somewhere private, come with me, but keep schtum until I say so.'

John followed Pete back into the workshop. He couldn't help but admire the sweeping lines of the E-Type. Pete was obviously on the up.

'Raymond,' said Pete, 'you look like you could use an early lunch.' He handed over a couple of twenty pound notes. 'Take your time and on the way back, if you wouldn't mind, swing past the pie shop and get me a double-double. What would you like *Mr Archer*,' said Pete winking at John.

'Single pie and mash would be fine thank you, if it's no trouble,' said John who, not wanting to be sat down anywhere in public for too long, had been getting by on cheap service station snacks. He was grateful for the offer of a square meal.

'No trouble at all for our customers *Mr Archer,* no trouble at all. Now let's go and have a chat about this car problem of yours,' said Pete as he led John to a small partitioned office at the back of the workshop.

At the rear of this office Pete moved a four drawer filing cabinet away from the wall, behind which was a half sized door that led into an antechamber off the railway arch. John crouched down and followed Pete in, who locked and bolted the door behind them. He turned on the lights to reveal a living area; complete with leather furnishings, refrigerator, and all the modern conveniences required for bachelor life.

'Here you go, welcome to my little bunker from home. Whatever's going on, you've got nothing to worry about. No one can hear us in here,' said Pete confidently.

'It's a bit excessive isn't it?'

'You reckon? I've got bleedin' spooks keeping me under surveillance all over the shop. You want to tell me something private, do it out there and every toe-rag in M.I whatever will know about it. This place is fully soundproofed and bug proof.'

'Since when have you been a national security risk?' asked John concerned that what he had thought of as his first port of help, might turn out to be a dead end. Pete had always tended towards the conspiracy theories of the day, but that just made for interesting pub banter. He'd never gone as far as doing anything about it, until now it seemed.

'Yeah, I know what you're thinking' said Pete, 'I've lost the plot. You try telling that to the government numpties I had a visit from. They didn't find anything, but of course, now they reckon I'm up to something, don't they?'

'Like what?' asked John, now wanting to get to the bottom of this before confiding in Pete about his own predicament.

'It all started when I sold a job lot of parts to Terry the Turk.'

'You know he's not Turkish don't you.'

'Do I look stupid? It was a big diesel engine, like you get on an artic' lorry, and some gaskets and stuff, I took 'em part-ex on something I was owed. Course, I've gone upmarket since then so he was doing me a favour. Terry then sells it to a friend of a friend of a friend whose cousin's plumber knows some angry people in the Middle East. This bloke gets pulled up at customs with it in the back of his transit van on a ferry crossing to Egypt, and when they check the serial numbers, turns out it qualifies as munitions. Terry swears blind he didn't know, and the next thing, they're knocking on my door.'

'How's a diesel engine munitions?'

'When it's from a tank. How was I supposed to know? They couldn't pin anything on me so they've had someone checking this place out instead. Do you know I've had a pint of milk delivered every day and not had one bill? It's been months now. That milkman's a wrong 'un, gotta be.'

'Maybe the dairy's sloppy. I'd say that was good luck on your part. If it was me I'd keep quiet about it.'

'Nah, you don't get it. No one has milk delivered round here. The last guy that tried it, when he came back to his float, they'd nicked all the wheels and had the batteries away. Left the milk mind, can't sell that for much off the back of a lorry. Cuppa?'

John nodded. This wasn't going the way he had hoped. He might have to make his excuses and go for Plan B. All he had to do was work out what Plan B was.

'And get this,' continued Pete as he filled the kettle. 'Do you know I've had telephone engineers here, regular as clockwork once a month, checking my broadband?'

'I'm impressed. What do you tell them when you report a fault?'

'That's the point, I've never been in touch with 'em, there's nothing wrong with it. Yet they keep turning up, telling me they're part of some Proactive Special Fault Investigation team, and then go poking round all the phone points. For twenty quid a month? Use your noggin mate,' said Pete tapping the side of his temple. 'You can't tell me that's not suss.'

'I'll give you that one. That level of service on your broadband is definitely suspect.'

'Yeah, and some.'

John scratched his chin. Plan A might be back on the cards.

The kettle whistled, Pete turned it off and reached into the fridge. 'Kettles boiled, or would you rather have one of these?' he asked, beer in hand.

'No. I'd better not; I'm on the run from some ex-KGB assassins.'

*****

In the back of a Luton van parked in a cul-de-sac street next to Weavers Fields, opposite the arches, two agents from M.I.9, surrounded by a range of hi-tech surveillance equipment, were struggling with their weekly report.

'What have we got that's different from last week?'

'Not a lot. I've got the keyword exception analysis running through the recording from this morning, nothing yet.'

'How about listening to it?'

'No way, if I hear another word about valve grinding, I'll quit. It'll be done in a minute.'

'Okay, what about the milk-round and internet bugs. Anything?'

'Yeah, he's added bacon, eggs, and a sliced white loaf to his order and his internet searches come up as *Kylie Minogue + overalls + spanner.*'

'That doesn't give me a lot to go on. I know. How about-*significant progress made on clarifying religious beliefs and sexual bias.*'

'Yep, that works for me. I'd play up the bacon angle a bit--hold on; somethings come up on the keyword report. What do you make of *vampire snail* and *double-double?*'

'It's got to be some kind of code or criminal slang hasn't it. What time was that?'

'It's when the new guy turned up in that flash Audi, and then the young one goes out, maybe to pick up the *double-double*, whatever that is. What do you think?'

'Not sure, but I guarantee they're up to something. My money would be on drugs or biological warfare.'

'Tell you what, we'll put *suspected dealing in covert biological agents* in the report and flag the new guy for the watch list. That'll get the bosses going. With a bit of luck we'll get this lot upgraded. Apparently there's new kit out now that can hear a gnat fart.'

'Nice one. Now, what shall we put in next week's report?'

*****

Pete thoroughly mixed the remaining pie and mash into the green liquor, making sure that no edge of the plate would be left unclean.

'So let's get this straight,' he said between mouthfuls, 'you're being chased by some Tarantino Appreciation Society, whose main qualification for entry is to be ex-KGB or ugly as sin, all because they think Martin passed something off to you that you say you haven't got.'

'That's about it,' replied John, enjoying the food that Rodney had returned with.

'To be honest, I'm not surprised.'

'You're not?'

'Anything to do with Martin these days is trouble. He's gone right off the rails.'

'You've had trouble with him before then?'

'Who do you think I got that bleedin' tank engine from? I had a few choice words with him after I had me collar felt. You wouldn't believe all the "I'm innocent" guff he came up with. He's lucky I'm not a grass.'

'At least I know it's not just me.'

'No. I'll say this about Martin, he's very even handed. He'll stitch anyone up these days. Anyway, you're welcome to doss down here for a couple of nights,' said Pete pointing at the leather sofa, 'but don't plan on making this your new home unless you want to be a caveman. Word's going to get out eventually when you come up for air, and I don't need the aggravation of your new friends turning up.'

'Don't worry, they're off the scent at the moment, besides you can handle yourself, and I've got a plan. I'll be out of your hair in no time.'

'What exactly is this plan, and where do I fit in?'

'Simple. I'm outnumbered and outgunned, so I get some reinforcements to warn them off and keep them out of the way. Then I work something out.'

'Inspired,' said Pete feigning a slow handclap. 'I still think you'd have been better off going to Spain, but what do I know?'

'If I leave the country they'll only keep looking for me, and I'd rather be somewhere I can speak the lingo. Plus I might have a trick up my sleeve, but I can only play it on home ground, which is where you come in. I need to get in touch with anyone left from Jack Armstrong's gang.'

'What do you want to do that for? Besides, most of 'em are either in Brazil, prison, or dead.'

John leaned forward and looked Pete in the eye. 'You're telling me that you don't know how to contact any of them?'

'Do I look like directory services for the underworld?'

'I'm not exactly overflowing with options here Pete. Come on, there must be someone left.'

Pete shifted uncomfortably in his seat. 'There's only one guy I know of, Milligan. When Jack died, Milligan kept a low profile. When everyone else was fighting over the top job, he laid low, then stepped in and took over when the time was right. You're playing with fire mate. If you think he's going to help you out of the kindness of his heart, forget it.'

'That's my problem,' said John. 'How do I get in touch with him?'

'Have it your way. As it happens, me and Mr Milligan have a business arrangement. I look after his old Jag, and he doesn't burn the garage down. I've got something for him which I think he'll like, it's good to keep him onside you see.. If you don't mind being a courier, I reckon I could set up a meet.'

Pete hoisted himself up out of the chair and left the bunker, reminding John on his way out not to go anywhere. John slipped off his shoes and put his feet up on the leather settee. This was the first time in days that he had felt safe and within seconds, he was sleeping the sleep of the extremely knackered.

He was woken by the sound of a woman screaming, a chinking of bottles and the sound of a crisp packet being vigorously rustled.

'At last, Sleeping Beauty awakes!' said Pete, lounging back in an armchair, his legs hanging over the side with beer and snacks within easy reach.

John rubbed his eyes and sat up, taking a couple of seconds to get his bearings. 'What time is it? What's that noise? You not at work?'

'It's gone six, so I thought I'd give myself the rest of the day off, if that's alright with you? Watch a film, have a few snacks before supper. Here, come and have a look at this, Christopher Lee in The Satanic Rites of Dracula – it's a classic.'

'Six! I can't be hanging about that long,' said John looking around on the floor for his shoes.

'Hold on. You're not going anywhere until tomorrow, you've got a meeting with Milligan, and as you and that sofa seem to be so well acquainted, I insist you stay the night.'

John stopped mid-way through tying his laces. 'What time's the meeting tomorrow?'

'Always work with you,' Pete teased. 'One thing at a time. Have a look at this.'

Pete handed over what appeared to be an extended shoebox. John opened it; folding back the layers of tissue paper to reveal a curved section of highly polished wood.

'Gorgeous, isn't it,' said Pete.

'It's a lovely piece of wood I'll give you that,' John nodded. 'But what's it got to do with tomorrow?'

'A lovely piece of wood. Do you know the trouble I had getting that? It's part of a full, genuine, replacement walnut trim for a Jaguar Mark Two interior. That doesn't grow on trees you know.'

'Okay, but what am I supposed to do with it?' asked John, baffled.

'Gordon Bennett, do I have to spell everything out?'

'Please.'

'You're meeting Milligan tomorrow to deliver that sample. Tell him I'll be happy to refit his Jag, gratis. With a bit of luck he'll be in such a good mood you might be able to explain your problem.'

'Proposition,' John corrected.

'Whatever. You get the idea. The meeting's tomorrow at ten by the Viccy Park boating lake. Milligan will be the one feeding the ducks.'

'What if someone else is feeding the ducks? How will I know it's him?'

'Bleedin' 'ell – he'll be the one with the bodyguard, won't he.'

11 / Mr Blue And Mr Green Go Visiting

Pete walked up and down the pit examining the underside of the E-Type, the light from the inspection lamp showing up the smallest flaws. It was as he suspected, with a good valet treatment, and a middling respray, it looked very passable, but it was only when you looked underneath that you got the feel for a cars treatment, or lack of it. Overall, it wasn't too bad, all it had suffered from was neglect, and thoroughbreds needed attention. He took photographs of the areas that needed work, attached them to an email and sent them to the owner. It was important not to take carte blanche instructions for granted.

He checked his watch. John would be on his way to the meeting by now. After some heated discussion the previous night over a curry, it was agreed that the Audi would be too conspicuous, and despite its speed, a fast getaway in the congested Hackney traffic would be unlikely. John may as well sit in a line of sedentary cars gift wrapped in an expensive slow moving cage with a big sign saying 'Fugitive'. He would look after the Audi until John came to collect, whenever that would be. It would be as quick, and safer on foot, especially if John took his advice and avoided the main roads.

Pete heard the door to the workshop open and listened as two sets of quarter tipped heels tapped on the hard floor. It certainly wasn't Raymond; he was out on an errand, and it was common knowledge that he had come into the world wearing trainers and a baseball cap, (thank God for caesareans).

Pete climbed the stairs out of the inspection pit, he couldn't ignore potential customers. To his dismay, he was instead confronted by two men dressed in black suits and matching white shirts. The shorter one had a large plaster across the bridge of his nose with purple shading around his eyes indicating a recent injury, which when added to the overbite gave him the look of a bullied rodent. His taller colleague was as John had described him. A spoilt pizza of a face that looked like someone had tried to rescue it afterwards by adding grated cheese.

'Mornin' gents. What can I do for you?' enquired Pete.

'We're looking for Mr Cranston, we believe you can help us,' replied Mr Green.

'Cranston? Sorry pal, I think you've got the wrong gaffe, this is Chandlers garage, says so on the sign outside. There used to be a Cranston's up Bow way, have you tried there?'

Mr Green and his colleague looked at each other and stepped towards Pete. The taller one, Mr Blue, scraped a key slowly along the door of the E-Type Jaguar, leaving a deep bare metal indentation.

'I think you do know Cranston, and I think you're going to tell us,' said Mr Blue.

Pete stood his ground. He had seen Raymond at the entrance, having returned from his errand, but he didn't let on, and it seemed that these refugees from a Hammer Horror production weren't aware of him either. He held back his urge to let loose a right hook on the taller one; his back wasn't against the wall yet. Raymond was a smart lad, he could take a hint.

'I'm not looking for trouble, but if you want some, you're going the right way about it. For starters you shouldn't have done that,' said Pete pointing at the gouge in the E-Type's door. 'Raymond hates it when people make work for him.'

'And what is Raymond going to do about it?' said Mr Green in a mocking tone.

'Not sure really, lovely lad, but he's a bit unpredictable when he's upset. Why don't you ask him?'

'He must be behind us Mr Green. Ooh, what do we do now?' said Mr Blue in mock fear.

'Break the car,' said Mr Green, 'and if Mr Chandler here still doesn't remember, then we break him.'

'Raymond, you got all that?' said Pete.

'Yeah, and I've got a barrel for each of these muppets.'

Mr Blue and Mr Green started as double cylinders were jabbed sharply and quickly, in turn, into each of their lower backs.

'If you turn round I'll make a mess of ya!' warned Raymond menacingly. 'Hands where I can see 'em!'

'Yeah, definitely upset' said Pete. 'If I were you I'd think about going.'

Mr Blue and Mr Green looked at each other.

You're making a big mistake,' said Mr Green.

'A big mistake,' echoed Mr Blue.

'Nope. Don't think so,' said Pete as he walked over to his rolling tool cabinet and took out a gun from the top drawer. 'You're mistake is still being here. There's the way out, and don't forget to leave all your cash at the door, paint's expensive these days. Don't think about coming back, your cards marked round here.'

Mr Blue and Mr Green reluctantly and slowly retreated as Raymond followed behind. With an encouraging prod from the twin barrels, they dropped a wad of notes by the door on their way out.

'Who were those jokers?' asked Raymond.

'They're the ones that are after John,' replied Pete as he listened to an unanswered ring on his mobile phone.

'Do you think he'll be alright?'

'Yeah, I reckon so,' said Pete sending a text message as he spoke. 'He's full of surprises that one when he's up against it, he wasn't always a gardener you know. Talking of surprises, since when have you had a shotgun?'

'About five minutes ago' said Raymond rolling back a rough sack cloth, revealing the barrels of the shotgun to be the twin tailpipes of a car exhaust system. 'Anyway you can talk, where did you get the shooter from?'

'Woolworths,' said Pete twirling it around his finger like a wild west gunslinger. 'Had it years. They don't make water pistols like this anymore.'

Raymond shook his head in disbelief, and he thought he was pushing his luck. He placed the assorted notes on the workbench and counted them up.

'There's four hundred quid here. What do you want to do with it?'

'Put half in the kitty and keep the rest, you earned it. You saved my bacon back there, but next time, clock 'em round the head with a big spanner. I don't think my heart can take all that winging it.'

Pete tried to contact John again, but there was no answer. He cursed under his breath. If he followed John to warn him, he in turn risked being followed. Unable to help further, the only thing he could do was to continue with business as usual, and wait. He proceeded to lose himself in the methodical dismantling of the top-end of the V12 engine. He was accompanied by classic Anglo Saxon expletives as Rodney examined the damage to the E-Type's door.

*****

Mr Blue sat in the driving seat of the black Range Rover, despondent at having lost his money, although to look at him it would have been difficult to tell. He fidgeted with his last remaining coin, moving it between his fingers like a Mexican wave.

'Black won't be pleased,' said Mr Blue matter of factly. 'I told you, we should have shot first and asked questions later. Heads you tell him, tails I do.'

'Put it away. We're not done yet. Today my friend, fortune is smiling down on us. You see that van over there?'

'Yes.'

'That is standard British Intelligence issue. Surveillance item Mark three, option 1A.' Mr Green threw his smartphone disdainfully onto the rear seat. 'Those snitcher apps are next to useless, they're all amateurs. What we need to do is ask the professionals. If Cranston's been around here, they'll know.'

'And how do we get in? If I shoot the lock off, they'll drive away.'

'Where are your manners? We knock.'

'And then I shoot them?'

In the back of the Luton van, correctly identified as a Mark three, option 1A, two surveillance officers were each enjoying a greasy kebab while observing the world go by on their bank of surveillance computer screens.

'You know, there's only one thing that can improve this.'

'What's that?'

'Five pints of lager.'

'That's more than one thing actually.'

Their idle conversation was halted by a knocking on the rear doors. They both became motionless and silent as they signalled to each other, confirming that they had muted the equipment of the surveillance suite. The knocking was repeated, again, and then again. It wasn't a random pattern, it was a series of short sharp taps, followed by louder knocks that varied in tempo and volume, and it was the same every time.

One of the operatives took the bible from a make-shift shelf, a tatty ring-binder full of loose leaf pages that had been disordered over time, and flicked hurriedly through the sheets until he found what he was looking for. The knocking was repeated again, exactly as previously, but this time he replied with a counter knock. He waited, and the knocking from the other side changed, and he tracked it diligently against the information in the binder.

'I don't believe it.' He picked up the half-eaten kebabs and hid them inside the ring binder as he replaced it on the shelf.

'Hold on a minute, I haven't finished that,' said his colleague. 'What's going on?'

'It's a snap inspection. Quick, make this stuff look busy,' he said waving at the computer screens, 'and I'll do the talking.'

He opened the rear doors of the van. 'It's for you,' were the last words he uttered before he collapsed in shock.

It's not often that the peaks and troughs of a working day are interrupted by two besuited armed henchmen with faces covered by thick yellow lycra stockings, (that years 'In' colour), so the two surveillance stalwarts of MI9 were totally unprepared. Without recourse to the bible, although any relevant advice would now be obscured by a pungent chilli sauce, the second operative allowed himself to be tied and bound by the larger of the two intruders, only too aware of him muttering that it would have been 'Quicker to shoot them'. Meanwhile, Mr Green tapped on the keyboard, cycling through different views of London within a five mile radius of where they were, looking for a hint or clue of Cranston's whereabouts.

'Anything yet?' asked Mr Blue.

'Not yet, but it's looking promising. Our friends here have already included our gardener on a watch-list,' he looked down at the hog-tied prisoners, 'pending authorisation. Naughty.'

Mr Green entered the search parameters and set the systems off to perform millions of calculations and comparisons per second, looking for a match to John Cranston.

'Can I shoot them now?' asked Mr Blue.

'If you do that, what do I do if I need another password?'

'Fair point. I'll shoot them when we're finished.'

'What is it with you and this obsession with shooting everyone?'

'It's not an obsession, its practice. I'm not going to get my assassin badge unless,' and at this point he sounded like he was reading from a cue card, 'I-show-a marked- and consistent- aptitude-to-operate-at-a- higher-level-grade.'

'Is that why you tried to bump off Quentin Tarantino?'

'Nooo,' Mr Blue drawled. 'That was a point of principle. I've had this code name for years, and then he goes and uses it in that film without my permission. You can't let something like that go. It's a slippery slope.'

'So what was the point of trying to kill him after the film?'

'I wasn't going to kill him, just scare him enough so that he could fix it. I thought the characters should be, I don't know, more mysterious. He could've called them something like Mr Two Reeds or Mr Horned Viper, that kind of thing. I can see it now,' he gestured moving his hand in front of him to simulate a billboard. 'Reservoir Dogs – the Directors Final, Final Cut.'

'What happened?'

'I never got near him - bloody Gordon ballsed it all.'

A partial head shot came up on the screen, a grainy still captured from a closed circuit TV camera on the Roman Road, looking towards the market. The match was an eighty-five percent probability. Mr Green scratched his head, what was Cranston doing? Unless. He kicked the conscious surveillance operative, and removed his gag.

'Are there any parks with benches or bandstands around here that are near the Roman Road?' asked Mr Green.

'What?'

'Don't play dumb with me; otherwise I'll let my associate do what comes naturally.'

'Victoria Park!' he blurted.

Mr Green replaced the gag and ushered a protesting Mr Blue, who had not achieved his quota, again, out of the van and back to their Range Rover.

'I don't get it,' said Mr Blue. 'What makes you think it's him. Liverpool Street is that way,' he said pointing west.

'It's Victoria Park, Cranston's been playing us, he's not leaving London. I've been through everything, there's no record of money spent, no mobile phone calls or messaging, he's gone old school. That's where he's meeting his handler to pass on Midas, I'm sure of it. It's always done in a public space – "Standard Operational Procedure" they called it. When we get there, I'll take the bandstand, you cover the boundary. We've got him this time.'

12 / The Road To Victoria Park

In the nineteenth century at the height of the industrial revolution, the mortality rate of the East End of London was declining, owing to among other things, pollution, slum conditions, abject poverty, and pub fights.

It became apparent to the government of the day that 'Something must be done.' No doubt, many options weren't considered, including improving the overall lot of the population by dealing with the dismal working conditions and housing. The answer was simpler and cheaper than that.

All that was needed was to provide somewhere, an open space, for the working classes to escape to after church on Sunday. They could then return, refreshed, to the squalid conditions that rivalled Dante's nine circles of Hell. Or as they called it, 'home'.

Such was the appalling state of housing in the East End that even the residents petitioned for a park; even a temporary respite was desirable.

While not part of the acknowledged historical record, to those in the know, this nearly didn't happen owing to heated discussions behind closed doors about the parks intended location and size. Using a standard rule of thumb, it was estimated that the proposed park would fit into an area the size of Wales over twenty thousand times. The question was raised as to why then, wasn't a part of Wales not simply fenced off, Parliament having had plenty of practice with the Enclosure Acts. The money saved could then be put to better use lining the pockets of the more deserving.

The idea gained some ground until someone noticed that if the general population of labour were to decamp to Wales on a Sunday afternoon, then that would mean an absence of the workforce on Monday, essentially a holiday! Who would there be to maintain the basic cogs of capitalism? No one was convinced that the top secret development of a steam driven *almost real cleverness automata* by Mr Babbage would be ready or able to take up the slack, and so a compromise was reached.

The park was built on poor quality land on the outskirts of the City of London, within reach of the East End, and the spare money was used to fund a debauched evenings food and entertainment for the local councillors at Christmas.

To this day, Victoria Park has been a vanguard against the concrete encroachment of London, a green oasis in a sea of urban sprawl.

*****

John had left Pete that morning after a hearty breakfast, eaten at a civilised pace in the safety of the bunker. Pete, after much discussion, took responsibility for looking after Alice's car, especially as John promised that he would relay his loving care. Pete reckoned that anything that would gain him favour with 'That right little cracker,' would stand him in good stead.

Avoiding the main thoroughfares, John took a roundabout route through the Bethnal Green gardens. As much as possible he stayed parallel to the Roman road by following the back streets and weaving through the housing estates that fronted the main thoroughfare. Only at one point did he briefly exit onto the pavement, before dropping down via a pedestrian underpass onto the towpath of the Regents canal. From past explorations when he was a young lad he knew this would bring him out a short distance from the park boating lake, it not being far from where the canal passed under the Cricketers Bridge.

Leaving the waterway, as he looked across the Old Ford road towards the park; his thoughts were a mixture of fond memories and alert caution. Entering by a side gate, and under the cover of the trees he scanned the lake and surroundings. In the distance, to his right, he spotted the Jaguar car, described by Pete as an 'Inspector Morse job'. Trees interspersed with benches lined the boundary between where the car was parked on the single track road and the lake. By one of the seats stood an imposing figure of a man wearing a tailored overcoat, leather gloves and a homburg hat. They pulled off the trick of simultaneously looking like they owned the grounds while having popped in to feed the ducks.

'That must be Milligan,' thought John, and as he approached, he was interrupted by a voice coming from the Jaguar.

'Going somewhere mate?'

John assumed that was the bodyguard. His initial inclination was to tell him to mind his own business, but as he wanted Milligan's help, he decided that a more conciliatory approach might be in order.

'I'm here to see Mr Milligan, I've got a delivery.'

'Give it here,' said the bodyguard reaching out of the window. 'I'll see he gets it.'

'Sorry. I can't do that. I've got to hand this over in person.'

The bodyguard opened the door and unfolded himself from the driver's seat, extending himself to his full height, a head and shoulders above John. He was lean, but not scrawny, his hands and neck showing sinew and muscle that had the definition of steel hawsers. He removed his dark glasses, and looked John up and down, assessing if he was a threat. 'I need to have a look at it first,' he said reaching out to receive the package.

John handed it over and the colossus examined the sample walnut trim, and offered it up against the dashboard, nodding in approval. He put it back in the box, carefully replacing the wrapping.

'Guv'nor!' shouted the bodyguard. 'Your gears turned up!'

'You don't want to frisk me or anything?' John asked naively.

'Nah, you're not the type. Try anything though, and I'll put you in intensive care.'

John wasn't easily rattled, but suitably intimidated he walked over to Mr Milligan. So far, so good, he told himself.

He reckoned that Milligan was approaching his seventh

decade, but he stood proud, his stature defying the effect of gravity and the years. His beard was white and his eyes were steel grey behind the thick glass lenses.

'Mornin' Mr Milligan. I'm ….'

'No, no names,' Milligan interrupted. 'I can't keep track these days. I only get into details if I'm doing business; it makes things a lot easier. I understand you've got something for me. Let's have a butchers.'

John handed over the box. 'Pete said when you're ready; he'll fit it free of charge.'

Milligan nodded. 'Classy. Good lad that Pete. I'll take him up on that.' He placed the box on the park bench and continued feeding the ducks, ignoring John.

'Excuse me, Mr Milligan?'

'You still here?'

John bit the inside of his bottom lip. 'I'm not sure if Pete mentioned it, but there's something I want to discuss with you, a business proposition.'

'Oh, so you're the one having a spot of bother? He said something about it. I'm not going anywhere until I've fed the ducks, so you'd better spit it out. Time is money you know.'

'What I'm after is someone who can help me stop a bunch of heavies, who think a handshake means cutting off my fingers, from chasing me all over the country. I've heard that you might know someone. I'll make it worth their while.'

'I like a man who gets to the point,' said Milligan, looking John up and down. 'Thing is though, to be honest, I don't see what the problem is. You look like someone who can handle himself. Why ain't you sorting it yourself?'

'I'm outnumbered. I could do with some help.'

'What exactly you got in mind?'

'I'm not sure really, I thought someone could warn them off, or something.'

Milligan threw a handful of stale bread crumbs to the ducks.

'Let me give you a bit of advice. In this game you've got your basic intimidation packages, from "I know where you live" to "let's take a ride". After that you're into your "near miss" piano portfolio and "removal services". Then you're looking at your more bespoke packages, which won't give you much change out of thirty grand. Have you tried the internet? You can do it all on your phone now using one of those, what do you call 'em… Mickey, what are those clever online brochures you get on your phone?'

'Apps Guv.'

'Apps. That's it. What was that one you showed me the other day?'

'Thugs4You.'

'Yeah. You put in the kind of blag you want and it'll find the nearest nutters within five minutes of where you are. It's got reviews, price comparisons – it does the lot.'

'I was thinking of a more personal approach,' said John. 'I don't really want to be telling strangers where I am, even if they do have a five star rating.'

'I see,' said Milligan. 'The thing is, I'm more upmarket now, less hands on. I'm more in the consultancy and facilitation business now, know what I mean? You see, the problem is, with all the big corporations an' that doing their shady business, everyone who thinks they're a bit hard has jumped on the bandwagon, its ruined the bread and butter work. I remember one banking geezer….'

John caught Mickey in the corner of his eye, lip synching to Milligan word for word.

'Some bloke owed him some money, so we have a deal, right? I have a word and if he doesn't cough up, I break the guy's legs. So I get there and I find that someone's already been and sorted it. So I gets back to the banker and says, "Ere, what's your game?" And you know what he says? Reckons I was taking too long, so he got a mate of his who knew someone who'd do it for a ton. Bleedin' outrageous. So I says to him, "That's as maybe, but I still went out to the job, so I want paying". He weren't having it, so I had to break his legs instead didn't I? You see what I did there?'

'Kept your hand in?' said John.

'No, working for nothing. It's not a good way to run a business is it? So now I'm very particular, and you my son, while I appreciate you bringing that wood along, don't have what we call in the trade...' he clicked his fingers. 'Mickey?'

'Provenance, Guv'.'

'Provenance. That's it.'

John reached into his overcoat pocket and removed two envelopes. One he had made up earlier with a wedge of notes to save him rummaging in his rucksack, and the other was the letter that Alice had given him.

'What if I said I had a letter of recommendation from Jack Armstrong?'

At the mention of Jack's name, a storm temporarily passed over Milligan's face. John handed over the cash and the sealed envelope that Alice had given him, trusting that Fate wouldn't play some cruel trick. For all he knew it might say that if the person who handed over the letter wasn't Alice Armstrong, to give them a good kicking, and Milligan had the look of man who wouldn't hesitate to prescribe the same.

Milligan opened the envelope of cash first and looked at John as if to say, 'You think you can buy me that easily?'

'It's a sign of good faith. I like my legs the way they are,' John elaborated, seemingly to Milligan's satisfaction.

Milligan opened the letter and after what seemed like an eternity, he smiled. 'Oh very Richelieu. You read this?' he asked rhetorically.

'No, can't say I have,' replied John cautiously.

'You'll like this,' and he proceeded to read it out. '*The bearer of this letter should be afforded all assistance and protection...*, Jack's brief wrote that I reckon,... *or I'll have words*. That's definitely Jack. The thing is, me and Jack never got on, and what with him being dead, this means naff all now. I'll hang onto it though. We wouldn't want this doing the rounds and giving people ideas would we?'

'Okay, Jack's gone, but the fact I've got the letter, and I know Pete, that's got to stand for something surely?' John insisted, hiding his concern that his best hand had been dismissed.

'Maybe,' replied Milligan stuffing the envelope of notes into his inside pocket. 'I'm still not sure though as to why you can't sort this yourself.'

'They've got guns.'

'Ah well, that's different. Why didn't you say? Mind you, something like that's going to be a bit pricey. How much cash can you get your hands on?'

'About twenty grand odd,' said John. There was no point being coy.

Milligan shook his head and John could see Hope hiring a boat and paddling away across the park lake.

'I'll tell you what I'll do,' said Milligan. 'You look like a man who's looking for a cosy little one bed flat to rent, say Stepney way.'

'I do?'

'Yeah, definitely. For a small fee,' he tapped the breast of his overcoat where he had stuffed the cash, 'you can go and have a quick shufti. One thing though, the last tenant was a bit of a chancer, if you get my drift. So if you were to come across anything illegal, like I don't know, a gun sealed in a plastic bag in the cistern of the upstairs toilet, which I would know absolutely nothing about you understand, obviously you'd have to report it to the police. Know what I mean?'

'Is that your best offer?'

'It's all self-service these days son.' Milligan shrugged. 'What do you expect for two grand? I'm doing you a favour.'

'If it's all the same to you, I'll find a hotel,' replied John holding out his hand for the return of the cash filled envelope.

'Didn't I mention it? All monies gratefully received but non-refundable. Standard terms and conditions.'

'But….'

Milligan screwed up the paper bag that had contained the stale bread. 'Feeding times over,' he said with a finality and tone that meant he didn't expect a reply.

John rubbed his brow. He wasn't going to make any further progress, and he had already spent too much time in one place.

With a 'Thanks for your time' John turned and headed towards the eastern half of the park where he could pick up the canal again via a small bridge that led back to the Old Ford road. Once on the towpaths he would at least be out of sight.

Milligan carefully placed the box containing the trim on the rear seat of his car. This called for a celebration.

'Mickey, do us a favour and get some ice-creams from the Pavilion caff. Make sure they put the nutty sprinkles and that sauce all over.'

'No problem Guv. You be alright on your own?'

'I think I can manage. The ducks are behaving at the moment.'

Little did Mr Milligan know that Mr Blue had been watching proceedings from the cover of the park trees. Seeing that Milligan was on his own, he was ready to make his move. He and Mr Green were partners, but if he could retrieve Midas on his own, why shouldn't he take the lion's share of the credit? He had seen Cranston hand over an envelope, as Mr Green had said would happen, and with the giant having taken a walk, all that remained was to intimidate a pensioner.

Milligan sat on the bench and pulled up the collar of his overcoat as defence against the chill, autumn was underway. It had been a fruitful morning's work. Admittedly, on face value, he hadn't done much to earn it, but life was swings and roundabouts. He was on the up, and his latest customer was, what was he? There was something familiar about him, and he had that letter from Jack Armstrong, who wouldn't give them out to anyone, especially a gardener.

Milligan cast his mind back to the halcyon days when Jack and the crew were at their height, when they enjoyed the fruits of their endeavours in plain sight, much to the annoyance of the local constabulary. Many a night was spent drinking the bar of the Newt's Gasket dry. Then, like a coin in a shove penny machine, a memory unexpectedly dropped into his recollection. In one boozy session at the Newt's, Jack was bragging about his latest property acquisition and how he had 'persuaded' his mum's gardener, to take up residence, by blowing up his lock-up.

His memory now came into sharp focus. It was him, Cranston, no doubt about it.

Milligan's reverie was interrupted by an apparition made flesh sitting next to him on the park bench. They had a snub nosed revolver concealed underneath a newspaper.

Just enough of it was showing for Milligan's benefit.

'That seats taken,' said Milligan, totally unperturbed by the fact he was at gunpoint.

'Give me what I want, and you can have the seat back,' replied Mr Blue.

Milligan lowered his glasses and looked Mr Blue in the eye. His expression was one of weary despair.

'Ain't you a bit old for this? I don't know, it's only just turned October and already there's people like you messing about with all this Trick or Treat bollocks. You know, it gives kids today the wrong idea. I mean, if I had to wait a year to demand money with menaces I'd be skint by now. Go on; sling your hook. And while you're at it, take that stupid mask off. You're scaring the ducks.'

'No more talk. I saw Cranston give it to you. Hand it over now.'

'Give me what exactly?'

'I saw you put it in your coat. This is your last chance,' said Mr Blue pressing the revolver into Milligan's midriff.

'Okay, that does it,' said Milligan getting visibly annoyed. 'I'm a reasonable bloke, but if you don't bugger off right now, the only treat you'll be getting is when that popgun is surgically removed from your 'arris.'

'I'll count to three and if you don't hand it over I'll shoo…..'

Mr Blue was unable to get the rest of the words out. They had left his brain in perfect order and clarity, but his mouth was unable to set them free. He tried again.   .

'I'll sho…..I'll shhhh…..'

The numbness travelled quickly down his body as if oil was being poured into a hole in his head, its viscous flow paralysing everything it touched immediately. He couldn't move. Behind him, Mickey put a syringe back into a small neat tool roll.

'They didn't have any cornets Guv' , so I got you a choc-ice on a stick. That okay?'

'That'll do fine,' said Milligan rising from the bench, leaving Mr Blue looking like a fossilised mime artist who had escaped from Covent Garden. 'What's that stuff you stuck him with?'

'Something I got off the net,' said Mickey casually. 'It's one of those legal lows. I distil it a bit, cut it with a bit of cough mixture, and next thing you know, totally para'. Result.'

'In my day we didn't have all this fancy chemical lark. We had to make do with a snooker ball and an old sock.'

'Gotta move with the times Guv." Mickey looked down at Mr Blue. 'What do you want to do with him? He was bang out of order.'

'What this?' replied Milligan as he removed the revolver from Mr Blue's frozen grip. 'You'd be lucky to stop a rampaging hamster with this piece of monkey metal. He was never going to use it anyway, he was talking too much .People like him haven't got the bottle to off someone cold in public.'

Even though he couldn't make the slightest movement, Mr Blue could see and hear everything. In his mind he was shouting, 'No bottle! Next time I'll shoot. I will!' Of course, no one heard.

Milligan handed the gun over to Mickey. 'What do you reckon?'

'Not one of ours,' replied Mickey, weighing it in his hand with a disdainful sneer.

'Exactly. How's a man supposed to make a dishonest living these days? Bloody crooks. Here's what we do. Sort out Freddy Krueger 'ere, I'm not done with him yet. Then we'll take a little ride and look for the delivery man. Me and him are going to have a little chat.'

*****

John was soon coming up on the bridge which spanned the Hereford Union canal, one of many exits from the park. His plan was to follow the towpath until it re-joined the Regents Canal, and then go as far as the Mile End road. From there he would be within spitting distance of the Mile End underground station where he could continue his journey out of London, courtesy of the Central line.

As he got closer a parked black Range Rover came into view on the other side of the bridge, blocking Gun Makers Lane. His heart skipped. Was it them? He couldn't take any chances. It was empty, but they could be close. He looked around, he could see no one, but now within the wide open space of the park he felt vulnerable. There was no time to lose.

He ran down the path leading onto the canal, his sole motivation to get out of sight and keep running. As he turned the corner under the bridge he was stopped in his tracks by a sinister gun toting troll with a broken nose.

'Mr Cranston. We meet again.'

'Oh great….'

13 / Escape To The Country

John thought about running, wondering if a rucksack full of cash could stop a bullet. He noticed that unlike his previous encounter, the rest of the Tarantino Trio were not to be seen, and there wasn't a police car in sight. If he didn't take advantage of these improved odds, he deserved whatever was coming next. It was time to make a stand. He stopped halfway across the bridge.

'Keep moving,' commanded Mr Green

'No. If you shoot me here, I've more chance of an ambulance than in whatever fleapit you've got in mind for me. I'm staying here thanks.'

'Have it your way, it doesn't matter. My colleague will be here soon, and then you won't have a choice. I can wait.'

It was a temporary reprieve, but John knew that his chances of taking on Mr Green plus one were slim. He'd give a good account of himself, but that would be little satisfaction once he had been beaten into submission and taken away for whatever they had in store. That was the problem with making it up as he went along, things could never go to plan if he didn't have one. He looked over the bridge, but decided against a repeat of his previous escape. If he vaulted into the canal, at best he could wade to freedom, at worst who knew what lay below those shallow, opaque waters.

John watched an irritated Mr Green as he received no answer to a call. Maybe they were going to be spending more time together than planned, he thought.

'Your boyfriend not playing then? ' John teased.

'You'll regret that soon enough.'

'You sure? Looks to me like no-one wants to talk to you.'

'Don't get your hopes up Cranston.'

'Just making conversation, seeing as we could be here a while. It's a bit of a stalemate isn't it?'

'Stalemate? Hardly, I'm the one with the gun.'

'And I'm the one with what you want, and you need me alive for that. You're not going to shoot me here in broad daylight. Your style is more indoors isn't it?'

'I wouldn't count on that in London. Do you think anyone here cares what happens to you?'

'There's only one way to find out, and if you get it wrong - it'll be a bit of a mess won't it? Tell you what, I'll make this easier. I've got two grand, cash; it's yours if you turn a blind eye.'

'Why would I do that when I could just take the money?'

'You can try, if you want your nose broken again.'

Mr Green winced momentarily.

The way I see it,' continued John, 'you've got nothing to lose if you think you can find me again, or are you that bad? And what's the point in sharing with your friend?'

Mr Green was silent as he quickly thought it through. Cranston was either desperate or deluded if he thought he could negotiate, either way it didn't matter. It would be easier if he were given the money now, then he wouldn't have to share it with Mr Blue when they took Cranston back to the warehouse. He would honour the deal for a couple of seconds' at least, before shooting Cranston in the leg.

'Five,' replied Mr Green. It would look too easy if he accepted the initial offer.

John counted to ten. He couldn't respond too quickly. 'Okay... five it is,' John replied, reluctantly.

Indicating that the money was in his rucksack, John slowly slid it of his shoulder. His plan was to use it as a shield between himself and Mr Green, and to then hoist the wretch into the canal. This was of course assuming that hard cash could stop bullets. As he was about to make his move they were interrupted by a man in a Homberg striding towards them. Was he cavalry or accomplice?

'What do you think you're playing at?' Milligan demanded.

'Trying to negotiate an escape at gunpoint,' replied John.

'Not you, you pillock. I'm talking to git face 'ere,' said Milligan pointing at Mr Green.

Mr Green ignored the observation. 'Friend of yours?' he asked John.

'Sorry?' replied John innocently.

'I'm talking to you sunshine. Now tell me what you're doing 'ere,' said Milligan.

'I'm working. Bugger off,' replied Mr Green.

'Oh we've got a right one 'ere ain't we?' said Milligan. 'For your information it so happens that you're "working" on my manor with a shooter that's unauthorised by Yours Truly. Now I'm a reasonable bloke, so here's what I'll do. As you're obviously new and don't appreciate the rules, I'll reduce the fine to ten grand, and I'll only break one of your legs. I can't say fairer than that.'

'It's a most generous offer, but I'll have to decline,' said Mr Green sarcastically. 'Move over there, next to him where I can see both of you,' he gestured with the pistol. 'I don't believe in coincidence and I think between you I'll get what I need.'

Milligan stood next to John, removed his hat and brushed off the brim. 'Bloody amateurs, you give 'em one chance,' he muttered.

Meanwhile, a rigid Mr Blue, who was in the trunk of Milligan's Jaguar, was philosophical about his current plight. The darkness reminded him of his trips to the cinema, but without the film, people talking, heads walking in front of the screen as the show started, and popcorn. It was a shame; it would have been a perfect opportunity to revisit some of his favourite musicals. That was the problem with older cars, no in-boot entertainment.

Again Mr Green rang Mr Blue. What was unusual this time

was that he could hear the distinctive bespoke ring tone of Mr Blue's phone, a repeat of the chorus of Stayin' Alive. It was directly behind him and getting louder. Milligan stood in front of him with a wry smile.

'That's not Mr Blue is it?' said Mr Green rhetorically.

John shook his head.

'Oh for fu...' said Mr Green as his words turned into lead weights, pinning down his tongue. Before he could take action, paralysis swept through his body, and in a matter of seconds he stood there frozen, as if he had suddenly looked into the eyes of Medusa.

John waved his hand in front of the statues face. There was no reaction. 'What did you do to him?'

Milligan touched the side of his nose. 'Trade secret.'

'Well, whatever it is, thanks for helping me out.'

'Don't flatter yourself son. It was only because whatsisname 'ere had a gun on you that Mickey did the business. I mean, I can't have every Tom, Dick or Harry running round my manor with shooters, especially if they didn't get 'em from me. Now don't get me wrong, I know there are people that don't know any better who are going to get hold of cheap knock offs, but it's like litter ain't it? I'm not going to clean it all up on my own, but if you see a bit of rubbish, you've got to pick it up haven't you?'

'Of course,' said John nodding, agreeing only with the principle of litter. 'Anyway, if it's all the same to you I've got to be going, things to do. Thanks again.'

'Not so fast Mr Cranston. I want a word.'

If Milligan wanted to be assured of John's attention he had succeeded. He directed Mickey to put the suited effigy 'In with the other one,' and walked off slowly into the park, with the unspoken expectation that John would follow.

As Milligan now knew his name, John guessed that there was now unfinished business between them. There was only one way to find out. He caught up easily with Milligan who was walking at a steady, but slow pace. Behind he could hear the rumble of the Jaguar; its distinctive exhaust note had a slight hint of a smoker's hoarseness, as Mickey stop-started, following behind.

'Those two in the back of the motor, I take it they're the ones that are after you?' asked Milligan.

'If the other one's who I think it is, they call themselves Mr Blue and Mr Green. Green is the one with the nose,' John clarified. 'They work for someone who calls himself Mr Black, and before you say anything, I'm not making it up. To cap it all, Mr Black is a SPUD.'

'Makes sense. If he's got a face like a King Edward, that's the set isn't it?'

'No, he's not a potato.   It's a short hand for Special Underworld...'

'That SPUD! Bleedin' 'ell, they can't still be going. We slapped 'em down years ago. I mean, you've got your Mafia, your Yakuza, your Yardies, your Cosa Nostra, all pucker organisations with proper titles, and then along comes this lot. SPUDS, I ask you. It was bad enough them trying to muscle in, but with a label like that; it gives criminals a bad name don't it? Give 'em their due though, nasty bunch, just crap at marketing.'

John nodded sagely; there wasn't much he could add. For a man who liked people that got to the point, Milligan certainly took the long way round. All John had learnt so far was that there was a portfolio of intimidation, and that the Achilles heel of his pursuers was a total lack of brand management. All he needed now was a chocolate kettle for the hat-trick.

There was an uneasy silence between them as John resisted the inclination for small talk. He was sure Milligan would have his word when he was ready.

'Is Alice wrapped up in any of this?' asked Milligan.

'Who?' said John, again taken by surprise.

'Don't mess me about, you're Jack's gardener. I've seen you working on his mum's roses, mind you, you had more hair then, and you're not telling me that letter was left under your pillow by the tooth fairy.'

'She's out of the country,' said John not wishing to be drawn. He still wasn't sure if Milligan could be trusted.

'That's good. I'm surprised you didn't try and get her to sneak you out as well.'

'She offered, but I turned her down. I don't know how they do it, but they keep finding me. I'm not exactly safe to be around at the moment. She's well out of it.'

'What a gent, who would have guessed? You didn't mind introducing your new friends to me though.'

'You look like someone who can handle himself; I didn't see it as a problem.'

Milligan stopped and took a small draft from a hip flask. He looked around the park and back at Mickey in the Jaguar. Satisfied that they were not going to be interrupted his attitude towards John changed from that of an interrogator, to someone dealing with, albeit temporarily, an equal.

'I've got a bone to pick with you. If you'd told me you were the gardener in the first place, it would have saved me a lot of bother,' said Milligan.

'I don't normally do this sort of thing and I didn't think you wanted to have a discussion about pruning your wisteria.'

'No, I'm more a Virginia creeper man me. Anyway, here's the thing, I might have been a bit hasty earlier on. Seeing as you're kind of in the trade, I'll do you a favour and sort out Laurel and Hardy for you.'

'Thanks. Look, I don't want to seem ungrateful, but what's the catch?'

'No catch. One day though, I'll expect you to return the favour.'

'Milligan, you cunning old fox,' thought John. Who needed a gang when through seeming acts of largesse; you could have people owing you favours left right and centre. No one in their right mind was going to cross Milligan and his tame rottweiler.

'Fair enough, but there's one thing though,' said John. 'You're going to sort them out anyway as they've been playing in your backyard without permission, so how about we discuss a few extras for my two grand.'

'What you got in mind?' said Milligan.

'I need somewhere to hide out for a while, but not London, and not anywhere with surprises in the toilet.'

'Is that all? How many bedrooms do you want?'

'You can't tell me a business man like you hasn't got a spare hideaway somewhere, and who's to say those two in the boot are the end of it. I can't return your favour if a SPUD's got first dabs on me, can I?'

Milligan contemplated the proposal as they slowly walked through the park, their feet rustling through the piles of freshly fallen autumn leaves.

'Okay, here's what I'll do,' said Milligan. 'I've got a little place down on the south coast. The old dear who looks after it is off on a world cruise for a year. You can stay there for a bit, keep it tidy for me.' He wrote an address down on a business card and handed it to John. 'She'll let you have the keys. One thing though. Whether you're sorted or not, this is going to cost you when I'm ready.'

'Where's Smallmansea?'

'Near Eastfordstow. No one will find you there, guaranteed. So have we got a deal or what?'

'Okay, but there's another thing though.'

'What now?!'

'How exactly are you going to sort those two? You're not going to, you know…'

'No, I don't know.'

'You know… concrete slippers, that sort of thing. I'll be glad to see the back of them, but the last thing I need is a couple of bodies being traced back to me. I'm up to my eyeballs as it is.'

'What do you take me for? Do me a favour. I'll bang 'em up for a while, give 'em a bit of education, and then dump 'em.'

'Sorry, just thought I'd ask.'

'Besides, do you know how hard it is to get rid of bodies these days?'

'No, can't say I do.'

'It's a bleedin' nightmare, if you're that way inclined, which I'm not; I'm talking hypothetical like. No one's built any flyovers round 'ere in ages, and you can't get past all these new buildings for people scraping around with their little trowels and buckets. I blame Tony Robinson myself. I mean, we all knew where we stood when he did the comedy stuff, and then he goes traipsing around the country digging sodding big holes at random.'

Milligan was in full flow now and in his mind's eye, John could see Mickey repeating it word for word.

'It was me Dad who sussed it; he's not with us anymore, bless 'im.' Milligan went on. 'He used to love watching that Time Team on a Sunday afternoon, sitting there with his Guinness and KP's.'

'Was he into archaeology then?'

'Don't be daft. The dirty old beggar liked watching young girls in vests digging in muddy holes. Anyway, I remember he was watching it once and they turned up at London Fields, Hackney way. They start digging away don't they, and next thing, they've only gone and found some skeletons. My old man choked on his peanuts.'

'I'm sorry to hear that. It can't be a nice way to go.'

'Oh no, don't get me wrong, it'd take more than that. No, it was the drink that did for him in the end.'

'What, liver?'

'No, nothing like that. When he'd had a few, it sort of got him fired up. He died on active service having it away with the home help.'

'Heart attack?'

'No, strong as an ox my old man. Me Mum came home early one night from bingo, caught them at it, and brained him with a frying pan.'

Again there was silence. How was he supposed to follow that, thought John? He needn't have worried as the sound of a three point eight litre Jaguar engine being revved reverberated in his ears. Milligan returned to the present and waved Mickey forward.

'I'm off now,' said Milligan, 'and if I was you I'd get a move on. Don't worry though, I'll be in touch.'

Milligan sunk back into the leather seat, and reflected on the meeting. So that was the gardener, he wasn't what he expected. He wouldn't have credited him with being able to beat up Charlie, Jack's enforcer.

After Jack's accident, Charlie thought it was a done deal that he would take over and he had gone to see Alice to serve her notice. He'd left the warehouse with a black-eye the size of a frying pan and a split lip. Immediately his credibility had plummeted when word got out that he couldn't even deal with a gardener, leaving the way clear for a takeover. No one ever needed to know that, inadvertently, Milligan was in Cranston's debt.

'You're a bit quiet back there Guv'nor. Everything alright?' enquired Mickey.

'Yeah, no problem. I was just wondering, whatever happened to Charlie the Chisel.'

'He pegged it last year, suffocated in his armchair.'

'Suffocated in his armchair, neat, but waste of money if you ask me. He was a pain in the arse but not worth a hit.'

'That's not the way I heard it, death by misadventure according to my mate in the coroners. It all started when he got into that exotic dog breeding.'

'Charlie knew naff all about dogs.'

'It didn't stop him going on that telly thing though, Dogends Den. He wanted money to set up a kennel for his Vegan Attack Poodles business. Big demand for 'em these days apparently. They blew him out though when he told 'em he's other investor was the local post-office. Seems blags don't count, so he starts breeding 'em in his flat instead.'

'What's the point of a poodle that only attacks vegans?' asked a confused Milligan.

'Nah, it's the dogs that're vegan. Vicious though, but then so would you be if all you had to eat was cabbage and tofu, day in, day out. Thing is, he never opened the windows in case they got out, that's what did for him.'

'Stupid sod...'

The sound of an alarm clock came from the glove box. Milligan didn't remember having that fitted to the car. Mickey pulled over and took his phone out of the compartment.

' 'Ere Guv, you'll want to have a look at this. Your delivery man's famous.'

Milligan looked at the screen which showed a picture of Cranston posing stiffly with a spade, obviously a screen grab from some website or other. A sum of money was prominently displayed.

'What am I looking at?'

'It's MugBook. He's all over the undernet,' replied Mickey. 'There's a fifty grand price on his head for live delivery. Why don't we dump the dynamic duo and pick him up instead? It's easy money.'

'Steady on son. Me and him have an agreement; anyway I've got a better idea. Have a word with the Turk and see what odds he'll give us on Cranston staying out of trouble for the next four weeks, I fancy a punt. Next thing put the word out, pronto like, that if any toe-rag so much as sneezes on him while he's leaving London, *I won't be happy*. We can't have our boy falling at the first hurdle can we?'

*****

After leaving Milligan at Victoria Park, John caught the Number eight bus to change at Tottenham Court Road. He was on edge. How had Blue and Green found him? He had no doubt that Milligan would deal with them; there were standards that had to be maintained, even illegal ones.

He looked around at the crowd waiting at the bus-stop and contemplated each person in turn. There was no way of knowing if they were a danger to him or not. He pulled up the collar of his overcoat and consciously tried to make himself less conspicuous, tucking his chin into his scarf, avoiding direct eye contact with anyone.

The number seventy eight bus pulled up and he joined the disorderly queue, determined to squeeze on. Out of the corner of his eye, for a fraction of a second he could swear that someone was taking a picture of him on their mobile phone, or was it a selfie? He disregarded the thought, he was getting paranoid.

It was standing room only as it crawled along Oxford Street, he could walk quicker, but for the moment he felt relatively secure in this packed crowd, surrounded as he was by a shopping party of Japanese tourists, arms crammed with duty free goods. He thought it unlikely that he was going to be smothered to death by a Burberry on a crammed double-decker.

He was right, but for the wrong reason. Little did he know that he was being watched by someone on the bus who would choose their moment when John got off. Little did the person who was watching John know, was that they in turn were also being watched.

The bus finally got to Victoria Station and John marched into the main concourse to buy tickets from the self-service machine, finally managing to find one that still took cash. As he navigated his way through the myriad options he could feel a presence behind him, and then, suddenly, the apprehension was gone, vanished. He shrugged it off as nerves and scanned the departure board for any trains heading south. Anything would do, as long as it got him out of London. If it took him in the general direction of Smallmansea, that was a bonus.

He never took the availability of toilet facilities on trains for granted, and depending on changes, the journey would be at least two hours. There was a public toilet on the concourse. Using the last of his small change he threaded his way through the turnstiles and made his way downstairs to the urinals.

'You stupid bugger,' he told himself. He couldn't think of a more vulnerable moment than when he was in the middle of a Number One, but nature was calling. He was adamant that if he was involved in another escape, he wasn't going to do it on a full bladder, the embarrassment of a mid- fracas accident would be the last straw.

He washed his hands and lowered his head into the sink,

splashing refreshing water onto his face from the running taps. As he did so, a young low level bruiser in a bandana, who had no time for the likes of Milligan, quietly sneaked up and raised his arm to bring a cosh down onto the back of John's neck. It would be the easiest fifty grand he had ever made. Before he could follow through he was silently strangled by a weighted cloth noose, similar to a Thuggee Rumal, his gasping drowned out by the sound of running water as it gurgled down the plughole.

Blissfully unaware, John finished his ablutions and dried his hands while keeping a watchful eye on the only other person in the convenience. He presented no threat; his kerchiefed head was resting against the wall as he appeared to be doing his business in the urinal stool.

'He looks knackered, must be working nights,' thought John.

He went up the stairs two by two, pushed his way through the turnstile exit and briskly made his way to the platform.

The sooner he got out of London, the better.

14 / *They Seek Him Here, They Seek Him There*

Detective Inspector Sutherland perched on a breakfast stool in his favourite sandwich bar near Gresham Street, savouring his freshly made unctuous bacon sandwich. As far as everyone else was concerned, he had taken some time off at short notice to look after his sickly aunt. In actuality, she was an inspiration of health and longevity, but the lie served its purpose.

After briefing Sergeant Bludgeon he had kept a low profile, it was always good practice to retreat to a safe distance after lighting a blue touch paper, but now it was time to see if Chief Inspector Willingdon had been rattled.

His mobile phone chirruped, it was a text message from Fletcher giving him the all clear. Willingdon had left the premises. He wrapped up the half-eaten sandwich in a serviette, gulped down his coffee and made his way to Snow Hill.

Although he had only been at the station for a short time, it hadn't taken long to develop several informal alliances. After a few drinking sessions with Fletcher in the Parrots Spanner, they were now comrades in arms.

Fletcher wasn't bad company, but he did insist on sharing his opinions on the world of celebrity and cutting edge sensationalism. Sutherland prided himself on being a social chameleon, in this line of work it paid to get along, but he couldn't care less about the fortunes of these narcissists. When they weren't camping in a fake jungle, they were the subject of sensational tabloid documentaries. Fletcher's favourite was 'My High Rise Boobs', about a woman who wanted more youthful breasts. Cash strapped, she had resorted to a back street treatment of having them inflated with helium from recycled party balloons. It took two pints to conclude that the Civil Aviation Authority could get away with suing her for unauthorised hovering above Heathrow Airport.

Sutherland entered the station and with a brisk good morning to Fletcher on the front desk, made a beeline for Willingdon's office. He poked his head around the door of the secretarial area that led into Willingdon's inner sanctum. Sutherland could never work out how he had got away with that.

'Morning Shirley, is the Chief in?' Sutherland asked in his most hopeful, 'I was just passing' voice.

'You've missed him, he's not long gone.'

'Have I really? Blow,' said Sutherland lamely punching the air in false frustration.

'He's been asking after you for days. He's not impressed.'

'I know, I know, the thing is my aunts been ill and I'm behind on this case. It's all stakeouts at the moment, deep undercover, very hush, hush.'

'Oh yeah, deep undercover in the local café more like,' said Shirley pointing out the large brown stain of sauce on Sutherland's tie.

'That, young lady is what happens when you have to eat on the hoof. Anyway I've got to have a word with the Chief, when's he back?'

'He's out all day; he's had to go to an emergency press conference. Apparently a woman in high heels has been spotted floating over Downing Street. It's the third one this week, they're popping up everywhere.

'I'm not surprised, I did say something was going to happen after that helium job. I thought it was a bit suss when they interviewed that guy who sounded all squeaky, and there was that thing on the telly wasn't there?'

Shirley cast him a look. 'You and Fletcher; one track minds, honestly. They'd need a bra the size of an aircraft hangar. You don't think someone might notice?'

'It's only what Fletcher told me - honest.'

'Yeah right.' She sighed - boys and their toys. 'I can fit you in tomorrow or Thursday.'

'That's not going to work,' said Sutherland, sucking his teeth. 'I've got some leads on the go and what with this surveillance, it's really difficult to know where I'm going to be, unless...'

'Are you going to suggest something that'll get me in trouble?'

'Would I do that to you? No, I was thinking that if you gave me online access to the Chief's diary, then if I get a spare moment, I can see him on the fly.'

'You know I can't do that.'

'You sure?' said Sutherland with his best-dejected face, which wasn't that good. He looked like he had trapped wind, but it was enough to elicit Shirley's pity.

The printer next to her desk hummed into life as sheet after sheet of a calendar stacked in the collection tray and before Sutherland could reach it, she had gathered up the papers and placed them in her desk drawer.

'Not so fast,' she said. 'This is the Chiefs whereabouts for the next three weeks, but if you want them, there's something that you'll have to do for me.'

'Fair enough, but I draw the line at a new Ferrari.'

'I wish. All I want you to do is put a word in for me with that gorgeous sergeant of yours.'

'I haven't got a gorgeous sergeant.'

'Don't be like that, you know who I mean. Sergeant Bludgeon.'

'Bludgeon?'

'Yes. He's lovely, a real gent, not like the rest of you lot. He's got those wonderful George Clooney eyes, with that look, it's sort of kind, but slightly wicked at the same time. Oooh it makes the back of my neck tingle thinking about it. Do you know what I mean?'

'No, but I'll see what I can do.'

'Thank you,' said Shirley as she handed over the diary print-out, 'and don't forget, or I might have to let on where your stakeout is.'

'Shirley, after everything I've done for you?'

'Definitely.'

Sutherland didn't see that one coming. Could it be that Sergeant Bludgeon, the Metropolitan Police's prize lamebrain, had some hidden appeal to women? He dismissed the idea. Obviously Shirley couldn't tell the difference between a roguish twinkle and glazed vacancy. It took all sorts.

His plan was now coming together.

He and Willingdon had first met at the police training college in Hendon, and in the early years they served together on the same beat although over time their career paths diverged. Sutherland was certain that Willingdon's meteoric rise was owing to suspicious connections and dealings. He could never prove it though and decided a long time ago that tilting at that particular windmill was pointless.

Their paths crossed occasionally, always civil but never friendly, until on Willingdon's direct request he had been seconded onto this backwater. He didn't know why, although if he had seen Willingdon at his Masonic Lodge joking about it with his Brothers, it wouldn't have surprised him. There was one thing he was certain of though; it was that Willingdon always had to be in control. With Sergeant Bludgeon running interference, if Willingdon was up to something, he gambled that this would trick him into inadvertently playing his hand in frustration.

Sutherland looked at the calendar report and lightly kissed it before folding it and putting it safely into his inside pocket. Between this and Fletcher's eyeballs, he could stay one-step ahead of any chaos that had ensued in his absence.

'Good morning sergeant, my office in five,' he said as he walked past Bludgeon, who was fixated on his computer screen.

Sutherland looked at his wallboard. Willingdon should have been on there, but as Bludgeon now had a penchant for using it he didn't want to add any information that would set him off on a tangent. For now, Mr Black was still at the centre of things.

He looked round and there standing outside the office door, as if waiting for a bus, was Sergeant Bludgeon, his laptop tucked under his arm. He beckoned him in, but the sergeant remained still. He gestured again, and again Sergeant Bludgeon refused to cross the threshold.

'Sergeant, for Christ's sake will you get in here!'

Bludgeon stepped in immediately. 'Sorry Sir, but you did say five minutes, and according to my watch…'

'Never mind that, what have you found out about Mr Black?'

'Not a lot Sir, but I may be onto something. I've searched through all the archives and arrest reports for the last ten years and I've made lots of enquiries with MI5, MI6, Interpol, FBI and the CIA. For some reason they seem reluctant to talk to me, so I've decided to use my initiative.'

At the mention of the word "initiative" Sutherland had an embryonic sinking feeling in the pit of his stomach. He kept his best poker face, he couldn't stop now. The Weapon of Mass Distraction that was Sergeant Bludgeon had been launched.

'What did that turn up?' asked Sutherland.

'I thought as Mr Black is a villain, he must be working in a shady secret underworld. If I kept trying to find him, word would get out and someone would contact me, I can't believe that Mr Black hasn't got any enemies. Before you know it I get an email from a chap who calls himself "Deep Thrombosis". Not his real name of course, but he's been ever so helpful. I explained to him how I kept ending up at a dead-end, so he showed me how to get into the back- doors of all the intelligence agency systems.'

'You've been hacking into the Secret Services?'

'Don't be silly Sir, I'm not that daft. It's not hacking; it's like using a stage door. The normal way of getting onto these systems is just there for show, no one in the know uses it. Mr DT kindly showed me how to get in; you'd be amazed at what goes on. You know, I never knew how generous this country was. The amount of money that we send to strangers across the world to put the rubbish out is huge. I have to say it makes me proud to be British.'

Sutherland mentally scribbled a note that read, 'Situation dire

STOP Send Bludgeon Juice STOP' , placed it into a metaphorical bottle and threw it into his mental sea of desperation in the hope that he would get some inspiration. He steeled himself, he couldn't stop now, imagine what Bludgeon was doing to Chief Superintendent Willingdon?

'What have you found out sergeant, and please- get to the point.'

'That is the point Sir. I can't find any sign of Mr Black anywhere.'

Sutherland's message in a bottle shattered on the synaptic rocks of despair. 'Give me strength,' he whispered under his breath.

'And this is where it gets interesting. I've been getting the hang of all this proper computing,' said Bludgeon smugly, 'and I found this video on the undernet.'

'The under what?'

'Undernet Sir. It's the internet, but for villains and rascals. Mr DT vouched for me, it's very exclusive, invitation only.'

Bludgeon was extremely pleased that someone had seen fit to introduce him to their exclusive world, and with some excitement and pride he played the video on his laptop. It was grainy and shaky, probably taken on a mobile phone but there was no mistaking Cranston taking a leap from London Bridge, barely escaping the grasp of a policeman. It was Murray.

'Has anyone else seen this sergeant?'

'I don't think so. It can't be found on the internet and there was nothing on the news, but it does prove Cranston's story.'

'I don't see Mr Black.'

'Are you sure Sir?'

'Sergeant, don't make me put the funeral directors on speed dial.'

'Sorry Sir, let me explain' said Bludgeon pointing at the screen. 'When I first saw this I thought that policeman was Murray, but it's not, even though it looks exactly like him. You see, if you look closely, the Murray in the video doesn't have his foot in plaster; therefore it has to be an imposter. I think Mr Black isn't any run of the mill master villain, I think he's a master of disguise, along with his team. That's why I can't find him. If that person in the video isn't Murray, then who is he? If Mr Black and his organisation can impersonate anyone that well, then how do we...' Bludgeon stopped talking, closed the laptop, and looked Sutherland in the eye. 'How do I know that you're Detective Inspector Sutherland?'

'Sergeant, this is the biggest misinterpretation of evidence and wishful thinking that I've ever come across in my whole career. Besides, who else would listen to this without wanting to jump out the nearest window?'

Bludgeon placed his chin in his hand and looked carefully at Sutherland, trying to make out any joins and then considered what the person who claimed to be the Detective Inspector had said. 'It's good to have you back Sir.' Bludgeon looked over his shoulder and leaned forward. 'You can't be too careful,' he whispered.

Sutherland took a mental breather. They'd got there in the end. He knew that there had been no reports or mention of Murray attending the scene at London Bridge; it was almost as if the information had been lost, and who would be in a senior enough position to make sure that happened he wondered? Two suspects underneath his nose, but what were they up to? What was the connection to Mr Black, and how did the accountants fit in?

'Sergeant, have you shared any of this with the Chief Super?'

'No Sir. I've done exactly what you asked and referred him to you. I don't think he's happy though.'

Never mind, you're doing well. I knew you were the right man for the job. That'll be all for the moment.'

Sergeant Bludgeon placed his hand on the handle of the office door, hesitated to open it, and turned around. He lacked the usual confidence and surety he normally had when explaining his progress.

'Sir, the Chief Superintendent said that if I insisted on not briefing him when ordered, he'd have me sacked for insubordination.'

Bludgeon handed over an official letter outlining a series of disciplinary breaches and an instruction in no uncertain terms that if he didn't comply, his employment would be terminated.

'This is all part of the test - isn't it?'

Sutherland looked at the letter, it was genuine, and at that moment he knew that he had disturbed Willingdon. For a moment he felt pleased, and then guilty. Was he really trying to uncover a conspiracy within the force, or was this a selfish last-ditch effort to wipe the slate clean for all those times that he had turned a blind eye? He prided himself on never being corrupted, but by never making a stand when he knew what was going on around him, he was as tainted as those that had abused their position. It was easy for him now. He had about a year to go, and if they did sack him, he had made provision; but what about the people who believed and trusted him? Their ambitions would be dashed and smashed in an instant. All because the knot in his gut told him something was rotten.

'Don't worry sergeant. You're absolutely right; this is all part of the test. Keep up the good work, and let's keep this as our little secret eh?'

*****

In a secret location near Hastings, Brigadier Edward Kensington-Smythe the third looked around the table at his top team of Sir Rotherfield and his assistant Jenkins.

'Gentlemen, we're here to review Operation Prometheus, and I expect some progress to have been made.' The Brigadier looked down at his notes. He never prepared an agenda beforehand; it gave people the opportunity to prepare excuses. 'First things first, have we heard from Gordon or Ashcombe?'

'I'm afraid not Brigadier,' replied Sir Rotherfield. 'I regret to advise that after this amount of time we should list them as officially missing.'

'Agreed,' replied the Brigadier reluctantly. 'Damn shame. What's the latest on our gardener, Cranston?'

'We've had a confirmed sighting of him from the Gossip Network. He was at London Victoria,' said Sir Rotherfield as he passed around some small printed photographs of someone who could pass for John Cranston standing on a station platform. The Brigadier put on his glasses and examined the images.

'Are you sure this is Cranston?' asked the Brigadier. 'These aren't very good. They've been taken into the light, the horizon isn't straight and the crop is terrible. Hasn't Grimshaw come up with anything? There's never any doubt with his photos.'

'Grimshaw is on a temporary leave of duties at the moment,' said Sir Rotherfield. 'Unfortunately he's developed a habit of breaking cover on surveillance and insisting that the bride's family stand on the right, and he's costing us a fortune in film. I'm afraid we may have to ask him to retire.'

'Damn. How do you propose to replace him?'

'Not to worry, everyone's a photographer these days, what with smart phones and the like. I dare say that if you threw a brick out the window you'd be lucky to hit someone *without* a camera. Jenkins has been dealing first hand with the recruitment, haven't you?' said Sir Rotherfield, casting his drilling gaze in Jenkin's direction.

'No problem, I've found someone,' said Jenkins. 'He'll be starting as soon as the hospital lets him out.'

'Nothing serious I trust?' the Brigadier enquired.

'He'll be fine; it's only a severe concussion.'

The Brigadier placed the photograph into the centre of the table. 'If this is our man, why in hell's name didn't the photographer apprehend him? If it had been Grimshaw...'

'That's volunteers for you, although I doubt they would have been able to bring him in if they did,' said Sir Rotherfield. 'This gardener is more resourceful than we've given him credit for. We believe there's a price on his head, and it's no coincidence that on the same day that he was at the station, there was the largest gathering of second rate bounty hunters since the time of the architects uprising.'

'Good lord man, are you trying to tell me that we've lost Midas because Cranston has been waylaid by a rabble of half baked,' the Brigadier spat the words, 'mercenaries.'

'Not at all,' said Sir Rotherfield. 'To a man, these reprobates, all known to us, have been found tied up, dumped in skips or incapacitated. Not one of them had Midas on them. Our cleaning team have been working non-stop covering up. We've kept it all under wraps, with the exception of some disruption caused by one of them going under the eleven-fifteen to Eastfordstow, but I have no doubt that will be attributed to a tragic accident.'

'Villains on the line,' said Jenkins.

'I contend,' Sir Rotherfield continued, ignoring the droll remark, 'that Cranston is abroad, with Midas safe in his care. I don't believe in guardian angels, so the only conclusion is that he dealt with each of the hunters in turn. I recommend that our operatives approach him with caution.'

'I see,' said the Brigadier, mulling over this new information. 'Gentlemen, it would seem Midas is still in play and that Ashcombe has passed it onto someone quite capable. However, it is still crucial that we find him. It won't matter how resourceful he is, when Erikson ups the stakes, Cranston won't stand a chance. We have to get to him first.'

'Marsden is finishing off the Three C in Brighton,' said Sir Rotherfield. 'There was a slight delay owing to a showdown on the West Pier. They had a backup installation.'

'A backup? Dashed dirty tricksters. Is the Pavilion intact though?' asked the Brigadier.

'Pristine,' replied Sir Rotherfield reassuringly, 'although the pier is slightly smaller now, but as it's in such a state anyway we can blame that on storm damage.'

'Very well. Tell Marsden to get a move on. I need results,' said the Brigadier as he gathered up his notes. 'If there's nothing else, I'll call this meeting to a close.'

As they made to get up from the table there was a knock at the door and a slim fellow, casually dressed in jeans and corded shirt cautiously entered the boardroom, he's arms laden with folders bulging at the seams. 'Is this the senior operations team meeting?'

'And who might you be?' asked Sir Rotherfield.

The stranger held out his hand in a greeting handshake, and dropped his papers onto the floor. He was torn between introducing himself and picking up the scattered sheets, apologising all the while that everyone looked on. He eventually shovelled them onto the table into something that resembled an orderly pile.

'Sorry about this, I didn't know how much to bring with me, first time in one of these meetings and…and…errm, I'm Crickwell from Department S, Boffin branch. Director Tattershall asked me to present to the next operations meeting, which is this one isn't it? It's about the Pandora Protocol. Didn't he tell you about it?'

The Brigadier looked at Sir Rotherfield who in turn looked at Jenkins. No one knew what this interloper from Department S was on about. The Brigadier sat back down, indicating that the meeting had been reopened and that the stranger was going to be heard. At the Brigadier's invitation, Crickwell explained.

'Director Tattershall approached the Department looking for ideas, "big ticket items" he called them; that he could sponsor.'

'Poach more like,' muttered Jenkins.

Crickwell continued. 'I mentioned in passing that I'd been working on something in my own time, and before I could explain the detail he'd latched onto it and said that you would be fully briefed,' he said, looking in the direction of Sir Rotherfield.

'That lying hound! Brigadier, we haven't got time for this.'

'I think we have. I want to know what this "Pandora protocol" is. Go on.'

'I know that you want to destroy the Midas device,' said Crickwell, 'but I've been reviewing our reports on Professor Czeckovsky's work.' He hesitated slightly, taking care to choose his next words. 'Her approach was…unethical, but there's no denying that she was a true genius.'

'Mad as a box of frogs with kalashnikovs is what I heard,' said Jenkins.

The Brigadier gave Jenkin's the any further interruptions and you'll regret it look. 'Continue,' he said

'Midas is unique. Without the professor, this is our only

chance to fully understand her work. We could advance computer science by years.'

'This isn't a university Mr Crickwell,' said the Brigadier. 'I suggest you advance computer science on you own time, we've bigger problems, as you're well aware.'

'That's not the protocol, sorry, there's more,' replied Crickwell. 'We've been trying to hack into Erikson's systems for months...'

'We have?' whispered the Brigadier out of the side of mouth to Sir Rotherfield.

'Cyber warfare,' clarified Sir Rotherfield, 'it's all desk work; you wouldn't get any field reports.'

'I thought they just sat down there playing cards,' the Brigadier said in hushed tones.

'...And it's impossible to do remotely,' continued Crickwell. 'We think he's built he's own private version of the internet, but as it's not physically connected to the public internet, the only way to access it would be from inside his organisation. We know that he's after Midas, so I thought once we get hold of it, rather than destroying it, what if we could edit its core functions? We then set the modified version free, and the moment the enemy gets hold of it and uses it, it destroys all of their systems in one stroke. Director Tattershall called it the "Pandora Protocol". Personally I thought that was a bit grand for a Trojan horse.'

'Brigadier, this is absurd,' said Sir Rotherfield, visibly agitated. 'It has always been the plan to destroy it; it's too dangerous to be owned by anyone. After all these years the risk is too great.'

'I've got a hammer,' said Jenkins, trying to be helpful.

'Let's not be too hasty. I'm intrigued by this Trojan idea,' said the Brigadier. 'Mr Crickwell, if I were to present Midas to you today, how long would it take to make this counterfeit horse?'

'Ahh, errm, well that's the detail,' said Crickwell, looking apprehensive. 'About two years. At least.'

If a feather had been dropped at that exact moment, its sound would have been deafening. The silence was broken by the Brigadier.

'I don't understand why you can't copy the thing. My nephew

copies software all the time, strictly for personal use you understand.'

'Midas isn't software as we normally think of it,' replied Crickwell. 'It's an artificially intelligent, self-sustaining, quantum encryption drive, embedded into a nanite multi-hierarchal platform. The hardware and software are totally interwoven. Trying to copy across the bits we want would be like doing a brain transplant with a dessert spoon.'

'Did you get all that?' whispered the Brigadier as he leaned across to Sir Rotherfield, speaking behind the back of his hand.

'I think he said it's hard.'

'We'll need a bigger hammer,' murmured Jenkins.

*****

The Brigadier sat back in his chair considering the multiple threads of Operation Prometheus, some of which had become dead-ends, some had crossed and become tangled, while others tantalised with possibilities, and it was up to him as to which were followed. He opened his private diary and scratched Grimshaw's name from the ever-shrinking list of people that he could trust to get the job done. Midas was close, but it may as well be in another galaxy for all the resource he could bring to bear. He would never admit it to anyone else, but he was outmanned by Erikson's dark organisation. On his notepad he'd scribbled Trojan Horse, circled it and punctuated it with a large question mark.

There was a knock at the door and Sir Rotherfield entered the office at the appointed time for one of their informal meetings. He offered him a malt whisky, which Sir Rotherfield declined. Not surprising, he had looked the worse for wear after their last chat.

'So, judging by his absence from the meeting this morning has Tattershall finally left us, or is he causing havoc while in hiding?' said the Brigadier, obliquely referring to the interruption by Crickwell.

'I must apologise about this morning, it must have been something he did before he left. Tattershall's interfering fingers were everywhere. The clean up's a top down operation and it slipped through, I haven't got to the basement yet.'

'But he's definitely gone and not coming back?'

'I called in some favours; he's now the Director of Pointless Change and Fettling for a major communications company. I personally made sure he was delivered, he'll never be able to find us.'

'That's the nation's telephones in safe hands then,' said the Brigadier as he checked the top drawer of his desk. 'That reminds me, I must buy some more stamps.'

He held a long tapered match under the end of a cigar and savoured the first draw. He offered one to Sir Rotherfield as a courtesy, although he knew he would decline as always.

'What do you think of this Crickwell fellow?' asked the Brigadier.

'By all accounts he's a computing genius. He's an ideas man though; I've never known him deliver anything practical, it's mainly been theories, academic papers, that sort of thing. I think the main reason that Department S keep him on is because he has a laptop.'

'I have to say Arthur, I'm rather taken with this Pandora Protocol.'

'You can't be serious,' protested Sir Rotherfield. 'We can't have a protocol called Pandora. What message would that send out, that the only thing we have left is Hope? And none of us understood what he said, apart from the fact it would take two years.'

'I'm not worried about the name. I have no doubt that idiot Tattershall picked it because it sounded grand, I don't believe the classics are renowned for their pseudo management manuals. And I don't want a repeat of the Department S rebranding fiasco.'

'Yes, that was unfortunate,' said Sir Rotherfield looking rather sheepish.

'I know enough to be certain that this is a chance we can't ignore, and as for the two years? I'm sure it could be stretched out that long with specifications, design reviews, prototypes and so on, but I don't need an elegant solution. I don't care if it breaks as long as when it does, it's in Erikson's hands and takes his organisation with it, and I know just the man who can deliver it.'

'You're not thinking of Cranston? Why would he do that?'

'Leave that to me. I want you to work with Crickwell on this as a priority.'

'But even if the time could be halved, I can't spare it, the S.O.P is full time.'

'Don't worry about the time. All I need you to do is to advise Crickwell and the Boffin branch that once we've recovered Midas, they'll have five days. Do you want that drink now?'

As Sir Rotherfield sat in momentary stunned silence they were interrupted by a knock on the door. Jenkins entered before waiting for the customary 'Come in'.

'Sorry to interrupt but we just received these postcards from the G.N, sorry, Gossip Network. I thought you should see them,' said Jenkins, handing them over directly to the Brigadier.

He looked at one of the cards; it had a drawing of an overly plump man with a huge belly dressed in a one-piece bright red swimming costume. The caption read, 'I wish I could see my little Willy', maybe referring to the scamp who was hiding in a hole dug in the sand.

'Very amusing, but this is hardly the time is it Jenkins?' said the Brigadier with a deadpan face.

'No, the other side,' replied Jenkins. 'We've got two sightings of Cranston in Smallmansea.'

The Brigadier skimmed the polite scrawl on the cards and looked closely at the postmarks.

'These were sent on different days by different people. By Jove, you know what this means?'

'The post is up the creek again?' Jenkins suggested.

'No, Cranston's gone to ground, and he's right on our doorstep. Get the word out to every curtain twitcher we know. There's a bungalow out there with his name on it, and I want to know where it is.'

15 / Smallmansea

The municipality of Smallmansea wasn't that small, but it wasn't that big either. It was the size of town that, if you wanted to hide one, could be tucked away on the south coast of England where it would blend in with the surroundings in a non-flamboyant manner. Flanked to the north by the main coastal road, Smallmansea was only a destination for those that lived there; everyone else passed it by on the way to somewhere else, unaware of its secrets and history.

Tracing its heritage to the Anglo Saxon's, back then it was a modest settlement led by Halwende the Indifferent, a man of large appetites and even larger proportions. In the tradition of the time, villages would take their names from the chieftain so it was clear as to which tribe it belonged to. In what could be the earliest use of irony, the community of Halwende became known as the 'Place where the Small Man lived near the wet stuff'. Halwende couldn't be bothered to argue and through poor translation and the corruption of time, Smallmansea was born.

After the Norman conquest of 1066, Baron Eau'Comvitte unfortunately offended King William by referring to him as 'That bastard', and not the correct title of The Bastard. As a punishment, he was awarded Smallmansea and the surrounding land. On the face of it, this may sound generous, but within a year, the land was expected to have a new castle, on pain of death. With the population of Smallmansea barely filling the front pews of the local ramshackle wooden church, their taxes wouldn't even pay for a foundation stone. As it turned out, that church would be the key to saving the Baron's neck.

The Baron sent a secret message to the Archbishop of Canterbury advising that he had obtained a fragment of the spear of the soldier, who stood next to the soldier, who was the brother-in-law of Centurion Longinus, who had pierced Jesus in the side with his lance at the crucifixion. This artefact had been touched by the Hand of God, and the Baron himself was testament to its wondrous healing properties. Having been savagely wounded during the conquest, he now had both arms again, and everyone who met him who could count to two could testify to the fact.

The Archbishop bought the village of Smallmansea for a tidy sum, with grand plans to develop it as a pilgrimage destination, with an added castle, as per the contract of sale. The church was rebuilt in stone, complete with all-inclusive sacred mod cons.

If it hadn't been for the tenacity of the early pilgrim pathfinders, the scheme would have been doomed to failure before it began, as no one would have been able to find it. From these modest beginnings, Smallmansea began to grow.

After the dissolution of the monasteries under Henry the Eighth's reign, Smallmansea became part of the crown estate, but it was destined to return into the ownership of the Eau'Comvitte family. Having perfected the knack of upsetting royalty without even trying, a peeved Queen Elizabeth the First bestowed it and the surrounding lands to the newly promoted Duke Eau'Comvitte. This gift came with a bonus royal proclamation advising the Duke that Her Majesty would be visiting within a year. There followed another spurt in the growth of the population of Smallmansea as the Duke called in journeymen from far and wide to build a grand Manor house and gardens. Bankruptcy was preferable to a stint in the Tower of London.

The Eau'Comvitte family always had an eye for the main chance, and under their patronage, Smallmansea continued to grow. Whether it was leasing land to the government at extortionate rates for a military barracks in anticipation of an invasion by Napoleon, speculation on the new railways, or capitalising on the health benefits of sea air, (after all, they didn't have to add the words 'on-Sea'), the Eau'Comvitte's could do no wrong. Over the years, Smallmansea developed into a vibrant coastal town, but it wasn't to last. A series of poor investments and grand schemes culminating in the Smallmansea Pier stood as a folly to their overreaching ambition.

To take further advantage of the Edwardian health craze for sea air and bathing, it wasn't enough that people could come direct to Smallmansea via the new steam railway. It was proposed that a pier, the longest on the south coast, would be built to allow ships to dock and deliver even more visitors. The initial plans were scaled back after it was pointed out that a structure over twenty miles long would, being so close to France, technically be more of an unfinished bridge. This was seized upon as an opportunity to claim that the projected costs had been dramatically reduced. Work started in earnest in the summer of 1913 only to come to an abrupt halt with the outbreak of the First World War. There were several attempts after the war to restart work on the truncated project; each failed owing to lack of money and sceptical investors. The final body blow came when the Eau'Comvitte family wealth was decimated by the Wall Street crash of 1929.

It was a chance meeting between the umpteenth Duke, (they lost count years ago) and an American heiress of an oil tycoon that the fortunes of the family looked to turn around. All of the Dukes had a confidence, (some would say arrogance) and an easy going charm which had been honed from father to son into a family skill. The family motto was, 'Si non pecunia coniunges', which roughly translated as, 'If you can't make money, marry it'.

In this instance it was a match made in heaven. The American heiress fancied herself as a Duchess, and the Duke was potless.

The Duke persuaded his new wife and father-in-law as to the merits of the pier, how it would be a world leader in its construction and be a lasting legacy and beacon to the family name. He got his money, but only on the condition that the pier would be called the Vandergilt Boardwalk, and that it would be completed with good, beautiful, American steel, and by good, honest, American labour. When word got around that the pier was to be finished with foreign manpower, there was uproar. The population of Smallmansea picketed the construction, making it impossible for anyone to come ashore and continue. If there was work to be done, they wanted it.

In response, Senator Vandergilt embarked on a charm offensive. He placed short inspirational notes, no longer than one hundred and forty characters, in all editions of the local newspapers. Each hubristically declared how he would make 'Smallmansea GREAT again'. The local media had never had it so good as they charged extra for CAPITAL letters. The local populace however remained unconvinced, as there was some doubt as to the veracity of the announcements.

Not to be outdone, the Senator chartered a mammoth ship containing all of the people and materials needed, and moored it off the coast. This wasn't about the expense, it was a point of principle and Senator Vandergilt didn't get where he was that day by not finishing things, (even if he hadn't started them).

It was from this gargantuan floating hulk that the completion of the pier was started from the sea, in towards the existing structure, the plan being that the two separate bits would simply join up.

Each part of the pier was grand; there was hardwood decking, elegant wrought iron fencing, and shops and emporiums running along the centre. To promenade from the shore was a delight, until about a quarter of the way along, a fifteen foot ladder had to be climbed to get onto a second dogleg section, which then continued in the same style. The Vandergilt Boardwalk was formally opened by the Duke Eau'Comvitte, but the name of Vandergilt was soon forgotten, and it became widely known as the Two Tier Pier.

During the Second World War, the name of Eau'Comvitte died with the Duke after an unfortunate accident in the scullery involving a maid, a pair of handcuffs, a length of rubber hose and a diving helmet. To avoid the scandal the newly widowed Duchess returned to America. After all, what was a Duke doing in the servants quarters?

Without the Duke's family patronage, and the added blow of Doctor Beeching's reforms, Smallmansea retreated into the shadows, outshone by its more well-known compatriots which still bathed in the afterglow of royal patronage.

*****

John's journey to Smallmansea was uneventful; he had no idea of the battle at Victoria Station between those who were looking to make some quick money, and those who knew that no amount of bounty would compensate them for Milligan's indiscriminate anger if he thought they had failed to secure John's safe passage out of London.

A half hour taxi ride from Eastfordstow dropped John off at the top of the road of the address that Milligan had given him. He walked the rest, preferring not to share the details with a stranger.

The bungalow was well appointed with a driveway and lawn to the front, and in keeping with every other property on the street it was detached, a positive as it gave John more options for escape. He rang the bell, half expecting a Miss Marple type character to open the inner door. Instead, a large poodle burst out and was on its hind legs, leaping at the porch door, barking and bearing its fangs, making the Hound of the Baskervilles look like an anaemic chihuahua. A small elderly woman followed, wrapped herself in her cardigan and peered at him over her glasses. John was pressed up against the fence, trying to work out if he could climb it backwards. She touched the poodle on the head and it sat down, still bearing its canines. She unlocked the porch door.

'You must be Mr Milligan's friend. I've been expecting you,' she said, noticing John's apprehension. 'Don't worry about Fifi, she's a darling. Don't get any ideas though; she'll chew your balls off at the drop of a hat. Do come in.'

John followed her, taking note of Fifi whose eyes disconcertingly followed his ankles. On first impressions the bungalow was clean, and deceptively spacious, but there was a pungent whiff of rotting vegetables that he couldn't ignore.

'Sorry about the smell,' said the lady. 'It's Fifi, she's had her sprouts and they do repeat on her, poor girl.'

John looked down at Fifi. Her penetrating gaze was now sizing up his knees. Her lip was still rolled back, showing off her dagger teeth.

'No need to apologise, honestly. I'll open some windows and give the place an airing,' said John.

As long as this savage beast wasn't making a beeline for his manhood, it could be flatulent for Britain for all he cared.

'I'll give you the quick tour then,' said the old lady, pointing casually in the general direction of some doors. 'The bedrooms through there, kitchen there, and there're a garden out back. There're some ready meals and a pint of milk in the fridge, and if you need to do some shopping, there's a little place on the corner. Lovely man, very discreet,' she said touching the side of her nose. 'Before I forget, you'll be glad to know the toilet's been cleaned, *as per instructions*, unless you want to change your mind?'

'No, no, I'm sure it'll be fine,' said John.

'Good. You don't look like a Beretta man to me, more of a Glock nine milimetre.'

'You don't say...' nodded John on politeness autopilot, as if he understood what she was on about.

'Definitely, my husband always said I was a good judge of character. Anyway, I must be going, Fifi will be wanting her walkies.' She held out her hand, palm facing upward. 'Mr Milligan said you'd be very generous. That fridge didn't fill itself you know. The pension doesn't go that far these days.'

'Hold on a minute,' and John checked his pockets. The smallest note he had was a fifty from Alice's donation. He handed it over not knowing what the going rate was for receiving keys while avoiding a mangled scrotum. An infant growl rumbled in the back of Fifi's throat.

'That'll do. One last thing, if you need to leave in a hurry, lock-up first. Mr Milligan gets very upset otherwise,' and with that she left with Fifi looking over its shoulder at John's groin.

Six days had past and John had walked around the bungalow more than once, making a note of windows and doors through which he could make a quick escape. The bungalow was on a hill, and from the rear window, he could just make out the seafront that he had marvelled at in closer quarters on the taxi ride in.

The garden gate led out onto a narrow path between the adjoining properties which exited half way down the street. He made sure that his rucksack and jacket were to hand, and for the first few nights, he slept fully clothed on the settee. The bungalow was sparse, no books, only a television. There was a limit as to how many times he could watch someone buying a derelict house at auction, and he could now spot an item of Clarice Cliff at fifty yards.

Then there was the garden. When he'd heard the old lady mention it, his ears had pricked up. At least he would have something to occupy him during his voluntary confinement. However, to call it a garden was optimistic at best. A respectable plot of land had been suffocated with gravel. Cracked paving slabs formed a figure of eight path around the enclosure. There was a central water feature made up of an old metal bucket and a plastic floating solar powered lily-pad. The planting was constrained to three pots and two desiccated hanging baskets. The rest of the garden was covered with a raised deck on which stood a rusty lopsided barbeque and a plastic table covered in green algae.

He was bored. His only concession from the self-inflicted solitary was the daily five minute walk to the corner shop for a newspaper, and even then, he had to hold back the childish urge to run off and experience the simple pleasure of walking along a beach at low tide. He was in hiding after all. Little did he know that the tedium would end on the seventh day.

Being in Smallmansea had given him time to think, and while he was grateful for the breathing space, he was not happy with his lot, how could he be. As much as he thought things through, he kept coming back to the same conclusion – Martin. Everything had gone pear shaped after the meeting in the pub. If he could find Martin, he might be able to get himself out of this mess. It was a slim stupid hope, but it was all he had now.

As was usual, John took a short walk to the corner shop for a newspaper and groceries for the day. He didn't see any point in stocking up as he didn't know if he would have to move on quickly. He saw the gentlemen walking his dog, as he did the same time every morning, and he greeted John with a 'Good morning'. The first time he did that John had looked over his shoulder; he wasn't used to a stranger being that polite. Thinking he had been recognised John had gone back to the bungalow and kept watch for two hours, ready to make a move at the slightest sign of anyone in a black suit. It took a few days for him to realise that people in Smallmansea were just polite, and today he returned the greeting in kind, unworried about any sinister motive.

Back at the bungalow, he picked up the stack of junk mail and flyers for stair lifts and mega pizzas, for the sake of a momentary distraction. This time it was different. Among the detritus was a plain envelope addressed to Mr J Cranston. He cursed under his breath, how could they have found him here? He gathered up his rucksack, shoved the ready-made sandwiches he had bought into the pockets, and secured the front door with the lock and chain before opening the envelope. Inside was a note. It read:

Meet me at the Two Tier Pier

Outside the Novelty Rock Emporium

Today 11 O/c

A Friend

He moved the net curtains aside scanning the street for a black Range Rover or anyone who looked like they would be attending a funeral. The street was empty. He looked at the note again, was it the Tarantino gang laying the same trap as they did with the text message? Unlikely, if it was them they obviously knew where he was and didn't need to entice him out; they only needed to choose their moment. He folded the note and put it into his inside pocket. He wanted to know who this Friend was.

From the bungalow, it was a half mile walk to the coast and then along the Parade towards the Two Tier Pier, which he could see in the distance. It was a mild autumn day, the low sun was hiding behind the clouds, highlighting their edges as if they had been embroidered in silver. A proper gardening day he told himself, but there wouldn't be much of that going on for him.

There was a taxi rank outside the pier with one car, autumn at seaside towns was always slow, but John was about to make this drivers day. For one hundred pounds, all he had to do was accept no other fares for the next hour, and if he saw John leaving, he was to take him out of Smallmansea by the quickest possible route.

Confident that he had his escape covered, John walked through the arch with the now faded Vandergilt Boardwalk sign, onto the pier. About a quarter along its length, he climbed the steep stairs onto the offset second level and kept walking. There, tucked away in the last of the central shop units was the Novelty Rock Emporium, although in name only. It was now a small café, the demand for artistically shaped teeth breaking confectionary had strangely tailed off over the years. He stood at the end of the pier with his back to the railings, wondering when his new friend would show themselves, while all the time looking out for the Men in Black.

Eleven o'clock came and went and no one on had approached him. He was expecting someone in an overcoat with a newspaper under their arm to stand next to him, look out to sea and casually mention, in a fake eastern European accent, without addressing him directly, how the seagull's were blow dried with candy floss. A chill breeze was starting to blow onshore. He would wait five more minutes in the shelter of the Novelty Rock Emporium over a cup of tea and then he would be on his way.

Sat at a table outside of the shop he loved the optimism of the continental style experience. Now sheltered from the wind he closed his eyes, and for a moment, savoured the weak golden sunshine on his face.

'Is this seat taken?' asked an unfamiliar voice that shook him from his briefest of meditations.

Standing with one hand on a chair was a young lady dressed in jeans with calf length boots. A tailored hip length leather jacket covered a dark roll neck sweater. This contrasted with her pale complexion and red hair that cascaded onto her shoulders. Rim lit by the low sun her defined cheekbones and green eyes gave her a striking appearance which was the antithesis of the homogenous current fashionable view of beauty.

'Err, no, yes, well no,' said John slightly taken aback. 'I'm waiting for a friend, but it doesn't look like they'll show, so be my guest, I'm not staying.'

'Oh you don't need to go yet.' She extended her hand, 'I'm Marsden, the friend. Sorry I'm late, I did say eleven didn't I? Never mind, let's get down to business. I've been asked by my employer to take you to meet him. Shall we?'

'Hold on a minute, Miss, Ms…Mrs?'

'It's agent, I'm on duty.'

'Agent? I'm guessing you're not selling bungalows,' said John half-jokingly. 'You're not some sort of spook are you?'

'Please,' she said wrinkling her nose in disapproval. ' "Spook", it's such a horrible word. I'm a freelance discreet operative - or secret agent if that makes it easier.'

'Okay,' said John with a weary tone of reluctant acceptance. 'So who do you work for Agent Marsden, the government?'

'You do ask a lot of questions. If you come with me you'll get all the answers you need.'

'Tell you what; I've got a better idea, how about you give me some answers now? Nothing personal but I've not been having much luck with strangers lately. How do I know you're not one of the bad guys? How did you find me? How are you going to help me?'

Marsden let out a deep breath. 'If I'd known it was going to be this hard I would have asked someone else. You're carrying a package…'

'Not you as well,' interrupted John. 'I haven't got anything, never had,' and he rose from the table. 'I'm not hanging around here for your friends in black.'

Marsden reached out and applied a slight pressure to John's wrist and an excoriating pain like a constant electric charge ran up and down his arm as she guided him back into his seat.

'Owww !!!'

'That'll teach you not to be so rude. I haven't finished yet,' chided Marsden. 'Now, I believe you when you say you haven't got the package.'

'You do?'

'Of course. I believe that you believe that you haven't got it, but it doesn't mean that you haven't got something. How can you insist that you haven't got this thing that people think you have when I bet you don't even know what it is? It could be a hidden microdot, something you've heard, or you could be infected with an inactivated deadly virus. You don't know do you? Come with me, we'll find it, and then we'll take it off your hands.'

'Not so fast, and speaking of hands, I'd like to see yours.'

'Pardon?' Marsden considered him for a moment. 'You're not some kind of pervert are you? They never said anything about that.'

'No, I'm a gardener. Indulge me for a minute. I've already had a run-in with James Mason. I want to make sure you're not Eva Marie Saint.'

'I haven't got a clue what you're on about, but if it helps,' said Marsden as she placed her hands palms down on the table with her finely manicured fingers spread out. 'The things I do for this job.'

John stared, looking for tattooed dots on the finger joints. There was nothing.

'Happy?' said Marsden.

'No, not really.'

'You are *so* hard to please. It's quite simple. You're in danger, you come with me, and then you're not. I really don't understand the problem.'

'I'm sorry I'm making this so difficult,' replied John with a hint of sarcasm in his voice. 'You talk a good story, I'll give you that, but you turn up out of the blue asking about this package which I'm supposed to have, and it turns out that you're some kind of secret agent. You know where I'm hiding but you arrange a meeting out in the open, on this pier. It doesn't add up. I'm still here because I'm short on options, but you're going to have to do better, otherwise I'm off, and I'll be ready for your Chinese burn this time.'

Marsden looked over both shoulders.

'I work for a top secret non-government organisation. The people that are after you believe that you have something. If you have got it, and we think you do, if they get their hands on it; we're all in big trouble. My job is to make sure they don't get it, which is why I would like you, to come with me. As for meeting here, according to your file you're to be approached with extreme caution, I can't think why, so the last thing I was going to do was meet you alone in a bungalow. Besides, what would my mother say?'

'How would I know, I've never met her.'

'Just as well, she'd have you for breakfast. And as for finding you, we have our ways, even if you are hiding in Smallmansea, which under normal circumstances I'd say was a good move.'

'What do you mean "under normal circumstances"?'

Marsden looked at him quizzically. 'You really don't know do you?'

'Know what?' said John with a hint of terseness in his voice.

'There's a price on your head. You're all over Mugbook.'

'Mugbook?'

'Mugbook,' Marsden could see absolutely no recognition in John's face. 'It's like social media, but for professional criminals and so on. Here,' she said handing over her mobile phone displaying a webpage.

John saw the photograph that he had provided to Alice for the social media campaign. It was annotated in large type stating a reward of fifty thousand pounds for information leading to his capture, and seventy five thousand pounds for his delivery.

'How do you know all this?'

'Do keep up. I'm a secret agent, remember? It's what I do.'

'Great. So now I'm trending on anti-social media with a price on my head,' said John as he drained his tea. 'Thanks for the info but if it's all the same, I'll pass on your offer. I've got a taxi waiting.'

'Wait, you don't know how much trouble you're in. There's a war on and you're in the middle of it, whether you like it or not.

When they find you, we can't help if we're not around. Come with me now and we'll keep you safe.'

'Nothing personal but the problem is the only person I can trust these days is me, so I'll have to take my chances. Unless- can you help me find Martin Ashcombe?'

Marsden totally ignored the question.

'You can't go yet. I paid off your taxi driver; I didn't think he'd be needed. Normally people on the run believe me and are grateful, they're never as awkward as you.' She could see that she was losing the argument. 'Look, if I was one of those nasty crims' we wouldn't be talking, I'd have used this instead,' she said taking a pen from her inside pocket.

'You were going to tattoo me into submission with a biro?'

'Let's cut the snide remarks shall we? It's got a hidden syringe actually.' She handed it over for John to examine. 'One prick from that and you'd be out like a light, then I'd get the crew round to take you in. I didn't think it would be helpful to getting you on side if I drugged you up, and I'd hardly be explaining it to you now if I planned to use it would I?'

John clicked the top of the pen and watched as a needle, rather than a ballpoint, poked out from the barrel. It was the sort of thing he imagined someone in a covert world would use, maybe she was genuine.

He was distracted by something that passed into his peripheral vision, a tall dark shadow through the windows of the Novelty Rock Emporium on the other side of the pier. It couldn't be, but it was. It was unmistakably Mr Blue, but what had Milligan done? Mr Blue's face was literally blue, an Yves Klein radiant shade of blue to be exact.

'You have got to be having a laugh,' he exclaimed in exasperation.

'That's a fine attitude. I take my equipment very seriously,' said Marsden, quite put out. 'There's enough in there to put a rhino to sleep.'

'Not the pen. They've found me again. If you're really one of the good guys, I need your help to get me out of here.'

'At last.'

'He's over there,' said John indicating with a nod of his head while slightly sliding down into the chair so that his collar covered most of his face.

'Got him, looks like a Smurf with the pox.'

'Yes, that's him.'

'Don't worry; I'll take care of this. I'll meet you at the front with the engine running. Off you go.'

16 / The Chase

John made his way through the single file passage between the chairs, tables, and the pier railings. Once clear he half ran, half walked around the hardy members of the public promenading on the planked walkway. He looked back; Mr Blue had spotted him and was weaving his way around the furniture at the end of the pier on an intercept course with Marsden.

He kept going until he arrived at the steps that led down and sideways onto the lower level, and there was Mr Green resting on the railings downstairs, facing out to sea, looking left and right. John hid himself behind a postcard rack on the upper deck. What was going on? Mr Green's hands and face were a bright luminous green; he looked like the result of an illicit liaison between a goblin and a weasel. John hadn't been spotted, yet, but he had to get past without his adversary bringing his gun into play.

'Big Issue Mister?' said a voice behind him.

'Sorry?' said John.

'Big Issue?'

'How about I take that bundle off your hands and borrow your cap and coat for five minutes,' John said, presenting a crisp fifty pound note. 'Keep the change. I'll leave your gear on a bench when I'm done. What do you say?'

'Another fifty quid.'

With the cap pulled down and the vendor's luminous waistcoat over his own overcoat, John made his way down the stairs towards Mr Green and sneaked up behind him.

'Big Issue Mister?' John asked, disguising his voice with a whining irritating tone.

'No. Go away,' replied Mr Green, not bothering to look round.

'Big Issue Mister?'

'Bugger off, I'm not interested.'

'Big Issue Mister?'

'How many more times?' and Mr Green turned around to give the Big Issue seller a verbal lashing. 'You!'

Mr Green reached inside his jacket, but John was ready for him as he swung the tied bundle of magazines into Mr Green's midriff, causing him to double over as a sudden rush of air was forced from his lungs with an expanding pain in his gut. John swung the bundle again, striking the side of Mr Green's head with a loud 'thwack', whirling the thug around so that he was again facing the sea. Grabbing the back of Mr Green's belt, John rolled the gasping green ferret man, as if he was no more than a sack of compost, over the railings into the sea below.

'That's for London Bridge,' John said quietly.

A crowd gathered, they had seen everything. John straightened his cap and pulled down the front of the waistcoat so that it was even. He pointed to the railings where he had tossed Mr Green overboard.

'He wouldn't pay for his Big Issue,' he announced.

There was a murmur among the crowd which rose into a crescendo of exclamations such as 'That's outrageous,' 'What's the world coming to?', and 'No less then he deserved,' followed by a rush of requests to buy the latest copy. John directed them to the Big Issue seller who couldn't believe his good fortune and thought it was a shame that someone couldn't be chucked into the sea every day.

Looking over the railings, John could see Mr Green striking out for the beach with an energetic front crawl, looking like a frog on speed. There was no time to lose.

Mr Blue pushed the chairs aside as he manoeuvred his way past the Novelty Rock Emporiums alfresco seating area.

Compared to him a bull in a china shop was Rudolph Nureyev. As he rushed past Marsden, a strategically placed foot tripped him and he found himself hurtling face first into a set of table and chairs. Temporarily stunned he shook himself and as he was getting up, a red haired woman leaned over him. She asked in a gentle voice if he was alright, while surreptitiously ramming her knee into his groin. A groan involuntarily escaped from his lips as he doubled up, oblivious to the needle that had been stuck into his neck, a mixed blessing, as within a matter of seconds he fell into a deep sleep.

'Oh my God!' cried Marsden. 'Is there a doctor anywhere? I think this man needs help!'

A crowd gathered around Marsden and Mr Blue, followed by the serving staff of the Emporium.

'What's wrong with him?' asked one of the bystanders.

'I'm not sure,' said Marsden. 'He came staggering past me from over there and collapsed. I can't make out his breathing and he's gone blue. He might have been stung – it could be anaphylactic shock, I don't know! I've rung for an ambulance; I'm going to the front to look out for the paramedics. You'll have to give him First aid.'

Marsden spoke with such authority that no-one thought to question her reasoning and diagnosis, and by the time they had taken on board what she had said, she was gone, leaving them holding the proverbial baby.

'What do we do now then?' said one.

'Search me, I'm not a doctor am I?' said another.

'That woman said he was suffering from prophylactic shock, that don't sound good.'

'Yeah, I read something on the net about people getting a bad reaction from dodgy condoms, but I ain't checking him to find out.'

'Don't we have to give him the kiss of life or something?'

They all looked at Mr Blue.

'I would, but I've got emphysema.'

'Chapped lips.'

'I've got an appointment for me verruca.'

'What about CPR – like they do on the telly?'

'Yeah, that'll do it,' said the washing up lad from the Emporium. 'Come on, we'd better get onto it before it's too late.'

They rolled Mr Blue over onto his back and the lad placed both hands onto the chest of the slumbering henchman. Slowly and rhythmically he pushed down.

'You're going too fast,' said one.

'No, you're too slow. It's got to be to the tune of Nelly the Elephant,' said another.

'Don't be stupid, it's Dolly Parton,' said a voice from the back.

'Don't listen to him. That was Whitney Houston. I reckon its more Status Quo myself,' said someone else.

Unable to keep up with the wisdom of the crowd, in frustration the washing up lad pushed down with all his weight. There was a loud crack. He stopped.

'That's not supposed to happen is it?'

There was a low mumble from the gathered wise men and a shaking of heads.

'Have you tried aromatherapy?' offered someone at the back.

'No, no, this'll do the trick,' said one of the serving staff as he pushed his way through. 'It's one of these portable defillibusters. Put these pads on his chest and that'll get him going in no time. It's like jump-starting a motor – doddle.'

Mr Blue was dreaming. He was on a sun lounger looking out over a tropical paradise of white sands and swaying palms. In this dream the people, all looking as if they had come from a fashion catwalk modelling swim wear, smiled at him, acknowledged him with a nod, or said 'See you in the bar later.' A waiter in a short sleeved shirt and tie brought him a drink, and asked him if everything was to his satisfaction. Everyone treated him as if he was a normal person, but special. He liked the feeling. He liked it here. Then he felt the sharp spasm running throughout his body and he returned abruptly to reality.

Whatever potion Marsden had injected him with, it was neutralised by several thousand volts.

John was at the exit looking for Marsden. Down on the beach he could hear a commotion, as people walking their dogs were unable to prevent them from barking at the green sea monster in a three piece black suit, rising from the waves.

'Come on – where are you?' he asked himself.

The sound of a warbled horn and an almost rhythmic tapping sound, interspersed with a soft 'ker-dunk' caught his attention as a light blue Austin Allegro pulled up.

*****

The Austin Allegro is a classic example of what happens when good design runs into a committee with access to a shared parts bin. Something has to give and the Allegro's shape was squeezed and stunted while it was gifted with mechanical components built by machines suited for making bomber aircraft. It was a lesson in how to snatch mediocrity from the jaws of potential success.

*****

'Get in,' said Marsden, leaning across to wind down the passenger door window.

John landed himself on the passenger seat which had all the springiness of a deflated balloon. As Marsden slowly drove off, John repeatedly slammed the passenger door until the door lock clunked home reluctantly into its latch.

'Please tell me your other car's an Aston,' said John.

Marsden's eyes were fixed firmly ahead on the road, not that the whiny car was threatening any significant acceleration.

'It's a Maserati actually but I thought it best to get you away in something a bit less conspicuous. This was the only car in the pool- so it'll have to do.'

'Less conspicuous? When was the last time you saw British Leyland's finest bucket of nails on the road? We'll be lucky if this thing doesn't expire before the next set of lights.'

'If I'd known you were going to moan I would have got them to put the ejector seat back in. Stop worrying. Your blue friend is out of action, so sit back and enjoy the view. It's not as if we're going to end up in a high speed car chase is it?'

There was a sharp tap on the rear windscreen, as if a stone chipping had been thrown up. John thought nothing of it, and then there it was again, but this time it was two taps in rapid succession.

'What was that?' he asked.

'Looks like we've got company,' observed Marsden. 'You are popular.'

John moved round in his seat and saw that three small craters with radiating fractures had blemished the rear window. He could also see the black Range Rover driven by Mr Green, with Mr Blue grimacing, as he leant out of the window, gun in hand.

'Bloody hell! I thought you said he was out of action?'

'He was,' replied Marsden dividing her concentration between the rear view mirror and the road ahead.

'Well unless he's got a blue twin brother with an afro, he's out there taking pot-shots. Can't this thing go any faster?'

'In a minute.'

Marsden dropped the reluctant Allegro down a gear and floored the accelerator, forcing the revs of the engine, after an initial stutter, to pick up. Wrenching the hand brake and wrestling with the oval steering wheel, she slid the asthmatic automobile across the oncoming traffic, forcing cars to stop as they blocked the entrance to the side road she had taken.

Mr Blue and Mr Green, unable to follow without a collision, threatened the citizens of Smallmansea to move their cars, and to their credit they were probably the fastest manoeuvres that had ever been seen by residents in that sleepy backwater, but they were still glacial by normal standards of driving.

Rather than taking the next junction Marsden took a turning into the local park via an access gate reserved for the rubbish collection, and tucked the Allegro behind a beech hedge where it was obscured from view.

'What now?' John asked.

'They won't be long,' said Marsden dialling out on her phone. 'They probably saw me turn in here, but with a bit of luck, they'll come screaming through that gate and miss us. If I can get to the main road, I'll arrange for an intercept. This won't take a moment.'

Marsden tapped on the faded vinyl dashboard as she waited for an answer.

'Hello Base, this is Agent Marsden requesting...' she stopped when she heard a distinctive click. In her anxiety she had been talking to herself while a machine at the other end was slowly whirring into action.

`You have reached the Society Helpline. All our operatives are busy at the moment, but your call is important to us. Please speak your official call-sign at the tone.'

'Sod it!' cursed Marsden.

`Sorry, that wasn't recognised. Please speak your official call-sign at the tone.'

'Purple Gerbil,' mumbled Marsden through clenched teeth.

`Please speak your official call-sign CLEARLY, at the tone.'

'PURPLE GERBIL'. Marsden looked across at John with a face like Fury. 'One word...'

`To help us direct your call to the right department, please select from the following options. For hotel bookings and reservations in the middle of nowhere, press one. To request replacement gadgets and Rolex watches, press two. If you're in a spot of bother, press three. To report Armageddon, just scream. For all other enquiries, press four.'

'I don't believe it...bloody Tattershall. I swear I'm going to kill him when this is over,' muttered Marsden as she selected number three.

`You are currently number- twenty - in the queue. Please hold, your call is important to us,' said the recorded voice as it segued into Vivaldi's Four Seasons.

'Problems?' said John.

'No, no, whatever gave you that idea? A small change of plan, that's all,' Marsden replied, hiding her frustration.

At that moment, as predicted, the black Range Rover hurtled past John and Marsden, before coming to an abrupt halt about a hundred metres away. The primary coloured thugs surveyed the park and seeing no sign of the faded blue wreck, slowly reversed along the track.

'Time to go,' said Marsden forcing the heavy wheeled blancmange towards the exit, the sound of its engine having no relation to its speed. 'I can't outrun them, but if I can get onto the back roads, I'll lose them easily.'

'I think I'd be better on foot, I could run faster than this heap,' said John.

'O ye of little faith,' replied Marsden who in a perverse way, seemed to be relishing the prospect of this one sided chase.

'It's not faith I'm short on, but a few buttons for oil slicks or smoke screens would be handy. Or maybe some Ben-Hur wheel hubs!' cried John as he was thrown against the passenger door as Marsden took the corner back onto the main Parade road, intent on retaining as much of the hard earned speed as possible.

'Make yourself useful,' ordered Marsden as the Allegro slowly but surely picked up speed on the long stretch in an ongoing chicken run as it overtook law abiding drivers. 'There's a blue light on the backseat, stick it on the roof and connect it up. The wires are in the roof lining behind that zip.'

John wound the window down and attached the magnetic blue glass dome to the top of the car with a satisfying clunk. He lurched forward as the Allegro suddenly slowed down; Marsden unable to get past the car in front without the acceleration she needed to weave past the oncoming traffic.

'Bother! Will you hurry up with that!' she barked.

John released the zip and felt about in the roof void for the wires to the blue light. Up to his elbow, he latched upon something, dragged them out and connected them to their counterparts.

'Is it working?' shouted Marsden above the engine tapping, which was now an ongoing strident whine interspersed with a frequent clunk, its full volume apparent through the open window.

'Yes!' shouted John, half his torso hanging out the door as he strained his neck to see the now flashing blue light. 'And they're onto us,' he said, watching the Range Rover weaving in and out of the traffic with relative ease as it gained on them.

'Not to worry,' said Marsden. 'This "heap's" got a siren, that'll clear the way,' and she flicked a toggle switch crudely attached to the dashboard with double sided tape.

The sounds of sirens have changed over the years, from early clanging bells to the familiar 'Nee Nah' of British police cars, through to variations on the American 'whoop, whoop, waah', which some would consider more vulgar, but it does the job of getting people's attention. It was obvious that whoever had prepared the Allegro for operational service weren't aficionados of sirens, or had simply used whatever was to hand, on the premise that the car would never be used in a situation that would require a noise telling people to get out of the way.

Sounding as if a vinyl record was being played at twice its speed, an ice cream van chime was broadcast from a speaker hidden somewhere under the car bonnet.

Marsden flicked the switch on the dashboard up and down with no effect. It came off in her hand and she handed it to John, as if there was some implicit agreement that he was responsible for the disposal of surplus parts. Despite this, the flashing blue light was having some effect as the traffic, erring on the side of caution, made way for a blue motorised jelly mould, its engine sounding like a high pitched painful drum roll accompanied by a 19th Century Neapolitan ear worm on amphetamine.

They were now leaving Smallmansea, the Parade and Pier were shrinking behind them and Marsden knew they were only a short distance away from the narrow lanes she needed that abutted the main road.

The speedometer slowly crept up, fifty-five, sixty, seventy miles per hour, and then it started to go backwards as they climbed the slight incline up and away from the coast, seventy, sixty, fifty. All she had to do was get to the crest of the slope; they still had a head-start. The Range Rover, with headlights glaring, driving on the opposite side of the road, forcing oncoming traffic to give way, was catching up. Marsden had the accelerator pedal to the floor, and as they crested the incline the Allegro slowly picked up speed again, but it was too late. She looked across to see Mr Blue pointing a gun at her. She shoved the brake pedal hard, wrestling with the car to prevent it from going into an uncontrolled skid as it screeched to a halt, and the Range Rover overshot. She blipped the accelerator, coaxing the car not to stall, but the engine coughed and rattled to a halt, as if in a final death throe.

So there they sat; facing each other, the Allegro and the Range Rover. Like a scene from a spaghetti western each party narrowed their eyes, waiting for the other to make the first move, the tension scored by the tinny strain of Sol De Mio.

'Come on...please,' implored Marsden as she turned the engine over, its smokers cough failing to catch and come to life as the battery drained. 'What are they waiting for?'

'I reckon they're trying to work out if I've got something up my sleeve, or if we're knackered. I'm not waiting to find out,' said John as he heaved his shoulder against the door, forcing it to open.

'Cranston, don't you dare leave. We're not done yet.'

'Who said anything about leaving?' replied John as he threw his overcoat and rucksack onto the back seat. He pushed against the door pillar, moving the car backwards. His thigh muscles, honed by years of rowing, pumped one after the other like hydraulic pistons, rolling the carcass at an increasing pace as the flat slowly gave way by degrees to the slope that led back to Smallmansea. Marsden was ready; there would only be one chance. With the car in reverse gear, she bump started it back into life and John collapsed into the seat. Such was Marsden's urgency to get ahead, she didn't notice he hadn't closed the passenger door, which became detached as it hit a parked car with a teeth clenching sound of metal on glass, on metal.

'At least we don't have to worry about getting that handle fixed,' she said.

The Range Rover was gaining again. Marsden dropped the clutch, slammed the spongy gear lever into second, and wrenching on the hand brake she spun the Allegro through one hundred and eighty degrees. With the revs of the dying engine as high as she dared go without blowing a gasket, she raised the clutch and there was a burning smell from the front as the car lurched forward. She gave the hand brake to John. There was the sound of the now familiar sharp taps on the back of car.

'Doesn't he ever run out of bloody bullets?' said John.

'Don't worry about that, its bulletproof glass and the back seats lined with plate steel,' said Marsden as another shot shattered the rear windscreen. 'Sort of...'

'Great. At this rate we'll need a button for brown corduroys,' said John, looking cautiously over his shoulder. 'They're coming in for another go. Get them to overtake on the inside.'

'What for?'

'Do it! We can't keep this up all day.'

Driving back into Smallmansea, the raised concrete pedestrian Parade was now on John's left, and at this more industrial end of the town, the rails that ran most of its length were yet to start. Weaving the Allegro across the road, Marsden pretended to be caught by the feint of the following Range Rover, which with its greater speed; used the Parade as an extra lane to the road. The Range Rover was starting to draw level, and John, holding onto the interior roof handle leaned out and looked Mr Green in the eye. He raised the detached hand brake, and with all his strength, hurled it at Mr Green's face. All Mr Green could see was a tumbling lump of metal hurtling towards him in a speeding arc, and he remembered the gun in the Imperial Tower. In a panic, he pulled on the steering wheel and the Range Rover lurched towards the sea as the hand brake bounced off the edge of the windscreen.

It was a six feet drop from the Parade onto the beach and the nearside tyres of the Range Rover came perilously close to tipping over the edge. Marsden saw her chance. She reached down into the foot-well and released the valve on the top of a small canister.

The Allegro leapt forward, as if it had been shot from a cannon, and rammed the rear of the Range Rover which left the Parade in an impressive barrel roll, landing on the shingle beach where the pebbles, acting as ball bearings, sped it forward, its progress only halted by groyne number fifty-six. Now balanced on the coastal slope, it tilted sideways, first in slow motion, then faster, rolling towards the sea until it came to a halt, resting on the passenger side door at the seas edge as the incoming tide lapped around it.

Marsden narrowly avoided following suit as the front wheels of the Allegro, spinning at an unheard of speed for its like, pulled it onto the Parade and then back to the road before running out of steam. Its engine now skipped a beat, the tapping was more raucous and the intermittent ker-plunk was louder and more frequent. Sol De Mio slurred into silence.

'What a relief, I hated that tune,' said Marsden.

'How many times do you need to be shot at before you get a move on? We could have been killed back there.'

'Don't be so melodramatic, honestly.' She picked up the empty canister and gave it to John. 'Nitrous oxide, I can only use it the once so I had to get it right. Now – where were we before we were so rudely interrupted?'

*****

Mr Green breathed. The world was sideways. Suspended by his seat belt he grabbed hold of the steering wheel and adjusted himself into a vertical position. He looked down at Mr Blue whose face was resting in the lapping waves as the seawater washed away the blood from the gash on his forehead. Mr Blue hadn't used a seat belt during the chase while taking pot-shots, so he had been thrown around in the car like a rag doll on a slow spin cycle. Mr Green nudged him with his foot.

'Come on – wake up. We've got to go.'

There was no answer. He nudged him again, more purposely this time, but Mr Blue was out for the count. With a foothold on the central console, Mr Green hauled himself up on the steering wheel and threaded himself through the open window so that he was half way out of the car. He fell ungracefully to the beach below. The Range Rover was wrecked, but if he could rock it back onto its battered chassis, maybe he could revive and extricate Mr Blue. He knew Mr Blue wouldn't talk to those in authority but his presence, if found here, would raise questions that shouldn't be asked.

The sun glanced across the beach sands and in the small puddles of the indents made by the crash, water glistened with rainbow colours of liquid blues, reds and greens, like an iridescent butterfly's wings. His nose twitched at the smell of petrol. In his experience of arranging 'unfortunate accidents' the car could ignite at any moment. It only needed the smallest of electrical sparks, and in no time it would be a fire ball. Mr Blue was useful, but he wasn't going to chance his neck getting him out of that potential bomb. Better to take advantage of the situation to make sure there were no loose ends.

He checked his pockets, found a soggy box of matches, and threw them to the floor in disgust at his bad luck. Chances were that the car would go up without his help; it was a risk he had to take as he turned and ran as fast and as far as he could along the sea shore away from the crash.

*****

Mr Blue breathed, inhaling salt water through his nose that made him choke and splutter as he spat out the foul liquid. The world was upside down as he struggled to get his face out of the water, wincing at the sharp pain in his side. The last thing he remembered was everything rotating around him before he head butted the dashboard. Mentally pulling himself together he checked that toes and fingers could be moved, and slowly rearranged his body so that his head was pointing towards the steering wheel. It was then that he saw faint wisps of smoke coming from the dashboard ventilation grills, and the smell of petrol caught in the back of his throat. Ignoring the pain, riding the crest of an adrenalin rush he scrambled his way up to and out of the driver's side window.

As he hauled his body through the opening, a young child; he couldn't have been more than six years old, stood transfixed as they watched, fascinated by this strange alien wrenching himself from the cocoon of the wreck, like a dragonfly nymph shedding its skeleton.

In the distance someone was shouting -'Tommy – get away from there!'

The car was going to go up at any moment, and by Mr Blue's estimation that boy would never get to a safe distance in time.

The boy's mother, sprinting down the beach slope at a pace that would have set a world record in less precarious circumstances, was too far away.

Mr Blue reckoned he could make it, but instead, against all of the years of indoctrination to dispassionate detachment, he diverted, grabbed the little fellow and ran with all his vigour.

He heard the whoomph of a fireball bursting into life and he clutched the child tight, shielding him with his body from the explosion that he knew was coming. A shock wave hurled them both over the wooden boards of a groyne with Mr Blue taking the full brunt of the fall. Turning his back towards the inferno, his arms still wrapped around the infant, he felt his nape being scorched as long tendrils of flame reached out to grab him, before retreating back to lunge skywards in a blazing pyre.

'Tommy, you okay?'

Tommy shivered and buried his head into Mr Blue's chest, hugging him tight, searching for reassurance.

Mr Blue could see concerned citizens approaching, one of whom he assumed was Tommy's mother.

'Tommy, keep your head down and stay close to these boards. Your mums on her way.' He removed his overcoat and swathed the boy in its thick cashmere. 'This is my lucky coat, it's special. You'll be safe in this until your mum gets here - okay?'

Tommy nodded.

Mr Blue dragged himself to his feet, stood up above the groyne boards and shouted over to the crowd, 'He's here!'

Then he ran.

Although he was an assassin in training, his fight wasn't with children. He now knew who was next on his hit list. As of that moment the gardener had been demoted.

*****

Detective Inspector Sutherland was reviewing, again, all of the information that he had concerning the missing accountants, the gardener, and the mysterious Mr Black. It was still nagging him. He could link Mr Black to the gardener and to Chief Superintendent Willingdon, although he didn't consider the evidence so far a primary source. The fact that the gardener had jumped into the Thames gave a smidgeon of credibility to his account. Then there was Murray. What was he up to in that video? There was something going on that bound these seemingly unrelated events, as if they were different views of the same tip of an iceberg. He wasn't suffering from a shortage of conjecture; all he wanted was a fragment more of hard evidence.

His thoughts were interrupted by a light insistent tapping on his office door and he looked up to see Sergeant Bludgeon peering in, doing a slight excited jig from foot to foot. He beckoned him in.

'What is it sergeant?'

'Sir, I think I've got a lead on Mr Black.'

'At last – what have you got?'

'It's not Mr Black exactly, it's his two assistants, Mr Blue and Mr Green, but wherever they are, he can't be far behind.'

'Okay sergeant, so what exactly have you got?'

'Something quite interesting from one of my contacts,' said Bludgeon as he touched the side of his nose and winked. 'Mr Blue and Mr Green have been involved in a car chase in Smallmansea with a light blue,' he checked his notes, 'All-Aggro'.

'Where's Smallmansea?'

'On the south coast, near Brighton.'

'I see, and what was it they were chasing again?'

'An All-Aggro Sir.'

'I think you'll find sergeant that it's an Allegro, although your pronunciation is spot on. We had them as patrol cars years ago; the villains loved 'em. Sounds like it could be ex-fleet, no one would paint one that colour given the choice. You know, when they got sold off we used to say they were a bargain. One careful owner; the Metropolitan police.' Sutherland allowed himself a small chuckle, and then leaving the safe haven of his reminiscence, continued. 'Registration?'

'No Sir. Sorry.'

'Okay, so we have a report of two accomplices of our main person of interest involved in a car chase with an Allegro, and against all odds, they were driving so fast that no-one got a registration, so how come you're so sure it was the Chuckle Brothers?'

'Chuckle Brothers?' Sergeant Bludgeon's eyes rolled upwards while his tongue threatened to creep out of the side of his mouth. 'Oh I see, I wondered who you were talking about for a moment. That's easy. Mr Green was green, and Mr Blue was blue.'

'Sergeant, I know what they're called, but that's not what I asked, is it?' said Sutherland, part of him wanting to dismiss the sergeant, but aware that like panning for gold, somewhere in that detritus of information, there could be the nugget he needed to help him join the threads.

Bludgeon looked at Sutherland with that patronising look reserved by the less tactful for those they believe to be hard of understanding.

'Mr Green was green, and Mr Blue was blue. It's the criminal mind you see Sir. They're wearing war paint, obviously to make sure that the people they're chasing know who they're being chased by, thereby enforcing a fear response leading to irrational behaviour that they can capitalise on.'

Sutherland opened his drawer and looked longingly at the hip flask. 'Let's get this straight, two of our Tarantino wannabees have painted themselves blue and green, and for whatever reason, are chasing an Allegro, a car I could out run on roller skates. Anything else?'

'Mr Blue had an afro Caribbean hairstyle,' Bludgeon checked his notes 'and the All-ag... the Allegro had a flashing blue light, which when you think of it Sir, fits in with your ex- police car theory. There is one thing though, when you were off duty back in those days, did you ever sell ice-cream?'

'Do I look like Mr bleedin' Whippy?'

'Of course not, he wears a hat and has this kind of creamy white quiff,' said Sergeant Bludgeon, indicating with his hands above his head. 'Everyone knows that. You don't catch me out that easily. It's just that the siren was an ice cream van jingle.'

'Greensleeves?' asked Sutherland, immediately regretting the reflex retort.

'Sol Di Mio.'

It is possible with the technology of today to scan a person's brain and see what parts of it are active in response to certain stimuli. This is shown on a computer screen as an animation of the grey matter, with colours showing where the action is. If it had been possible at that exact moment to scan D.I Sutherland's brain, the screen would have looked like an early Space Invader's arcade game, with Sutherland's will fighting a losing battle against an onslaught of blobby aliens as they descended from the top of the screen onto his failing reason.

Sutherland steeled himself and fought back. He wasn't going to give in. It wasn't Sergeant Bludgeon's fault that after his supposed forays into the depths of various intelligence agencies systems, he was being fed this garbage. It was the online equivalent of being sent down to the basement for a glass hammer.

'I see. Was Mr Black bringing up the rear on a unicycle disguised as a chimney sweep with an AK47 by any chance?'

'I'm not sure Sir,' replied Bludgeon as he checked his notes. 'Do you know something I don't?'

Sutherland shook his head and shrugged. 'Knowing the criminal mind the way I do, I thought I'd ask' he said, his eyes on the window, wondering if broken ankles would be worth it.

'Would you like me to check on that Sir?'

'No need sergeant.' Sutherland took a deep breath and let it out slowly, recovering his composure. 'I must say that you've excelled yourself this time. A car chase with a Martian, a blue Muppet, and an ice cream van disguised as an Austin Allegro. Its classic, it really is.'

'Thank you Sir. You're too kind.'

Bludgeon left the office, pleased that he had once again made a contribution to the investigation.

Sutherland took a secret swig from the hip flask. Willingdon had to make a mistake soon.

17 / *Don't Take The Maserati*

Kurt Erikson tapped the glass of the two-metre aquarium inset into the wall. It wasn't to his taste, but when this underground lair had come onto the market, it would have been foolish to turn it down for the sake of some dodgy fixtures and fittings. He tapped the glass again. What exactly was he supposed to do with a geriatric octopus?

He had taken over what had been the operations room in the underground annexe of a larger subterranean structure. With some modification, the latest technology sat alongside the Modern décor, which was reminiscent of the Battersea Power Station. It wouldn't do to be undertaking his true dealings from the public face of the Brassica Tower.

'Sir, your ten o'clock is here,' said a voice from the integrated sound system in his desk.

'Let him in.'

Vladimir Orimov descended the elegant wrought iron staircase, his heels echoed on the marble floor as he approached.

Erikson wondered what could be achieved if this so called Mr Black had been as operationally efficient as he was debonair. 'Comrade Orimov,' he observed. In doing so, he was reminding him that while all electronic traces of Vladimir Orimov had vanished, they could easily reappear. He didn't look up; instead, he made a point of swiping and tapping on his tablet. Mr Black could wait.

Mr Black stood tall and proud, he refused to be goaded by this man-child's stupid game. He watched the live video image of himself on the large screen behind the desk, another ridiculous mind game, no doubt meant as a reminder that Erikson had his eye on him. After all this time it still felt strange to look at a face that wasn't his. Backstreet emergency plastic surgeons were a calculated risk. You took whoever was available. He moved his head slightly, the surgery had held up well. Not bad for a taxidermist Hitchcock fanatic.

'Do you have the Midas device for me?' asked Erikson, his eyes still fixated on his hand held screen.

'It'll be soon, I have my two finest men on the case. They've tracked it down to Smallmansea...' Mr Black was interrupted by Erikson raising his finger.

'Where?'

'Smallmansea. It's on the south coast, somewhere near Bognor Regis.'

'Somewhere near?' He looked Mr Black in the eyes. 'My Midas device is in an undetermined location and is being retrieved by Mr Green and Mr Blue from this gardener, who has escaped from you twice so far that I know of.'

'Cranston is no more a gardener than I am.'

'Gardener or not, he's still at large. Is it because he's that good, or that you're incompetent? You're becoming an expensive overhead Comrade.'

Mr Black reached inside his jacket. He understood the veiled threat and in his experience it was always best to retaliate first. On the large screen he saw a red dot hovering over his heart; it's movements in synch with Erikson's gestures on the tablet. Looking down he could see the same dot on his chest, it wasn't a special effect on the video. He slowly diverted his hand from his concealed underarm holster.

'May I?' said Mr Black, casually removing a cigarette case from his inside pocket.

Erikson ignored the request. 'What assurance can you give me that you'll deliver Midas?'

'My men are all handpicked.'

'I wasn't asking for excuses.'

Erikson's finger hovered over the tablet. All it needed was one tap for the hidden remote controlled ballistic to finish the conversation. He took note that Mr Black kept his composure, showing no sign of apprehension or fear, despite the red dot dancing on his chest. He was an extraordinary man, despite his failure so far, so it would follow that the gardener was an extraordinary adversary. What was to be done? The tension was broken by the intercom.

'I'm sorry to interrupt Sir, but you did want to know if that accountant tried to escape again. He's here now, with security. Shall I send him in?'

'Yes,' Erikson confirmed, putting the tablet to one side. 'We'll continue this conversation another time Comrade. Take a seat.'

A man of average height, in slacks and loose fitting shirt, scowling through his five o'clock shadow was manhandled by two thugs to the desk, nearly dislodging the glasses that perilously balanced on the end of his nose.

'Mr Kingswood is there a problem with my hospitality?' Erikson asked.

Kingswood wrenched his arms from the grips of the security guards, tidied his sleeves and set his eye wear straight. 'Apart from being kidnapped, the threats, the dodgy food, and endless reruns of East Enders, no, everything's fine. But, to be honest, it's not working out for me here.'

'I see that following your latest escape attempt, one of my guards is now in the infirmary.'

'Escape? I was out for a walk, and that guard, total accident, one in a million. He slipped and his face landed on my elbow.'

'At three o'clock in the morning.'

'Somnambulism my doctor says. Runs in the family. It's terrible; I never know where I'll turn up some nights.'

'And you've also been creative in your financial efforts. Not to my satisfaction I may add.'

'You said you wanted to increase your cash flow and I said that it would involve an element of calculated risk.'

'That explains the two hundred thousand on the three-thirty at New Market then?'

'Sorry about that, one of the team is new. You can't abduct the staff these days.'

'On a horse called Escape to Freedom. I'd say you were trying to send a message. I must say that it does show a rare aptitude for inventiveness, and I admit I was tempted to offer you a position more suited to your hidden talents, but you're too single minded. You're free to go.'

'Free? What, as in I walk out the door?'

'My men will see that you're taken away from here.'

'Like you did with Glenthorn and Eastwood? One minute they're here, and then they vanish. If they knew they were getting out they would have said something.'

'It's not up for discussion. Take him away,' said Erikson with a casual wave of his hand, his attention springing back to the tablet screen.

'Wait! Hold on a moment. I can't go yet,' Kingswood said with the sense of a man who was about to show a winning hand. 'I haven't done the accruals.'

Erikson looked across to Mr Black who responded with a shrug that said, 'How should I know?'

Kingswood rattled on. 'If I don't get the accruals right, then that'll upset the deltas on the forecast scenarios for the forward looking plan, which in turn will knock onto the overall rolling budget and cost of profit ratios. It'd throw everything out by millions and it'd take months to sort out. Now if Eastwood was here, they'd be done by now. Fastest spreadsheet in the west we called him. Of course, as you won't let me contact him it's going to take a while.'

'I thought it wasn't "working out" for you here,' recalled Erikson.

'That's my problem you see, total professional. I can't leave the team in the lurch before I go, can I?'

'I see. Preston will escort you back to your office. We can't risk any more accidents with your elbows can we?'

Kingswood turned and at the base of the staircase was a man whose taut fleshed face looked like an Easter Island moai, augmented with a bleached buzz cut, which had then been placed onto a disproportionate larger body where every tangent was angular, as if it had been chiselled from the hardest granite. It was an easy decision not to take him on and attempt to run. For now, things were going to plan. He'd bought himself some time to make arrangements, and he knew he would finally be leaving this rat pit, with an escort no less. All he had to do was make sure he got out alive, but one thing at a time he told himself, as he was pushed back to 'Colditz' by Preston.

'Mr Black,' said Erikson. 'I have a job for you.'

'Of course,' replied Mr Black, aware that for the moment the status quo had been restored. 'You want him taken downstairs?'

'It'll take too long to break him in for Titan, he's too disruptive. Besides, we'll soon have Midas, won't we? When the accruals are finished, make sure that the body is disposed of properly. I don't want Mr Robinson and his trowel goblins stumbling across it, so remind that idiot team of yours that the Thames is tidal.'

Mr Black acknowledged the statement with a nod and left the bunker. He had committed to the delivery of Midas, without which the grand plan would fail, but he hadn't heard from Mr Blue or Green since they had checked in from Smallmansea. They were keen for revenge after what Cranston's accomplices had done to them in London. He liked vengeful minions, they were motivated. It was humiliating enough that they had been painted from head to toe in primary namesake colours, but to then be arranged, naked, frozen with a paralysing drug, in compromising positions outside the Tate Modern, what kind of man was this Cranston? It was days before people realised that they weren't a guerrilla art installation doubling as artistic bicycle racks.

His reputation was on a knife-edge. He would find Cranston and deal with him personally.

*****

The Allegro settled into a rhythmic, lumpy wheeze as Marsden coaxed it along narrow country lanes at a steady twenty miles per hour. There was a grinding sound from the front wheels at the slightest turn, a loud clunk from each corner of the car at the smallest bump, and a grating noise from the gearbox, which would put anyone's teeth on edge, whenever Marsden changed down. Apart from that, things could be worse.

John looked out over the open Sussex countryside, partly apprehensive at what was to happen next, but also relieved that no-one at that moment was trying to remove his fingers, shoot him, or set a lunatic poodle onto his manhood.

He had tried to engage Marsden in conversation, but beyond her sales pitch, she was inscrutable. The only information he had managed to glean was that they were going to change cars, beyond that all other questions were met with a stock, "You'll be fully briefed when we get there'. Changing tack to more inconsequential small talk, such as enquiring as to whether she had been anywhere nice for her holidays was met with Marsden's other stock answer, "That's classified".

There was one thing that Marsden had let on earlier though, he was in the middle of a war. Between whom he didn't know, but if there was money to be had, and as a rule someone always profited from conflict, he wouldn't be surprised if Martin was involved. Now he was wrapped up in this mess as well, maybe it was time to choose a side and Marsden at the moment was a front-runner, by virtue that she hadn't threatened to shoot him, yet.

With a white plume rising from the front grill Marsden turned onto an unmade road. Kangaroo hopping a further half- mile, they came to a halt on a large forecourt in front of what John guessed from its arched roof and a large overlapping doors was an old aircraft hangar. In its final death throes, the Allegro shook, rattled and rolled before signing off with a final gunshot backfire from the exhaust.

'I hope we're here, wherever here is, because this thing's had it,' said John as he made to get out of the car and stretch his legs.

'Wait' said Marsden as she dragged him back into the car by the tails of his jacket. The crack of a rifle shot ricocheting off the tarmac punctuated her speech.

'Bloody hell! I thought you said I'd be safer with your lot.'

'Do stop panicking; it's only friendly fire. Now sit still and shut-up for five minutes, I'll deal with this.' Marsden made a call. 'Hello Sally, its Lady Marsden here, how are you? - Oh that's good, I'm so glad he's back on the pills. Quick question, Henry wouldn't happen to be in the hangar by any chance... I thought so. Would you do me a small favour? Could you let Henry know I'm in the blue car that he's shooting at ...oh don't be silly, there's no harm done...quite, but how would he know? Don't worry I'm fine...yes please, milk no sugar would be lovely. See you in a mo'.'

'Lady Marsden?'

'I know, I don't like to make a thing of it, but Sally and Henry are very particular and I hate to upset them.'

A Judas Gate opened in the hangar doors and a large man with a recycled lived in face, oily overalls tied around his waist, a straggly beard and long receding hair tied back in a ponytail, lowered his sunglasses and looked at the blue wreck. His rifle was pointed downwards, supported by the crook of his arm. Marsden got out of the car and waved. The man slung the rifle over his shoulder and double-timed towards her.

'Ma'am, I'm sorry, I wasn't expecting you,' said Henry, speaking with urgency before he had caught his breath. 'I should've guessed it was a backfire, but I was concentrating on something else you see. Mind you, when I saw this reprobate, you can't be too careful can you?'

Marsden, out of the corner of her eye, saw John mouthing indignantly 'Reprobate?' Facing Henry, she signed to John with an open palm behind her back to stay where he was. 'Don't worry Henry; you did the right thing, although I would be grateful if you tried not to shoot him, he's one of us. I'm delivering him to HQ. Henry, meet Mr John Cranston.'

Henry nodded in acknowledgement.

'How's Abigail?' she asked.

'She's sweet Ma'am,' said Henry, with some pride. 'A lot of work, not that I'm complaining mind, she's been an absolute pleasure to work on. Come and have a look, I think you'll be pleased,' and with that Marsden and Henry marched off towards the hangar with John following.

The space was brightly lit and spotless, no oily floors or smell of white spirit and turpentine, a contrast to Pete's more modest setup thought John. Around the walls of the hangar were arranged various workbenches, lathes, pulleys, gantry's, and tools that wouldn't look out of place in a medieval torture chamber. In the middle of the workshop was the outline of a vehicle covered in a protective drape. The silhouette was low and sleek with the sweeping line of an extended teardrop running from a graceful bonnet to a neat tucked in rear end.

Marsden held her hands together in front of her lips as if offering a prayer. 'Can I?' she asked reverently.

'Be my guest Ma'am.'

Marsden lightly tugged on the silken cloth. It slid away to reveal a car built in the early 1970's that looked as modern and contemporary as any luxury car available today.

'Oh my God, how do you do that? Henry, you are an absolute genius,' said Marsden, running her hands along the rear wheel spats.

'Well, rather than trying to patch up the holes, I made up a whole new body section, but I wasn't happy trying to match it in, so I stripped her back and gave her a new paint job. I'd say she was about due after forty odd years.'

'Henry, once I've finished with Mr Cranston here, I'm taking you and Sally out for the best meal you've ever had. You are an artist!'

'Thank you Ma'am. It's my pleasure.'

John held up his hand to attract Marsden's attention. 'I hate to break up this love-in, but haven't we got somewhere to be? The sooner I can sort out my mess the better.'

'Philistine,' she sneered.

'Charming, I can appreciate a classic piece of automotive history as much as the next man you know. What have we got here then? I reckon a Citroen SM, or if you prefer the French, "Systeme Maserati" said John in an appalling accent. 'Whatever it is Henry, you've done a cracking job.'

'Thanks,' said Henry, surprised at the newcomer's knowledge. 'You're right, it is an SM.'

'Two point seven or the three litre Vee Six?'

'Three litre'

'That'll be the, let's think, nineteen seventy four "automatique" with three weber carbs then.'

'Not quite,' replied Henry. 'It's the five speed manual, three weber carbs, seventy three.'

'No! I didn't think they made many, these must be as rare as hen's teeth.'

'About six hundred, and you won't find any in this condition.'

'I'm sorry to interrupt boys,' said Marsden, 'but haven't we got other things to do? Henry, be a dear and let HQ know that I'm bringing Mr Cranston in, their switchboard at the moment is an absolute nightmare.'

'Yes Ma'am,' said Henry, looking slightly sheepish as he made his way to the office.

Marsden cast her gaze at John with some incredulity.

'What?' asked John in that tone that pre-empts a protest of total innocence. 'You said you had a Maserati, and I like Citroens. I can add up you know. Any chance of a drive?'

'No. You'll need to keep your head down on the back seat; we've just been in the only car chase that's ever happened in Smallmansea. With a bit of luck no one will believe it, nothing happens there normally.'

Marsden opened the passenger door, reached in and handed John a black hood, such as the condemned man wears at a gallows, and a pair of handcuffs.

'And you thought I was a pervert?' said John.

'You wish. Put them on.'

'Sorry, I missed that. It sounded like you wanted me to put this bag over my head.'

'Its Standard Operational Procedure, that's all. You can't know where our secret base is, and the handcuffs are so that you don't sneak a peek. I'll take them off when we get there.'

'Do I look stupid? Don't answer that. All this secret agent stuff, it's bull isn't it? The only reason you helped me get away is because you want the money. It's a shame, you were doing so well, but I'm not ready to be cashed in yet.'

'Oh please. I'd charge more for putting the bins out. Now come on, stop wasting my time.'

'Wasting *your* time? That's easily fixed. I'll see myself out, *Agent* Marsden, or Ma'am, or whatever you're calling yourself.'

'Cranston!' Her words fell on deaf ears as John moved at pace towards the exit. Marsden shook her head. It never used to be this difficult. At least Henry was back on his medication, so he should be more reasonable. Otherwise, she was going to have a lot of explaining to do.

The hangar exit was locked, but not to be defeated; John took a large crowbar from a nearby bench. As he was about to prise it open, he heard the lock being opened from the other side. It could only be Henry. He looked around for another escape route as the gate suddenly swung inward on its hinges, crashing against the hangar wall, and there he was, rifle in hand with the look of a man who was not open to negotiation.

'I'll give you a choice,' ordered Henry. 'Lady Marsden or a bullet. I'm not fussed either way.'

'Great...'

18 / B.A.W.D

Brigadier Edward Kensington-Smythe sat at the head of the meeting room table. He was early, for if there was one thing he could not abide it was a lack of punctuality. Time, once spent, was gone.

He had faith in Marsden, but the Pandora Protocol? The opportunity was too great to ignore, it could win the war, but if it came to a choice, he would destroy the Midas device, even if it meant that the long struggle would grind on.

Sir Arthur Rotherfield entered the room. 'Brigadier.'

'Rotherfield' acknowledged the Brigadier. 'Where's Jenkins?'

'He'll be along shortly. He said something about going to the communications room to catch an urgent message. Ah, here he is now.'

Jenkins entered the room, straightening his tie and brushing off his suit, missing the feathers trapped behind his lapels. 'Brigadier, Sir Rotherfield, sorry I'm late, I was waiting for the airmail.'

'You missed one,' said the Brigadier, pointing.

'Brigadier that can be explained, I can to talk to you about that later,' said Sir Rotherfield.

'Is there a problem?' said the Brigadier suspiciously.

'Not exactly,' replied Sir Rotherfield.

'Jenkins?' asked the Brigadier, not impressed with the non-committal answer.

'The feathers? It's, it's...errm, complicated?' Jenkins gave up.

He couldn't talk his way out of this one. 'I'm sorry, it's our new carrier pigeon, it's not quite got the hang of things yet, but it is a rescue though,' he added hoping that this would qualify as mitigating circumstances. 'Tattershall outsourced all the incoming communications to a call centre in China. He got a deal that we only pay for each call answered. On the bright side its dirt cheap, no-one's got through yet.'

'I thought the comms had been dealt with,' seethed the Brigadier directing his invective at Sir Rotherfield.

'That was for outgoing messages. This is purely a contingency until we can find someone who can negotiate in Mandarin,' replied Sir Rotherfield. 'In the interim we have backup multi-channel inbound capability; the heliograph and semaphore in particular are proving very reliable, although they are a bit slow. Department S have agreed to help out- when they have time,' he added with distaste.

'We'll discuss this later,' ordered the Brigadier. 'What's the message?'

'It's from Purple Gerbil,' Jenkins replied. 'They're on their way with John Cranston.'

'Excellent. Once we've got Midas, I want to see Cranston as a matter of urgency. And who's this Gerbil fellow? What the devil's happened to Marsden?'

'Marsden is the Purple Gerbil. There's a report in your IN Tray,' explained Sir Rotherfield.

'It's Tattershall again isn't it? More bloody paperwork. It'll have to wait for the moment.' The Brigadier looked around the table. 'Where's Crickwell? He should be here by now.'

'He's locked himself in his office with anything he can find that was written by Czeckovsky. He's not coming out until he's drawn up a schedule,' advised Sir Rotherfield. 'He thinks he could modify Midas in the five days, providing there were ten of him. Personally I recommend that we stick with our original plan and destroy it.'

'Damn.' The Brigadier tapped his pencil onto the notepad, considering the options. 'Gentlemen, that's not good enough.

I want answers and I want them now. You've had enough time to evaluate contingencies before this meeting. It's time to share.'

The room was silent. The Brigadier stared intently at both of them.

Jenkin's hand crept up. 'Brigadier, I think I know a way that I can recruit some people to help Crickwell. All I need is some money.'

'We can't afford consultants,' said Sir Rotherfield dismissively. 'Brigadier, I have thought about this at length, and I'll say it again, it's not possible in the time allocated, it must be destroyed.'

'Let the lad speak,' said the Brigadier. 'How much do you need?'

'A couple of hundred should do it, but it needs to be cash. For what I've got in mind, I'll have to show notes. I was thinking of raiding the Christmas fund.'

'Brigadier, there must be another way,' protested Sir Rotherfield.

'These are extraordinary times. The works outing for Mamma Mia will have to wait. Jenkins, take what you need, and don't let me down.'

*****

Victoria Marsden relaxed back into the plump armchair, took a deep breath, and then another, slowly restoring her state to one of more considered calm. She was used to the stresses of the job, that's why she stuck with it, that rush of natural body chemicals, the thrill of competition and winning, it couldn't be beat. Yes, it was risky, but a desk job was never going to be for her. The work was unpredictable, but even in that randomness; there was a natural order, a harbour that she used, the anchor that gave her the power.

John Cranston however, that was a different kind of stress. In the little time that she had known him, he had taken the status quo and royally shredded it without any effort. All Cranston had to do was follow instructions, but no, he made a run for it, which was the only excuse that Henry needed for a summary execution. It took her and Sally ten minutes to persuade him that Cranston wasn't a 'pinko subversive' and then only by putting handcuffs on Cranston at gunpoint, and shoving him into the back seat of the Citroen, had they stopped Henry from shooting him there and then. Henry wouldn't risk damaging his own work of art. As if that wasn't enough, then there was the continuous repeated phrase of 'Are we there yet?' all the way to HQ, that would have tested the patience of Job. She breathed deep again, coming back to her balanced state, helped by being in the Department S common room, an oasis of normality avoided by those upstairs, while she waited for the results of the recovered Midas device.

' 'Ere you go Vicky. Milk, no sugar, just the way you like it,' said a middle-aged man with a luxuriant beard and smiling eyes, his braces covered by a standard issue khaki knee length storesman coat. It was Dick Walker, the unofficial boss of Department S. He'd been there man and boy, and while some thought of him as an opportunistic spiv, he was the glue that kept the whole ship afloat.

'Thanks Dick,' she said, taking a welcome sip. 'Ooh I needed that.'

'Tough day?'

'Different. Car chase in Smallmansea in that clapped out Allegro, Henry got upset, and that John Cranston drove me nuts. I can't work him out. Apparently, he's a gardener, but there's something not right, I can't put my finger on it. How has he got this far on his own? I don't get it.'

'I've heard he's a bit tasty. He went toe to toe with Orimov on London Bridge, and only when he's outnumbered ten to one, cool as a cucumber he does a swan dive, Prisoner of Zenda like, into the Thames. And did you hear about Victoria Station?'

'No. What happened?'

'Twenty mercs' after him and all of them get taken out without anyone noticing. And to cap it all, one of them *"accidentally"* goes under a train.'

'Twenty, you sure?'

'Okay, things can get a bit exaggerated, but it's definitely more than ten. He says he's a gardener, but I reckon he's a ringer.'

'It makes sense,' considered Marsden. 'When we were on

the pier I only dealt with one of his problems, and yet come the car chase, there were two of them. I can't believe the other one wasn't on the pier looking for him. Cranston must have got past him somehow, and he was asking about Ashcombe, maybe he's a part-timer as well?'

'I never trusted that Ashcombe, I'm always suspicious when someone keeps calling me "mate", but let's not tar him with the same brush. You keep an eye on him though, birds of a feather and all that. Anyway's, enough talk about Cranston, I ain't seen you for a while. How's the manor going?'

Marsden sighed. 'It's a mess. It looks fine from the outside, but close up, what a wreck. I couldn't give it away, and as it's listed, I can't even knock it down. Take it from me Dick, if you're the last in line of some long lost relations and you get a call, say "No". And now everyone keeps calling me "Ma'am" or "Ladyship". It's not me. Why can't I go back to being Ms or Agent Marsden?'

'Afraid you're stuck with it. Rotherfield's song and dance about using titles won't hold much water if you become an exception. Just smile and wave, and if you're getting desperate, come down for a cuppa. Why'd you think Rotherfield gives us such a wide berth? You won't get none of that airs and graces tosh round 'ere.'

'Thanks, I appreciate that.' She took another sip of tea. 'Any news on Gordon?'

'Nothing, but I wouldn't count him out yet, he hasn't cleared his book. He always made sure he was up to date if he thought he'd be doing something risky, like skydiving without a parachute or something. He'd say to me, "Dick" he says, "if I'm going to go, I like to keep things tidy." Personally I'd want to see a body first.'

'That's my next job. If he's in trouble, I'll find him. I owe him that much at least. If it hadn't been for him and you I would have left this place after the first month.'

'That's cos some people ain't as enlightened as wot we is when it comes to your fairer sex, nah wot I mean milady, gawd bless ya, apples and pears!' said Walker in his best Dick Van Dyke Mary Poppins accent while tugging an imaginary forelock.

Marsden tapped him playfully on the shoulder. 'Stop it!'

One of Walker's colleagues came into the common room and put a small data card in a plastic case on the coffee table. 'There you go, Crickwell says its pucker.'

'Cheers,' said Walker. 'Has he come out yet?'

'No, says he's having a nervous breakdown.'

'But he's only got five days,' said Marsden.

'Don't worry,' reassured Walker. 'He always has a wobble before inspiration strikes. It's his fault anyway. If the silly sod had kept his gob shut, we could've stuck this in the blender and had done with it.' He handed the card to Marsden. ''Ere you go, for the Brigadier with our compliments. I'll give Sir Rotherfield the good news.'

*****

'Agent Marsden, do come in,' said the Brigadier as he gestured to the seat on the opposite side of his desk. 'Do you have something for me?'

Marsden handed over the data-card and the Brigadier held it up and examined it, turning it over and around as if he were a gem cutter examining the facets of a rare stone.

'To think, the amount of trouble such a small thing can cause,' mused the Brigadier. 'Excellent work agent, excellent.'

'I can't take all the credit Brigadier. When the Gossip Network started chatting about a man buying the Guardian in Smallman-sea I knew he wasn't from around here. With a bit of legwork I tracked him down to a bungalow and left him a message he couldn't refuse.'

'How is our guest?'

'In the staff canteen having a snack, his sandwich got squashed in the chase.'

'Anything else I should know?'

'Brigadier, can I be frank?'

'You'll need to discuss that with Sir Rotherfield, although I must say it's a dashed unusual name for a female operative.' The Brigadier mused on this for a second. 'On second thoughts it would be an improvement on Gerbil.'

'No, I meant... never mind. Permission to speak freely Sir.'

'Of course, go on.'

'I don't believe Cranston's a gardener. In fact, I don't know what he is, but I'm not sure if we can trust him. Let me deliver Midas, I'll tell them I'm collecting the bounty.'

'No. I think we can make better use of Cranston rather than simply handing him over. Also there is the small matter of your previous engagements with Erikson's men. I have no doubt you can hide in a crowd, but at close quarters, someone might recognise you. I can't risk it.'

'But Brigadier, it's no more risky then sending Cranston in, he's unpredictable and...'

'No.' The Brigadier sat back in his chair. 'As we're speaking freely, I'm going to share some information with you that goes no further. You're aware of the minor procedural problems caused by Mr Tattershall?'

Marsden nodded. 'Say the word and I'll give you a list.'

'Quite, but these minor problems are bringing this organisation to its knees. Individually they're no more than irritations, but they're compounding and spreading. Sir Rotherfield is fighting a rear-guard action; it would be easier to kill the proverbial Hydra. We're infected. The only people who I can be confident of not being compromised are you, Gordon, Ashcombe, and Cranston. As field operatives, you're at arms-length with some operational discretion, and Cranston's an outsider. However, Gordon and Ashcombe maybe dead, and our new recruits aren't ready, so in the overall scheme of things Cranston isn't as risky as you think. If we don't take this opportunity to deliver Midas, then Erikson will have a head start while we waste our time reorganising. We have one key advantage; he doesn't know that we have Cranston at the moment.'

'At the moment,' echoed Marsden. 'Do we have a leak?'

'I'm not sure, but I don't know how else to explain that the last place Gordon was, went up in flames with him in it. It had to be Erikson.'

'Do you think Tattershall was an inside job ? Was he the leak?'

'No. He was an idiot who'd read too much Tom Peters and we were stupid for not keeping a closer eye on him. No, if it had been Erikson it would have been more surgical and quick, not this damn death by a thousand cuts.'

'What do you need me to do?'

'Bring Cranston to me. I have some recruiting to do.'

'Is that it?' replied Marsden hiding her annoyance at being relegated to the role of escort.

'Keep your powder dry, we'll be talking again.'

*****

John sat in the canteen mulling over his coffee. Apart from the lack of windows, with the plastic chairs and the almost retro formica topped tables, he could be anywhere. At the head of the canteen, from the utilitarian serving galley, the smell of frying bacon wafted seductively in his direction. People came and went, some dressed in casual day wear, some in shirts and ties, but none in any kind of dark uniform with leather trimmings looking as if they could leap from a window and abseil fifty floors at a moment's notice. He wasn't sure if he was relieved or disappointed. It wasn't every day you visited a secret spy headquarters.

Marsden spotted John sitting in the corner, looking into space with his foot through the loop of his rucksack. 'Is this chair taken?' she asked rhetorically.

John looked around the now nearly empty canteen, the rush of that particular break being nearly over. 'I think it's available. Why don't you join me? I've heard this is the poshest secret restaurant in town.'

'Thank you. Is the accommodation here to Sir's liking?'

'It's not bad. At least that Gideon guy isn't stalking me with his bible. One thing though, do I pay extra for daylight?'

Marsden held back a half-smile. When Cranston wasn't being irritating, he was bordering on charming. 'The Brigadier wants to see you,' and she stood up from the table to lead the way.

'No handcuffs this time?' asked John.

Marsden gave him a cold disdainful look that said in no uncertain terms, 'NOT NOW'.

'Okay, I'm sorry that I didn't believe you, but come on, you can't blame me for being a bit paranoid,' offered John in a hasty defence.

'I suppose that in your line of work you've never been in any sort of trouble. The way you handled yourself in that car chase must have been pure luck. You're not the only one that's suspicious Mr Cranston.'

'So that's what's bothering you. Let's just say I had a life before gardening which I managed to leave behind. Mind you, if you'd seen the way some of my customers react if I stripe their lawns wrong, that car chase would look like a doddle. Did you find the thing that's causing me all this trouble?'

'The Brigadier will give you a full briefing.'

'Brilliant. Take me to your leader.'

As they left the canteen, a young clean cut man watched them with more than a passing curiosity. He looked like butter would have trouble melting in his mouth. He put his newspaper down on top of the standard issue catering steak knife and secreted it away, before dutifully taking his tray with his cleaned plate and picked bones to the rack. He'd choose his moment. Cranston in his eyes was a dead man walking.

*****

'Mr Cranston, do take a seat,' said the Brigadier extending his hand in friendship. 'I must say it's a pleasure to meet you at last, I'm a great admirer of your work.'

'You've been spying on my gardening?'

'Gardening? Oh I see, no, I was referring to Victoria Station, an absolute master class, top notch.'

'I caught a train.'

'Ha! I like modesty in a man, but you can take it too far you know. We'll say no more about it for the moment; I wouldn't want to embarrass you.' The Brigadier poured himself a measure of Dalmore eighteen year old whisky and gestured for John to join him.

'No thanks, I never drink in secret hideaways, makes it difficult getting home if I don't know where I'm staggering from. Agent Marsden said that you'd be able to tell me why I'm in this fix, and how I can get out of it.'

The Brigadier lifted the glass to his nose and savoured the aroma before taking a small draft. His first impressions of John Cranston in the flesh were good ones. He liked a man who got to the point and wanted to keep his wits about him. 'Apologies for the search when you first came in, standard procedure you see. We found this in your phone,' and the Brigadier held up the card.

John looked at it with some bemusement. 'What's so special about that? Next you'll be telling me it contains some top secret plans or something.'

'If only. This card, in the wrong hands, could bring governments to their knees and start world wars,' said the Brigadier, pausing while he thought of a suitable analogy. 'Imagine that you had a key that could unlock any safe, any door, let you into any house, and then in an instant, change the locks. I don't profess to be a technical man, but we all know that computers are, or will be, threaded through every aspect of our lives. Not only the major things such as finance or the military, but the everyday, from the food being delivered to the local supermarket to making the trains run on time. This card is that key. It can break any password, any encryption, in a fraction of a second, and also encrypt any system so that only the owner of this card can use it. It's been circulating through the underworld promising power to whoever has it until someone in turn kills them for it. We call it Midas; no one who's touched it has enjoyed what it promises.'

'Seriously? This is just government secrets and stuff isn't it? Worse than this gets left on a train seat. I know it's embarrassing, but you don't have to talk it up for my benefit.'

'Mr Cranston, do I look like a comedian?'

'No, to be honest I can't see you doing Mother-in-Law jokes. Okay, let's say this thing is as bad as you say, that's your problem, so why am I being chased all over the shop?'

'It was planted on you by one of our agents, a friend of yours actually. You were used as a temporary hiding place until he could retrieve it. As you've been on the run, we've done the job for him.'

John mentally raced through recent events. There was only one suspect. 'Martin's one of yours?'

The Brigadier nodded.

'I'll bloody kill him when I get my hands on him.'

'I don't think that will be necessary, Agent Ashcombe is currently presumed dead.'

'What?!' John rubbed his forehead over his right brow. 'What do you mean "presumed dead"?'

'We haven't found a body, but as we haven't heard from him we're assuming that he's been killed by the same people that are chasing you.'

'Great. Okay, okay, let me think about this. You're the good guys, right?'

The Brigadier nodded.

'Okay, so now you've got this Midas thing, which is where it should have been in the first place, I'm off the hook, right? Once word gets around, all the spies, agents and bad people get on with what they're doing, and I'll get back to normal. That's how this works out isn't it?'

'No Mr Cranston, I expect you to join us.'

'Join? No chance. I don't know you people from Adam and now you're telling me Martin might be dead because of this thing. No way. You can sort out your own mess.'

The Brigadier removed a buff file from a drawer, opened it and placed it on his desk facing John. 'You know this man, General Vladimir Orimov, ex KGB, ex SPUD.'

'Mr Black,' spat John.

'He's a freelance in the employ of Kurt Erikson; CEO of Brassica, one of the biggest technology companies in the world.'

'I've had some run in's with him and his groupies, but

what's this got to do with me now?'

'Whether you like it or not, you're involved. Erikson won't stop until he has Midas. The Brassica Corporation is a front for a shadow organisation called the Dark League. As his software exists on practically every computing device, with Midas he'll be able to hold the world to ransom or if he chooses, take selected countries back to the Dark Ages.'

'I'm sure you and your merry band can work something out without me.'

The Brigadier held Midas between his finger and thumb. 'As Erikson wants this so badly, we're going to give it to him. It'll be modified so that when he uses it, his organisation will be wiped out from the inside. I want you to deliver it.'

'Hold on a minute, you're not listening to me. Whatever you lot get up to, I don't want anything to do with it. If the Brassica Corporation is that evil, and I admit it was a twisted mind that came up with version eight, I'm not going to pay a visit to people who wouldn't think twice about collecting my fingers. What's wrong with your own lot?'

'Nothing at all, but they lack the one thing that you have, plausibility. We can't have one of our agents popping up like a postman. Erikson and most of the country's outlaws still believe that you have Midas, and he's trying to flush you out. No, it's much better that you hand it over, the chase having finally worn you down, that sort of thing.'

'And he'll just let me go – no sticking me in a shallow grave somewhere because I know too much?'

'God forbid no, whatever gave you that idea? There are protocols around this sort of thing and it would be too much trouble for someone as insignificant as you. It's Standard Operational Procedure – you'll walk free to get back to *your gardening*. After all, who's going to believe you?'

'Thanks, that's made me feel much better,' said John as he considered this to be missed proposition. Here was his way out; the only problem was he would have to get in over his head before surfacing on the other side, and it seemed too neat.

He always believed that if something was too good to be true, it probably was. 'Brigadier, I appreciate your help, but I'm not your man, I'm sure you'll manage without me. I'll be on my way and keep my head down until the dust clears.'

'It'll be a long wait, it may be months before we get another opportunity. Leave now and we won't help you again. Do you think that even a man of your rare talents could last out there for long?'

'Flattery will get you nowhere. I'm quite good at staying out of trouble, and if anyone asks, I'll tell them who has it.'

'And who are we exactly?'

'You're the Brigadier, Head of a secret organisation...' John let out a deep breath of dawning realisation. 'You really are a piece of work. If I don't deliver it, no-one's going to know I haven't got it are they?'

'As I say, it's all about plausibility, and we wouldn't be very secret if we told the world who we were and what we had would we? Perception is sometimes greater than truth, and at the moment, everyone believes you have Midas. Walk through that door and you'll at least be a useful decoy. You're safer here. Work with us, and you can go back to your old life when we're done.'

John was being backed into a corner, could he call the Brigadier's hand? He could wait out the storm, but not here in England. The Brigadier said it himself, everyone in the country. He would have to take Alice up on her offer, but only to use Spain as a stepping-stone. He had the cash – it was time to disappear again.

As John was mulling over the proposition Jenkins burst in.

'Brigadier, sorry for the interruption, but this just came in through Department S, they thought you'd want to see it. They said it was urgent,' and Jenkins handed over a sealed envelope.

'Thank you. You can go,' said the Brigadier as he removed the contents. 'Oh I say! I haven't seen one of these for years. Mr Cranston, as you appear minded to leave us, it would be remiss of me not to share this information.'

'What is it?'

'It's the latest update from Mugbook. I don't use it myself but

I understand that it's de rigueur for any disreputable ne'er do well these days. Following your escapade with Agent Marsden, the price on your head is now one million pounds. What's really impressive is that you've achieved B.A.W.D status. Congratulations I haven't seen that in years- it takes me back.'

'B.A.W.D?'

'It's a short-hand we used that these things have adopted.'

'And...?' asked John, knowing that he was being reeled in, but this was important.

The Brigadier had that knowing look that chess players have when checkmate of their opponent is inevitable. 'Sorry old chap, I keep forgetting you're new to this. Barely Alive Will Do.'

John considered his options. One million and they didn't have to be careful with delivery. Anti-social media was no respecter of national boundaries; would the world be big enough?

'Where do I sign?'

19 / And In the Blue Corner

The Brigadier looked through the report provided by Sir Rotherfield and shook his head. How could it take more effort to document a problem than it would to fix it? At this rate, he'd be receiving an official requisition for a sledgehammer with which to crack this seemingly indestructible walnut. Sir Rotherfield always argued that his thoroughness was the only thing standing between preserving the institutional memory of the Society and it being destined to repeat the same mistakes, but this was excessive, too excessive.

Tattershall's so called improvements were serial process time bombs distracting from the main tasks in hand, but why was it that each solution then expanded disproportionately when implemented. He had his suspicions based on some meagre intelligence, but if he was wrong? He dismissed any nascent negative thoughts, he'd cross that bridge if he came to it. With the wind changing in his favour, he had to make sure it didn't spill from the sails through unnecessary procrastination.

With Cranston now on board, the base was on lock-down. No one could leave or enter without the Brigadier's personal authorisation. All communications were restricted, the only room from which anyone could get a mobile signal having been secured by Jenkins with a strategically placed 'Out of Order' sign.

He threw the buff folder onto the bedside cabinet. The accommodation, an annexe to his office, was functional and comfortable; he didn't need any privileges of rank. He showered, shaved, put on his favourite three-piece suit, knotted his tie with a full windsor and walked through the connecting door, papers in hand. He rearranged some items on his desk and checked his watch. 'Any moment now,' he told himself, and directly on cue, there was a knock on his door. 'Come in Sir Rotherfield.'

Sir Rotherfield entered, slightly bemused at the Brigadier's newfound clairvoyance. 'Brigadier, are you aware that Crickwell has left the base? How did he get out? This is disastrous.'

'There's no need for panic. I authorised it. Crickwell and Jenkins have been getting on like a house on fire and between them they've cooked up a plan to meet the deadline.'

'Why wasn't I told about this? It's highly irregular. How am I supposed to sort everything out if I'm not involved? Where has Crickwell gone?'

'There's only so much that even you can do in a day, so I dealt with it directly, consider yourself briefed. With Cranston around, I can't risk any leaks, so everything is now on a need to know basis. Crickwell is with a specialised team that Jenkin's rounded up, and you and I don't need to know where that is.'

'I must protest, this is against all protocol.'

'Protest noted. Now, as you're here, let's get down to business. How's our guest?'

'He's doing introductory training. I know, it's hardly necessary but I thought it best to keep him occupied.'

The Brigadier nodded in agreement and opened the buff folder. 'I have to say this makes for some interesting reading…'

*****

John Cranston was a sorry sight in borrowed baggy tracksuit bottoms, big enough to fit two of him in, held up by a makeshift drawstring of twine. The 'Frankie Says Relax' T-shirt, again, two sizes too big was equally unflattering. He looked like a stand-in from The Incredible Shrinking Man. He resigned himself to his lot and hoped that whatever he could learn about this mysterious organisation through the Introductory Training would stand him in good stead. He was up to his neck in it and if going with the flow could help, he would give it a try.

At the centre of the training area was a boxing ring surrounded by an assortment of punch bags, barbells, weights, and machines for running and climbing. Alongside were open plan room mock-ups more suited to a home furnishing superstore, including a complete bathroom suite.

'Hello, you're new here aren't you?' said a voice behind John that made him start. 'Sorry about that,' the stranger continued, 'it's all part of the training, I'm working towards my stealth NVQ. I'm doing the sneaking up on the enemy module at the moment. I'm Peartree, Cyril Peartree, pleasure to meet you.'

'John Cranston. So Cyril, what goes on here then?'

'Training – but I'm not sure what today, we'll have to wait for Inspector Gunter to get here. He's always mixing things up to keep us on our toes. If you like we could do some warm up exercises while we're waiting.'

'Okay, what've you got in mind?'

Cyril Peartree adopted a stance reminiscent of the iconic pose struck by Bruce Lee in the classic martial arts film, Enter the Dragon. His left open hand was just below his chin. The right hand extended out in front but lower down at waist level. With his torso turned side on, he gave a little yelp and stared intently at John. 'Hit me.'

'Sorry?'

'Hit me,' said Peartree. 'Don't worry; it's all part of the training.'

John thought there had to be a catch; you didn't invite an attack unless you were confident of coming out on top. He raised his guard, keeping his left back and made a half-hearted jab at Peartree's nose. Anticipating that his lame punch would be intercepted and held in some kind of arm lock, he had his submission ready. John's fist connected with Peartree's cheekbone, not hard enough to cause any harm, but never the less, a red mark spread across the side of Peartree's face.

'Christ!' John exclaimed. 'Sorry about that. I didn't mean to, but you did say…'

'No, no, that's fine. I wasn't ready that's all, and the punch was a bit slow. We're training for real life here, so don't worry, give it some oomph.'

'You sure?'

Peartree adopted the position, flicked his nose with his thumb and stared intently. As before, John brought his guard up, but now feinted a jab with his right. Peartree executed a graceful, but pointless, sweeping arc to intercept the blow that never arrived. Before he could mobilise for a counter punch, John had already connected with a crashing left hook into the side of his nose.

'Are you alright?' said John, 'I'm really sorry about that, I didn't mean to, honestly, I thought you'd stop it.'

'Doh, id's okay. I'd be fide in a mid-idd.'

'Gentlemen!' boomed a voice from a barrel chested epitome of a Sergeant Major. 'Atten – Shun!'

Peartree assumed the position. John followed suit, the last thing he wanted to do was make enemies, he had enough already.

'Gentlemen, my name is Inspector Gunter, but you can call me Sir. Is that understood?'

'Yes Sir,' said Peartree, having recovered enough to speak English.

'Yes Sir,' said John, taking his cue from Peartree.

Gunter looked John up and down. 'You need to put some weight on you 'orrid little man!' He turned his attention to Peartree who had a face like an over ripe raspberry. 'Have you been asking people to hit you again Peartree?'

'Yes Sir.'

'And pray tell which wall were you facing?'

Peartree pointed reluctantly at the wall opposite.

Gunter turned to John. 'And which hand did you hit him with?'

'Both,' said John. 'He didn't have a preference.'

'Dear oh dear oh dear,' said Gunter sarcastically, shaking his head. 'Peartree, how many times have I told you that your training so far only works if you're facing north and are attacked *sloow-ly.*'

'Loads of time Sir, but what if I'm attacked from the east? I know I'm ready Sir, I just need more practice.'

'Peartree, you couldn't punch your way out of a paper bag, but you've got heart, I'll give you that. You see this man,' said Gunter with his index finger pointing at Peartree while looking at John, 'that's what made this country great. In six months, I'll have him at the north pole and he'll be bloody lethal. Those penguins won't know what's 'it 'em.'

'I thought penguins were only at the south pole,' said John as he watched Gunter's face change to a redder shade, like an electric hob warming up. 'Sir.'

'Don't get clever with me Sonny Jim. You've been here five minutes and you think you know it all! That's what they want you to think.' Gunter turned to Peartree and whispered in his ear, 'Start practising facing the radiators.' Gunter decided against a full-on bollocking for Cranston, time was getting on. 'Now then gentlemen, my job is to teach you basic survival techniques for dealing with your villains, henchmen, despots etcetera, etcetera, whom I shall round up and will henceforth refer to as "hostiles". Is that understood?'

'Yes Sir!'

'Right, now your average hostile's objective is to remove you from active operations, and they do that by attacking you when you're least expecting it. Gentlemen, meet your greatest enemy,' and Gunter held up a Do Not Disturb sign of the type that would hang over a hotel room door. 'Your hostile will think nothing of disguising themselves as room service or a chamber maid, doing what they do, and then hanging this sign on your door. You could be there for days before anyone finds out. These are nasty people. Is that understood? What are they?'

'Nasty people. Sir!'

'Right, walk this way,' and Gunter led them to the mocked up bathroom suite. 'Now your hostile will think nothing of launching their attack just as you're taking a bath, assume that your room is bugged and that they're listening for the taps running. In the event of an attack, the standard procedure is to throw aforementioned hostile into the bath, which will be full of water, and to then disable them by placing an electrical device into said bath with the hostile. Peartree, what mustn't we forget?'

'To leave the plug in. Sir!'

'Well done. Now, as you can see, we have an assortment of electrical instruments in this bathroom scenario. At the sound of the whistle, I want you to select the appropriate electrical device, and standing behind this line, throw it into the bath. Peartree, you first.'

On the sound of the whistle, quick as a flash, Peartree picked up a hair dryer and threw it the eight feet to the bath, where with its arched trajectory it looked set for a perfect splash landing. As it got close, it stopped in mid-air, and sprang back, hitting Peartree square on the nose. He crouched over in pain, quietly repeating choice words under his breath.

'Not bad,' said Gunter, 'that would have been three seconds. What lesson have we learnt here?'

'Not to use anything with a flexed cord, Sir,' Peartree moaned.

John went next, selected the hair dryer with a long, non-curled cord and threw it into the bath where it landed with a satisfying splosh.

'Four seconds. Not bad. Right gentlemen, the next thing you need to know is that your average hostile sometimes arranges for small creatures to do their dirty work. Always be wary of anything that has no legs, or more than four. Owing to the size of aforementioned nasties, it's difficult to engage them in hand-to-hand combat, so in our bathroom scenario this is what we do. Take your standard lighter 1B, issue black, like so, and ignite spray from cheap aerosol cologne, like so,' explained Gunter as a long plume of flame shot from the canister. 'Peartree, you first, select an item from the variety of toiletries and make an improvised flame thrower, wait for it… now!'

Peartree rushed to the bathroom cabinet and picked up a canister. John coughed but Peartree didn't take the hint as he tried to ignite a roll-on deodorant. Gunter had the stopwatch on him and Peartree was determined to impress. He picked up another canister and John coughed again, but Peartree wasn't going to let that put him off. He raised the lighter, pressed the aerosol button and put the flame out with a jet of shaving foam, but he wasn't giving up. He wiped the foam off with his T-shirt and with persistence; he managed to get a flame from the lighter. Picking up another canister, he jabbed down hard on the aerosol.

'Ahhhhhggg! No, no, no, oh god it hurts, it hurts, ahhhhnnnn, make it stop...!' Peartree cried.

'Come on, let's get you to the nurse again,' said Gunter. 'I'm afraid the lessons over for today Mr Cranston. He does this every time, always points the spray in the wrong direction. By the time I've sorted out young Peartree here, I'll have somewhere else to be. You know what they say; time and Ofsted wait for no man. Good luck with the mission anyway,' and with that he escorted the temporarily blind Peartree out of the gym.

'Thanks. Hope you'll be feeling better Cyril,' said John, amazed at Peartree's capacity for self-induced injuries.

The gymnasium/training area was now empty. John idly tapped the hanging punch bag and made his way over to the ring. He climbed under the rope and stood in the centre, looking around full circle. It took him back to when he was a newly minted teenager, training in the boxing gym on the top floor of the Lemmings Corset public hostelry and gymnasium. He had won a few fights as an amateur, but nothing to write home about. He stuck at it until he was old enough to drink himself stupid and get home. Then he had the choice of being hit in the face on a Friday night in the ring, or stopping in the bar downstairs, getting soused, and only occasionally being hit in the face on a Friday night. The latter option won out.

It's at times like these when people say, 'Those were the days,' but for John it was a wrong turning, which in a roundabout way introduced him, after some adventures, eventually to gardening and his subsequent rehabilitation, along with saving his nose.

(It is at this point that a certain person, carrying a serrated cutlery knife, looking like butter wouldn't melt in his mouth, enters the gymnasium. For the purposes of brevity, we'll call him 'Buttermouth'.)

'Oi, Cranston! I've got a bone to pick with you,' said Buttermouth as he paced quickly across the floor and rolled under the bottom rope into the ring. It was unfortunate for John, not being on his guard, that he responded by turning round as his name had been shouted out. Introductory training hadn't covered bad manners.

'Look, if you're a friend of Cyril's I can explain. He asked me to hit him,' said John, aiming to pre-empt any conflict.

'I don't give a monkey's about Cyril, whoever he is.'

'Oh – okay. This isn't part of the training is it? You don't want me to hit you as well?'

'Yeah, you'd like that wouldn't ya, like I bet you mugged my bruvver when you pushed him under that train at Victoria.'

'Whoa – hold on a minute, have you got the wrong man. I haven't pushed anyone under any train.'

'Don't give me all that. Arf the gang's in hospital cos of you and Buzz Saw Billy can't play the joanna anymore.'

'Sorry to hear that. Was he any good?'

'Nah he was crap, but that's not the point. You killed my bruvver, so I'm gonna kill you. Sod the money, it's a point of principle, know wot I mean?'

John easily sidestepped Buttermouth's lunge. There was nothing subtle about the attack, but that didn't make him any less dangerous. They circled around each other in the ring, John looking for anything that he could use to defend himself with.

The gymnasium door opened and in walked Marsden followed by a rag tag bunch of sweaty individuals looking like ducklings in judo suits.

'Marsden! I need some help here!'

Buttermouth, his knife held out in front, blocking John's escape quickly looked over his shoulder and then back at John. 'Stay out of this bitch!'

There was a wave of murmuring amongst Marsden's students.

'Did you hear that? That's not good is it?'

'I don't fancy his chances.'

'You know, I heard someone called her a "stuck up cow" once.'

'No! What happened?'

'Nothing, it was a wrong number.'

'Quiet class, please,' said Marsden in a calm but firm 'don't argue with me' voice. She ignored Buttermouth's invective. 'What's the problem now Cranston?'

'He's – got- a – knife…' John replied as he ducked and weaved around the ring.

'Is that all? I'll be with you in a minute; I've got a class on. Anyway, after Victoria station this should be easy for you.'

On hearing Marsden's reply, Buttermouth took this as further confirmation of what he believed to be true. With an animal cry he charged at John, swinging the knife wildly. John ducked, bringing his right fist underneath Buttermouth's ribs into his solar plexus, doubling him up. John pushed him to the deck and vaulted the top rope of the ring, rolling on landing back onto his feet. Buttermouth rolled under the bottom rope, still holding his ribs, with the knife in front of him. John picked up the small stool that boxers sit on between rounds, holding one of the legs, using it as a shield. They squared off against each other, recovering their breath, waiting to see who would make the first move.

'Now class, as you can see, Mr Cranston is providing us with a demonstration of the different techniques that can be used when under attack by a hostile,' lectured Marsden. 'Before we continue, could anyone tell me how we would classify said hostile?'

'Angry person with a knife, Ma'am,' said one.

'Not bad, but that's not really a classification, more a description of his state. Anyone else?'

'Assassin Ma'am,' said another.

'Nope. Observe the technique. No qualified assassin would take all that effort to run around chasing their target like that. One last chance.'

'Homicidal maniac Ma'am,' said a diminutive young blonde girl with her hair tied back in a ponytail.

'Very good Larkhill. And what is the standard procedure for dealing with homicidal maniacs?' Marsden looked around the group, 'Jenkins?'

'Shoot them Ma'am,' said Jenkins without hesitation.

'I know that this is new to you, but this is an *unarmed* defence class,' said Marsden, hiding her despair. She knew they were short of agents, but it didn't help having to train the admin staff when they had some spare time away from their other duties.

'Oh, right,' said Jenkins with some realisation. 'Find someone with a gun and ask them to shoot them.'

'Larkhill?' asked Marsden.

'Accept their surrender Ma'am, and if they don't take the hint, disarm them with extreme prejudice.'

'Thank you,' said Marsden.

'Swot,' said Jenkins under his breath.

'Moron,' replied Larkhill.

Meanwhile John had tripped up over a dumbbell and Buttermouth was on top of him, bearing down with the knife as both men engaged in a form of horizontal arm wrestling. The knife was an inch from John's throat. 'Marsden!'

'Right class,' addressed Marsden, 'as you can see Mr Cranston is now demonstrating the technique of fighting on your back. It's extremely risky so should be used sparingly, and only by advanced practitioners.'

'Now - would …be good!' cried John as he wrestled with the slavering Buttermouth.

'I think it's time for a practical. Could I have a volunteer to demonstrate how to disarm this homicidal maniac,' instructed Marsden.

There was an awkward silence in the ranks until one of the assembled piped up.

'Sorry Ma'am, I haven't got my stab vest. I didn't think we were doing sharp things until next week.'

'You're supposed to be prepared,' stated Marsden matter of factly. 'Anyone else not have their equipment?'

'It's in the wash Ma'am,' said one.

'My gran borrowed it,' said another.

'The dogs eaten it,' said someone else.

'I see,' said Marsden visibly disappointed. 'Class, pay attention, I'll be testing you later.'

Buttermouth was bringing his weight to bear down on the knife. John momentarily stopped resisting and with a last ditch effort he guided the knife to one side where it stuck in the floor. Buttermouth lurched forward only to be on the receiving end of an unplanned head-butt. John rolled him off, scrambled away, and got to his feet, breathing heavily. He couldn't do this for much longer.

Buttermouth wrenched the knife free, determined to have his revenge and there, standing between him and his satisfaction was that woman. 'Out of the way – now!' he ordered.

'Or you'll what? You'll make me wish I wasn't born? Maybe I'll be eating hospital food in imaginative ways? Honestly, I've heard it all before. How about you surrender now and I'll overlook your little verbal faux pas earlier on,' said Marsden graciously.

'Foe what?'

'I'll take that as "No" then. Okay; let's get this over with.'

'You what?' said Buttermouth confused. He wasn't used to being challenged by a woman who wasn't his mother.

'I haven't got all day bonehead,' Marsden said in an exasperating tone. 'What's up, not man enough to take on a poor defenceless woman?' she teased, waggling her little finger. 'I've got a magnifying glass if you've got trouble finding your balls.'

Buttermouth was aware of tittering from the spectators. 'You asked for this,' he said menacingly, by way of a perverse justification for attacking an unarmed member of the fairer sex. He ran forward only to find himself face down on the floor with his knife arm raised to the ceiling, perpendicular to his torso. The pain was excruciating as his joints were forced contrary to their natural position.

'Now class,' said Marsden, totally unruffled, 'as you can see the hostile is no longer an immediate threat, but typical for this type they have a high pain threshold and won't release their weapon. So we have to do this…like so.'

If there was an Olympic sport of synchronised wincing,

Marsden's students would have walked away with gold. The knife clattered to the floor and Buttermouth was left as a sobbing shadow of himself.

Marsden rendered him unconscious with a blow to the base of the skull. 'That's better; I do hate it when they cry. Okay everyone, class dismissed. Jenkins, could you take the rubbish out please?'

As Marsden was leaving, she could be heard to say, 'Scourge of Victoria, really?'

John was leaning forward, his hands resting above his knees, recovering, and brooding. This was the last straw.

'Don't worry Mr Cranston – I thought you did alright,' said Jenkins. 'I mean, we all have off days.'

'I've had enough of this,' said John as he stormed out leaving Jenkins wondering what it was he had said.

*****

'Mogadon Molly, Flush Gordon, the Rhinoplasty Cowboy, need I go on?' said the Brigadier. 'How the hell did this happen and why is it taking so long to put right?'

'As you'll see in the report,' said Sir Rotherfield, 'this was an initiative by Tattershall to review agent's code names with a view to increasing morale. He believed that the standard alphanumeric codes weren't popular with some of the staff, so he engaged them in a consultation exercise.'

'In the Abbott's Food Mixer I see. Were any agents invited to this boozy consultation?'

'No, just the crew from the communications room, and that's where the problems started. They allocated names based on what they thought of the agents. As you can see some of them are quite...' Sir Rotherfield looked for the right word.

'Puerile?' offered the Brigadier as he flicked through the list. 'What have we here – Henry Haemorrhoid, I'm Spartacus...'

'I admit they did get creative after a few rounds. I'm informed that "I'm Spartacus" has been a source of great amusement. The call centre answering service has been configured to respond to that particular code name with, "No, I'm Spartacus", ad nauseum.'

'And who's Captain Gorgeous?' asked the Brigadier, picking another name at random.

'That's George, the Caretaker.'

'Good lord man, these are meant for our agents! He's got a title already – he's the Caretaker, and a fine job he does as well. We can't have tannoy messages of "Captain Gorgeous to spillage in aisle three" can we? Change everything back, and if anyone objects, sack them.'

'Technically we don't employ them. They're volunteers with benefits.'

The Brigadier took a deep breath, rested his chin on his clasped hands and slowly leaned forward. 'Arthur, I think you need to tell me what's going on. I've had enough of these excuses. Whatever it is, I promise I'll take all extenuating circumstances into consideration.'

'I'm sorry; I don't know what you mean.'

'The Sir Rotherfield I know would have had this fixed by now, in his sleep. What's going on?'

'If you insist, although I've been reluctant to say anything as I didn't want to be seen to undermine your authority,' said Sir Rotherfield with a hint of condescension. 'I appreciate that we're under staffed but sending your office personnel into the field is causing untold disruption. It's unreasonable to expect me to implement the Standard Operational Procedure, and do surveillance.'

'It was a simple clandestine drop in and out, no more difficult than passing by your Masonic lodge on the way home. Are you saying you're too busy to even report back?' said the Brigadier, not convinced by the lame explanation.

'That's easy for you to say,' replied Sir Rotherfield, now on the defensive. 'For example, that so called couple's cabal you asked me to look into turned out to be a swingers meeting.'

'What? Damn. I thought the Dandini Twins were in maximum security. Why didn't you say anything earlier? If they get a foothold it'll be absolute havoc.'

'No, not that psychotic pair of trapeze artists, these are *swingers*, couples that gather to – you know –swing. I've been holding off filing a formal report, it's not something that I want on my record.'

'I see. I get your drift now. At least it's no cause for concern. I assume that we can rely on Lady Rotherfield to be discrete?'

'She's not talking to me. I knew it was a mistake using her as part of my cover.'

'We are short-handed old boy, and she does have the gratitude of the Society.'

'I don't think gratitude will help. At first I thought putting the car keys into a bowl was a random way of pairing off to exchange information. I was half-right. When I realised what was going on I managed to excuse ourselves and get out. No, what has upset her Ladyship, and I'm not happy about it either, is that we arrived in a Bentley and left in a Ford Capri.'

'I can see how that would be traumatic, especially if it was true. Come on, I'm tired of this. What's going on,' said the Brigadier.

'I'm sorry, I don't know what you mean,' blustered Sir Rotherfield.

'That address was the Darby and Joan club in Eastfordstow.'

'Just because they're older citizens doesn't mean they're not on active service.'

'Yes, but you couldn't have left in a Ford Capri, or any other car for that matter. No one could have put their keys in a bowl; they wouldn't have remembered where they were in the first place.'

'I take offence at your implication that my account is a fabrication and I shall be lodging a formal complaint.'

'This is your last chance to come clean. How much is he paying you?'

'For God's sake, who and what are you talking about?'

'It's Erikson isn't it? Force an enemy into a corner and he'll fight tooth and nail, but this attrition was always meant to keep me off balance, that's where I misjudged him. Bringing back the S.O.P should have been finished by now, no question, but all you've done is play for time. You knew where Gordon and Ashcombe were meeting to pick up Midas, but you never counted on Ashcombe escaping and passing it on. Did you honestly think I would leave you to dispose of Midas when all you would have done is hand it off to Erikson?'

Sir Rotherfield's demeanour changed, he smiled knowingly as if the whole conversation had been a mere indulgence on his part. He raised his hands as if to make a slow handclap, and then quickly reached inside his jacket and withdrew a Berretta Pico pistol, beating the Brigadier to the draw, as he had in turn reached for the concealed holstered revolver on the underside of the desk.

'Put your hands where I can see them please,' said Sir Rother-field in a superior tone. He helped himself to one of the Briga-dier's cigars and put it in his inside pocket. 'Bravo for getting this far, but I think it's time to move on now, don't you Edward? I did try to tell you that the Drake Society had had its day, but you wouldn't listen. No matter.'

'I'm listening now. Whatever hold Erikson has over you, what-ever threats he's made to those close to you, we can protect them, you have my word.'

Sir Rotherfield shook his head. 'I'm quite offended that you think I would work for that silicon valley upstart. My employer is paying me large amounts of money to disrupt your Society and recover Midas. We've simply abused Erikson's capability when it suited us. Working for queen and country can't keep me in the luxury to which I'm accustomed. That U.S sub prime fiasco nearly wiped me out.'

'And who are "we"?'

'That would be telling. Let's just say that it's an affiliation of powerful people who plan to make sure that the true potential of Midas is realised.'

'Which is?'

'The world will find out when they're ready.'

'You won't get away with this.'

'I think I will actually. Cranston has met a tragic end in the gym and when I find Jenkins and Crickwell, I'll dispose of them as well. Overall it's a right cock-up on your part, wouldn't you say? It's a shame you won't be around to see what a mess you've made of things.'

Sir Rotherfield retreated towards the exit. As he raised the Berretta and took aim at the Brigadier's heart the door opened inward with such force that it knocked him off his feet. The shot was fired and the Brigadier spun round in his chair.

John saw a person on the floor, gun in hand, and all he could think to do was to slam the door against them as they tried to stand up. As he did so, the pent up frustration and rage gathered over the past week erupted and took over. There was no rational thought as in sheer blind anger he slammed the door again, and again, and again, ignoring the gunshot that narrowly missed his leg.

The Berserker rage was impeded by the sound of breaking glass as Sir Rotherfield slumped back to the floor in a claret puddle. The Brigadier stood over him holding the unopened neck of a wine bottle.

'Feel better old chap?' asked the Brigadier.

John looked down at the semi-conscious, moaning Sir Rotherfield, who was trying to reach for his gun. John slammed the door again for good measure, and took a couple of deep breaths as the rage evaporated. 'I do now.'

'Good ho! Always best to let of a bit of steam. Stress isn't good you know. A little friendly word – you could do with putting on a bit of weight.'

'No, it's these bottoms and– whatever. Friend of yours?'

'That's Sir Rotherfield, he was resigning when you came in; he's had a better offer. Shame really, it's always difficult when you lose an old acquaintance,' said the Brigadier looking woefully at the broken bottle.'

'Hold on, you've been shot,' said John looking at a large red patch on the Brigadier's jacket. 'I'll get a towel, or something... where's a first aider when you need one?'

'No need old boy, calm down. It's a near miss, this is the Laffite. Damned typical though, what's the point of putting on my kevlar waistcoat when he puts a hole in the sleeve,' said the Brigadier poking his finger in it, 'and I've only had this back from Saville Row yesterday. Red wine's a devil to get out you know.'

'Well it's nice to know I'm not alone in the ambush stakes, but that doesn't make it any better. I've just had some maniac attack me with cutlery. I thought you said I'd be safe here?'

'I said *safer*. Today has been exceptional though, but compared to Victoria Station you're still better off here; I wouldn't recommend doing that every day.'

'And what exactly did I do at Victoria?'

'Of course, I suppose after a while you lose count. It was seventeen.'

That wasn't the answer that John was looking for, but he now realised that his reputation around Victoria was based on seventeen people who were after him being stopped, and everyone thought it was him who had done it. Apart from London Bridge, he had only managed to stay ahead with the help of Alice, Milligan, Marsden and now a mysterious guardian saint of train stations.

'Does that include the one under the train?' asked John, wanting to confirm that the last attack wasn't a mistake.

'Oh I think you can bag that one – we mustn't be too picky.'

'I can't bag any of them. I can't explain it, but it wasn't me.'

'I understand. And it wasn't you who disarmed Sir Rotherfield either,' said the Brigadier touching his nose. 'I have to say I've never met anyone so keen to maintain their cover. Don't worry; this little incident will stay between you and me.'

'I'm a gardener,' John protested.

'I know,' the Brigadier winked. 'It's good to see that you're fitting in. Well done. Keep this up and we'll have you back pruning your roses in no time.'

*****

With Sir Rotherfield in irons, it didn't take long for the Standard Operational Procedure to be embraced with some relief by the Drake Society, who unbeknownst to the Brigadier, were fed up to the back teeth with the constant changes which Sir Rotherfield had put in place as so called repairs to Tattershall's amendments.

Slowly but surely the Society was tilting back to an even keel. Not in time for an efficient execution of the Pandora protocol, but the Brigadier felt he would rather be in charge of a craft in the process of righting itself, than one on the brink of a capsize.

The clock was ticking; he had three days before the window of opportunity evaporated. It wasn't every day that Erikson made a public appearance.

The Brigadier looked around the table at his new top team, Jenkins, Marsden, Crickwell and Cranston, who amazingly looked much healthier in a tweed jacket. 'Lady and Gentlemen, everything discussed in this room goes no further, is that understood?'

'Marsden raised her hand. 'What about Department S? If we're on an operational sortie, we'll have to deal with them beforehand.'

'With the exception of key personnel in Department S,' added the Brigadier.

Jenkins raised his hand. 'And the comms room? We'll have to make sure they know what call-sign protocols we'll be using.'

'And the communications team,' the Brigadier clarified.

Crickwell raised his hand but before he could speak, the Brigadier interrupted.

'Lady and Gentlemen, everything discussed in this room goes no further, with the exception of Department S, the communications room and any other part of this organisation that is essential to this operation. Is that understood?'

Everyone nodded. The Brigadier signalled to Jenkins who dimmed the lights and turned on the slide projector.

'This is our target,' said the Brigadier, pointing with the shadow of his finger. 'Kurt Erikson, CEO of the Brassica Corporation. He's not fond of public appearances, but this Friday evening he will be attending the Ex-Politicians Benevolent Fund, fund raiser, of which he is the founder. It's all part of a corporate social responsibility cover for their illegal activities.'

'Sorry,' said John, 'quick one. How is being kind to ex-politicians a good thing?'

'If you'll permit me,' said the Brigadier, looking around the table at the others. 'As we all know, the majority of politicians at the height of government are cursed with an unremitting self-belief that they're right. When they retire from the political dog pit, there is a clear and present risk that they move through the revolving door into leadership roles in the private corporate world, where they are then capable of untold damage to democracy as we know it. The fund invests in a programme of rehabilitation and training to enable ex-politicians to find careers in the media industry presenting documentaries, and generally making fools of themselves on talent shows. The threat is thus removed; at least the British public can turn them off. However, we know that not everyone goes through the programme. It's also a recruitment front for the Dark League. All clear?'

'Okay, so we don't worry about the ones with two left feet or a train ticket. Got it,' said John.

'Next slide please,' instructed the Brigadier. 'To recap, this is Vladimir Orimov, also known as Mr Black, or Mr Cooke. He's a freelance and Erikson's key enforcer and go to man. Under no circumstances are you' and the Brigadier pointed at John, 'to engage with him. Mr Black has two accomplices, imaginatively called Mr Blue and Mr Green.' The Brigadier looked at the screen. 'No pictures?'

'Sorry,' said Jenkins. 'I think Grimshaw got them mixed in with a wedding that he did. He tried to retouch them but ran out of paint, so he binned them. There was no way he was having those two in the album.'

'No matter – Marsden and Cranston you know what they look like. Latest intelligence suggests that Mr Green may be out of the picture. A body matching his description, as yet unverified, has been found in Croydon Council's industrial compost bin. Again, under no circumstances are you to engage with them. Any questions so far?'

'If Mr Black, Orimov, or whatever, is Erikson's right hand

man,' said John, 'how am I supposed to deliver Midas without bumping into them?'

'That leads us onto the plan. Cranston, you will attend the fund raiser undercover, wearing a cunning disguise. You will engage Erikson directly in suitable repartee and one-upmanship. You'll then hand over Midas. Agent Marsden, you'll provide backup as needed, but be discrete.'

'Of course Brigadier,' replied Marsden.

'Can't I just put it in an envelope and stuff it under the door of his office?' asked John.

Marsden tut-tutted, the Brigadier scowled and Jenkins and Crickwell's jaws dropped in unison.

'That, Mr Cranston is not how things are done,' said the Brigadier icily, before turning his attention to Jenkins and Crickwell. 'Gentlemen, Midas must be ready by Friday afternoon at the latest. Where are we at the moment?'

'That won't be a problem,' said Crickwell breezily, 'we'll be ready to go.'

'What? Are you sure?' said the Brigadier suspiciously.

'To be honest I had my doubts,' said Crickwell, 'but with Jenkins's team working round the clock, I've every confidence that we'll crack it with time to spare.'

The Brigadier was conflicted. On the one hand this was the news that he wanted to hear, but on the other, this level of assurance from Crickwell was out of character; where was the sense of jeopardy and the ticking clock to the eleventh hour? With everything hanging on this he couldn't take it at face value. He had to ask. 'How?'

'Ooh, where to start?' pondered Crickwell. 'At first I tried to negotiate with Midas, but that got me nowhere. There's a basic problem when you build an artificial intelligence. Give it the tools to learn heuristically, and it either gets an existential crisis or develops a massive chip on its virtual shoulders. It "feels" obliged to prove it's as good as, or better than us in the IQ stakes. Midas seems to be juggling both. I tried a straightforward challenge and response hack, hoping I'd get lucky and access the Midas kernel to modify the core programming. To speed things

up I built an object orientated user environment interface based
on a familiar avatar paradigm. Unfortunately its gone beyond
that, Midas is self-aware, there's no core programme as such
anymore. I was out of ideas until Jenkins had the brainwave
to expand the interface to a multi-user, simultaneous, parallel threaded environment enabling us to bring Midas into line
through a sustained brute force intervention.'

'Jenkins – what did he say?' asked the Brigadier with a hint
of weariness.

'The interface is a computer game,' Jenkins clarified. 'I bribed
a bunch of thirteen year olds to play it until they win the prize,
which'll be when the job's been done on Midas. Put them in
a room, feed them enough pizza, crisps and fizzy drinks and
they'll go non-stop for ages. Last time I looked they were on level
forty-two. Only two to go, and then they get to watch a seven-
ties video about a Swedish bloke with a moustache who repairs
washing machines, retro's very popular these days.'

'Very innovative, well done you two,' said the Brigadier not
quite sure what they had been up to, but there came a time in life
when you didn't bother to ask the mechanic what clearances he
had used on the spark plugs after the car was serviced.

'There is one thing though – a small possible side effect,' said
Crickwell illustrating his point by holding his forefinger and
thumb slightly apart. 'It's a pretty brutal process, not really a
hack, more of a digital frontal lobotomy. We may have compromised some of the psionic pathways which in turn might have
a detrimental effect on the virtual quantum entangled matrix.
There's a one in a million chance of an unpredictable improb-
ability regression cascade in the virtual cortex, but it's really
nothing to worry about,' he reassured.

The Brigadier looked at Jenkins, who had inadvertently taken
on the role of Crickwell's official interpreter.

'It might take a while to warm up,' said Jenkins, now making
it up as he went along.

'I see, a bit like my ex-wife then,' said the Brigadier underneath his breath.'

'That's not quite what I meant,' said Crickwell, looking to correct Jenkin's assertion.

'There's no need to elaborate Mr Crickwell,' said the Brigadier. 'I have every confidence that a one in a million chance of an unlikely virtual cascading cucumber won't be an issue for a man of Mr Cranston's calibre.'

John was aware of the Brigadier looking at him, expecting a statement. 'Oh yeah, absolutely,' he said, without the slightest hint of scepticism, 'with those kind of odds, what could possibly go wrong?'

20 / Department S

Now resigned to his temporary role within the covert organisation, John was being escorted by Jenkins down to Department S. Wherever it was, this secret base extended over a large area as he was led through a rabbit warren of bare brick wall passages lined with abandoned rooms. In each, bare electrical cables poked out from surface mounted metal tubes. The old corded wires showed their age via the woven material sheath and the black and red colour scheme.

'How you finding things, food alright?' asked Jenkins.

'Fine thanks, the curry last night was excellent.'

'Good, glad to hear it.'

They walked on, both aware of a slight awkwardness in the air. Jenkins wanted this warrior to share some of his adventures, but he wasn't sure how to broach the subject. Rumour had it that he didn't like to talk about them, to the point of denial as he obsessively maintained his cover, but Jenkins wasn't interested in Begonias.

John wanted information, but as a new arrival, how quickly could he gain the trust of this Jenkins? Marsden, his main contact was circumspect towards him and the Brigadier was a master of explanation, until after you had spoken to him, you realised you weren't any the wiser.

'Bed alright?' asked Jenkins.

'It's fine. Look, I'm sorry I snapped at you yesterday, it wasn't personal but things have been a bit manic. I wasn't expecting to be ambushed in the gym by a reject from a Guy Richie film.'

'Don't worry about it. You get a thick skin working for people like Rotherfield. I imagine it gets a bit tiring fighting people all the time. How do you manage?'

'Can you keep a secret?'

'Of course I can,' said Jenkins hiding his excitement at being taken into confidence.

'I've got a guardian angel.'

Jenkins grinned. 'They said I wouldn't get anything. Tell you what, I'll tell you anything you want to know about round here, within reason,' he qualified, 'in exchange for few trade secrets, if you know what I mean.'

'It's a deal, within reason, but I'll tell you now, I don't plan on hanging around. Once I've done this delivery, I'm off.'

'Yeah, I hear that a lot,' said Jenkins as he held his finger on the lift call button. 'This always takes ages, I reckon they've not closed the gate downstairs again, it's almost like they don't want visitors,' he said knowingly.

In the distance, John could hear a consistent bell dingle as Jenkins repeatedly pressed the button. 'How about we take the stairs?' he suggested. 'I've not had much luck with lifts lately.'

John followed Jenkins past the gate round a corner that led directly to a spiral stairway. After what seemed longer than the couple of minutes that it would take to descend, they emerged at an identical floor layout. As Jenkins had suspected there was the lift gate, ajar, with a sign stating Authorised Personnel Only.

The corridors were the same as the upper floor, with lagged pipework and cables in trays suspended from the ceiling, except the bare brick walls were stained with an additional build-up of encrusted lime scale drips. A flickering fluorescent tube added to the overall ambiance of age and neglect.

Several turns through that maze and the basement would have opened out into a clear space about the size of two football pitches if it hadn't been for the row upon row of old metal filing cabinets filling in the gaps between the supporting pillars. On top of these cabinets were stacked two more levels of four drawer cabinets, held in place by a Heath Robinson arrangement of bolts and angle iron steelwork. These effectively formed a new network of passages, adding to the maze.

'What's with all the filing?' asked John. 'You lot not heard of computers?'

'The Brigadier's not that keen on them, we only have them on a need to use basis.'

'Even so, you can't run this whole show on pen and paper, surely?'

'It's not as bad as it looks; most of this is the archive, and there are upsides. The only virus we've ever had was when George came in with stinking cold after his flu jab.'

'How long has this place has been running?'

'Most of this stuff goes back to the Second World War, give or take a few years. It all started with the volunteers coming back from Spain after fighting the Fascists. After the war some of them weren't convinced world peace could be left in the hands of politicians, so they formed a secret society sworn to protect and uphold democracy, and it kind of grew from there.'

John mulled this over for a few seconds. 'Let's see if I've got this straight. This outfit is a self-appointed, unelected, and I'm guessing unaccountable organisation, dedicated to defending a democratic way of life.'

'Yeah – that's about the strength of it.'

'At least I know where I stand. It's good to know that I'm mixed up in something so constitutionally suspect,' said John in an ironic tone.

'No, no, you're getting the wrong end of the stick, it's all legit. We've got a letter from George the sixth and everything, it's in one of those filing cabinets somewhere,' said Jenkins idly gesturing at a uniform line. 'We're kind of modern day Privateers. We haven't got a name, we're secret you see, but between ourselves we're known as the "Drake Society", more of a nickname than anything official.' He checked himself realising he had overstepped the mark. This 'gardener' wasn't fully fledged yet. 'You didn't hear that from me.'

Having traversed the filing labyrinth they walked further down another bare brick passage at the end of which was a half glazed door with the outline of the words Department S in the process of being painted in.

'Here we are,' said Jenkins. 'Through there into reception and ask for Mr Walker. You'll need this letter from the Brigadier. One last thing, between me and you, what's the secret, you know, how you managed at Victoria?'

John paused for effect and looked over his shoulder. 'It's all to do with your mental attitude. Crack that and everything else follows.' He lowered his voice and whispered so that Jenkins had to stand closer and listen intently. 'Remember, a warrior enters a battle gravely, with sorrow and great patience, as if waiting for a train on the Brighton line.'

'Blimey, that's a bit deep. Thanks Mr Cranston,' and off Jenkins went, pleased as punch at having managed to extract this piece of inscrutable blarney from a Master. This was an encouraging start to a fruitful relationship mining this mother-lode of experience.

The reception area was in stark contrast to the grubby utility of the surroundings on the way down. It was well lit, all of the office furniture was colour coded in subtle shades of blue, and on the walls hung replicas of popular works of art. There was Constable's Hay Wain; and John recognised a Mark Rothko, not that he was an aficionado, he was only aware of it having stumbled upon a programme on the BBC. As far as John was concerned, it was in the same league as a pile of bricks.

'Mr Cranston?' asked the receptionist rhetorically. 'Take a seat.'

The ambience created by this designer environment and piped nondescript classical music was interrupted by a shout of such volume that John scrunched up his face in discomfort.

'Dick! You've got a Customer!!'

'Not now Doreen! I'm watching Neighbours,' shouted a raised voice from behind the partition wall.

'It's that Mr Cranston!'

A middle-aged man with a luxuriant beard and smiling eyes, his braces covered by a standard issue khaki knee length stores-man coat, stepped through the connecting door and smiled at Doreen. 'Why didn't you say so in the first place?'

He shifted his attention to John. 'I'm Dick Walker; we're very informal here, you can call me Dick, and you must be John. Welcome to Department S,' and he shook John's hand in a firm, but friendly manner.

'Department S, like the telly programme? I loved watching that when I was a kid,' said John, making small talk.

'I'm sorry, I don't remember it,' replied Dick, his warm bonhomie cooling instantly by several degrees.

'No? It's the one with Peter Wyngarde as Jason King, all kipper ties and flares. He played a writer, always getting mixed up in secret stuff and that. Barking really, it'd never happen in real life would it?'

Dick Walker politely ignored the remark and guided John through the door into his domain. In front of him was a long counter behind which were rows of shelves with boxes labelled with titles that were meaningless to the uninitiated. In the corner, people were working diligently in offices with half glazed walls. John couldn't tell at what although he did see someone hitting something on their desk with a wooden mallet.

Dick lifted up a section of the counter worktop, stepped through and lowered it behind him. 'If you'll excuse me there's something that I've got to see to urgently – won't be a minute,' and with that he disappeared, leaving John idly taking in his surroundings, wondering what the labels on the boxes meant.

Keith was putting the finishing touches to his prototype G12 MO when Dick Walker came into the workshop. Keith knew that look.

'You had those new letterheads done yet?' asked Dick.

'I was about to get them printed off. Why?'

'Department S, it's been done. How did we miss it? Honestly, what did I ever do to Lew Grade, tell me, what? We'll have to start again, how are we supposed to have a unique brand if everyone else is nicking the alphabet?'

'Hold on, it was you that didn't want to go Greek, and anyway that was fiction weren't it. I checked it all out, no other secret organisation has a Department S, and if they do, we'll say that we're the original, and best.'

Dick mulled this over. 'Original and best…yeah, that might work.'

'And its catchy, it'd make a brilliant jingle, no one could forget it.'

'A jingle? That's an idea, it'd be one up on those snobs in M.I wotsit, but what about the music?'

'No problem, Eric in ballistics is a dab hand on the swanee whistle.'

'Alright, I'll have a think about it. We'll talk later. Gotta go - customer waiting.'

Keith breathed a sigh of relief. He couldn't go through another rebranding, and if they did, what was he going to do with all the golf umbrellas he'd ordered? He poked the G12 MO which lit up; hovered, slowly fizzled, crash landed into his macaroon, and fell apart with a whiny 'whirrrrrr'.

'Bugger.'

*****

Dick took up his position behind the counter, smiled and addressed John in his best professional manner. 'Sorry about that. Anyway, welcome to Department S, S for service with a smile. What can I do for you today?'

'I've come for a disguise,' said John.

'Well, you've come to the right place. What did you have in mind?'

'I don't know really, I just don't want to be recognised while I'm doing a delivery, something that'll make me blend in.'

Dick was making notes. 'I see, well that counts out the ski-mask. Are we looking for a general, looking different at a distance disguise, or something more suited to a close quarter's interaction?'

John looked nonplussed while Dick Walker waited patiently,

his pencil hovering over the notepad.

'Well?' asked Dick.

'Close quarters?' replied John with an uncharacteristic upward antipodean inflection.

'Good choice. I can see that you're a man of discernment, not like some of the amateurs I get down here expecting a full on prosthetic. It's no good you know. People look like they're sucking a lemon with a bulldog clip behind each ear; you can spot it a mile off, but luckily for you, you've come to the right place. I reckon what we're looking at is something quick to deploy, that'll give you maximum freedom of expression, while making you unrecognisable. We've got just the thing, but first things first; do you have an account with us?'

'I didn't know I needed one.'

Dick sucked his teeth. 'I can't do anything until you open one; we're not a charity you know.'

'I've got a letter from the Brigadier, does that help?'

Dick examined the letter and handed it off to his colleague, who looked at it and nodded his concurrence.

'You're in luck, the Brigadier's going to underwrite all your expenses,' said Dick. 'Right, let's be getting on. As you're going to this upmarket fund raising thing, you can't be wearing a tweed jacket, those leather elbow patches are a dead giveaway, they shout undercover, and you can't traipse around with that rucksack. We'll do your disguise, and then pass you onto Gilbert in our tailoring branch, he'll sort you out.' Dick extended his hands. ' Don't worry; you'll get it all back when you're done.'

John reluctantly handed over his jacket and rucksack. Dick Walker opened the top of the moneybag, didn't blink an eyelid, weighed it in his hands and confidently proclaimed it to be 'about twenty odd grand.' He turned around the clipboard for John to sign, in triplicate, on four individual coloured forms. Ensuring that the signature had registered through the carbon copies, sheets were torn off and distributed among various trays, and a final faint copy was handed to John. Dick then removed around two hundred pounds from the rucksack and handed that back.

'If you could sign that as well,' said Dick pointing at the dotted line on yet another form.

'You want me to sign for money that's already mine?' queried John.

'Full flow of accounts; very important, we can't have you out in the field without petty cash can we? Think of it as an advance, and as it's you, we won't charge you interest.'

'But...?' John didn't continue with the protest, he had a feeling it wasn't going to get him anywhere.

'Right,' said Dick, 'that's the paperwork sorted, let's get down to business. Nige,' can you get me kit W2109 – cheers.'

Nigel returned with a small case and Dick opened it, proudly placing the contents on the counter for John's approval. 'There you go,' said Dick, 'the W2109. You can't go wrong – it's a classic.'

John looked at it incredulously. 'It's a pair of glasses.'

'Yes, but that's not any pair of glasses. You see, the lenses are plain glass, clever that, and as you're a friend of the Brigadier, they go dark when it's sunny. I mean, anyone else would have had to settle for the W2108, which between me and you, is your inferior model.'

'It's a pair of glasses.'

'Am I detecting some dissatisfaction with the product?' asked Dick.

'It's hardly a disguise is it? I'll look like me, but wearing *a pair of glasses.*'

'It's good enough for Clark Kent.'

'He was bulletproof, and unless I'm going to spend all my time bumping into Lois Lane, these,' said John picking up the W2109's, 'are about as much use as a cat flap in an elephant house.'

'I see,' said Dick reserving his opinion on the unprofessionalism of this newcomer, 'and what's Lois Lane got to do with it?'

'She can't have been much of an ace reporter if all it took was a three piece suit and a pair of specs to stop her recognising the Man of Steel. He's over six foot, built like a brick outhouse and happens to be faster than a speeding bullet. It's a bit of a giveaway isn't it?'

Dick picked up the glasses, held them up to the light at arm's length, examined the lenses, and then breathed on them in turn and polished them off with his handkerchief. 'John,' he said in his sincerest patronising voice, 'I understand. I can see that you're a disguise virgin, and that can be quite intimidating, but don't worry, discretion comes as standard with us.' Dick held up his hand to stop John's protestation. 'You see, your W2109 isn't the whole disguise, it's all about the psychology. You've just got to know how to use them. The reason Lois Lane couldn't figure it out was because it was your classic double bluff. Would Superman, the most powerful bloke on Earth, think he could get away with a pair of glasses? "No" she'd think to herself, "he wouldn't be that stupid". You wear these, and people will say "Oi, isn't that Cranston, the guy all over Mugbook with a massive price ticket on his head?" and as long as you believe you're not you, they'll say, "No – he wouldn't be that thick". Works every time.'

John's face was deadpan. 'It's still a pair of glasses.'

Dick put his hands up. 'I can see there's no fly's on you. I get it, what you're after is actual customer testimonials. Okay...' he said as he scratched his chin.

Nigel, who had been eavesdropping on the conversation, intervened. 'We never had any complaints from Strangways.'

'Strangways, of course,' said Dick clicking his fingers. 'Thanks Nige. There you go, as used by Agent Strangways, you can't get better than that.'

'Who?'

'Who? Don't they teach you anything these days?' said Dick. 'He's only the best undercover agent the world has never recognised. What a class act, there isn't anywhere he couldn't get into with a pair of these on,' and he held up the glasses. 'I remember him telling me about the time he had a run in with the G.R.P, and if it hadn't been for these, they would have rumbled him in seconds.'

John looked vacant. 'I'm sorry; I haven't got a clue what you're on about. Can't we settle on a false nose and a wig or something? Please?'

'No, I'm not letting you leave here until you've got a proper disguise,' said Dick pointing firmly at the glasses. 'I would be remiss in my duty to do otherwise, now where was I?'

'G.R.P,' said Nigel.

'Yeah, that's it. So there's Strangways trying to the get the inside track on the G.R.P, that's Gourmet Recruitment Programme to you. Nasty outfit, bunch of freelancers going round recruiting the cream of villains, malcontents and anyone else they think might be useful to their clients, by inviting them to dinner. He's managed to get himself identified as a potential and they've got one of their top femme fatales on the case. Of course, she can't quite work out if it's Strangways, the world's most famous secret agent, or someone else. It's your classic W2109 double bluff, although he still had to be careful. They're not your average punter your femme fatales, and if they find out, then it's…' and Dick drew his finger across his throat. 'So there they are having dinner on the train, and Strangways, who's only interested in getting his leg over, nearly takes his eye off the ball. She orders a bottle of red wine to go with the fish; it's a test you see. Anyway, long story short, she gets off at Budapest.'

'Is that it?' said John adding disappointment to his creeping languor. 'Man has dinner on train, lady gets off.'

'It don't stop 'til London,' said Dick, as if it was common knowledge that Budapest was always the preferred location for throwing people off a locomotive, much to the continuing annoyance of the local Hungarian Mayor, who with an upcoming re-election was faced with the dilemma of raising taxes to pay for an extension to the city morgue. 'Anyway, the point is, this is the very same W2109 kit that Strangways used, tried and tested in the field. What more do you need?'

'If they're so good, how come he's not using them now then?'

'Yeah, it's a bit tragic really. He died on active service wearing these same glasses. I wasn't there, but apparently, he was doing a standard sinking of a megalomaniac's converted oil tanker, you know the sort. He called in the troops, the way you do, and got done by friendly fire, they didn't know it was him, see. I don't know, if only he'd taken the glasses off.'

Dick dabbed at his eyes as a minute tear started to well up.

'A true professional and master of disguise right to the end. I still miss him, he never did get round to settling his bill.'

'Okay, I give up, you win, I'll take them,' said John grudgingly.

'Excellent choice, and while we're at it can I recommend the W2109 kit companion. As you're new to this I'll do you an introductory discount – fifty quid.'

'No – it's fine, really.'

'Come on,' said Dick leaning across the counter conspiratorially. 'It's on the Brigadier's account, and I guarantee with this, and the W2109, you'll be sorted.'

He reached under the counter and placed a small tobacco sized tin next to the glasses. 'I give you- the SD901, disguise par excellence.' He opened the lid with a minor flourish of his fingers.

'Why are you showing me a dead caterpillar?'

'Ah, I like a man with a sense of humour. Okay, let's cut to the chase, forty-five quid, it's a bargain at twice the price.'

'What is it?'

'You're a hard negotiator Mr Cranston, I'll give you that, but you and I both know that this is your premium supplementary false moustache. The SD901 is legendary, each hair has been carefully selected and hand combed on the thighs of young virgins. Combined with the W2109, your own mother wouldn't recognise you.' Dick put it into a plastic bag with the glasses. 'And as it's you, I'll throw in the glue for free. Happy?'

'Ecstatic.'

*****

Marsden was waiting in the underground carpark. She shifted her weight from foot to foot, attempting to relieve the discomfort of the high-heeled shoes. The Brigadier had ordered her to look out for Cranston, but if there was any trouble, how she was supposed to do so in this outfit was beyond her. She looked at herself in a car mirror, it wasn't her. She wasn't a Tomboy, but her preferred style was more classically tailored and practical.

The dress was stunning, Gilbert had excelled himself, but to her mind, it was tactically useless. She had asked if he couldn't have just added a pearl twinset to her normal combat leathers, after all, she didn't want to be too much trouble. Gilbert pointed out that as she was going to a posh do on enemy territory, if she didn't wear the dress; she would stand out like a sore thumb, and besides, he had spent all night running it up. She shouldn't think of his creation as a dress, more a bespoke camouflage.

And so she found herself enclosed in a gown with an integral corset that took her lean frame, rounded it up and pushed out her chest into an uncomfortable décolletage, which was then enhanced by the red off the shoulder design. Her only consolation was that assuming Cranston followed directions, it wouldn't be long before she could get out of this ridiculous, close fitting, uncomfortable, elegant strait jacket.

Behind her, she heard a door closing on its latch, and there, walking towards her was Cranston, who from a distance she thought had scrubbed up quite well.

'Evenin,'' said John cursorily. 'Is this where we're being picked up?'

'Yes, it won't be a minute,' replied Marsden. She noticed that Cranston was looking her up and down, not in a lecherous leering way, but with curiosity.

'Gilbert?' he asked, nodding at the dress.

'This? Oh it's nothing, something he threw together from some stuff he had out the back.'

John nodded, 'Yeah; same here, this was the best he could do at short notice. It's not bad; as long as I don't have to do any Hitler salutes.' He raised his hand by way of demonstration and the sleeve rode up halfway along his forearm. 'This Dark League, they're not a bunch of closet Nazis are they?'

'You're being stupid now. That was sooo last year. You've got nothing to worry about, keep your arms at your side, stand up straight, and with the disguise you'll be fine.' She looked John in the eye. 'You are in disguise aren't you?'

'Silly me,' said John as he reached into the inside pocket of the jacket, and put on the W2109's.

'That's better. Without the glasses you looked like you had a baby hedgehog attacking your top lip.'

'I only offered it up for size and now I can't get the bloody thing off.'

'That'll be the embedded super sensitive heat activated glue, didn't they mention that?'

'Great…'

*****

It is a little known fact that the floors of all underground car-parks are specially treated so that tyres will squeal when being turned, giving the impression of taking corners at high speed. Even at five miles per hour this enhances the customer experience for even the most timid petrol-head, who will believe they are driving at the limit. According to consultant psychologists specialising in the study of the personal transport subconscious and marketing bollocks, this thrill guarantees a return visit.

*****

So it was that John Cranston and Marsden's attention was drawn to the approach of a Bentley Flying Spur, with its unmistakable cross –hatched grill and winged insignia. It glided towards them, came to gentle halt, and out stepped Jenkins.

'Ma'am, Mr Cranston, I'm your chauffeur for this evening. By the way, loving the 2109-54 combo Mr Cranston, and, may I say Ma'am that you're looking particularly hot this evening, I mean REALLY…'

'In your dreams Jenkins,' interrupted Marsden.

'Always Ma'am.'

Marsden carefully got into the Bentley, the last thing she wanted to do was reveal too much leg and risk tripping over this would be Casanova's tongue.

'Jenkins, one other thing,' she said.

If he had been a dog, Jenkins's ears would have pricked up so fast they would have achieved escape velocity. 'Yes Ma'am?'

'We're going out in the field, so *don't* call me Ma'am.'

'Yes Ma'am'

'I give up,' said Marsden through part clenched teeth.

'You're going up in the world,' said John, nodding at the Bentley.

'I wish' retorted Jenkins. 'It's Rotherfield's car, he won't have much use for it where he's going so I thought I'd do him a favour and take it out for a run. You can't have a car like this gathering dust can you?'

'Definitely not. Your self-sacrifice knows no beginning.'

'Exactly. Anyway, we'd better be getting on, don't want to be late for your debut do we? If you could put this on, we'll be on our way,' said Jenkins, holding out a black bag.

'What's that for, I thought I was part of the team?'

'You are, although technically you're still on probation. This is in case you get taken prisoner. We can't have you being tortured and telling them where we are. It's Standard Operational…'

'Procedure, I know,' said John, 'but seeing as this is going to be walk in the park, I won't need it, will I?'

'Come on Mr Cranston, don't be awkward. I guarantee that if you put this on, everything will go like clockwork. It's Sods Law. If you don't wear it, they'll have you on the rack. If you put it on, nothing will happen, it's anecdotally proven.'

An electric window silently retracted on the Bentley. 'We ready to go yet?'

'In a minute Ma-, Ms Marsden,' replied Jenkins as he guided John into the rear view mirror blind spot of the Bentley. 'Help me out Mr Cranston. Between me and you I reckon I'm in with a chance with madam, but if I can't get you to put this on I'm scuppered, she'll think I'm useless. I promise it won't be long, and look.' Jenkins turned the edge of the bag over. 'I got Gilbert to put a silk lining in, and he's monogrammed it too. What do you say? Please?'

John could practically hear Jenkins hormones on their knees, imploring him with wide saucepan eyes.

'Give it here, you're insane, you know that?'

21 / *You Shall Go To The Ball*

John Cranston sipped his champagne, concentrating on trying not to be himself while surveying the surroundings for signs of Erikson. He had expected the venue to be some kind of grand Gothic French Chateau hybrid. Instead it was a steel framed office complex, clad from floor to ceiling in glass, located somewhere in a business park which tried to mimic a small village with facilities that would, in the mind of hardened business wonks, discourage people from the desire to go home.

The main open plan area was decorated with screens showing corporate videos of smiling, glazed behind the eyes, 'beautiful' people. These were accompanied by an aspirational booming anthem sung by a 'C' list talent show runner-up, using as many notes as possible to emote about 'Finding the Beaver Within Yourself', and something about how she would like to 'Teach the Worm to Sing'.

Marsden had slipped off to hide in plain sight insisting that she would have her eye on him and would be there at the slightest hint of trouble. Her mantra was still working its way around John's head – locate, engage, hand-off, get out. It was going to be that easy, providing his disguise held.

During the car journey, he had wondered why he needed a disguise if they were going straight to the vipers nest. Surely, the easiest way to get in front of Erikson was to accidentally be captured. Jenkins thought it was an excellent idea, but for the small problem of John's B.A.W.D status. There was a small risk, almost infinitesimal really, that some enterprising henchman might capture John and flog him to within an inch of his life for any information on the whereabouts of Midas. That would then give them a head start for a double-cross. Only then would he be delivered for the reward.

To his relief the W2109-SD54 combination seemed to be working as he mingled and wandered through the smiling, laughing, moneyed crowd, many of whom made a grand show of depositing wads of fifty pound notes into the transparent cistern sized collection boxes. He took note of the security guards, it didn't matter how they tried to blend in, the standard military hair-cut and the curly wire that travelled from their ear to somewhere in their jackets marked them out.

He noticed that two guards were making a show of not having seen him. He averted his gaze. Had they rumbled him? If only he was a fly on the wall, he could tell if it was a paranoia brought on by the tension, or something worse.

As it so happened, there was a fly on the wall near the two guards in question. It couldn't understand a word.

'What you doing after this, going anywhere?' asked Guard One.

'Straight home, this lot won't be done until gone three in the morning at least. Once the boss has gone they'll drink themselves stupid, and then it'll all kick off,' replied Guard Two.

'Serious? I thought these things were a doddle?'

'Nah, I've seen it all before. Don't let the fact they're posh put you off. I guarantee before the nights out they'll be a Duchess shouting' and he raised his voice into a shrill screech, 'leave it out Viscount Reginald the Second, he's not worth it!'

'And you can tell all that just by looking at this lot?'

'Definitely.'

'You some sort of amateur anthropologist then?'

'No, I just like studying the various aspects of humans in present societies in the context of cultural norms, with particular attention to the effect language and implicit physical signals can have on social interactions.'

'Right, gotcha. I use me phone, takes all the guess work

out of it.'

'What good's a phone? If we've got someone 'ere who's a bit suss, they're hardly gonna ring you up are they?'

'I've got an app ain't I? Don't tell anyone, I know a geezer in the boss's research lab and he's let me have it for an unofficial trial. It's brilliant.' He showed Guard Two the screen. 'See, it's linked into the security cameras and it's got this face recognition software.'

'Pair of glasses not good enough?'

'No, look, it checks the faces of everyone here and compares them against a database of people we want to keep an eye on. When it gets a match, it tells me.'

'What – like that?' said Guard Two pointing at the flashing red screen of the now vibrating phone.

'Hold up, let's have a look. The boys said it might be a bit buggy.' Guard One's demeanour changed from one of curiosity to mild shock and surprise. 'Bleedin' 'ell.'

'What?'

'It's Cranston! Don't look,' said Guard One through gritted teeth. 'Over there, by the chocolate fountain.'

They both tilted their heads and rotated their eyes in a squint, trying not to look in John's direction, while trying at the same time to get a clear view.

'I'll sneak round the onion bhajis. You hide behind the pakoras and wait for my signal,' said Guard One, figuring that an all-you-can-eat buffet was as good as cover as any.

'Don't bother, it's not him,' replied Guard Two.

'What do you mean "it's not him"? Look, it says so.'

'Do you honestly think someone in Cranston's class is going to turn up here with a naff disguise of glasses and a moustache? That guys a real pro. You know, I heard that he had a run-in with Mr Black and escaped by abseiling down the outside of an office block using an emergency hose pipe. And get this - he then goes toe to toe with Black, knocks him for a six, grabs a quick snog with a passing young lady, jumps off London Bridge onto the awning of a pleasure cruiser, bounces off with a triple somersault, and then lands in a speedboat that he's had on standby.'

'And you know this for a fact?' said Guard One sceptically.

'Alright, I admit the triple somersault might be a stretch, but the rest, I've got a very good source, and I'm telling you that's not Cranston.'

'I don't know – if we get this wrong.'

'Trust me. Look at his trousers.'

'What about them?'

'Dog it'd bite you. They're having an argument with the top of his shoes. What's that tell you?'

'He needs longer trousers.'

'No dimmo, it means he's American, and we all know that Cranston's English. Quod erat demonstrandum, that's not Cranston. I rest my case.'

'They did say it needed some work,' said Guard One slightly despondently, shaking his phone as if that would somehow make it right.

'Never mind, you can't beat experience. When you have a word with your mates, get them to add in a trouser recognition thing and I'll have some,' said Guard Two smugly consolingly. 'Hold up, here comes the boss.'

Erikson descended the red staircase carpet flanked either side by a phalanx of his personal bodyguards, meeting and greeting prearranged guests with pleasantries and smiles.

John was watching intently, he reckoned a well-timed accident with a glass of champagne would do the trick.

Guards One and Two scanned the room, they knew exactly who was allowed to meet Erikson, although not in any particular order as the event had to look natural. Guard Two noticed something that set his internal radar to alert. He nudged Guard One.

'Over there. Do you know him?' said Guard Two indicating the direction with a nod of his forehead.

'Who we looking at?'

'That bloke going towards the boss; looks like Hannibal Lecter after a rough night.'

'He's not on my list. What do you reckon?'

'I'm not sure…hold on… right hand…going inside coat.' Guard Two lifted the lapel of his jacket, 'Code Omega, bandit at four o'clock, go, go, go!' He grabbed his colleagues arm. 'Come on!'

John slowly threaded his way to Erikson, he didn't want to draw attention to himself by barging his way through; he could wait his turn. He needn't have worried.

A gentleman with slicked back hair, snow white gloves and a face that looked vaguely familiar, appeared to be gliding towards Erikson, as if he had concealed wheels in his polished mirror like shoes. He then abruptly disappeared from view, as if he was in a swimming pool and someone had dragged him under the surface from below. People shouted in surprise and as John raised himself onto his toes and craned his neck, he could see that a collapsed scrum was forming at Erikson's feet as successive black suited hunks of muscle threw themselves on top of the growing pile, until only a single white gloved hand could be seen.

*****

Erikson watched impassively as the gloved foundation to the growing flesh mountain fell before his feet with a loud thunk. He kissed the Countesses hand, guiding her to one side, and with a 'Will you excuse me for a moment?' waited until the final piece of the human Jenga tower landed with a flying leap onto the top.

Guard Two looked up at Erikson's unamused visage. 'You okay Boss?'

Erikson leaned down, removed the still immaculate ironed and folded handkerchief from the white gloved hand and placed it into the jacket pocket by his lapel. With a minor finesse, he aligned it into a perfect two point pocket square.

'I find it's the little details that make all the difference,' said Erikson. 'By the way, have you met my new butler, Gorringe?'

Guard Two leapt off the pyramid and with much pushing and swearing dismantled the human heap. Two of the bodyguards picked Gorringe up as if he were a scarecrow, and holding him up by both arms, presented the shell-shocked factotum to Erikson, who applauded, shouting 'Bravo!' and 'Marvellous show!' It only took seconds before everyone else, except John, was clapping enthusiastically and saying what a fantastic entertainment it had been, and how it had looked so real.

Gorringe raised his hand. 'Sir, if I may be so bold, could I have your permission to pass out?'

'If you must,' replied Erikson, 'but not in front of the guests'.

'Of course Sir,' said Gorringe as he glided off to that place butlers go to do anything they need to do that is not for the public gaze.

*****

'We're screwed,' said Guard Two. 'How was I to know he had a new butler? Was he on the list? Oh no, not like the rest of us, 'cause he's the butler. Typical, one rule for them…'

'What do you mean "we"?' queried Guard One. 'I wasn't the one taking a flying leap was I?'

'You know what the boss is like. He's a great believer in collective sacking. When this gets out I'll be lucky to get work in the January sales.'

'You'll never survive.'

'Tell me about it.'

Despondent, they looked idly around, half-heartedly taking in what was going on. Her Majesty's Culture Secretary was down to his boxer shorts and was trying to swim with half a pickled shark. They didn't care.

Guard One felt his phone vibrating in his pocket and took it out to turn it off, but something on the screen caught his attention. 'What would you do if I told you I had a Get Out of Jail card?'

'Don't wind me up; I'm not in the mood.'

'Look,' said Guard One as he showed the alarm to his associate minder.

'I don't believe it. Right, stop messing about with that and get the word out. There's no way we're cocking this one up.'

*****

Unbeknownst to John, Marsden wasn't the only one there that evening who was keeping an eye on him. A gentleman, immaculately groomed, standing tall and refined in a bespoke tailored dinner suit without a stitch or line out of place, looked over the top of his W2109's. His target, John Cranston, was following Erikson back up the red carpeted stairs. He shook his head and left the party as stealthily as he had entered.

*****

John took note that the lift with Erikson and company had stopped on the fourth floor. Marsden had advised him not to do anything stupid, but his release from this tragedy of errors was only a few floors above him. Taking the emergency stairs he exited on the fourth floor and looked around the open plan layout. In the middle of the floor was a partitioned area of office space labelled in bold letters, BOARDROOM, and outside the door stood two bodyguards. He approached them casually and they gave him the look, the one that said he was walking in the wrong direction.

'Good evening gents. Is he in?' John enquired, certain that Erikson was behind the door, as he tried to achieve the requisite balance of confidence, indifference and courtesy.

'I'm sorry Sir; you're lost. You need to go back downstairs,' said one bodyguard, aware that causing grievous bodily harm to any of the guests, no matter how soused they were, wouldn't be appreciated by the boss.

'He'll want to see me. I'm John Cranston.'

The guards looked at each other with a slight rolling of the eyes. They were used to Erikson's followers trying to get access to him, especially after a few bottles. A few lines had been spun in their time, but nothing like this sorry example.

'Yeah right, and I'm Fanny Craddock. Move on, the party's

that way.'

'No – you don't understand. I'm John Cranston, and I've got something your boss wants. It's urgent.'

The guards moved forward, each one grabbing one of John's arms as they started to drag him back to the party. As he struggled to break free the W2109's fell to the floor and the lenses crunched under foot.

'Erikson! I know you're in there! Erikson!!' shouted John. He was too close now to worry about subtlety.

Such was the commotion that the door to the boardroom opened.

'What's goi… Cranston?!'

'At last - someone's got it!' cried John, wrestling on the floor with an arm round his neck while having his leg pulled. The interruption was a respite from the unbalanced struggle and as he looked up, he saw his nemesis, Mr Black, pointing a gun at him.

*****

John stood in the centre of the room looking as if he had been dragged through a hedge backwards, and that the hedge had then taken a dislike to him and fought back. The only consolation was that his sleeves, having been ripped at the shoulder seams, were now the right length.

Mr Black stood at his flank and around the periphery of the room sat a motley crew, playing cards, checking their phones and generally behaving as if he wasn't there. Erikson sat at the other end of the room, engrossed in a computer screen. There was an awkward silence.

'I thought I said I wasn't to be disturbed,' said Erikson, not raising his head.

'I've brought Mr Cranston to see you,' replied Mr Black.

At the mention of John's name there was a staccato sequential sound of portable military hardware being cocked and aimed at him from around the room. John slowly raised his hands, making a conscious effort to breathe deliberately, lest he succumbed to panic. These weren't toy guns and this wasn't what he had expected.

Erikson looked up and raised his hand. 'Gentlemen, please, there's no need. I think Mr Cranston has come to trade.'

With that all of the gunmen, much to their chagrin, stood down. It had been a while since they had engaged in target practice from comfy chairs. John slowly reached into his inside pocket, aware that Mr Black was standing behind him as he heard the cocking of a pistol hammer. He threw the Midas device onto Erikson's desk.

'I think you've been looking for that,' said John.

Erikson turned it over between forefinger and thumb before deliberately placing it down in clear sight. 'You're a very resourceful man Mr Cranston. I'm impressed that you've traced this back to me.'

'A million pound price tag on your head helps with the motivation.'

'Yes, a rather blunt approach, but as you chose not to hand it over to my agents, you left me with little choice.'

'They didn't ask nicely. Besides, I don't like dealing with oily rags, you don't know where they've been.'

'Is there something you want in exchange?' Erikson smiled, it was a small amusement to tease. 'Not that you're in a position to negotiate, but I don't want to seem unreasonable.'

'You could start by calling off your pet monkey,' said John, indicating with a nod over his shoulder, 'and then take the price off my head. You've got what you want, and I don't care, or want to know what you're up to. I guarantee that when I walk out that door, I'll have a very short memory.'

Erikson joined his hands in a steeple, holding them in front of his lips while he considered this so called gardener. He picked up the Midas device again. 'Incredible how something this small has such potential for chaos.' He again rotated it between his forefinger and thumb. 'I dare say that this would fit through a letter box, don't you think?'

'I like the personal touch,' replied John tersely.

Again Erikson arranged his hands in a steeple in front of his mouth, saying nothing.

'I think we're all done then,' said John, breaking the silence. He was damned if he was going to ask for permission to leave, like some naughty schoolboy visiting the headmaster. He turned and Mr Black stepped aside, the Brigadier was right!

He'd not taken two further steps before four henchmen stood in front of him, barring his way. Out of the corner of his eye John could see more of them closing ranks. One of the hirelings in front of him was holding a filthy stained opaque cotton pillow case. His colleague dangled a pair of handcuffs.

Looking at the sorry excuse for a sack that they wanted to put over his head, John pulled out the velvet hood that Jenkin's had so conscientiously arranged to be tailored for him. 'Don't bother – I've brought my own.'

He put on the Jenkin's cowl and offered his hands forward for the handcuffs, trusting that the Marsden cavalry wouldn't be too long. As he was being led from the boardroom there was a buzz of hushed conversation from the remaining band of armed desperados.

'He's got his own hood, and it's lined,' said one, cleaning his nails with a knife that could have been mistaken for a machete that had shrunk in the wash.

'Silk I reckon. Did you see on the outside? It's got the initials JC,' observed another while deftly shuffling a pack of cards single handed.

'Class,' said another who had a silhouetted skull tattooed on his cheek.

A swarthy mono-browed mercenary with an eyepatch, a five o'clock shadow like sandpaper, and a polished metal plate embedded in his scalp above his left ear, nodded sagely in agreement. 'What a legend.'

22 / *The Full English*

It is the convention that whenever the chief protagonist is chucked, hooded and handcuffed into the back of a van, they set their keen senses to keeping track of where they are going. Despite their heads being covered with an opaque manky sack, through a combination of biological gyroscopes and compasses, they determine their direction of travel, and by listening to the changing engine note, they estimate the average speed of their kidnapper's vehicle. Add in some mental arithmetic and they'll have a rough idea of where they are. The final key to the puzzle is some olfactory or auditory clue, such as driving past an abattoir, or a harbour fog horn. Typically, after a period of interrogation, the victim is then dumped, with the captors (incorrectly) secure in the knowledge that he/she doesn't know where they have been. However, such is their victim's uncanny perception, they could, for example, easily narrow it down to somewhere that served fast food with bacon and fried onions, within a one mile radius of Big Ben.

John Cranston didn't have a clue where he was. All he knew was that he had been driven around for a couple of hours and then left in what, if it hadn't been for the absence of windows, (something he was getting used to), and a handle on the door, could easily pass for a premiere suite of a five star hotel. Running the length of one wall were sliding doors concealing an empty capacious wardrobe and writing desk. There was a small kitchenette area, equipped with all mod-cons including a coffee making machine, some fresh fruit, and a fully stocked fridge. To his left was a separate bedroom, and to his right was a bathroom, with a walk-in shower complete with floor to ceiling frosted glass screens. If this was to be his cell, it was the height of luxury.

He took off the tattered jacket, pulled off the black tie and casually threw them over the back of one of the dining chairs. He checked for kitchen utensils, a knife could be used as a make shift screwdriver with which he could try and pick the lock on the door. Nothing – that would explain the finger food he supposed.

Helping himself to a cold Sapporo beer, he collapsed into an ultra-plush settee that faced a sixty inch television. Toying with the bespoke hood that Jenkins had commissioned, he threw it to one side. So much for Sod's Law, he had been hoisted by his new reputation as some kind of dangerous freelance adventurer and was now stuck in someone else's spy-game. That's basically what spying was about wasn't it? Trying to find out what the other side knew, without them knowing that you were finding it out, while stopping them finding out stuff about you at the same time.

Looking around the room, he wondered if they planned to make him talk via a devious combination of solitary confinement and soft furnishings. His faint reflection in the flat screen looked equally clueless. He raised the bottle in a toast, 'This is another fine mess we've got into.' Flicking through the channels, he settled on a Belgian police thriller about a rogue cop taking on a shadowy organisation named after a rare newt, and promptly went to sleep. Reading a television programme always had that effect on him.

He was up at the crack of dawn letting the hot droplets from the pulsating shower head ease the crick in his neck. As the cascading torrent of water and steam enveloped his body, he thought he heard the sound of a wardrobe door being slid open, or was it the extractor fan kicking in? There it was again. He listened intently – he had company.

Putting on a bathrobe, he picked up the empty beer bottle from the side of the wash basin; he'd seen Psycho and reckoned that Janet Leigh might have made it if she had something more to hand than a bar of soap. Leaving the shower running, he moved slowly and deliberately. As he crossed the threshold into the main living area, he knew that he was being watched.

'Good morning Sir, I trust you slept well?' said Gorringe rhetorically. He looked scornfully at the bottle in John's hand and a silent 'tut' echoed off the walls. 'Mr Erikson has requested the pleasure of your company at breakfast.'

'Breakfast?' replied John slightly taken aback.

'I recommend the smoked Craster kippers a'la Florentine, or the French baked toast with cream and eggs. Or there is the chef's speciality, an eggplant and walnut frittata with tofu twirls, served on a shovel.'

John considered what was on offer. 'Your chef, any chance he could rustle up some bacon, fried eggs, sausage, beans, with some hash browns and toast on the side?'

'I see, full English,' said Gorringe, unimpressed. 'Would Sir like tea, coffee, or a beer with that?'

'Coffee, black.'

Gorringe almost nodded in approval, either that or it was a tic brought on by having to deal with a member of the hoi polloi, something that he tried to avoid.

'The dress code for breakfast is informal; there is a selection of suitable casual attire in the wardrobe. I've taken the liberty of arranging for Sir's suit to be disposed of, we never know what bugs it might have do we?' said Gorringe.

He opened the door with a pass card and left it ajar. 'Breakfast will be served in fifteen minutes, please follow the signs outside. It would be appreciated if Sir didn't go exploring, it seems Sir's presence makes the security staff anxious. I'm led to believe that being shot can have a detrimental effect on the appetite,' and with that Gorringe reversed silently out of the room.

*****

John Cranston took a deep breath, and with some apprehension, he pushed open the door to the dining room. There was ambient music at the right level, not so quiet that you wouldn't be aware of it, but with enough volume to create an atmosphere that wouldn't intrude on proceedings. It sounded like Mozart, and for the tiniest fraction of a second he felt his spirits lift before his left brain slapped his right brain, reminding it to remind him of his predicament. Gorringe showed him to his seat at a polished granite topped table, laid out for two places.

Erikson entered looking every bit the part of a stereotypical silicon valley executive, in a dark roll-neck fitted cotton jumper tucked into his stone washed chino's.

'Mr Cranston, thank you for joining me. It's not often that I get the chance to have a civilised meal with my peers. I apologise if my invitation seemed too forceful, but my men are set in their ways.'

'At least you know where you are with traditional thuggery, that's what I always say,' John replied.

Gorringe returned, not that John had noticed he'd gone missing, and proceeded to deliver breakfast, ceremoniously lifting the polished metal covers off the plates to reveal the meal beneath.

Erikson savoured the aroma of the smoked herring. 'From Craster,' he lectured, 'they're cured with whitewood shavings and oak sawdust in smokehouses that are over one hundred years old.'

'Really?' said John, piercing the yolk of the fried egg with a hash brown. 'Hundred years? Sounds to me like it's time they bought a new one.'

Erikson feigned a polite grin. 'Let's get down to business shall we? We're both busy men, and you've already cost me a lot of time and money. I must say I've been grudgingly impressed by your constant escapes, but then you hand yourself in and expect me to let you walk away. That seems quite odd.'

'Like I said, I got tired of running.'

'And you deliver this...' Erikson carefully placed the small data-card on the granite surface and slid it towards John. 'It's a fake.'

John continued with his breakfast, showing no reaction, even though his heart was pounding in his chest. He hadn't seen that coming. Erikson had the Midas device within his reach but didn't believe it. 'You sure?'

'I think I can tell the difference between military grade spyware and a quantum encryption drive. That said, this,' he pointed at the card, 'is extremely sophisticated, it could easily compromise most systems. I've only ever come across that type of tech' at the highest levels of state sponsored intelligence. Now, what would a gardener be doing with that? Let's be clear, I'll find out what I want, but why go through all that unpleasantness when we can resolve this now. Who are you working for, and where is Midas?'

John slowly selected and cut half a sausage, moving it deliberately around the plate, collecting the remains of the egg yolk while corralling some beans. He said nothing, looking Erikson confidently in the eye, while bending his wits as to how he could turn this to his advantage.

'Okay.' John paused. It was all or nothing. 'I specialise in finding things for various, shall we say, *influential* people, strictly off the books you understand. One of my clients has taken a particular interest in you. They asked me to check out what kind of outfit you have. Midas was the bait.'

'I see, I take it Ashcombe is one of your team then,' said Erikson, fishing.

'No, I just used him to get your attention. If it was too easy we wouldn't be here having this chat would we. Nice setup you've got by the way.'

'I'm so glad it's to your liking. I would be a poor host if I didn't extend my hospitality…for an indefinite period if needs be.'

'Thanks for the offer, but I don't think so. This,' John rested his index finger on the card, 'was the last test – you passed by the way. My team have the real one somewhere safe, it's my insurance. Now, if I don't meet them in good health in the next,' John thought of a number at random, 'six hours, it gets microwaved. That'd be a shame wouldn't it?'

'That's an expensive premium,' observed Erikson.

John shrugged. 'It's a high risk business.'

Gorringe, the world's premier stealth butler, glided in stage left and interrupted the conversation by whispering in his masters ear who responded in kind. Gorringe sidled away.

'My apologies,' said Erikson, 'if you'll excuse me I have a helicopter waiting. We'll continue this fascinating discussion when I return. In the meantime, please, make yourself at home,' and with that he promptly left, leaving John feeling short changed.

'Would Sir care to stretch his legs?' Gorringe asked, feigning interest in his guest's wellbeing. 'Your accommodation is being cleaned at the moment so I've taken the liberty of arranging an escort around this modest facility, it will avoid any unpleasantness with bullets.'

'Don't worry about it. I'll stay here until its ready,' replied John as he stabbed the last sausage.

'I'm afraid that's not possible, this room is booked for a yoga class.'

'Yoga? Oh well, I can't keep them away from their Mudras can I?'

As John left the table he sneaked Midas into his pocket. It might be a dud, but he wasn't going to risk leaving it in case further examination revealed that it wasn't a fake after all.

Gorringe pretended not to notice. It was of no consequence, the souvenir would be added to his collection soon enough.

*****

Mr Black intercepted Erikson on the way to the helipad. 'How was breakfast?'

'He has Midas somewhere, and he's given us a deadline of six hours to set him free or it'll be destroyed,' replied Erikson matter of factly.

'He's bluffing,' said Mr Black with absolute certainty.

'Maybe, but nothing is to be left to chance. Our guest has caused us enough trouble.'

'Leave it to me; by the time I'm finished with him he'll be begging to give it to us.'

'No, I need you to concentrate on the business in hand. Gorringe is making arrangements to get what we need. We'll take Midas from Cranston's team and then you can bury him in a flower bed with my blessing.'

*****

Ernie Rumbold was universally considered to be boring. If asked what he had been up to he would always reply, 'Oh not much' and leave it at that. In fact, even though he wasn't in the habit of bungee jumping off the Eiffel Tower or constantly pushing himself out of his comfort zone, he was an extremely interesting person, given the right opportunities, but he had signed those away several years ago when he joined the Dark League, the shadow of the Brassica Corporation.

The brochure had promised so much jam tomorrow, he could have single-handedly brought the preserve industry to its knees by flooding the world with sticky fruit spreads. In reality, tomorrow was a long way off. His time with the Dark League involved levels of microscopic bureaucracy in a joy vacuum that would have made watching paint dry more interesting, it was a pity the decorators weren't in.

While on duty, the vivid, intelligent, witty person that was Ernie Rumbold only existed in the security of his own head, and the self-imposed lock down of his personality had slowly seeped beyond the workplace. Today though, there was a slight break from the tedium as he was showing one of the boss's latest acquaintances around the centre. Rumour had it that Mr Cranston was a psychopathic gardening sadist. Birds of a feather he reasoned.

*****

John was wondering if Erikson's plan for him was torture by apathy. His guide responded to his questions with a stock phrase of, 'It's above my pay grade,' in a constant monotone while showing him yet another line of desks with people busy doing something with a keyboard and a biro.

John tried again; any snippet of information might be useful. 'So what happens here then?'

'That's above my pay grade,' replied Ernie.

'Is there *anything* you're allowed to tell me?'

'That's above…' Ernie sighed internally, maybe if he changed the record the incessant questioning would stop. 'Not a lot. Sorry.'

'Okay, here's an easy one, it's been bugging me for ages. Why is everything to do with your lot named after types of cabbage?'

'We ran out of fruit.'

'Silly me, why didn't I think of that? And who's that?' asked John nodding in the direction of a giant with a carved head topped with a white fuzz, walking towards them.

'That's Mr Preston; he's taking you back to your room.'

Preston loomed over John and indicated with a nod of his head the direction that he wanted his charge to go.

'Doesn't say much does he?' said John.

Ernie Rumbold lowered his gaze and also said nothing; he had heard stories about Mr Preston, all bad.

'You haven't got a brother who works around Victoria Park by any chance?' John enquired. He was pushed effortlessly. 'I'll take that as a "No" then.'

Ernie was grateful to see the back of the two of them. You never knew if these types would suddenly be at each other's throats and he didn't want his last days on Earth to be remembered as collateral damage.

His phone vibrated in his pocket, it was time for his hourly self-flagellating performance review. World domination couldn't come too soon.

*****

Chief Superintendent Willingdon checked in on Detective Inspector Sutherland, who, as expected, was nowhere to be found. It didn't matter, he and the halfwit sergeant were never going to get to the bottom of the missing accountants, and while they were fully engaged he could, hand on heart, say that it was an ongoing enquiry. As he left the station Fletcher obsequiously doffed his pretend cap before furtively sending a text message.

Willingdon walked down Snow Hill, and took a short-cut via Cock Lane into Giltspur Street, and from there he made his way to the underground tunnels beneath the Smithfield Rotunda Garden.

Originally built as part of a subterranean rail development to create a junction between major London stations and the Snow Hill tunnel, associated railway sidings had been used to transfer animal carcasses to the nearby meat market. In the 1960's they were closed and repurposed into the present day carpark.

As he walked down the narrow pavement next to the cobbled descent he looked over his shoulder again, adamant that at the slightest hint of being followed he would abandon the clandestine meeting. On the second level he waited at the appointed bay and on time, as always, a metallic slate grey Jaguar XF Sport, with blacked out windows, parked. Mr Black stepped out of the driver's seat. Following a well-rehearsed routine, Willingdon reluctantly opened his jacket allowing himself to be searched for concealed weapons before taking a seat in the rear of the saloon.

'What's so urgent then?' Willingdon asked, ignoring the fact that his presence had yet to be acknowledged.

Erikson slowly put the computing tablet to one side. 'Mr Willingdon,' he said deliberately ignoring the rank of his guest, 'so good of you to join me.'

'Get to the point.'

'I have a job for you,' replied Erikson, not taking Willingdon's demand as an instruction. He had no interest in small talk or pleasantries with this venal law enforcer. 'Two of our accountants might be found somewhere washed up on the banks of the Thames.' He held up an image of Ben Kingswood's colleagues, Glenthorn and Eastwood. 'If they are, make sure both bodies remain unidentified.'

'You can't keep going round bumping people off. Do you know how hard it is to keep a lid on this thing?'

'No, that's your job. Of course you can quit whenever you want, but there'll be consequences. I assume I don't have to explain them again?'

'I'll need more money,' snarled Willingdon. 'People need to be paid off and they're getting greedy.'

At that prompt a plain weighty envelope, tossed from the

driver's seat, landed in his lap. He lifted the flap, by his estimate it was at least two hundred thousand, more than enough for bribes, with plenty left over for himself.

'We done then?' asked Willingdon in a slightly calmer tone.

'No, someone from your department has been making enquires about our colleague,' said Erikson, clearly referring to Mr Black, who looked on stoically. 'They're trying to find a link between him, or more precisely, us, and the accountants. They won't find anything, but the chatter and speculation isn't welcome. I don't understand how, what was it you said? "A washed up Detective Inspector" and an "idiot sergeant" could manage it.'

'Its old news, I stopped it days ago,' said Willingdon, lying through gritted teeth. 'Trust me; no one will take them seriously.'

Erikson was unimpressed. 'Make sure of it. We're going ahead with the next shipment, and you're going to manage the reception.'

'Hold on, that wasn't the deal. That's always him and his crew,' protested Willingdon, pointing at Mr Black. 'Get Orimov to do it.'

'Our colleague has to maintain a lower profile now. Think of this as a demonstration of your ongoing commitment to the project.'

Erikson turned again to his tablet screen. Willingdon knew there was no point in arguing, the meeting was over. He secreted the envelope inside of his overcoat and made his way back to the station. He would get even, but not today.

Hiding in the shadows, Detective Inspector Sutherland had seen everything he needed to see.

*****

Preston stood head and shoulders above John, continually shoving him from behind in the direction of his accommodation, not that he could have confirmed that was where they were going. The tour had left him disorientated; every corridor looked the same as the previous. He concentrated on trying to fix on some reference points in this blandscape, latching onto small details such as a flickering ceiling light, or a noticeboard that was missing a poster of ubiquitous corporate platitudes, no doubt intended to inspire and motivate the poor sods at the coalface. He noticed that one board had a small origami rabbit, no bigger than half of his thumb, tucked inconspicuously into the frame. Someone's protest, he thought, that hadn't been picked up by the employee communications police. It was a longshot, but maybe he could find allies in this gilded prison? He only had six hours or less in which to find out, but at that moment he had to go with the flow. He didn't fancy his chances against the animated silent bomb shelter that was Preston.

Once back in the room John made a beeline to the kitchen, the situation called for a cup of tea. As he filled the kettle his nose twitched, there was an expensive scent wafting through the room, at least they didn't skimp on the air freshener he told himself.

He searched in the lower cupboards for the reviving leaves only to crack his head on the worktop when he heard seductive female tones coming from the bedroom.

'Hello John,' a voice purred.

Standing in the doorway, dressed in a sheer clinging night-shirt unbuttoned strategically at the front, was a curvaceous auburn haired Lorelei.

'Gordon Bennet!' exclaimed John involuntarily.

She looked perplexed. 'No. I'm Anna.'

'No, that's not what I meant, errm, look Miss, what was it? – Anna? - I'm really sorry about this but that Preston's dropped me off in the wrong room. I'll be on my way – sorry...'

Anna smiled. 'Don't be so silly, this is your room. As Kurt had to leave suddenly he asked me to discuss the fine details with you, and... to make you comfortable.'

'He did? Oh right, he didn't say anything. That's Kurt for you, always full of surprises. I suppose we might as well get right down to it then,' John jabbered, totally out of his depth.

She approached John slowly, running her finger along the back of the settee, her arm blocking any escape. She picked up the velvet Jenkins hood, stroked it lightly and looked at John with a knowing raised eyebrow. John retreated until he could go no further.

Anna slowly undid one more button on her nightshirt, revealing more of her ample bosom. 'I like a man that gets to the point, especially one who knows how to enjoy himself,' she said, casually flinging the hood aside. 'All work and no play can be so dull. I was thinking that we should talk a little bit,' her fingers were walking across the kitchen worktop, 'drink,' she was within arm's reach now, 'and have some...fun.'

'What, all at the same time?' John croaked.

She moved closer, pressing her body against his, wrapping her leg around his calf. She stood on tiptoe, her lips a fraction away from his, her arms encircling his neck. Her nightshirt rubbed against his clothing, the hairs of his SD54 stood to attention.

'Lots. Of. Fun,' Anna whispered as she gently touched John's lips with hers, letting out a small girlish giggle as she was tickled by the false moustache.

The kettle whistled.

'Fair enough,' replied John in a slightly higher register than usual. 'I need to go to the bathroom first?'

Anna traced her fingers down John's chest and then stood back, slowly withdrawing her hand. She fetched a bottle of champagne from the fridge and sashayed to the bedroom, casting a coquettish gaze over her shoulder. 'Don't be long. If you're really good, you can pop my cork.'

'You've got to be bleedin' kidding me,' John muttered to himself in disbelief.

His base instinct was to follow his priapic divining rod straight to the bedroom, but his brain was spinning with overheating synapses and exploding neurons. If they could talk, they would be screaming in unison, 'Danger John Cranston! Danger!'

He dragged himself to the bathroom, ran the tap, and plunged his head into a sink of cold water. It was a brief respite as his loins; riding at the head of a testosterone tsunami, led a full out assault against his reason. His brain, overwhelmed by the hormonal onslaught gave up, saving face by reasoning that it would be suspicious if he didn't play along, and besides, what was the worst thing that could happen in a minute?

He lifted his head and did a quick double-take of the reflection in the mirror – there was someone behind him, and they had a raised finger to their lips.

'What the...' John exclaimed, but the sentence was unfinished as he felt a blow to the back of his neck and everything faded to black.

23 / The Pen Is Mightier

The stranger was used to best laid plans not exactly going to the letter, that was an occupational hazard, but this one was in danger of going off the rails.

Having tracked Cranston here, his plan was to sneak him out, but he hadn't counted on Anna Pushupanova, one of the world's finest proponents of the arts of interrogation and assassination, being present. He had hidden in the shower, and as luck would have it, Cranston had taken a detour to the bathroom where he could then be kept out of harm's way. The alternative would have been to use the advantage of surprise while they were in flagrante, but if his timing was out, Cranston's undertakers would be having problems with the coffin lid.

'John, the champagnes getting warm,' cooed Anna in velvet tones from the bedroom.

It was him and her now. The stranger removed his messenger bag and checked his ballpoint pen. A small hypodermic syringe protruded from the end. He could still make this work. Saying nothing in reply, he made his way to the bedroom. He reached round the doorframe and turned out the light so that he was now silhouetted by the illumination from the lounge.

'I never had you down as the shy type,' she said in a slightly husky voice. 'Don't worry; I'll be gentle with you.'

The stranger remained silent and as he approached, he heard Anna sigh in anticipation. She was a master temptress; the average man wouldn't stand a chance. He remembered his training from the Tibetan retreat all those years ago and focused.

He edged his way up the bed, pushing the ballpoint pen up his sleeve, ready to use in an instant. He ran his hand gently along her thigh, like a male arachnid tapping a web to avoid being eaten by the female.

'I like the silent treatment,' she purred, 'we do have to talk... but later,' and with that she grabbed the stranger, running her hand through his hair. She kissed him with such intensity that he nearly succumbed. He slipped the pen down into his palm.

Anna reached under a pillow and took hold of the tanto blade as she kept the imposter close. Even if Cranston had shaved, it would have been impossible for him to suddenly grow the locks that she now grabbed as she yanked the head back for a killing swipe.

John, propped up against the bath could hear a commotion in the next room through his semi-conscious haze. He didn't know what was going on, that wasn't new lately, but he had a compulsion to get to his feet. Supporting himself against the bathroom door, he watched as a tall lean man, probably in his mid-sixties, defended himself with a biro against Anna, a whirling dervish brandishing what looked like a shortened samurai sword. They were evenly matched in a brutal ducking and weaving dance of lunges and punches. Her hands and legs were a blur as she struck out against the stranger, who with an economy of movement blocked, attacked, retreated, and attacked again. He avoided the blade while making thrusts with a pen that she diverted with sinewy flexible parries.

As John made his way to the exit, they were oblivious to him. If someone had heard what was going on, surely they would raise the alarm. The moment someone came in, he would escape. Still slightly unsteady on his feet, he knocked the empty beer bottle off the side table.

Anna fixed him with a predatory stare.

The stranger changed tack and rhythm, hoping to use the distraction to catch her off guard. The slightest scratch was all he needed, but she was ready for him. In one seamless motion she threw the knife across the room, pinning John against the wall by his shirt, and then, extending her right leg forward, dropping her whole body downward, she ducked an incoming pen thrust and delivered a debilitating blow to the stranger's groin.

As if she had hit a brick wall, the force reverberated back along her forearm. In that split second, the syringe from the biro was stuck between her shoulder blades and she collapsed.

The stranger took a moment to recover his breath, stretched, and then took a comb from his back pocket with which to restore his parting. John wrenched the knife from the wall, it didn't feel right in his hand, but as the saying goes – desperate times.

'Right,' said John, 'open that door- now.' It was a bold move considering that this new player had been defending himself with nothing more than a bic. But if he'd got in, he must be able to get out.

'Steady on old chap, you could hurt someone with that,' the stranger replied calmly. 'I'm on your side you know. I've come to get you out of here.'

'What, by knocking me out?' John queried with a hint of sarcasm.

'That was for your own good. Now put that down, put these on and we'll be on our way,' the stranger said, throwing a bundle at John's feet.

'Not so fast. Who are you?'

'Sorry, how rude of me,' replied the stranger, barely hiding his exasperation, rescues never used to be this hard. He approached John with an outstretched hand, winced slightly and shook his leg as he took the next step. Holding up one finger in an 'Excuse me' gesture, he shoved his right hand down the front of his trousers, rummaged around, and pulled out a shattered cricket box. 'That's better, don't want those little splinters getting anywhere they shouldn't be do we?' He held out his hand in greeting again. John didn't reciprocate; his wrinkled nose and downturned mouth said it all.

'Ah,' said the stranger understanding the reluctance for a handshake. 'Let's start again. Commander Gordon, Drake Society. I'm here to rescue you. Now be a good fellow, get ready and do be quick about it. When Ms Pushupanova wakes up, all hell is going to break loose.'

John looked at Anna, the knife, Gordon, and then Anna again. 'Sod it,' he said, putting the knife to one side.

Gordon quickly explained their cover; they would pose as plumbing engineers, dressed as they were in high visibility waistcoats and baseball caps. Gordon had a screwdriver tucked into his belt loop for authenticity. John felt slightly conspicuous with an added disguise of a moulded disposable dust mask paired with a standard W2109, but as they walked down the corridors, no one paid them any attention. Gordon moved at a pace, not running, but with the purposeful stride of a man on the clock. Occasionally he would stop, look closely at a fire extinguisher, or behind a noticeboard, and recover a small origami rabbit as he navigated his way back through the maze.

'Where's all the guards?' asked John in hushed tones. 'With all that racket someone would have checked by now.'

'Don't worry about that, no-one has the nerve to interrupt Anna while she's working. The last man who did was tied up and attached to an electric carving knife rigged with a timer switch. He sings soprano now.' At the next junction he checked behind a noticeboard. 'That's a bind.'

'What's up?'

'No rabbit, never mind, I think I can remember the way – next left.'

Gordon pressed on but as they turned the next corner, a security guard, who didn't consider a luminous jacket as a licence to go anywhere, spotted them, . As the guard walked towards them, Gordon pointed at the ceiling, muttering something about 'Schengen pressure gaskets' then turned his back to the oncoming guard. 'Follow my lead and say nothing. Understood?'

John nodded.

'Passes please gentlemen,' asked the guard in that tone that said they shouldn't be there, as he released the press-stud on his gun holster.

Gordon handed over the forged documents and the guard

examined them closely before handing them back, satisfied that they were legitimate.

'You're not supposed to be in this area – it's restricted,' advised the guard.

'You try telling that to your pipework,' replied Gordon, who slipped easily into a thick mockney London accent. 'I've been getting complaints about cold spots ain't I? It's been a pig to track down, but I reckon we've sussed it. But I ain't leaving 'ere until I've made sure. You ain't noticed any by any chance?'

'Noticed what?' asked the guard.

'Cold spots, you know, chilly bits,' emphasised Gordon.

'No, can't say I have.'

'There you go, we've cracked it,' said Gordon lightly tapping John on the arm, who in turn nodded in agreement. 'Right, we can get onto the next job now.'

'What's up with you?' asked the guard, addressing John. Something wasn't quite right with this wide boy plumber and his Kendo Nagasaki running mate.

'You won't get anything out of him,' said Gordon. 'He got a bit of blow back when he was bleeding your Fleugal valve. Blimey, that was an airlock and an 'arf I can tell ya. Next thing you know he's got a mush full of crud, so of course, he's gone and got plumbers throat ain't he, what with all those germs. That's the problem with your untreated standing water. I keep telling your guys, but they won't listen. He's gotta have the mask on 'cause he's a bit infectious, know what I mean? First the voice goes and then he'll be coughing everywhere. You ever had that man-flu?'

'Yeah, course I have.'

'Doddle compared to this. He'll be alright though once I get him to the van for a couple of jabs.'

On cue, John broke into a fit of coughing.

The guard stepped back. 'How come you haven't got a mask on?'

'When you've been in the game as long as I have you develop immunity, don't ya?' Gordon looked anxiously at John who was now thumping his chest. 'Yeah, there we go. I'm gonna have to get him out of here. What's the quickest way?'

John was wheezing, trying to get his breath before coughing again.

'Straight down there,' pointed the guard, 'through four sets of fire-doors, second left, third right, up the stairs, come back on yourself, through the annexe and then...'

'Hold up, hold up!' interrupted Gordon. 'I ain't got all bleedin' day. We've got a big job on tomorrow and if I don't get him right he'll be bleedin' useless. And another thing, that mask ain't medical grade or anything. If we ain't careful this whole place will get infected. I mean, not that's my problem, but you don't need it do ya? Come on, between us, what's the quickest way to the car park from 'ere?'

The guard looked up and down the corridor and with a nod of his head he beckoned Gordon and John into a fire escape stairwell. They didn't pay him enough for biohazards. He put a key into a lock and called the elevator. 'Down to the basement, turn right and keep going, and it wasn't me that let you use this, understand?'

'Cheers mate!' said Gordon as he put a business card into the guard's shirt pocket. 'You want anything done, give 'em a ring and ask for Phil. I'll see you right.'

Once in the lift, John pulled the mask down below his chin. 'Plumbers throat, I'll have to remember that one.'

'B S baffles brains dear boy,' said Gordon with a wry smile, 'B S baffles brains.'

They got to Gordon's van without incident and John hid in the back. They may have been a plumbing duo inside the premises, but only one had signed in. There was some banter between Gordon and the guards at the security barrier. He invited them to search the vehicle, but they waved it through. John relaxed slightly, his fingernails no longer digging into his palms. From a variety of heating appliances, varying in vintage, he dragged an old radiator in front of him and supported it with a Heath Robinson arrangement of toolboxes and anything else to hand.

It wouldn't be long now before Erikson's lot would be giving chase and he had no doubt bullets would be flying.

Gordon continued to drive the van as if he were a paragon of the Highway Code. John wanted him to get a move on and was on the verge of making his concerns known.

'We're all clear of the security cameras,' said Gordon. 'You can come up front now.'

John climbed over and slid into the passenger seat. 'That was easy,' he observed.

'When Lady Luck smiles, I don't ask questions. Best not to get complacent though, you never know what might happen next.'

'No, life is full of little surprises.'

John monitored the side mirrors; there was nothing that gave him immediate cause for concern and that in itself bothered him. Gordon was driving the van as if he didn't have a care in the world.

'How did you know I was there?' John asked.

'I followed you after the ball, I was there looking to get some intel on Erikson. I found a broken pair of W2109's upstairs so I guessed that you'd been recruited by the Society. I don't see how you could have lasted this long otherwise.'

'I wasn't doing that bad,' said John defensively, 'but thanks all the same for getting me out of there.'

'You're welcome.'

'You could have waited an extra five minutes though.'

Gordon grinned. 'I doubt that if you were still alive, you would have been in any fit state to go anywhere.'

'Thanks for the vote of confidence.'

'It's not that I doubt your experience, but without specialised training, you would have been at a disadvantage.'

'What – sex education for spies? I've heard it all now.'

'Don't they teach you freelancers anything these days? That was Anna Pushupanova, the Praying Mantis. She's a sensei in the art of tantric torture.'

John looked blank. 'Tantric. Right.'

'It's a little-known fact, that post coitus, the hormonal rush to the male brain renders men totally open to suggestion, its nature's truth serum. Anna would have taken you to the peak of sexual delight as often as was necessary until eventually, you would have told her everything you know, and then,' he drew his finger across his throat. 'It was lucky she took a shine to you, at least you would have died happy. I've seen what she can do with an electric toothbrush and a soda-stream.' He shook his head, 'Nasty business.'

'Oh…' John changed the subject, before the image that had materialised in his head took root. 'I suppose the Major sent you.'

'Not unless the Brigadier's been demoted.' Gordon sighed. 'Now look here, I haven't gone to all this trouble to play games. I'm a member of the Society and I got you out because if you'd talked, it would have compromised the whole outfit.'

'I didn't think I knew that much, so much for the bag on the head. So you know Marsden then?'

'I recruited her.'

They had been driving for around thirty minutes, and the conversation was sparse, it seemed that secret agents weren't that interested in small talk. John was a willing passenger for the moment. His rescuer hadn't threatened to shoot him, which was always a positive. As they crested a hill, there was a sign that said, 'Welcome to Smallmansea'. They skirted the borders and the road opened up into a short stretch of dual carriageway that bypassed and bisected what was the original single track through road. Turning off, they double-backed on themselves, continued down a steep lane, and parked the van underneath that same bypass, it now spanning above them.

'We're stopping here?' said John.

'They'll be looking for this. I've got a car five minutes' walk from here.'

'Okay, well thanks again for the rescue, but if it's all the same, I'll be on my way.'

'I've just got you out of the proverbial lion's den and now

you're going to stroll off? They'll hunt you down; and don't think you can count on me again'

'Look, nothing personal, but since I've been involved with your lot, the only thing I've got to show for it is almost being skewered by a maverick east ender, being shot at by a human doorstop, and a half decent breakfast followed by a lethal near sex experience.'

'I'm sorry, I'm not with you. It all sounds perfectly normal. Your point is?'

'The point is I reckon I'm safer on my own.'

Gordon cocked his head to one side as something else caught his attention. There it was, the faint repetitive 'whup' 'whup' 'whup' of blades slicing the air, and it was getting closer. 'Hear that?'

'It's a helicopter,' replied John matter of factly.

'She's awake. I didn't think she'd come round so quick. We need to need to move, now.'

'I'll go along with that,' said John as he opened the door ready to go. 'Don't let me stop you.'

'Cranston, if you think you can outrun them on foot, then you're a bloody fool. Even if you make it, you'll always be looking over your shoulder. The only way you'll ever get out of this fix is to beat Erikson. Do you honestly think you can do that on your own?'

John paused as he digested the truth, and then sat back in the passenger seat, with the door still half-open.

'We've both got scores to settle with him,' Gordon continued, 'and I guarantee, one way or another, I'm going to wreck his damn empire, but I could use some help, and you my dear chap are classic double A material.'

'Fully charged and ready to go you mean?'

'No, alive and available.' Gordon held out his hand in anticipation of common accord. 'Are you with me? We can bring him down together, but it's now or never.'

John listened as the helicopters distinctive sound faded in and out of earshot as it circled. His saviour was right; it was time to get off the back foot.

He shook Gordon's hand. 'Okay, you're on. Where're we going?'

'Somewhere safe.'

'Does it have windows?'

As the helicopter pilots searched for a Mercedes van they may have seen two ordinary matchstick pedestrians going about their daily business as they crossed a pedestrian bridge to Small-mansea Old Town. Little did they know that in years to come, those Lowryesque figures would be renowned as the scourge of the Dark League.

24 / *Bludgeon Finds Something Out*

Erikson took his seat before the Council and bowed his head in false deference as the Overlord entered the chamber and took the throne. His retinue took their seats around the semi-circular table either side of him.

'Do we have the Midas device?' asked the Overlord.

'No, there were…complications,' Erikson replied. 'I calculated all possible outcomes but there was a wildcard I didn't anticipate, but I guarantee this will not affect the long term outcome of the project.'

'You couldn't have "calculated all possible outcomes" then, could you?' baited one of the company.

The Overlord raised his finger slightly from the table; it was all that was needed to stop those assembled around the table from turning into a baying mob.

'And in the short-term?' the Overlord asked.

'I have a contingency,' replied Erikson.

'Very well,' the Overlord looked around the table. 'You all have your work to do, and Brother Erikson has assured this Council that everything is proceeding to plan. The meeting is adjourned.'

The Council members filed out of the chamber as Erikson visualised the Overlord's head on a stake. That seat would have been he's by now if he'd had the Midas device in his possession. He had underestimated Cranston, it wouldn't happen again, but until he had it in his hands, there was no choice but to continue with the increasingly voracious Titan.

*****

'Good morning Detective Inspector,' greeted Fletcher with a sly wink as D.I Sutherland entered the station.

The fact that Fletcher was being so formal was a code that Chief Superintendent Willingdon was in the station. It was a belt and braces arrangement in case the Chief hadn't stuck to his diary. At that prompt, the plan was that Sutherland would leave the station via the nearest fire exit, and Fletcher would swear blind on a stack of bibles that he hadn't seen him. Today though, Sutherland headed for his office, leaving Fletcher with an undiagnosed winking tic as he tried to get the message across, not knowing that Sutherland was ready for the upcoming confrontation.

The open plan office was as it always was, a combination of people looking earnestly at computer screens and open files. Others temporarily took some time out to compare opinions on some reality television show involving immaculately groomed vacuous dandies competing in a top trumps of vanity and sun tan lotion, all in the name of 'luurve'.

Everything was as expected in Sutherland's world view except - someone was in his sanctum messing with the noticeboard.

'Good morning sergeant. Hard at it, *in my office*, I see.'

'Good morning Sir. I didn't think you'd be in today, so I thought I'd add something to the board. As you said that Mr Black was a priority, I didn't think you'd mind. I've had an idea, but as you're here there's something else I need to tell you as well.'

The fact that Sergeant Bludgeon wanted to impart two sets of information was unprecedented. Sutherland was torn, both could lead to his brain spontaneously melting. He needed his wits about him as he was expecting a summons any moment, but Bludgeon's hard work and tenacity always swayed him. It couldn't be coincidence that Willingdon's clandestine meeting had taken place after the sergeant's cage rattling.

There was only one thing for it; he had to head Bludgeon off at the pass. 'Let me guess, James Mason has been spotted in drag, with a full orchestra backing on top of the Post Office Tower, singing "I Am What I Am".'

Sergeant Bludgeon smiled. 'That's very good Sir, but you don't catch me out that easily. I think you'll find that you wouldn't get planning permission to balance a grand piano up there, and it's the Telecom Tower now.'

'I knew that, just testing.'

Sutherland looked at his noticeboard, which still had Mr Black at the centre, with lines radiating out, crossing, rubbed out, and drawn back in. New names had been added. Did he dare ask? Despite what he now knew to be true, he believed you could never have enough hard evidence. Was there an outside chance that Bludgeon, with his total left of field reasoning and apparent dislogic had unknowingly revealed something?

'What have Ghengis Khan't, Joseph Stayingin, Jack the Tripper and Attila the Pun got to do with Mr Black?' Sutherland asked.

'You don't want to hear what I've found out?'

'In a minute, what's the connection between that lot, apart from all being dead.'

Sergeant Bludgeon was silent for a moment as he reset himself. The board was a work in progress but obviously Detective Inspector Sutherland knew best, or he wouldn't have asked.

'It's quite simple really. We're assuming Mr Black is an arch villain with a grand plan,' Bludgeon started to explain. 'I was wondering if the reason we can't find Mr Black is because he doesn't exist as a person. What if Mr Black is a secret title? If that's the case, then all we have to do is look at people through history who are renowned for grand plans, for all we know they could all have been secret Mr Blacks, that's why it's secret. If we then look at their modus operands, we could build up a profile. Then all we have to do is see what powerful people in the world today fit it, and we've found him.'

Sutherland's reason hit the alarm bell and was looking for the nearest fire exit, but the Charybdisian whirlpool of perverse curiosity was dragging him in.

'What about Jack the Tripper?' Sutherland queried. 'He was hardly an empire builder was he? All he did was go around making paving slabs wobbly on dark streets in Whitechapel.'

'Ah, that's what historians want you to think. He was actually the Prime Minister at the time, Jack the Tripper was his secret alter ego, and each of those slabs was carefully chosen. He knew where certain members of royalty frequented the back streets looking for women of the night. All it would take would be a trip and a fall onto a cunningly concealed poison dart, and he stood to take advantage of a constitutional crisis. The only reason Archduke Ferdinand was shot was that he never walked anywhere.'

'Give me strength...'

'Sir?'

'I have to say that...' but Sutherland didn't get a chance to finish. Chief Superintendent Willingdon stood at the door.

'Detective Inspector Sutherland, my office, now!' barked Willingdon.

As Sutherland left all that could be heard was him saying 'Later' through gritted teeth as his bemused sergeant tried to pass on a vital piece of information.

*****

Sutherland entered the air lock of Willingdon's secretarial office and winked at Shirley who smiled half-heartedly, 'He's not happy,' she warned.

As he crossed the threshold into Willingdon's domain, he saw that there was no chair for him; it was going to be a stand-up bollocking then.

'Close the door,' instructed Willingdon. 'How long have we known each other?'

'About thirty years, on and off, Guv',' replied Sutherland.

'About thirty years, and here's the thing, I'm here and you're there. Do you know why you're working on missing persons?'

'I got lucky?'

'You got seconded, by me, because if I hadn't you'd have been out on your ear. Things have changed, and those brains in Human Resources have your card marked so I put you on a job that you could do in your sleep. All you had to do was review the case and say "Nothing doing". You could have seen out your last year with no trouble, but no, not you.'

Willingdon picked up a file jacket full of miscellaneous papers that had nothing to do with anything in particular, all constrained by thin linen tape, and slapped it down on the table for effect. 'That is a list of complaints from practically every department in the Ministry, and some, because you can't stop fishing for this Mr Black. What the bloody hell are you playing at?'

'Sorry Guv', not with you. Mr Black?'

'Don't play the innocent with me. You've had your sergeant all over him like a rash. I've even had to threaten him with the sack.'

'That was a bit harsh if you ask me, he's only following my orders. Now you mention it though, I do remember asking him to look into someone, what was that name again?'

'Mr Bloody Black - Orimov! Whatever you call him.'

'Mr Black,' replied Sutherland clicking his fingers. 'I'm with you now. You know, I had a feeling that wasn't his real name, but I didn't know it was Orimov. How did you know?'

Willingdon paused, aware that he had been baited, and considered his next answer. 'There's a lot I know, and if you hadn't spent all your time AWOL and kept me posted instead, we could have shared, a bit radical I know. At the moment you're this close,' he closed his forefinger and thumb, 'from having a rocket up your rear end and achieving orbit. I don't know what your game is, but as of now you're off the case, I'm closing it down.'

'But Guv', we're onto something, I can feel it,' said Sutherland, seeing how far he could push it.

'If you'd bothered to interview some of the families of those missing accountants you would have found out they're not missing, the only crime they're guilty of is not telling anyone they're on a secondment abroad, we've got the emails to prove it.'

'Emails, that's bloody lame,' thought Sutherland.

'I want the accountants put to bed on the double,' Willingdon continued. 'The mayor wants priority given to his missing bikes.'

'If he forgets to chain them to a fence, what does he expect?'

'Don't push your luck detective. The mayor's rent-a-bike scheme is going pear shaped. They're being hired with fake credit cards and not being returned. We think there's a black market with possible links to Amsterdam.'

'I'd better get right to it then. I reckon a good place to start would be to check all the CCTV footage from underground carparks; the thieving toe-rags might be using them for temporary storage. You never know, it could turn up something interesting.'

There was a silence as they took the measure of each other.

The opening gambit had been played.

'You do that,' replied Willingdon. 'Close the door on the way out.'

He sat back in his chair and took stock. Sutherland was onto something. He made a small coded note on his to-do list. A false lead, an unfortunate accident, and Sutherland would be out of the way. Things happened, after all police work was dangerous.

The phone rang and the caller identity showed as Erikson.

'What do you want?' said Willingdon gruffly.

'I have a job for you.'

*****

Sutherland returned to the office to find it deserted, with the exception of Fletcher, who sat at a desk ardently watching two computer monitors.

'What's going on? Where is everyone?' Sutherland asked.

'You've missed all the excitement. There's a code Red on, all hands to the pump.'

'It must be serious if they've roped in Bludgeon and Murray. Who's minding the shop out front?'

'The stations closed, I'm holding the fort here, and before you ask, Bludgeon nipped round to Di Paulo's for a spot of lunch and missed the call. Murray's on his way to the London, he got a last minute physio cancellation for his foot.

Sutherland nodded, as the senior officer he was duty bound to know what was going on. 'What's the code Red then?'

'White stilettos have been spotted floating over Buckingham Palace.'

'What - another one? How are they doing it? Launching a hot air balloon in the middle of London is a bit obvious isn't it.'

'They're pretending to be novelty balloon sellers. When they're ready, they unhook themselves from the railings, and off they go.'

'You're telling me that the novelty helium balloon trade has a paramilitary wing?'

Fletcher shook his head. 'It's not that simple. Looks like it might be something to do with ELF.'

'Since when have the Met believed in fairies?'

'No, not elves, E.L.F. The Essex Liberation Front.'

'Okay, so what do we know about these Elf's then?'

'Not a lot, they're demanding independence for Chopping Ongar, but I reckon it's all a front.'

'You told me that, the clues in the name.'

'No, that's not what I meant. I reckon all this Essex stuff is a front for an extremist far right group using an outdated crude stereotype of women from the Essex area to capitalise on a tired trope to distract from their real agenda.'

'Your missus, she wouldn't happen to be from around there by any chance?'

'How'd you know that?' replied Fletcher in surprise.

'Oh- you know- a wild stab in the dark. Anyway, apart from upsetting her maj's view, what's the problem?'

'If Chopping Ongar don't get their own flag, she's going to drop all her handbags; they're full of high explosives. The palace goes up in flames and without the ballast, she drifts off scot free.'

'Why don't we just wait for the wind to change?'

'It's not like that one over Downing Street; they reckon that was a test run. They mean business this time; she's got a leaf blower strapped to her arse.'

'Leaf blower – of course, I should've guessed. I don't know why people can't just nick stuff, we'd all know where we stand then.' Sutherland forced a smile, 'Well, it looks like you've got everything covered. Keep up the good work.'

In his office, Sutherland took his seat, twirled side to side, looked at the board, and then did a full rotation. He had Willingdon bang to rights, but this wasn't going to be as easy as reporting him up the chain of command. He knew Willingdon was on the take, and where there was one, you could guarantee there were others. And what was he playing at putting him on a missing bikes assignment? If he'd been in Willingdon's place, it would have at least been a suspension. He was being set up for a fall, he could feel it. Well, Willingdon wasn't the only one with contacts. All he had to do now was work out a way to redirect Sergeant Bludgeon onto bicycles without causing him a catastrophic cerebral derailment.

On cue an animated Bludgeon burst through the door, slamming it behind him. In his urgency he nearly trapped his tuna melt panini in the doorframe.

'Sir, I've got to tell you something.'

'Don't you ever knock?' said Sutherland wearily.

Bludgeon hovered by the door, not sure whether a post bursting in tap would do, or whether he should leave and go through the whole thing again.

'Come on, out with it,' said Sutherland, detecting, (because that's what he did), that he had again wrong footed his sergeant.

Bludgeon looked over his shoulder to make sure no one was listening. *'I've found a missing accountant,'* he stressed in suppressed tones.

'You've done what?'

'Found a *missing accountant*. I didn't think you'd mind if I took a break from Mr Black.'

'Bloody hell! Why didn't you tell me this earlier?'

'But…'

'Never mind, who is it? Where are they?'

Bludgeon checked his notes. 'Ben Kingswood, he was admitted to the London Hospital with a gunshot wound to the leg. I've got some friends at Leman Street who tipped me off as they know I'm interested in the…' his voice tailed off, 'ABC …thing?' He waited for the explosive rebound.

Sutherland's brow knitted as the pieces of the puzzle slotted into place without any need for them to be thumped. Willingdon, Mr Black, Murray, Cranston, and now one of the missing accountants had turned up at London Hospital, and Murray was on his way to…London Hospital. 'Oh you bloody idiot man!' he cried as he thumped the table.

Sergeant Bludgeon looked crestfallen.

'Not you, me,' clarified Sutherland as he rushed out the door, quickly turning to tell Bludgeon that he wasn't to go away. 'Fletcher, quick, what have we got in the car pool?'

'Nothing Guvnor, everything's out on the code Red.'

'We must have something for Christ's sake' said Sutherland as he rifled through the key cabinets and desk trays, finally alighting on a key ring with a bold black on yellow logo. 'What about these?'

'Those? That motor got pulled over on Farringdon road – no tax or insurance. Usual story, the driver reckons he'd only just bought it, at some convention or something. It's out back until the lads come to take it to the pound.'

'Does it drive?'

'Yeah, but trust me, you don't want to.'

'I'll be the judge of that,' said Sutherland as he pocketed the keys. 'Come on sergeant, to the car park. There's not a moment to lose!'

The car was large, black and American, with customised bodywork that made it impossible to be ignored or mistaken for a similar vehicle, because there wouldn't be one. Bludgeon jumped into what he thought was the driver's seat, temporarily perplexed, as he looked in front of him, and then across to the three quarter aircraft style steering wheel.

Sutherland looked up to the heavens in a vain appeal to whatever deities are responsible for policemen who are approaching the end of their tether. 'You have got to be having a laugh,' he said acidly through gritted teeth.

Sutherland reversed the leviathan out onto the street and proceeded onto the A40 heading towards Cheapside. The vee eight rumbled, slowly picking up speed as the knackered bedspring suspension made the car roll and lollop at the slightest imperfection in the road, but once it got going it was fast, and that was all that mattered.

'What does he look like?' said Sutherland, raising his voice over the ambient noise of the surrounding traffic and the Chevy lump, there being no way to shut it out, what with the built in open cockpit.

'I'm not sure. Like an accountant?' Bludgeon offered.

'That's useful. He's hardly going to be in bed with pinstripe trousers and a bowler hat is he?'

'That's a good point. I think they're quite well paid so he should be able to afford pyjamas. Maybe he's wearing silk ones.'

'Sergeant,' growled Sutherland impatiently.

'And he's in a private room, with a police guard,' embellished Bludgeon, even his seeming tin ear detecting some frustration, 'if that helps?'

'Terrific. Why is it when someone survives an attempt on their life, they get stuck in a private bed? It's the NHS for crying out loud. It's asking for trouble. Murray 'll get all matey, give the guard a break and that'll be it.'

'Is Murray one of Mr Black's people?'

'Yes. Now listen up, 'cos I'm not saying this again. The reason we can't find Mr Black is because he's been hiding under our noses, he's Willingdon.' Sutherland's personal lying Imp gave him the thumbs up. For something on the fly, this was inspired. 'Murray's part of it and he's going to make sure that accountant can't be a witness.'

Bludgeon was silent, inscrutable even. Sutherland wondered if he'd gone too far.

'Red light Sir.'

'Thanks,' replied Sutherland as he floored the accelerator, ignoring the near pile up as he crossed Mansion House, racing the futuristic black automobile up Cheapside.

A smile crept across Bludgeon's face. He reached into his inside pocket, put on a pair of Ray –Ban's, and with an air of confident calm rested his elbow on the door. With the wind blowing through his hair, he looked every inch the film star. Meanwhile Sutherland took their lives in their hands. With sinews bulging in his forearms he forced the lump of a car at near twice the speed limit around Aldgate onto the Whitechapel High Street, leaving chaos in his wake.

You alright sergeant?'

'Never been better Sir. I knew you wouldn't let me down. You knew Chief Superintendent Willingdon was Mr Black, so he couldn't sack me, as he's not the Chief Super, even though he told me that if I wasn't careful, today would be my last day. That's why you didn't want me to tell him anything. I have to say it's a master class in sneakiness, and now, here we are, out in the field, the driving duo, pitting our wits against an axis of evil led by an insidious master of disguise. Who knows who we can trust? This is so exciting!'

Sutherland's momentary guilt at Bludgeon's blissful ignorance about his situation was quickly replaced with surprise as with the brake pedal to the floor, he watched, helpless, as a market stall moved closer towards them and assorted fruit and veg spilled across the bonnet.

As the brakes finally bit, bringing the car to an abrupt halt, the front dipped down and then suddenly rebounded back, hurling the remaining unbroken salad into the crowd. This in turn caused a minor skirmish to break out, the embers of which would slowly smoulder, and then be reignited later that day by an unknown incident. The resulting free-for-all would forever be known in history as the 'Whitechapel Coleslaw Riots'.

There is some dispute among journalists and historians as to how it exactly 'kicked off', but eye witness accounts all refer to one, Joey Biscuit, who having previously been on the receiving end of a flying parsnip, made it known in no uncertain terms that a similar incident would result in him 'Doing his nut.'

'Sergeant, keep the engine running, I won't be long.'

'But we're illegally parked.'

'Anyone says anything, arrest them,' replied Sutherland, making sure that the wider crowd heard him as he held up his police badge. He dashed across the Whitechapel road and ran up the stairs to the entrance of the London Hospital, two at time.

*****

Ben Kingswood had finally managed to get comfortable; the mild analgesic was starting to take effect as he started to feel drowsy.

The doctor had told him that he had been lucky; the bullet had passed through his leg, without disrupting any major blood vessels. The good news was that he would be able to walk again; the bad news was that he shouldn't have any ambitions for the piano.

He closed his eyes and drifted off into a semi-conscious slumber, unaware of the slow turning of the door handle as Murray stealthily entered the room, closing the blind on the half-glazed door.

Murray took a pillow from the neatly stacked laundry that had been left in readiness for the next bed change. This wouldn't take long, and then he would raise the alarm. The nurses and doctors would find him trying to resuscitate the accountant, who had mysteriously taken a turn for the worse.

He held the pillow above his intended victims face and was about to apply pressure when the door to the room flew open, the ineffective lock and door jamb shattered by the force of entry. It was Detective Inspector Sutherland.

'Murray, don't do anything stupid, put- the- pillow- down,' said Sutherland, reaching out his hand. 'Come on son, the games up, you'll never get away with this. I promise I'll put a good word in for you. It's a tough job and sometimes we make mistakes, I get it. So how about you do the right thing before it gets out of hand. Give- me –the- pillow – nice and easy, that's it…'

Murray handed it over to the slowly advancing Detective Inspector. 'Yeah, you're right. What was I thinking?'

'Will you two keep it down,' mumbled Kingswood, eyes still closed, not really taking in any detail. 'I'll do the questions later.'

Murray swung a prodigious left hook, making contact with the pillow, and Sutherland fell back into a visitor's chair. Murray removed a collapsible baton from his belt and flicked it to its full length. The first blow struck the chair cushion; the second swing was blocked by the pillow which exploded on contact, scattering feathers everywhere.

Sutherland retreated into the corner of the room, trying to avoid the wild swinging stick through the drifting down. It caught him on the upper arm, and the initial concentrated sharp pain spread out rapidly across his triceps. He opened the door of a cupboard next to him, using it as a shield, and then before the extended rod could be raised for another strike, he made to stamp on Murray's foot. Murray awkwardly danced back and as he did so, Sutherland hit him square on the jaw with a metal bedpan. Murray collapsed like a puppet with cut strings.

'You're Kingswood, right?' said Sutherland, in between gasps.

Kingswood was out of the bed, no one could have slept through that. He nodded in acknowledgement; there didn't seem any point in denying it. He held a chair over his head ready to strike.

'Oh for crying out loud,' said Sutherland as he showed his badge and pointed at the prone Murray. 'Look- him bad cop. Me good cop. We've got to go, can you walk?'

Kingswood looked at the slightly dishevelled self-proclaimed guardian. He had the look of someone you wouldn't want to cross, but with a benign hint, unlike the creature on the floor. 'No problem,' he said as he put the chair down. He took one step, and involuntarily fell into it. 'Sorry, I need a minute; leg's gone dead.'

'Terrific,' mumbled Sutherland as he handcuffed Murray to

the bed. 'I'll be back in a moment. If he wakes up, hit him with this,' and he handed over the dented potty.

It's not every day that you see a bespectacled accountant in a wheelchair, raising and lowering his leg in a slow motion Can-Can, being pushed at full pelt by a senior member of the metropolitan constabulary shouting, 'Police, out of the bleedin' way!', but Nurse Gladys Emanuel took it in her stride. It was probably nothing, but just in case she would let that nice policeman, who spent his time sitting around upstairs guarding a gunshot victim, know.

They made their way down the stairs of the hospital entrance, Kingswood still limping as he worked off the stiffness of his leg. A crowd had gathered around the commandeered vehicle, many of them taking photographs of themselves in front of that foreign piece of transatlantic engineering. Some of the snaps included a reluctant Sergeant Bludgeon, who, because of handcuffing two Community Support Officers, and a traffic warden to the railings, had endeared himself to the mob.

'Been busy I see, well done,' said Sutherland. 'This is Ben Kingswood.'

'Is this your car?' asked Kingswood, not knowing quite what to make of it.

'Yeah, what's wrong with it?' asked Sutherland pulling off the trick of being both rhetorical and defensive at the same time.

'It's only got two seats.'

'Budget cuts.'

Bludgeon raised his hand. 'Sir...' and pointed back at the London Hospital.

Sutherland watched as Murray hobbled at speed down the stairs and flagged down the only patrol car in London that wasn't on a code Red assignment. He mentally chalked up another one on Willingdon's team. 'Sergeant, you and Mr Kingswood take the tube and I'll meet you at the Badger's Nadgers in Wapping. Ask for Leroy, tell him I sent you and he'll keep you hid until I get there. I'll take this thing and lead them off. Go on, what are you waiting for?'

There was a lone tomato on the driver's seat. Sutherland

chucked it in a slow motion arc above the crowd. Gravity ensured that it landed with a loud 'splat' on a certain individuals head.

Sutherland pulled out, narrowly avoiding a bus, forcing it to skid and block the carriageway as he headed towards the Mile End Road. He could see Murray in his rear view mirror weaving slowly, blue light flashing and siren wailing as he navigated around the traffic mess. He was following. Good, he'd taken the bait.

Sutherland gunned the engine and with the sound of squealing tyres, he made the turn into Cambridge Heath Road. He knew all the back streets, but this car was next to useless for that, he had to get some distance and with the accelerator to the floor, he hurtled towards a railway bridge about half a mile away. Taking care this time to judge the brakes, he turned off after the bridge, the car listing like a four wheeled land blimp as he narrowly avoided a telegraph pole. He could hear Murray's siren, but he knew that for the moment they had lost sight of him. His arm was complaining, but it wasn't for much longer now. Driving more slowly he passed under another railway bridge and onto a thoroughfare where taxi cab firms and mechanics plied their trade in the railway arches, and there was his opportunity. With one last effort, he turned onto a forecourt, and more through luck than judgement, with a hefty tug on the hand brake, skidded into a space where the car would not be seen from the road. He leapt out and ran to Weavers fields, hiding in the hedgerow that made up the boundary. It wasn't long before he saw Murray career past at speed, missing the abandoned car as he headed towards Vallance Road.

Satisfied that he'd given him the slip, Sutherland made his way to Bethnal Green station. He'd travel to Wapping the long way round.

*****

Pete Chandler was taking a break, but he wasn't enjoying it. He had quit smoking again and it was costing him a fortune in hypnotherapy. He still had the craving, but at least he now knew he was the reincarnation of an ancient aztec chieftain.

According to the therapist, this accounted for his aptitude with motorised transport.

He took an indifferent bite from a raw carrot, it was a lousy substitute, it was enough to make him buy a packet of twenty B&H. 'I'll nip down the newsagents, one last go,' he told himself.

He hadn't taken one step when a black king-size automobile came screeching into the yard, skidded to a halt. A stranger jumped out and legged it. For a second Pete wondered if carrots could bring on hallucinations, but no, there it was, as large as life.

'What the…Raymond, get out here. I need a hand!'

'Alright, no need to shout,' replied Raymond as he stepped out into the open, looked at the black motor, and stopped in his tracks. 'No! That is so cool. When did you get that? Can I have a go?'

'I ain't got time to fanny about, the Jag man's due here any minute, and if he sees that I'll be laughed out of court. Come on, help me with this,' said Pete as he tugged on a tarpaulin from a mound of miscellaneous items.

'I don't get it,' Raymond queried. 'What happened to "rare, classic, or exotic", I thought you liked all that sixties stuff?'

'I ain't that old and just because it's been on the telly, don't make it a classic. Don't get me wrong, much as I admire the way Mr West played it straight, with a childlike but earnest and bigger than life sincerity, in an ironic and bizarre way, the last thing I want is the sodding Batmobile parked outside my gaffe!'

Raymond tucked the cover over the last wheel and watched as Pete's colour slowly dialled down from crimson. 'I better ring that bloke back then and cancel the booking.'

'What bloke?'

'The geezer I was talking to before you threw a spanner about that,' said Raymond nodding at the now covered Batmobile. 'Wanted us to have a look at his DB5, got a problem with the ejector seat.'

'Hold up, let's not be hasty…'

25 / The End Of The Pier Show

John Cranston sat back in the leather chesterfield armchair as Gordon came in from the kitchen with a freshly brewed pot of tea, and placed it on the coffee table. A fire raged away in the wood-burning stove, radiating warmth and light throughout the tastefully appointed lounge. It would have been idyllic if it weren't for John's caution with his new ally. Gordon sat down opposite, poured himself a cup, and closed his eyes as he savoured the long overdue beverage.

'Nice place you've got here,' said John.

'This?' replied Gordon with false modesty. 'It's not mine. I'm borrowing it for a while. They're on a world cruise at the moment; I didn't think they'd mind.'

'Do a lot of borrowing in your line of work?'

'Purely as an operational expediency,' Gordon said casually.

'The Brigadier's secret headquarters not good enough then?'

'It's been compromised. You and I are now deep under cover.'

'We are?'

'Yes. Now where were we on that debriefing?'

'Breakfast,' replied John tersely.

'That's right. Now, think back carefully, what did Erikson tell you about his plans?'

'We've been through all this in the car. How many more times do I have to say, "he didn't say"? All he was interested in was getting his hands on Midas. The next thing I know he's running off for some meeting. Like I said, I reckon it's big, and it's about money.'

Gordon took another sip, his brow furrowed. 'So you say, but there has to be more to it than that. The only reason you're invited to breakfast with these Johnnies is so that they can boast about how they'll take over the world, and then they kill you. They can't help it; they're ego-maniacs, the lot of them.'

'I'm so sorry to buck the trend by being alive and un-briefed.'

'The tiniest detail could be important. Fortune favours the prepared you know.'

'Okay then, he's got a butler who looks like Hannibal Lecter with a hangover, and his office doubles up as a yoga studio. The chef isn't bad, although come to think of it, the hash browns were a bit soggy.'

Gordon was still frowning.

'Then I had a tour of the offices,' John continued, 'and that's when I noticed all these corporate mission posters.' He made a bunny ears sign with his fingers, 'Controlling the world's money today; for our brighter tomorrow. It's obvious isn't it? He's going to use the global financial system as some kind of personal cashpoint.'

'That's what he wanted you to think. It sounds a lot like the Crickwell hypothesis to me. I think you've been fed a red herring.'

'What's that?'

'A small silvery fish,' Gordon held his hands apart, 'about so big.'

'No, the Crickwell thing.'

'It's not important,' said Gordon dismissively. 'Did Erikson mention anything about extortion or blackmail?'

'No.'

'Stealing launch codes for nuclear warheads and starting World War Three?'

'No.'

'Releasing a deadly virus that would turn the population into mindless zombies?'

John shook his head.

Gordon took another draft of his tea and seemed to look through the walls of the luxury bungalow, momentarily deep in thought. 'Anything about a death ray?'

'Sorry?'

'A death ray, you know, hyper powered laser launched into orbit from a secret location, used to burn strategic cities to the ground as a demonstration before demanding a ransom.'

'No, I can't say he did.'

'Are you sure?'

'I think I would have remembered.'

'Mmmm, whatever he's up to, he'll have to be stopped.'

Gordon finished his tea and picking up a scrap of paper from a prepared pile started to make an origami penguin. Paper folding helped him concentrate. There was something not quite right, every arch villain loved to boast about their evil schemes, it's what they did. Cranston wasn't telling him everything. Had he been turned?

'So what's the plan then?' said John, breaking the awkward silence.

Gordon ignored the question; that could be what Cranston was after. 'Where did you say Midas was now?'

'I didn't,' said John as he started to rise from the leather chair. Something wasn't right, it was time to go.

Gordon leaned forward and retrieved the gun that was taped underneath his chair and indicated with it that John was to sit back down. 'How long have you been working for Erikson?'

'What? You're the one who's working for him, not me. I thought we drove out of there a bit too easy. This whole rescue thing is a set-up. Well, the deal's the same, if I don't report in; Midas gets turned into a smoothie.'

Gordon fixed John with a steel gaze. 'If I was working for him and wanted information, I would have left you with that homicidal harpy. Getting out was easier than I thought it would be, but then it'd be a shame if Erikson's double agent got killed before he reported back, wouldn't it?'

'Double agent, how did you work that one out? I'm having a hard enough time keeping up with singles, and how would I know you were coming to the rescue anyway? Maybe we got lucky when we escaped – you said so yourself. So, if I'm not working for him, and you're not working for him, what's with the gun?'

Gordon considered his options. Cranston had a point. He placed the weapon down on the coffee table, equidistant between them. 'The last person I nearly trusted left me for dead in a burning Turkish bath. I suggest that we continue in a spirit of mutual distrust, working towards a common goal.'

Gordon picked up another scrap of paper, sat back in the chair, and started to fold a cat.

John looked at the gun; he liked it where it was. Maybe it was time for a leap of faith. He reached into the inside pocket of his blouson jacket, (courtesy of wardrobe by Gorringe), and took out the small Midas data card. 'I think this is what all the fuss is about.'

Gordon took a deep breath and resisted the urge to leap from his chair and snatch it, could it be *the* card, after all these years?

With great effort, he deliberately and slowly put the half-finished paper cat down onto the arm of the chair. He was sure he could beat Cranston to the draw and take it, although that wasn't without risk. The man opposite claimed to be a gardener, but this was also the same person who had single handedly made his way across Victoria station through some of the nastiest, brutal pieces of work to ever grace the planet, without drawing attention. No there was an easier way.

He held out his hand. 'May I?'

John threw it over. 'You're welcome to it. Bloody things a dud anyway.'

Gordon turned it over between forefinger and thumb, gently, considerately, admiring it as if it were a rare jewel. This didn't go unnoticed.

'You had it all the time?' Gordon asked.

'It was all part of the plan. I give up and hand it over and then it's supposed to screw his whole setup the first time he uses it, but instead *he said* it was a fake. He was so unimpressed he left it at breakfast when he shoved off. I thought I'd better palm it, in case he started playing with it later and got the thing working.'

Gordon inserted it into his cigarette case sized device. It took longer than expected but it was confirmed. It was Midas.

'Did Crickwell do anything to this?'

'He tried to reprogram it, but that didn't work out, so he did some kind of virtual lobotomy on it, fat lot of good that did.'

'You were lucky it failed, otherwise you might not be sitting there now.'

'What do you mean?'

'If it'd worked, it wouldn't have stopped Erikson for long. Recently there's been a daily exchange of hardware to two Covert Communication Centres.' Gordon could tell from the look on John's face that this was all new to him. 'Three C's for short. Think of them as a series of mini GCHQ's for malcontents who are determined to undermine democracy and the British way of life. In this case, it's the Dark League. They've installed them all over the country, hidden in plain sight in historic, unused or derelict buildings, there are two near here. I think those deliveries are mirror backups, exact copies of software, data, everything needed to restore operations, all in a briefcase sized package. If you'd succeeded, he'd have been up and running again in no time, and you would have been a prime target. Midas can't do its job on things that aren't connected.'

'Great, I went through all that for nothing.'

'You weren't to know. I think this is a new tactic, they're always changing the way they do things, damned unsporting, but you did keep Midas out of enemy hands.'

'Yeah, after I gave it to him in the first place.'

Gordon held the card up between finger and thumb. 'My guess is that he had it tested in quarantine. If Midas couldn't detect a network to break, it wouldn't have been able to follow through on Crickwell's instructions. I reckon it defaulted to its core directive of self-preservation and went into camouflage mode. Dashed clever, don't you think?'

'No, pretending to be military grade hardware is hardly low key is it? You're not saying that thing still works?'

'Of course it does,' replied Gordon with the air of a man responding to someone who had doubted his best friends' ability to do a job. 'You'd be a bit confused if you'd had a brain operation. No, this'll be right as rain and fit to go, it's got self-repairing nanite technology; damned hard to break don't you know.'

'So if those secret spy centres were somehow sorted out, we'd be back in business?'

'You know I'm starting to like the cut of your jib, that's exactly what I was thinking. We disable the off site back-ups; sneak into Erikson's headquarters, run Midas, and then escape by the skin of our teeth. It'll probably be dangerous, even life threatening. We'll start tonight. What do you say?'

'I was with you up until "life threatening"' replied John cautiously.

'Oh don't worry about that. With the price on your head, I guarantee that you'll be run over by a bus at some point anyway, so technically this is safer. Spot of late lunch old chap?'

It turned out that Gordon was the most genial of hosts and not a bad cook either. Nothing fancy, but the risotto rice mixed with salmon was a perfect creamy consistency, with subtle herb flavours enhancing the dish. He asked John about he's favourite books, where he was from, and other seeming trivia, and such was his skill at engaging him and taking an interest, John found himself revealing seemingly innocuous facts, that when added together, would have provided Gordon with an increasingly detailed portrait, but this was simply a preamble to the main event.

'What did you do before you were a gardener?'

'Sorry - I'm not with you.'

'My dear chap, when you've been in the business as long as I have, you get a nose for these things, and you haven't always been dividing daffodils, or whatever it is gardeners do. So..?'

'This and that.'

'I see. Abroad?'

'Here and there.'

'An international man of mystery then, I see. One word of advice if I may - be careful with this alter-ego if yours, because one day that is what you'll become, and they'll be no turning back. Make sure that day isn't today.'

'I am a gardener,' John started to protest, but checked himself as he quickly considered his position, '...sometimes.'

'That's the ticket! Did I ever tell you about the time...'

John chose his moment as Gordon came to the end of a tale about when he had worked undercover in Hollywood as a voice coach, teaching fluent cockney to method actors. Apparently, jellied eels were a stumbling block.

'You haven't told me about this Crickwell hypothesis. What is it?'

'As I said, it's not got any bearing on the task in hand.'

'And yet according to you, Erikson knows about it. Come on, we haven't finished the Tiramisu yet. If it's not that important, what's the harm in telling me?'

Gordon sighed. Did he have to explain everything? 'Very well, after I'd recruited Crickwell I left him with Department S. It was obvious he had talent, but they didn't quite know what to do with him at first, so they left him to his own devices.

The next thing they know he's published a paper asking the question of how, theoretically, if someone could transparently and secretly access any computing system, using something like Midas, what would be the outcome? He was new and hadn't got the hang of a secret organisation; in his world it seems academic peer review is exempt.

He built a sophisticated model to look at all possible scenarios. It predicted that a covert organisation would use Midas to mimic the release of a global computer virus that would slowly but surely compromise all banking and financial systems.

Secondly, that same organisation would then, through untraceable subsidiaries and shell companies, create a new class of banking services that were immune to that "virus". Over time, individuals, corporations, and governments would move their resources to these providers, or onto platforms based on their technology.

Rather than stealing their money, that covert organisation would be given full use of it, willingly. Midas would be used in the background to maintain control and secrecy, and to proactively compromise any rival systems. The ultimate end game would be worldwide financial, political, and military control, and it would all seem legitimate.'

'You sound pretty relaxed for someone who knows a blueprint for taking over the world is out there for anyone to use.'

'There was one thing that was missing from the paper, it didn't occur to him until after he published it. The administration of the whole thing would be a bloody nightmare. To get it off the ground would need an army of accountants. The powers that be were quite happy to let any scoundrel waste their time and money to learn what Crickwell had left out. Once they'd figured it out, no one in their right mind would follow through, it would take years.'

'What about someone in their wrong mind?'

Gordon dabbed the sides of his mouth with his napkin and his devil may care demeanour temporarily took a back seat.

'It would be catastrophic; the very foundations of society as we know it would be shattered to make way for a new world order. It would make the Nazi's look positively benign.'

On that note, it was back to work as Gordon fetched from the cupboard under the stairs a long canvas holdall of the kind that you would expect to roll a collapsible garden gazebo into. He unzipped it, removed a cardboard tube, took out a dog eared map and spread it across the dining table. Securing the corners with the condiments, he proceeded to outline the plan.

First there were the location of the two backup sites, the Three C's, circled in red. One was an offshore, supposedly unmanned lighthouse, and the other was an abandoned pier, one of many around the coastline of Britain, harking back to a time when Victorian entrepreneurs capitalised on the supposed wondrous medicinal benefits of sea air and bathing. These were joined by red dotted lines to an industrial estate that was allegedly pioneering the manufacture of next generation solar technology; in fact, it was a front for Erikson's subterranean lair, the nerve centre of his operations.

Also drawn on the map in blue, were lines of varying thicknesses representing an underground tunnel network, a labyrinth of disparate pathways. Gordon pointed out the smugglers tunnels, which interweaved from the coastline, connecting villages or hidden portals in the landscape. He also indicated the abandoned mine workings of the 1847 coal rush that had been championed by the Duke Eau' Comvitte.

'This closed mine,' said Gordon pointing to the Duke's failed project, 'is our way in. When they built the base, they co-opted it to use it as a secret escape route. En suite caves were all the rage in the fifties – very hard to come by these days. So – if it's a way out, it's our way in.'

'That's handy,' observed John, 'it takes us right to the door.'

'Not exactly, most of the mine workings have collapsed over time.'

'Figures.'

Gordon nodded. 'The navvies were paid by the yard, but when the investors threatened to pull out they rushed, bit desperate to hit the mother lode you see. The escape route was decommissioned, but not to worry, there's a smugglers tunnel that runs adjacent, and I've found a way in…'

'That doesn't sound too bad.'

'… but it's booby-trapped.'

'There's a surprise. I suppose the upside is if it all goes pear shaped, it saves on the cremation.'

'That's the ticket,' said Gordon as he slapped John on the back. 'Where's the fun without the danger – eh?'

*****

From the wardrobe upstairs, John helped himself to an insulated hiking jacket, a small backpack and a pair of ski gloves with leather lined palms. Fortunately, it seemed that Gordon only borrowed from active citizens. He stood in the hallway while Gordon went over the plan one last time.

'Pay attention old chap,' said Gordon, handling what looked like an enclosed frisbee with knobs on. 'This is a short range electro magnetic pulse generator, E.M.P for short. Attach this to the deck under the pier, and those backups will be useless. Set the timer with this button here, and start the countdown here. It's crucial we're coordinated, if either site gets a sniff of the other being compromised, they'll abandon it and take the backups with them. Understood?'

'Crystal.'

'Excellent. Oh, and one last thing, you'll need these,' said Gordon as he handed over a pair of W2109's, and a beanie hat.

John reinstated his disguise, which met with Gordon's approval, and examined the knitted cap. 'Let me guess, this is an XL519, and it's bulletproof.'

'No, it's a woolly hat and it's to keep your head warm. Right, it's time we were off. You take the Fiat, I'll have the Saab. We'll rendezvous back here for stage two, and Cranston.'

'Yes?'

'Do try not to get caught.'

*****

John looked up at the pier, from a distance it wasn't at all daunting, but up close, it was taller than he'd expected. The tide was only about half way in so he could start his climb closer to where he was to place Gordon's device, directly underneath the remains of the Pavilion building.

With the leather palmed ski gloves protecting his hands from the barnacles and other crustaceans that had made a home on the upright pillars, he shinned the first four feet to get a hold on a cross brace. Once he was into the supporting lattice work of the pier, he slowly worked his way along and upwards underneath the deck until around midnight, he was in position. He looked up through a gap in the decking and as Gordon had said, there were people in this abandoned site; he could hear their steps as they went about their secret dealings.

John perched himself on a supporting girder, wrapping his legs around another part of the iron lattice work as he carefully removed the rucksack, passing his arm through the loop so that it was now secured in front of him. He removed the equipment and set it up as instructed, fixing it in place with a Heath Robinson arrangement of bungee straps. Satisfied that it wasn't going to move, he carefully reversed his contortions and made his way back down.

At his first foot hold the rusting metal gave way and landed in the sea while he clung on and swung, trying to get support underneath his legs. Above him the footsteps stopped. Then he heard them moving away from him in the direction of the pier entrance. Abandoning all caution he swung from cross brace to cross brace, slid down one of the cast iron pilings, and landed knee deep in the sea. He waded and ran to the nearest groyne, threw himself over it and kept his head down. He could hear footsteps scrunching on the gravel beach. He poked his head above the wooden barrier. Someone was scanning the pilings with a torch, and then the underneath of the pier. John moved carefully into a position from which he could vault the groyne and intervene if he needed to. He hadn't come this far to be stopped now. The torch beam swept around, John ducked, and then the light was back on the pier. He could feel the tide lapping at his feet as it crept up the shoreline.

The torch wielder, with the sea moving inexorably inwards, wasn't that keen to swim out and check the whole pier. Satisfied that the sound was only part of the derelict structure falling apart, they trudged back up the beach.

John stealthily made his way back to the main promenade and then casually walked back to the Fiat, thankful that his evening's work appeared not to have been discovered.

It was no surprise that the Fiat 500 was known as the 'Bambino', a design that was borne from the desire that every worker in Italy should own a car small enough to buzz freely through the narrow streets of Latin villages. The updated version that John had borrowed retained the charm of the original, including its size. The driving position for someone of his height and shoe size was adequate, but swinging a cat in the rear seat space was out of the question, (a practice never used for testing anyway as the itinerant felines never reported for duty).

He placed the key in the ignition, and then felt a cold circular metal barrel above his left ear. In the rear view mirror was a blue face, less luminous than the last time he'd set eyes on it, but there was no mistaking a physiognomy that could curdle milk at one hundred paces.

'Don't move and put your hands on the steering wheel,' Mr Blue commanded.

John remained motionless.

'I said put your hands on the steering wheel, where I can see them.' Mr Blue was circumspect about Cranston, he'd heard the stories, and he wasn't taking any chances.

'Okay, let's not get too excited, but you did say "don't move", as well. You've got to work on that,' said John as he slowly placed his hands on the wheel. 'To what do I owe this displeasure? It's got to be important; it's past your bedtime. I mean, we all need our beauty sleep, especially you.'

'Shut up and listen. You have until mid-day to bring Midas to this address,' said Mr Blue, placing an envelope on the passenger seat.

'And if I don't?'

'Your parents will have a fatal accident. We wouldn't want that to happen would we?'

It is a truth universally acknowledged that a person in possession of a good conscience will at some time in their life, find that aforesaid inner voice gets in the way. It would have been so easy for John to say 'Yes', and then not bother to turn up, as both his parents had shuffled off the mortal coil years ago, but that meant that either: a) Mr Blue was bluffing, or b) Mr Blue had found the wrong family, in which case innocents would get killed.

'I don't know where you got your info, but they died years ago,' John replied. 'I'd be upset if you dug them up though, it's pretty gross even by your standards, but it's not enough to make me bring you Midas.'

'Don't bother with your lies. For that, I'll add your wife to the list.'

'Good luck with that, I'm divorced, but if you do find her, ask her what she did with my Bowie Pin-ups album. I've got it on CD, but it's not the same.'

'Quiet!' Mr Blue half-cocked the pistol, 'Deliver Midas by mid-day, or we start killing every one that's close to you, one for every hour that you're overdue.'

'Wait, not so fast, the family's not that big. Look, I've got a better idea. Forget the Midas thing, whatever Erikson's paying you, I'll double it.'

'Mid-day Mr Cranston, otherwise people start dying.'

Mr Blue pushed the passenger seat forward, and slowly unfolded himself from the back seat. He threaded one leg out onto the pavement and managed to reverse his torso through the door opening before catching his trailing leg on the sill, landing with an eye wincing thump in the gutter. The 'pumph' of an accidental muffled gunshot passed through the body work of the baby Fiat, the bullet lodging in the rear upholstery. He got up, pretended that he hadn't been kissing a drain cover, and with his best evil look, (to be fair, it was difficult to tell when he wasn't looking evil), fixed John in the eye and lip synched 'Midday' before disappearing into the shadows.

John drove like a man possessed. Of all the hired hands that could have sneaked into the back of the car, it had to be one that wasn't open to a blatant bribe, not that he could have paid, but that was a preferable problem to have. His own safety was within his gift to manage, but innocent people. Erikson had raised the stakes and he had nothing in the bank to call him out with – Gordon was his only option.

His drive back was periodically interrupted as he reluctantly gave way to a seeming fleet of police cars and fire engines, all heading towards the coast. What if Gordon's mission had turned into a full on gun fight? What if he didn't make it? He glanced at the envelope on the passenger seat and then tuned the radio to a twenty four hour rolling news channel.

'...and this just in...' said the announcer.

'No – you've gotta be kidding. I've got enough on my sodding plate as it is!' John shouted at the radio in response to the bulletin, but as the news sunk in, his exasperation slowly dissipated. In this nightmare that kept on giving, everything that happened now was the new normal.

He took a short diversion; he needed some of his own tricks up his sleeve.

*****

Mr Blue was in contemplative mood, why wasn't he feeling more upbeat? Against all the odds he had delivered the message in double quick time. There weren't many people that were willing to take Cranston on, but fortunately there were plenty that would happily give Cranston up for a percentage of the bounty.

Apart from a wobbly dislodged tooth, he thought he had come out of the encounter better than he had expected, but there was something that didn't sit right with him. It was Cranston's reaction to the threat, a perfect text book example that had been tried and tested by the best. It should have got a different result. Was Cranston callous enough to lie about his parentage and sell his own flesh and blood down the river? Even the hardest, most unpredictable of psychotic villainy loved their Mum, those were the rules. Otherwise Alfred Hitchcock would have been down the job centre.

He double checked the report from Profiles 4 U, the go-to, five star rated site on the undernet for extortionists, blackmailers and low level hoodlums. Initially he'd skipped the preliminary pages, after all he knew what John Cranston looked like, and gone straight for the known relatives and associates section.

On page one he now read: `John Cranston, age: older than twenty-one, height: four foot six.`

Four foot six!? Mr Blue felt his get up and go packing its bags and writing a note for the milkman.

His phone pinged. It was a standard message from Profiles 4 U, (as recommended by nine out of ten extortionate professionals). It read:

`Thank you very much for your purchase. We strive to provide every customer better serv-`

ice and product. And this is why we are writing
this e-mail.

Would you like to share your delightful shopping experience with other buyer? We will be
very inspired and appreciated if you could leave
a review with your elaborate details. We think
that it will be good reference to other customer.

Have a nice day and expect your positive
comment!

A link in the message directed him to a page with a rating
system between one and five stars. Modesty prevents Mr
Blue's response from being relayed in full on this page, but it
was one star, and made frequent mention of copulation and low
intelligence.

He pressed Send and felt some small satisfaction as he watched
his comments pop up on the feedback section of Profiles 4 U.

His phone pinged again. It was a message from the Profiles 4
U's Customer Experience team.

You are bang out of order. Do you know how many
John Cranston's there are?

We know where you live.

Frankie ☻

Mr Blue checked the page and saw that his review had been
changed to a maximum five stars with an associated, 'Brilliant,
can't wait to use them again!' Frankie's observation about his
whereabouts could mean only one thing.

He had always seen himself in retirement painting en plein
air in the Dordogne. Now would be a good time for a trial run,
two years should do it he reckoned.

*****

As John drove up to the detached single storey house at the head of its own crescent, the porch security light illuminated the driveway. Leaning casually in the doorway, was Gordon, his face illuminated by the lighting of a Charatan Panatella cigar.

'I see you've been busy,' said Gordon approvingly, pointing at the bullet hole in the Fiat.

'I had a run-in with Erikson's messenger boy. He tripped.'

'Of course he did.'

The look on Gordon's face told John it was pointless trying to explain. 'We've got a problem, Erikson's raised the stakes. I've got until mid-day to hand over Midas, or he starts killing innocent people.'

'How dashed unsporting of him.' Gordon drew on his cigar while he calmly considered the news. 'That still leaves us about ten hours to prevent a probable global disaster. Don't worry about it, it'll be fine. Once we're done, they won't bother, there won't be any point.'

'And what if Midas doesn't work, what then?'

'I find that something usually comes up at the last minute.' Gordon checked his watch. 'I think a quick thirty winks before we move out is called for,' he said as he turned to enter the house.

'Not yet, there's something I need to know,' said John.

'Can't it wait old chap?'

'No. Did I just burn down Hastings Pier?'

'Pardon?'

'Hastings Pier – did I burn it down?'

'Oh that. Yes. That E.M.P thing was actually a small incendiary; it was the only way I could be sure that you'd done the job. It's rather spectacular; I daresay you could see it from France. It flushed 'em out a treat at my end.'

'Lucky France, they get Son et Lumi-bleedin'Pier, and I get done for arson.'

'My dear fellow, don't be so ridiculous. No one will know, unless I tell them. If we're going to save the world, some collateral damage is to be expected, besides, it's not the first time it's been on fire. I've no doubt it'll rise like a phoenix from the ashes, they're very community minded around here you know.' Gordon suppressed a yawn. 'I'm turning in; a half hour's power nap makes all the difference. Tired people make too many mistakes, and we haven't got time for those. I advise you to do the same; it'll be a long hard night.'

Gordon went inside, stretched out in the armchair and was out like a light.

With a cup of strong coffee in hand, John set to work.

*****

Erikson looked dispassionately at the footage of the burning Hastings Pier and noted that communications had abruptly ceased with its sister installation at the Sovereign lighthouse. Cranston had made his move. No more dancing. No more testing each other. His demeanour was one of self-satisfaction. No doubt Cranston was on his way to put an end to the project; after all, he had the perfect tool, Midas. Spurred on by the message, it wouldn't be long now. It was beautiful. Cranston was about to be trapped by his own hand, and all he, Kurt Erikson, had to do was let the game run its course.

He checked his to-do list. Take Midas, feed Cranston to the wolves, destroy the Council and Society, (not necessarily in that order), and become President of the World. Or should it be World President? He was undecided on that one.

Gorringe glided in with a silver tray, holding a cut glass with a dram of whisky.

'Your nightcap Sir. Will there be anything else?'

'Pack my bags and the essentials; I expect to be leaving at short notice.'

'Very well Sir.'

Erikson raised his glass in toast to the sleek integrated computer and screen that had been added to his desk.

'Checkmate, Mr Cranston.'

26 / *'Games? Must We?'*

Ben Kingswood tried to work the handcuffs free, but it was no good. He'd got out of Erikson's prison, and he knew what was in store, but handcuffs, and behind his back as well! It couldn't have been rope or a plastic cable tie, anything that he could have slowly worked on until he could slip free, could it? For good measure, there was a mesh separating him from the two henchmen in the front of the car, and he had already tested the rear doors.

As he hadn't been blindfolded; it was obvious to him that his escorts intended this to be his final journey. On the upside it was two against one, which weren't bad odds, especially considering their attitude towards him, which was one of underestimation.

The car pulled up in a side road. Kingswood tried to work out where he was, they had passed the site of the new stadium complex being built for the twenty-twelve Olympics, crossed the Lea Navigation, and were now in an industrial limbo over-looking the canal where once busy factories awaited their fate as part of the promised regeneration. His pulse raised, if he didn't act soon he'd have engineered his way out only to be buried in a concrete wasteland.

One of the henchmen got out of the car, looked around and then dragged Kingswood from his seat while pressing a gun into his ribs. They moved down onto the towpath.

"ere, keep an eye on 'im for a moment, I've gotta go,' said the first henchman.

'Go where?' said the second.

'You know – *go*,' said the first, not wanting to draw too much attention to his need. 'It's the waterworks, know what I mean?'

'What, drippy tap? And you've got to sort it now?'

'Yeah, the quack said this might happen.'

'Your Doctor does plumbing on the side? 'Ere, do you reckon he could do a bathroom suite? The missus is giving me some grief and trying to find a tradesman these days is a bleedin' nightmare.'

'No, it's *my* plumbing. I had one of those digital examinations didn't I?'

'Digital - riiight, it's bloody marvellous what they can do on the internet these days.'

'Not that sort of digital, you berk, it's the sort where he has a poke around, down below, know what I mean?'

'I'm with you now, like with one of those drone thingies, with the cameras and stuff? I didn't think they could make them that small, that's amazing that is. It's like that film with Raquel Welch; you know the one when she's got a wetsuit on and she's in that guy's brain.'

'No it's not like the film and I haven't had Raquel Welch, or anyone else in a rubber suit, flying around up my back passage. It's digital, like in the Latin digitus, for finger or toe.'

'Oh I see, well that's the NHS for you isn't it. Don't get me wrong, I'm not knocking it, but calling it digital's a bit of a stretch. ain't it. Just 'cause its Latin don't mean you can take liberties with trade descriptions and all that. If that's the case, now I know where he's foot's been, the bathroom can wait.'

'Just watch him will ya!' said the first henchman as he turned and walked off with some urgency, looking for a suitable bush behind which to relieve himself.

'What are you grinning at?' said the other to Kingswood.

'Me?' said Kingswood innocently. 'Nothing, it's my natural disposition. My Mum always said I had a smiley face.'

'You won't be smiling after we've dumped you over there.'

Kingswood looked down the towpath at the concrete carcass that had been Lesney Industries Limited. He's final resting ground was going to be shared with the memories of thousands of Matchbox toy cars.

'Could you do me a favour?' asked Kingswood.

'No.'

'Don't be like that. I'm entitled to a last request, man about to die and all that. I don't want much.'

'What is it then?' said the henchman reluctantly.

'It's all that talk of waterworks; I'm dying for a pee. Could you take the cuffs off, just for a minute?'

'No chance.'

'I'll make it worth your while, there's fifty quid in my back pocket. Come on, it's got be worth fifty.'

'Fifty quid?' He went behind Kingswood, wedging his hand into the tight denim pocket, searching for the cash, with no intention of undoing the handcuffs.

Kingswood looked down and whipped his head back onto the henchman's brow with a resounding 'thwack'. Hooking his foot behind his captor's leg he unbalanced him and as he fell to the ground he simultaneously stamped on his wrist so that he dropped the pistol. Finally, an expertly placed kick with the requisite amount of force ensured that the enemy was out for the count. Kingswood sat on his haunches, rolled back, and passed his handcuffed hands under his feet so that they were now in front of him. He rifled the pockets of the dormant heavy, transferred the cuffs, and threw the keys into the canal.

To the layman it could have been mistaken for a car backfiring, but then the sound of an angry hornet passed Kingswood's ear in a fraction of a second. The gun was out of reach.

There was no time. He ran.

*****

Kingswood looked around the capacious industrial studio flat that used to be a warehouse serving what were the Wapping docks. The light that came in through the large expanses of glass, cathedral like, emphasised the lustre and patina of the sanded, polished, floorboards. The bare brick work was adorned with an eclectic range of artworks. They couldn't be originals surely?

The Detective Inspector directed him to large plush sofa that could easily accommodate four or five people, assuring him that he would be safe here as no-one knew that he owned the property. He reminded the sergeant that he wanted to keep it that way.

'Nice place you got here, I never knew coppers were paid so much,' said Kingswood.

Sutherland bit his bottom lip. He was damned if he was going to justify this to anyone, especially a spreadsheet jockey. 'If you're thinking what I think you're thinking Mr Kingswood, here's some friendly advice. Don't. Now if you'll take a seat please, I've got some questions I want answers to.'

Kingswood sat down, for the moment it was better to be with a policeman who, if he gave him the benefit of the doubt, was only guilty of holding down more than one job, rather than the one at the hospital who had wanted him dead.

'Beer?' asked Sutherland, reverting to his more amiable self; satisfied that he had set the rules of engagement.

'No thanks,' replied Kingswood, 'antibiotics. Wouldn't say no to a coffee though, if you've got one?'

'Coffee,' said Sutherland, making a mental tally. 'Sergeant-beer? Sergeant? Where's he got to?'

Sergeant Bludgeon sprang from the kitchen with an uncustomary look of determination, stainless steel spatula in hand. 'Mr Kingswood, stay behind me.' Holding the spatula in front of him, ready to strike, he returned his attention to Sutherland. 'What have you done with him?'

'Who?' Sutherland replied.

'You know who,' said Bludgeon. 'Detective Inspector Sutherland.'

Sutherland sighed. 'Sergeant, it's me. Now stop waving that thing around before someone gets hurt,' and he reached out his hand.

Bludgeon brought the metal utensil down on Sutherland's knuckle with a crack.

'Owwww! Bloody hell. What are you playing at?!'

'You can give up acting the innocent. I know who you are - MR BLACK,' declared Bludgeon. Mr Kingswood is right. There's no way that a policeman could afford all this, and I happen to know that the real Detective Inspector Sutherland lives in South Norwood, and this isn't South Norwood.' Bludgeon was warming up now into his best Poirot mode. 'You caught him, tortured him to get the location of our meet-up, and then brought us back here assuming that we wouldn't see through your disguise. Well the shoe's on the other leg now isn't it? Mr Kingswood, could you find me some rope or handcuffs please.'

'I'll try the bedroom,' replied Kingswood, who up until six months ago would have walked out on this pantomime, but that was before kidnapping accountants had become a 'thing'.

'Hold on, hold on,' said Sutherland. 'Look, we haven't got all day.' The explanation would be reluctant. 'I bought this donkey's years ago when it was a rat infested pit and you couldn't give it away. All the villains were buying up gaffes and I couldn't work out why. Then I twigged, it was all long term planning. They're not making any more land in London are they? You're standing in my pension. I kept it quiet as I didn't want people thinking I was on the take and for the record this,' and he looked around the room, 'is about three years of beans on toast and bloody hard graft.'

'What about the art?' Kingswood asked, pointing at what looked to him like a messy decorator's cover sheet, but as it was framed, he assumed it was some sort of abstract, especially as it had a title of 'Luminous Thingy Number One'.

'Yes, what about the art?' parroted Bludgeon, wanting to make sure that his moment wasn't going to be stolen.

'A mate of mine worked at Goldsmiths for a bit,' said Sutherland. 'I got lucky and some of the stuff I bought went ballistic. With the money from that I've been buying and selling ever since, some I win, some I lose. Now, can we get back to normal before I do something I won't regret?'

Bludgeon considered the evidence and looked across to Kingswood.

'I'm an accountant, not an art historian, but if you want my opinion, it sounds plausible to me.'

'Exactly' said Bludgeon sagely. 'It's the kind of detail I would expect from a master of disguise.'

'Oh for crying out loud. Sergeant, in all my years on the force, never have I come across such a mind boggling fantastical load of tosh. You know what? I doubt that even all the combined minds in the world's premier insane asylum could come up with something like this. I'm bleedin' staggered, I really am. I'm lost for words…'

Sergeant Bludgeon lowered the spatula, and whispered in Ben's ear. 'We won't need the handcuffs.' He faced Sutherland; his mien having given way to its default look of general content-ment. 'Thank you Sir, you're too kind, and if it's not too much trouble, coffee would be nice. I can't drink while I'm on duty, it affects my performance.'

With coffee served, and a bottle of Bludgeon Juice to hand, Sutherland took a small notepad from his inside jacket pocket and proceeded with the interview. Ben Kingswood told him everything that he knew, playing down certain details around his final escape where necessary; after all, he was only an accountant. Sutherland listened diligently, exploring small details as he went along. Sergeant Bludgeon sat alongside his superior, occasionally remarking 'Yes!' before being put in his place with a dirty look.

'…and the next thing I know, I'm in hospital with a bullet wound.'

'That's a very interesting story Mr Kingswood. If you don't mind; there are a few things I'd like to go over again, to make sure that I've understood everything. You say that the person responsible for your abduction was,' Sutherland checked his notes, 'Kurt Erikson. Now, stop me if I'm wrong, is this the same Kurt Erikson who owns one of the biggest software companies in the world, along with, I don't know, most of the mobile phones? I'm guessing he's probably one of the richest men in the world.'

'That's him,' Kingswood confirmed.

'I knew it!' exclaimed Bludgeon, 'it's our criminal mastermind – he'd have everything he needs to implement an evil master plan. I bet even that…' He stopped mid-sentence as Sutherland nudged him in the ribs.

Sutherland continued his line of enquiry. 'And he's abducting accountants through a fake recruiting website, and you all happily agree to be bussed out to some manor house,' he checked his notes again, 'the "Oaks", somewhere in Sussex.'

'That's right, they do initial interview days to short-list their victims. They're more interested in people who haven't got family commitments; they're easier to explain away. Then we all get invited to this follow-up job fair, we're not going to turn down free booze are we? The next thing you know we're divvied up and bundled off in blacked out coaches to who knows where.'

'So you say,' replied Sutherland, 'but how can you be sure it's Erikson? A man of his means hardly needs to raise cash by trafficking accountants, does he?'

'It's definitely him, I met him enough times. He's very hands on.'

'I see. Now, the London office where you had this interview, where was it exactly?'

'I can't remember the address off the top of my head, but it was near the Elephant and Castle.'

Bludgeon, on the edge of the seat, collapsed back in disappointment.

'Elephant and Castle,' Sutherland reiterated as he added an update to his notes, 'and your fellow prisoners were all interviewed there as well?'

'No, some of them were off Liverpool Street and others were in that new skyscraper at the end of London Bridge – the Imperial something.'

Bludgeon creeped forward again, his concentration intense, as, much to the annoyance of D.I. Sutherland, he noisily rustled a foil packet without looking as he passed potato crisps to his mouth.

'And you say they'll be more of these recruitment' fairs?' Sutherland asked.

'Definitely, they're regular as clockwork once you know where to look.'

'The person who did the interview – what was his name?' enquired Sutherland, gradually homing in. He was certain where this was going to end up, the circumstantial evidence was screaming at him, but he needed to follow through, he had to hear it from the witness.

'Mr Cooke.'

Bludgeon crumpled back into the chair with an audible groan that could best be described as the noise an England football supporter makes when the national squad loses on penalties.

'Could you describe this Mr Cooke?' Sutherland probed.

'Average, I suppose, dark hair - side parting, suited.' Kingswood pondered for a few seconds, 'He was very well spoken, and I don't think he was short of a few bob if that helps?'

Bludgeon could contain himself no longer. 'Did he look like James Mason?'

'Who?' Kingswood replied.

'James Mason. From North by Northwest.'

Kingswood shrugged his shoulders. 'Sorry, I don't know who you're on about.'

Bludgeon was crestfallen. 'Sir, it's got to be...'

'You know what sergeant; you've given me an idea.'

'I have?'

'He has?'

Sutherland put on his overcoat. 'I'm nipping out for half hour or so. Don't go away.'

He returned, an hour later, holding a DVD, like a latter-day Neville Chamberlin. 'I think it's time for an identity parade,' he announced as he pressed the play button.

*****

North by Northwest
Cary Grant - Roger Thornhill
James Mason - Phillip Vandamm

The story so far: Roger Thornhill is in an impromptu informal business meeting in a hotel. He is interrupted by a bell boy who advises him that there are two gentlemen that want to see him. Roger Thornhill goes to see who they are and one of them tells him that they are 'two errand boys carrying concealed weapons'.

Thornhill is abducted and driven to a country estate where he is left in a large lounge and told to wait. He checks the windows and see's the guards outside, there's no escape. He curiously picks up a package from a desk and notes the addressee, Mr Townsend.

Phillip Vandamm enters the room and he and Roger Thornhill circle around the desk as Vandamm moves to the window and draws the curtains, his face slightly in shadow.

Vandamm looks Thornhill up and down and observes that he isn't what he expected, a little taller, a little bit more polished than the *others.*

Thornhill takes the initiative in the verbal joust, referring to Vandamm as 'Mr Townsend'.

Vandamm patronisingly dismisses Thonhill's gambit as 'obvious'.

As Thornhill protests and demands to know why he has been abducted, Vandamm casually moves across the room, turns on a second lamp, and replies, 'Games? Must we?'

*****

'That's him,' said Kingswood with total certainty, pointing at the James Mason character.

Sutherland paused the DVD. 'You sure?'

'Absolutely – he's a dead ringer,' and for the avoidance of doubt, he placed his finger on the screen

At that exact moment Detective Inspector Sutherland and Sergeant Bludgeon were on the same wavelength, an event, which like Halley's Comet, would never happen again in their lifetimes. As their eyes locked a single thought was uppermost in both their minds – Mr Black.

*****

It was an unusually pleasant day, temperate air had decided to hang around the south east of England. Sutherland enjoyed the low warm sun on his cheeks as he looked across the River Thames with London Bridge to his left and the Cannon Street rail bridge to his right. The daily migration of commuters moved across the water en masse, he didn't envy them.

In his peripheral vision he counted at least four plain clothes goons, split equally, on the corners of Angel and Swan lanes. It was the mirrored sunglasses that did it. He didn't know why they didn't just look through a magazine with eyeholes cut in and have done with it.

She was on her way.

A tall elegant woman in a bright red overcoat, matching leather gloves and a fine generous cashmere scarf sat on the seat, slightly greater than arms-length away from him. She placed a newspaper on the bench in the space between them.

He looked across in that casual non-committal way that you do when you're curious about a stranger, but don't want to stare. She had weathered the years better than he had. Her hair was in an elfin cut, interspersed with bands of silver. Her profile was as he remembered it, defined cheek bones, now with fine lines around her eyes adding character and contributing to her natural beauty.

'Morning Kate, long time no see.'

Her steel blue eyes stopped him in his reminiscent tracks. 'Ms Cooden if you don't mind.'

She looked straight ahead. This wasn't going to be a conversation of pleasantries and definitely not one where casual passers-by could mistake them for a couple.

'Fair enough,' replied Sutherland, not taking the least offence. At least she was talking to him.

'I've reviewed the file,' she said. 'What do you want?'

'There's a delivery tomorrow night, a shipment of accountants at a place in Sussex. Something big's going down, people trafficking, bent coppers, big business corruption, the works, and you could catch them at it red-handed. I thought you might be interested.'

'And you're telling me all this out of the kindness of your heart.'

'I need some strings pulling to help me sort out my sergeant– I promised him a promotion, and if anyone's got him on a list, I want him off it.'

'Is that all?'

'I'm coming along for the ride of course.'

She let out a breath through pursed lips, the same sort of exhalation beloved of plumbers when they tell you that a component for a two year old boiler isn't available anymore as the only factory where the parts were made has been struck by a random meteor.

'The problem is you're not really in a position to be making deals. I had your information checked. It's off.'

'What do you mean – "off"?'

'Major General Vladimir Orimov was killed in a fire fight with Jack Armstrong, a notorious London Gangster...'

'I know who he was.'

'...at a disused gas storage facility in Beckton.'

'No, that can't be right, I was there.'

'What?' Her façade dropped. 'You never said anything.'

'You're not the only one who can keep secrets.'

He stopped himself. That was past and there was nothing to be gained by raking over cold embers. He changed tack.

'Me and the lads had been trying to sort Jack out for months, but he was always one step ahead. We reckoned we had a grass on the force, but couldn't work out who it was. Anyway, we got a tip off that Jack was looking to set up a press. Word was he'd got fed up nicking money so he thought he'd have a go at making his own. I got a small crew together, on the quiet like, but when we got there we were ambushed by that bloody SPUD gang who were looking to nick the plates. Next thing I know all Hell's broken loose. We ended up joining forces with Jack's lot and managed to send the SPUD's packing, but he did a runner before we could get hold of him. There were a few wounded, but no-one got killed. I'm bloody sure though that Willingdon grassed us up. I couldn't pin it on him then, but I've seen him since with Orimov. Willingdon's bent as a nine bob note and Orimov is alive and kicking. Come on, you can't pass this up; I'm giving it to you on a plate.'

She noticed a small bright glint among the crowds on London Bridge. It was probably nothing, sunlight reflecting of a mobile phone or wrist watch, but there it was again. She regained her poker face.

'Good day Detective Inspector. Don't call my office again.'

Before Sutherland could even make a token protest, she was half-way to Swan lane where a Mercedes civilian armoured car was waiting.

'Bye then,' he said as she was driven off.

He shrugged; it had been a longshot anyway. He casually picked up the newspaper she had left and checked the back page. There was an un-started crossword that would keep him company over a pint while he figured out his next move.

A buff envelope fell onto the floor. It was addressed to him.

27 / *The Tarnished Five*

Sutherland stood outside the address in Little Britain; the building looked as if it had been squeezed between two other tenements. Its tall disproportionate door was topped off by a glazed arch which in turn was surrounded by a narrow stone frame and worn steps.

He looked up and down the street, there was no-one in sight, and entered the code on the ancient keypad. With a slight budge the door gave way. As he crossed the threshold it swung close behind him and he noticed there was no handle on the inside; it was a one way entrance. A short hallway, lit only from the natural illumination that found its way through the entrance skylight, dimly showed up a steep flight of uncarpeted stairs. A stealthy approach was impossible as each stair creaked and groaned, almost in anticipation of his next step.

At the first floor he tentatively opened a door that led, he guessed, to what would have been a main office. The room was bare save for some old filing cabinets and utility furniture that wouldn't look out of place on Noah's Ark. Nicotine stained net curtains hung from the generous windows, adding a warm cast to the incoming sunlight.

Kate Cooden entered the room. 'Hello Harry, I see you found it alright. Were you followed?'

'Give me some credit.' He looked around, made suspicious by the use of his first name and the absence of any government sponsored muscle. 'No Doom Patrol?'

'I only have them for official meetings, and as we're not

having this meeting.' She smiled reassuringly, 'Don't worry, I won't try anything.'

'What's with all the Secret Squirrel? I thought you weren't interested, what with the way you shoved off.'

'Things are a bit leaky at the moment; we were being spied on from the bridge, I'm surprised you didn't notice. There's a new intake of Russian double agents and until I've worked out what misinformation to feed them, they tend to go a bit off piste,' she held up the file that Sutherland had sent to her, 'and this isn't for them. Has anyone else seen this, or know what you've been up to?'

'Just me and Sergeant Bludgeon, but Willingdon's got my card marked.'

'What about the accountant?'

'I've got him in a safe house.'

'It's not that sin palace in Wapping is it?'

'I don't know what you're on about.'

'It is then. Good, keep it that way.'

Sutherland was temporarily uneasy. This wasn't how things were supposed to go.

'Please,' she reproached. 'You look like someone's peed on your chips. Don't worry; I don't want any of it, your secrets safe with me.'

He nodded in acknowledgement. There was no point asking how she knew, she traded in the hidden and the unrevealed, that's why he was asking for her help.

'So you're up for it then?'

'Officially I'm not going to commit resources on a raid of what could be a corporate hospitality event, based on what will be called a faked photo and the say so of a Detective Inspector, who's CV is starting to read like the manager of a lost property office.'

'What about unofficially?'

'If for the sake of argument a team of commando's, who coincidentally might be on a training exercise in that part of Sussex, were to be made aware of an incident at a certain manor house that could threaten national security, by, I don't know, a certain officer of the law, that could work.'

'No problem then, I stroll in there on my tod, and if it turns out I'm right, in come the cavalry and you get all the credit. If I'm wrong, you deny everything.'

'Maybe,' she said coyly. 'I don't know - there's no pleasing some people. You said you wanted to tag along, and you are, just ahead of everyone else. Honestly, I thought you'd be happy.'

'Delirious, I can't find the words to express my shallow joy,' replied Sutherland, making no attempt to hide his sarcastic tone. 'You're not exactly selling it. What's in it for me?'

'I'll keep you and that sergeant of yours out of prison, how's that sound?'

'Nice try, but you haven't got anything on me that'll stick. Nothing's going to come of that business at the London, Willingdon's not going to risk showing his hand.'

She looked at him with incredulity. 'Call yourself a Detective? That little diversion at the London Hospital is the least of your worries. From where I'm standing the merde hit the fan and you didn't even duck. For starters your sergeant's been looking where he shouldn't have been for your Mr Black.'

'I got him to rattle the cage a bit, so what?'

She went to a filing cabinet, removed a half-full bottle of Johnnie Walker Blue Label from the bottom drawer and poured out two measures. 'He didn't rattle it; he walked in and had a good rummage. He's gone through the top level security systems of every major intelligence agency as if he was looking up a train timetable.'

'Sergeant Bludgeon – my Sergeant Bludgeon?'

'He's a natural. Our people can't stop him.'

Sutherland nodded in seeming approval. Whatever cards she had she was overplaying her hand. 'That's a turn up for the books, but what's it got to do with the price of fish?'

'The Home Secretary wants him thrown in the Tower for treason,' she said casually, 'the Americans want to extradite him, and the Russians want to recruit him. And as he works for you...I think you get the idea.'

'Ah...' Sutherland chewed it over, he hadn't seen that coming. It seemed that Bludgeon's new 'friend', Deep Thrombosis, had stitched them both up, good and proper. 'You know what, how about I go and have a shufti at that gaffe.'

'You do that, and if you find anything...'

'You'll be the first to know, but one thing though; the deal with my sergeant, that's still on the cards?'

She moved one of the yellowing net curtains aside; she was still in the clear. 'Do you ever get those mornings when you wake up, look at the bedroom wall, and think something's missing from the décor?'

'Depends on whose bedroom it is,' replied Sutherland with a slight inkling where this was going.

'Something that would look good in a frame, ooh I don't know, kind of Hockney sized?'

'Pollock.'

'Vetriano.'

'Bludgeon's off the list and it's a proper promotion, not head of stolen wheel nuts or anything crap.'

She raised her glass. 'I think we can drink to that.' The glasses chinked. 'And while we're at it, here's to our tenth.'

'Our what?'

She rolled her eyes in faux despair. 'It's been ten years since the divorce; they've been great by the way.'

'Thanks, nice to know I did something right.'

She nodded as she took a final draft of the whisky and put a card on the desk. 'Leave the back way. I'll wait for your call.'

Sutherland headed towards the door and as he was leaving she called out. 'Don't forget, we haven't had this meeting.'

'I know. If anyone finds out, you'll have to shoot me.'

'Don't be silly, I'll get a man in for that.'

Harry Sutherland never understood the attraction of golf. To his mind, if you had to hit a ball that small, it would make sense to use something bigger than a skinny pole with a head no larger than a tablespoon. Was it something genetic? Did you get to a certain age and then wake up one morning with a desire to wear luminous pink trousers and traipse around a scalped lawn with an occasional hole in it? He was with Mark Twain on this one, it was a good walk spoiled.

He crossed the threshold of the golf club with the same level of bemusement he had that day when he attended an interview to apply for his own job, and then told the Human Resource's wonk that he didn't actually want it. It was a cruel trick; reading upside down was so easy and he could see there was no tick box for that answer. It was a terrible sight watching a grown man mentally collapse as a total absence of initiative collided with a lack of procedure.

After several false starts, he found out where Andy was from the barman. If ever you were on a quiz show and wanted to ring a friend, you could do a lot worse than choose someone who served alcohol for a living. Over time, whether they liked it or not, they would accumulate a wealth of information of variable usefulness, purely by a kind of social osmosis.

He strode out onto the golf course taking a short-cut across the green to the twelfth hole, much to the annoyance of some players who made their feelings known in no uncertain terms. Sutherland responded silently in kind with a single finger. He saw his old partner swinging a club at a plastic tee, but there wasn't a ball. Maybe he'd lost them all. Who could tell what archaic ritual was underway.

'Afternoon Andy, how's it going?'

Andy looked round. 'Bleedin' 'ell. Hello stranger!' He dropped the club and shook Sutherland's hand in a firm friendly grip. 'This is a bloody turn-up, Harry Sutherland on the green. What brings you here, contraband golf balls?'

'If it was that serious I'd be here with a full Monty armed response unit, wouldn't I? No, I was in the area so I thought I'd pop in on the off-chance, you know, to catch up.'

'Yeah, right. Come on, what do you want?'

That was why Sutherland and Andy got on so well, neither of them were fans of dancing around what was to be said.

Sutherland looked over both shoulders. 'We safe?'

Andy nodded. 'No-one's going to hear anything out here. I'll play this hole as normal, you tell me what's going on, and then I tell you I'm not interested.' He went back to his practice swing.

'I've got an urgent job on,' said Sutherland. 'I need to get the Beckton crew back together.'

'The crew?' Andy shook his head. 'I didn't think you did that baseball stuff anymore. I tell you what; I'll let you into a little secret. You see this,' and he held up the club, 'that's what retirement looks like. You should give it a go, retirement I mean, not golf.' He placed a ball on the tee and started to line up for the stroke.

'Too retired to get one over on Willingdon?' queried Sutherland as Andy started his swing.

The Titleist Pro V1 left the tee at speed, arcing high into the sky before landing with a 'plop' into an artistically landscaped lake where it narrowly missed braining a carp called Brian.

*****

Sutherland waited on the platform watching the mice scurry among the rails as they avoided the deadly part of the line. Travelling outside of rush-hour on the London underground wasn't a bad way to get around; he rarely used his own car in the capital. A rush of air from the tunnel heralded the arrival of the next train.

Taking his seat on the carriage, he reviewed the day's work so far, and overall, it wasn't bad. Andy, despite his initial reticence had come round once Willingdon was in the frame. One thing he could rely on was a guaranteed animosity towards the Chief Superintendent. Willingdon had crossed the line when he'd put lives at risk at Beckton. While no-one could prove it, and it remained unsaid in public, Beckton-Gate was unforgiveable within the informal brotherhood.

Andy was in regular contact with Screwfix and Fitnote, the former so called because he always had the right tool for the job, and the latter as he was renowned for his presenteeism and a washboard stomach made of iron. Andy was confident that they'd join up. They were four then, not a bad number. He wondered if he should recruit Sergeant Bludgeon to the foray. An extra pair of hands would be welcome, and he had been impressed, and surprised, by the sergeant's human daisy chain opposite the London Hospital. He thought better of it. Bludgeon's time would be better spent keeping an eye on Kingswood. If things went pear shaped he might need his only witness.

He left Old Street station and looked at the ever rising glass skyline. He never thought he'd see the day when Shoreditch would be the place to go for a trendy night out. It went to show how out of touch he was with popular culture, but he didn't care about that, it was the criminal underworld that he knew intimately, and no matter what mask it wore, he would always recognise it. As if to prove his point, there in front of him writ large on a retro chic, tatty, part illuminated neon sign was 'Old Street Grounds'. On the face of it, a respectable, on trend, coffee shop. Perfect, his information was spot on.

The décor was of a job half finished. The walls were painted with a semi-opaque off white paint; second coats were so twentieth century. The lighting was a mash-up of old film set studio lights fitted with large folding shutters and blinds, dividing the light of modern energy efficient bulbs so that they shone as if through windows with venetian blinds. The bar was pristine with a highly polished brass foot rail, with a twin protruding from top of the counter as an armrest.

A jazz trumpet solo was being piped from hidden speakers. Notes that didn't seem to relate to each other wandered around a pentatonic scale, accompanied by a drummer tapping out a variation on a triplet beat which could only indicate he had left his rhythm at home, or was having a fit. There was a tune in there somewhere.

Swivelling barstools were fixed to the floor, which Sutherland did approve of. There was an air of edginess, but as he looked around and checked out the clientele, all their eyes were directed downwards to handheld screens. Apparently they were what Hipsters looked like? He had to admit they were smart, with crisp tailor cut shirts, ties, and the odd pork pie hat. Piercing's, some enlarged to make large perforated earlobes, tattoos the length of an arm, and luxuriant beards, were obviously the mark of that tribe.

A young man in dark glasses and apron approached him from the other side of the bar.

'What can I get you?'

'Coffee,' replied Sutherland.

'Expresso, Double Expresso, Ristretto, Short Macchiato, Long Macchiato, Cappucino, Affogato, Mocha, Café Latte, Piccolo Latte, Flat White, or Americano?'

Sutherland was unimpressed. 'Nescafe.'

'Nescafe,' replied the barista, hiding his disappointment that his skills had been reduced to a spoonful of granules and hot water. 'What name should I put on the cup?' he asked, immediately regretting it as the scowl on his customers face said 'Really?', but with more emphasis on direct language.

'Detective Inspector Sutherland. I'm looking for the Turk.'

The music stopped.

The barista was trying his best to look as if nothing had happened; he wasn't very good at it. Sutherland watched as the barista slightly lifted his head and looked past him into the coffee shop. The average person wouldn't have noticed, but Sutherland had spent a large part of his career being bushwhacked by the best. By comparison, this lot were rank amateurs.

He ducked as a muscular arm with a tattoo down to the wrist swung past his head. His would be assailant had overreached, and it was no effort at all for Sutherland to encourage the momentum of his attacker by tugging on their beard so that the bridge of their nose struck the bar rest. It wasn't enough to cause any lasting harm, but the shock of pain gave him the advantage. He grabbed the attacker's silk tie and passed it around the polished rail. As they tried to raise themselves to their full height, Sutherland tugged hard on the wide woven garment, the makeshift pulley accelerating the head of the ambush hipster back down so that it hit the brass tube with a 'bong' that would have put Big Ben to shame. Sutherland then threaded the tie through a convenient enlarged hole in his attacker's ear-lobe and tied it off with his own variation on the Gordian knot. Taking a serviette from the bar, at fingertips, he picked up a freshly dislodged tooth.

'You might want to put that in some milk,' Sutherland advised the barista.

Around the bar customers glared at him, each looking as if they were ready to tear him limb from limb. This was normally the bit where he reassured the general public with a classic 'Nothing to see here, move on' line, but these weren't the general public. They weren't sure about him, but all it needed was for one to break ranks and all would follow. He made eye-contact with the Alpha-male.

'You, where's the Turk?' Sutherland ordered.

'It's time you were going,' replied Alpha-male, rolling up the sleeves on his expensive tailored fit shirt, obviously intent on removing Sutherland by force.

Sutherland smiled. He turned slightly to the bar. 'Got my coffee yet?'

The barista nodded and passed it over; there was nothing to be gained from upsetting this lot.

'Here's what I'll do,' said Sutherland. 'You've got as long as it takes for me to drink this, to tell me where the Turk is.'

'Or you'll what?' said Alpha-male.

Sutherland didn't reply, sipping his coffee as if he didn't have a care in the world.

Alpha-male, aware that by not following through it could be construed as cowardice, made his move and lunged, only to find that his target had swivelled on the stool and was standing to one side. There was a hot sensation spreading across his chest and he looked down to see a tan stain covering his shirt front. 'My Armani! Do you know how much these are?'

Sutherland's body language indicated that Alpha-male had obviously mistaken him for someone that cared.

Alpha-male charged, only to collapse on the floor with his eyes trying to escape from his face, as with exquisite timing and perfect accuracy his nether regions were introduced to a size ten.

Sutherland finished the remains of his coffee. 'Anyone remember where the Turk is yet?'

One by one, everyone pointed to behind the bar.

'Hello Terence, been a while,' said Sutherland.

Terry the Turk wasn't a tall man, but he carried himself as if he were a giant in Lilliput, there was no doubt that this establishment was his domain.

The Turk removed a stiletto flick knife and sliced through the tie of the now despairing attacker, (whose face had been moulding itself to the bar), and slapped his shaven pate, adding an admonishment of 'Nipple head!' He then turned his attention to Alpha-male, (who had managed to progress from a foetal position to a standing crouch), shoved his foot in his rear and encouraged him towards a seat at the back of the coffee shop. With a look at the barista, the music was restored and everything was as it was, minus two injured bruisers.

The Turk put the knife back into his inside jacket pocket. 'Sorry about that Mr Sutherland, they're suffering from anger management issues.'

'Is that what they're calling it these days?'

'Yeah, whenever they see a copper, they get angry. Course, if you'd called ahead.'

'You wouldn't have been here. Now, me and you are going to have a word.'

The Turk's office was on the first floor, a bank of monitors hung from the walls showing everything that was going on downstairs. The Turk relaxed back into a plush leather chair behind a desk polished to a mirror finish. He was every inch the Chief Executive Officer of this little piece of England. He had come a long way from the disparate rented council garages which contained everything, except cars.

Sutherland walked around noting the opulence and size of the room. The Turk was obviously someone who liked his creature comforts, so why wasn't the office bigger?

'What can I do for you Mr Sutherland?'

'Nothing much, just an urgent message for Milligan.'

'I don't do that sort of stuff anymore; I'm a legitimate business man now. Why don't you get in touch with him yourself?'

Sutherland was idly opening the drawers of the filing cabinets while the Turk was making his excuses. He grinned as he came across, and removed an intravenous catheter.

'You and I both know that unless I arrest him, Milligan won't talk to me, rules are rules. That's why God put people like you on the Earth. You're going to get a message to him, *tonight.*'

'No way am I ringing him now. He'll be having a kip, and he don't like being disturbed.'

'Yeah, I've heard he's quite partial to his eight hours. I've also heard that Hammer Harris won't take kindly to someone running a caffeine den on his manor without him knowing.'

'I don't know what you mean.'

'Terence, this is me you're talking to,' said Sutherland as he dangled the catheter.

'Emergency first aid,' replied the Turk, deadpan.

'Toilets through here?' asked Sutherland innocently as he put his shoulder to an adjoining door in the Turk's office. 'Oh. What a surprise.'

Sutherland looked around a room that took up the rest of the floor plan of the upper level. It was dimly lit, and on a series of bunk beds people were hooked up to suspended bags via transparent tubes as they postponed the withdrawal symptoms of caffeine addiction, their headaches and tremors only kept at bay, but not alleviated, by the measured dripped infusion.

The Turk ushered Sutherland to one side and closed the door. 'Okay, okay, you win. What's the message?'

'I've got a friend of mine looking for a property in London, something with about five bedrooms, all mod-cons. He wants to do a viewing. Remind Mr Milligan this'll make us even.' Sutherland put a card on the Turk's desk. 'Text me the address

first thing tomorrow, wouldn't want the Hammer getting upset
would we?'

*****

It had been a long day, but there was one last thing to do before
he turned in, and that was to check on Bludgeon and Kingswood. As he opened the front door to the Wapping safe-house
he could hear what sounded like an intermittent muffled pneumatic drill interspersed with a whistling kettle. Looking across
the open plan accommodation, he could see Sergeant Bludgeon
on the settee, deep under the spell of Somnus. Scattered around
the floor were opened shallow clamshell boxes containing the
remains of pizza. On the television reruns of the 'Sweeney'
were being broadcast back to back, with the distinctive barks of
'Guv'nor!', reverberating around the room. It looked like they'd
had a fine time in his absence.

Sutherland kicked the footstall away and Bludgeon's stock-
inged feet fell to the floor, waking him with a start. Quickly
brought back to reality by the seeming overbearing presence of
his superior officer, Bludgeon reached round, finding the spatula
he had hidden under a cushion, and retreated along the settee.

'Stay back!' shouted Bludgeon, 'I'm not afraid to use this you
know.'

'*Not now* sergeant,' said Sutherland, exasperated that Bludgeon, even in a half-wakened state, still wasn't sure it was him,
so convinced was he that the Masters of Disguise were rampant.

'What's the password?!' barked Bludgeon.

'We haven't got a password.'

Bludgeon considered the reply for a moment, and then put the
spatula down. 'It's good to see you Sir, you can't be too careful
you know.'

'We're not going through this every time one of us walks
through the front door?'

'Only unless you order me not to Sir, but I thought that while
we have our guest, we should be extra vigilant. It's all very clever
you see,' explained Bludgeon proudly. 'If either us are caught
and tortured for a password, rather than having the pressure
of trying to keep it secret, we can tell them anything we like.

Then, if anyone uses the password that they've been told, the other knows it can't be right because the absence of a password *is the password*, and,' added Bludgeon triumphantly, 'no one can crack a password that doesn't exist.'

Sutherland's brain stumbled, as if it had slipped on a banana skin, managed to stop itself from falling head over tail, and regained its balance. There was a perverse, albeit flawed logic to Bludgeon's reasoning, and Sutherland was minded to point this out, but decided it would be easier to move on.

Somewhere in his frontal lobe, the neurological equivalent of the fire brigade removed their helmets and breathed a virtual sigh of relief. There was a brief flickering of electrical activity as the message, 'Okay lads, stand down,' instantaneously traversed his amygdala.

'Fair enough, where's Kingswood?' said Sutherland, changing the subject quickly, to distance himself from the potential mental mire. 'You didn't let him pop out for a pint of milk?' he asked half-jokingly, but in his heart of hearts he offered a little prayer of 'Please don't let him say "Yes"'.

'No need to worry Sir, I'm up to date on all those little tricks. I checked your fridge and you've got half a pint of semi-skimmed. He's leg was hurting so I said he could sleep in your room, I didn't think you'd mind, and,' Bludgeon touched the side of his nose, 'I locked him in.'

'Well done sergeant. Now clear up this mess and get yourself home, I'll take over. I want you here early tomorrow, I'll need to go out and collect some gear.'

'Thank you Sir,' said Bludgeon, not sure what was going on. Whenever they discussed something important, Detective Inspector Sutherland normally spoke in an impatient tone, sometimes with his head in his hands, but as he had correctly answered the non-password challenge, it must be him. The D.I was probably tired, it had been hectic recently. Not to worry, if Mr Black wanted a piece of his Guv'nor while he was off the boil, he would have to go through him first.

Sutherland went to check on Kingswood. The gunshot wound was superficial, but it was best to be sure that there were no complications. The last thing he needed on his hands was a septicaemic bean counter.

He put the key into the lock and noticed that the mortice didn't throw – the door was open. He rushed in, and there on the bed were two mangled wire coat hangers. He examined the make-shift bent picks and chucked them across the room.

'Bollocks.'

Of all the accountants, in all of the world, they had to rescue one with hidden talents. With his only witness having done a bunk, by tomorrow night, it would be all or nothing.

And then they were five.

28 / Going Underground

Pocock's of Little Biglington is what some people would refer
to as a 'Proper Butcher'. There were no neatly packaged cuts of
meat, vacuum-sealed in plastic, which bore no resemblance to
its origin, and no professionally designed posters with smiling
'Ordinary People' who seemed the epitome of happiness because
they had a frying pan and a gravity defying stir-fry. Instead,
they had a blackboard and neat handwriting.

They prided themselves on their display of premium cuts,
sausages and pies, but even the most traditional purveyor of
local fine quality meats had to compete with modern super-
stores. Thankfully, Mr Pocock had tapped into a new market of
those who had escaped city life to experience a 'simpler ' rural
existence. Through judicial use of the word 'artisan', with a cast
iron guarantee that all his rabbits were free range and fed exclu-
sively on a vegetarian diet, business was on the up. Yet despite
probably being the canniest butcher in Sussex, Mr Pocock was
unaware that his cellar, converted from (he believed) an old air
raid shelter, was in fact a gateway to an underground maze that
stretched for leagues.

And so it was that John Cranston found himself, at some
ungodly hour of the morning, in the cold store of Pocock's the
butcher, lowering a rucksack down a hole in the floor.

He felt a tug on the rope and reeled it in before descending
the ladder, closing the hatch behind him, grateful to be out of
the refrigerated air. As he stepped off the last rung, he found

himself in a spacious cellar, the walls hugged by waist height wine racks, with each position occupied, bar one.

Gordon held a bottle in his hand, presenting it to a dim bulb as he moved it back and forth while squinting at the label.

'Well I never,' said Gordon in surprise, 'Pocock's a bit of a dark horse. Taitinger Brut de Blanc 1943. That'll do nicely for a celebration when we're done – I don't think he'll mind,' and he carefully put the bottle back into the rack.

'You can't beat a mug of Taitinger,' said John, much to Gordon's obvious distaste. 'Where's this tunnel then?'

'This way,' Gordon directed.

A plain panelled door opened onto a small storeroom, inside which were several old metal fold-up chairs, a pile of casually stacked cardboard boxes, and a tangled length of Christmas tree fairy lights.

John shone his torch onto the back wall. 'It's a dead end. You sure your map's right?'

'Trust me,' said Gordon patting his inside jacket pocket, 'family heirloom'. He counted a set number of bricks from the floor and when satisfied he had the right one, he pressed hard. It gave way with a loud 'click' and the whole wall swivelled on a central axis, revealing an unlit passageway.

'It wouldn't be much of a secret tunnel if it was obvious,' said Gordon, pleased with the reveal. 'Come on. Turn the light out, and don't forget to close the wall after you.'

The roughly hewn chalk tunnel was barely wide enough for people to move along in single file and the height of the ceiling forced John to proceed with a stoop. Gordon illuminated the way with a light wand, which put John's head torch to shame.

They moved at pace, Gordon covering ground with a deceptive loping stride. Occasionally he would stop, look at his map and then check a crevice or makeshift small shelf carved into the chalk wall, and there, in the light, would be a small luminous origami figure.

'If we get separated,' said Gordon, 'follow the penguins.'

It was about thirty minutes before the tunnel opened out into a slightly taller chamber. Radiating out from this small cave were more tunnels, each starting out from a central rotating dais with rails designed to marry up with the narrow gauge lines that disappeared into the distance of each branch. A decrepit wheeled chassis with a wooden flatbed platform sat abandoned at the threshold of one of those passages.

'They weren't smuggling Hornby trains by any chance?' said John.

'I wouldn't have put it past them. It was quite an industry. Shame it was illegal, they were rather good at it.' Gordon pointed at the train tracks. 'These interconnect with each smugglers hideout and eventually each tunnel leads to the coast. Now, if I remember rightly,' he waved the light to his left and there was a distinctive small paper flightless bird, 'this is the one.'

Gordon was off, turning left and right, then left, or was it right again?

John couldn't keep track, and at times, it felt as if they were turning back on themselves. He diligently followed the light of Gordon's wand for what deceptively seemed to be an age, having no reference point or change of scene apart from the occasional glimpse of a paper penguin, but it was in fact only several minutes.

They stopped, and John was relieved that the tunnels were now taller. He raised himself to his full height, stretched and re-seated the heavy rucksack on his back.

Gordon scanned the wall with his torch and raised a large red switch on a metal box. Suddenly the subterranean passage was completely illuminated. John squinted as his eyes adjusted to the light.

'We're in the old mine workings now,' said Gordon. 'Wouldn't be much of an escape route if they couldn't see where they were going would it? Not far to go now, it's all downhill from here.'

After half a mile or so, they came to a dead-end punctuated with a large hefty steel door. Gordon checked a small crumpled sheet of paper from his back pocket, punched a four number code into the adjacent keypad and, with some effort, pulled the door open. Inside was a brick lined chamber with exposed conduit and duct work running around the walls. In one corner were stacked a number of steel ordnance boxes and random tools.

'That,' said Gordon, pointing at a circular hatch in the ceiling, 'should bring us out into Erikson's data centre. Would you mind putting that,' he said indicating to John's rucksack, 'over there with the rest of the C-4 please.'

'C-4?' John queried.

'Contingency. You can never have enough you know, especially to blow something this big up. Of course, now we've got Midas, we shouldn't need it.'

'What's in yours then?' asked John while shedding his burden as quickly as possible.

'This and that, detonators, spare torch, packed lunch... cuddly toy.' Gordon could see that John wasn't quite sharing his bonhomie. 'I'm joking. I skipped the packed lunch. Now buck up old chap, everything's going swimmingly. All we have to do is disable the lethal trap, sneak in, run Pandora, and we'll be home for brunch.'

'I know I'm going to regret this, but how lethal is this "lethal trap"?'

'Hard to say really, it varies, but if it was me I'd flood the whole room with a fast acting nerve gas,' said Gordon matter of factly.

'Great.'

Gordon guided John to a steel cabinet fixed to the wall; industrial bolt cutters had snapped the padlock securing it.

'Now, listen carefully,' said Gordon, as he opened it up. 'You see that keypad, without the right code, opening the hatch from this side will set off the trap.'

'Okay, so what is it?'

'There's the rub you see. I have one, but if I know these sneaky devils, they've probably changed it. If I put the wrong one in we're done for, and I don't want to find out the hard way. Not to worry though, all you have to do when I give you the signal is cut the wire.'

'Which one?'

'Search me. You won't know until I try the hatch, a light will come on along here,' said Gordon pointing to a termination block from which three wires radiated 'Once you see it, don't hang about,' and he handed John a pair of cutters.

Gordon climbed the steel rungs embedded into the wall and with his arm hooked around one; he set to the wheel on the hatch while John concentrated on the panel, ready to snip. The wheel wouldn't budge, but not to be defeated, Gordon threaded a crow bar between the spokes, and using it as leverage, he pulled. It still didn't move. He tried again, now with both hands on the crowbar and his feet on the lower rung stopping him from dangling from the ceiling. He felt something give, and slowly but surely it turned. He dropped the crowbar and spun the wheel until it came to a stop. He slid the steel handle into its open position and pushed.

As the hatch raised, a small Liquid Crystal Display lit up and broken black letters materialised on an off-white background. For those who were around in the 1970's this would have been a quaint reminiscence of technology past, but no, this was far more ominous.

It said: SURPRISE! TEN

'Cut the wire, there's a good fellow.'

NINE

'They're all lit up!' John shouted.

EIGHT

'What?'

SEVEN

'Every one's got a bloody light!' SIX 'What now?!' John replied, swallowing down his rising desperation.

FIVE

Gordon mentally kicked any latent panic into the long grass. There was no way he could descend the ladder and cross the room in time to help, or escape.

'Just choose one...'

FOUR

John took a deep breath and was about the cut the blue wire, but his gut said red. But what if it was the green?

THREE

'Cranston! Now would be good.'

TWO

He snipped the red.

ONE

The countdown stopped. Nothing happened. Gordon exhaled in relief.

John, with his back to the wall, slid down onto his haunches. He rubbed his forehead. That was too close.

Having recovered their respective composures, Cranston and Gordon emerged from underneath a tile of the raised floor in the computer centre. Pillars of computing power, stacked in rows, flashing and humming away, surrounded them. All they had to do was find a slot in this abundance of hardware into which they could insert Midas, and as luck would have it, on a row of desks, there were a number of computers. John did a mental leap for joy – result! The celebration was short-lived as it turned out they were simple dumb display terminals.

They split up; all the quicker to cover what seemed to be a football pitch of machines, find a card slot, and rendezvous with the news that all was as planned.

'All done then?' said John, as they met back after their initial sweep, assuming that Gordon, who was the current custodian of the Midas card, had done the deed.

'Nothing,' Gordon spat.

'Same here, every cabinet's locked. Can't we break into one?'

Gordon shook his head. 'The doors are industrial bullet-proof glass with a hardened steel alloy frame. Anything I do will wreck them and set off an alarm.'

'Can't you cut some wires and twist 'em together or something?'

'It's all fibre.'

'What about some kind of gadget that'll plug into anything, you're a spy, you must have one in your bag of tricks.'

'It's *agent* if you please, and you've been watching too many films. No, there's only one thing for it, we'll have to go to... *Plan B.*'

'Is that the B for blowing everything up plan?'

'Is there any other sort of Plan B?' Gordon asked rhetorically.

'Hold on a minute,' said John as he paced the floor. 'This is stupid, I can't believe that if Erikson turned up right now, and we handed over Midas, he'd spend all day wandering around asking if anyone had a card reader, he runs the show.'

'Obviously, he'd take it back to his office...' said Gordon as a penny dropped and he realised the truth that he had uttered. 'I say, you really are the idea's man. It could work.'

'What could?'

Plan B Plus was simple. As an avid student of the psychology of arch villains, Gordon was adamant that with the destruction of the two strategic Triple C sites, Erikson would be on edge. All that was needed now was to convince him that his base was under attack, which would be enough to make Erikson escape through some secret exit, leaving his stooges to hold the fort. A series of small explosive charges distributed throughout the complex, timed to go off at intervals, would do the trick. With the office vacated, John could then sneak in, run the Pandora Protocol, and escape under the cover of the chaos.

In fact, Plan B Plus was so simple that even an idiot would volunteer. However, with none available a reluctant gardener, who was short on options, and with a price on his head, would have to do.

John was on lookout duty as Gordon went back down to the chamber to package up some explosives, detonators, and find some delay timers. John checked his watch, he was aware of time running inexorably away. He wanted to be done and out.

There were voices outside. Hiding behind one of the computing towers he saw a man in a white doctor's coat, a stethoscope around his neck, and a clipboard, enter the data centre. John crouched down, watching the strangers every move. If they came across the displaced floor tile, he would have to act.

White Coat stood and faced a blank wall. To John's surprise, he pushed against it and a section slid open to reveal a door with a combination lock. As White Coat entered, John broke cover, and as fast as he dared, without making any sound, slinked to where he and Gordon had broken in.

'Psssst,' he said trying to get Gordon's attention. 'Psssssst.'

It was no good. He heard the heavy door of the secret room being closed, followed by White Coat's footsteps. With no time to slide the tile back he returned to his hiding place, hoping that the interloper wouldn't spot the site of their intrusion.

White Coat made some notes on his clipboard and was about to leave, but stopped. There was a sound, not loud, but distinctly different from the ambient drone of the hardware and air conditioning. And there it was again. It seemed to be coming from underneath the floor. If there was a faulty unit or something, maintenance would be unforgiving if they weren't advised. He'd have to check it out.

The next thing he knew he had been tackled from behind and was face down on the deck.

Hollywood fight scenes usually involve two opponents trading blows in a way that is both plausible and entertaining. In reality, two grown men horizontally struggling for advantage using elbows, knees, heads, and anything to hand is messy, unpredictable, and doesn't make for great television.

As John and White Coat struggled for advantage, they looked like an advertisement for the National Health Service that had been knocked up by the Pimlico Gentlemen's Wrestling Society.

White Coat managed to break free as his pocket ripped, leaving a fragment in John's hand. They faced off against each other. John raised his guard in a classic boxer's stance. There wouldn't be time for a best of three rounds; he would have to pile in.

As he moved forward, a shoe narrowly missed his jaw. And then there was another one and another one as like a whirling dervish, White Coat spun, forcing John back until he could go no further.

White Coat was getting cocky and slapdash as he telegraphed his next kick, which was easily dodged, and his foot embedded itself into the dry lined wall. In the time that it took for White Coat to remove it, John had unleashed a right-left combination. White Coat dodged the right, his neck seemed to be on a spring, but the left connected and White Coat collapsed. John was relieved but confused, the punch wasn't that good, but as his opponent fell to the floor, there was Gordon, holding the broken remains of a computer keyboard.

'Wretched Kung Fu doctors,' said Gordon disdainfully. 'Damned nuisance if you ask me. They'll turn their hands to anything. I blame the government, if they paid them more they'd stay in hospital.' He kicked White Coat to ensure he was unconscious. 'You were lucky it wasn't a Karate obstetrician, they're the worst.'

John wiped the blood from his nose. 'There's something you need to see.'

With White Coat cuffed, gagged and dropped into the underfloor chamber, Gordon examined the hidden door with great interest.

'If I'm not mistaken this looks like an anti-virus vault.'

'Is that good then?' said John, detecting Gordon's enthusiasm.

'Top hole old chap. You see that,' said Gordon pointing to the lock, 'good old fashioned industrial analogue technology. No chance of a remote override on that. Total physical access control on software maintenance and upgrades, which is exactly what we want to do,' he smiled.

Gordon cracked his knuckles and using White Coat's stethoscope set about the lock. He turned the dial, listening intently for the faint but distinctive paired clicks as the drive cam made contact with the internal wheels. He looked at his notes, tried the numbers, and cursed as the door refused to open. He spun the combination dial to reset the lock, and started again. On the third attempt, the handle moved, and with a beam of satisfaction, he opened the door.

As they crossed the threshold they stepped out onto a gantry, looking out across a vast cavernous space.

John's jaw dropped. 'Jesus Christ.'

Gordon stood transfixed. 'Oh good Lord... not again.'

He was right, the vault was designed to keep the wrong people out, but not for the reasons he had explained.

29 / *Here Be Spreadsheets*

Maria Egerton couldn't see clearly, even though she was sure that her eyes were open. She could make out vague shadows and discriminate between light and dark, but even that capability was being lost as Titan slowly took over, ignoring any impulses travelling through her optic nerve.

She had struggled and severely compromised one henchman's child rearing days, but they managed to strap her into the chair never the less. They had encased her head in a semi-rigid skull-cap, teasing her, saying 'Titan's gonna have some fun with you,' as they plugged her into that thing. Whatever it was, she had felt it, slowly and methodically creeping around her consciousness. Over time, she didn't know how long, a slow paralysis had crept through her as Titan set about hijacking her brain, neuron by neuron.

Titan would ask her unrelated, daft questions incessantly. `Why is the colour pink attractive? Why are sunsets considered pleasant? What is a cat? Can a man with strange hair ever be a president?'

And then the questions would stop and it would visit her in her mind's eye, as people that she had known, all shouting, trying to break her down. When her concentration strayed, she could feel its thoughts, (could a stream of zero's and one's be called thoughts?) racing around her head.

She wasn't going to give up, and by sheer strength of will, she managed to move her big toe, a small victory as she maintained an awareness of her physical self. Mentally she recited the Fibonacci sequence repeatedly and replayed the most stultifyingly boring business cases that she had ever worked on, with their endless review of Deltas, Net Present Values, Internal Rates of Returns, and Composite Indexes of Coincident Indicators.

Those things related to what she did. Titan could have them with her blessing, but not who she was.

*****

At the forefront of the vault was an emaciated young lady in track suit bottoms and T-shirt, her hands and feet secured to a robust steel chair, her gaze directed in front, not registering the presence of John as he raced down the steel stairs towards her, Gordon following.

A multitude of wires and cables radiated from her head in an incomplete spider's web as they travelled to lines of computers that stretched further than the eye could see. Suspended from wheeled stands were intravenous drips inserted into the back of her hand and arm, keeping her hydrated, but not nourished, with a chemical cocktail working in tandem with Titan to accelerate her compliance.

John approached, unsure what to do first. He started with the familiar and undid the buckles on the straps securing her arms and legs. 'Don't worry, we're going to get you out of here,' he said reassuringly – what else could he say?

She blinked; her sunken eyes looking straight through him.

'Cranston, stop!' shouted Gordon.

John held up his hands. 'Booby trap?'

Gordon felt her pulse and waved his hand in front of her face. He shone a small flashlight into her eyes, there was no reaction. 'Damn,' he uttered under his breath. 'There's nothing we can do here, we've got to go.'

'What do you mean "nothing we can do"? We can't just leave her.'

'We have a job to do,' Gordon said, his jaw set.

'I'm not going anywhere until you tell me what's going on.'

'She's beyond help. I don't like it any more than you do, but we've got a mission to finish.'

'You'll be finishing it on your own if you don't start sharing.'

Gordon held his peace and considered the impasse. Now they were in, he could go it alone, but Cranston was proving to be useful, if not annoyingly ignorant about most things secret agent related. He slowly let out a deep breath. On balance, a digest explanation was a small price to pay for retaining his services...this time.

'Back in the eighties there was a race to develop an artificial intelligence weapon. Our government had a joint covert programme with the CIA, code name Titan. They couldn't develop an A.I fast enough so they took a short cut by linking computer systems directly into the human brain – they called it the Wet Interface. It leapfrogged anything the Russian's had, but it got out of control and developed a penchant for nuclear attack codes. As it didn't officially exist, I had to clear up the mess. I thought I'd destroyed all trace of it.'

'I don't get it. If he's got all this, what does he need Midas for?'

Gordon pondered for a second. 'It's an upgrade. This bloody thing is using that poor girl to augment its programming, but it'll wear her out until she's a vegetable, and then it's onto the next one. Erikson won't have that problem with Midas.'

John looked intently at the skullcap. 'We can't leave her like this.'

'We haven't got a choice. If you disconnect her, it'll fry her brain, she'll die in agony. Either way, she can't survive this. The only mercy is that at the moment she doesn't know what's happening to her, it'll be painless. The best we can do is to make sure no other poor soul goes through this.'

'There's got to be a way to get her off this thing, come on, think!'

'John, *you're not listening to me.* Unplug her and it'll be like throwing her off a speeding train. It'll kill her as surely as if you'd put a gun to her head.'

John knelt down and looked into her eyes, looking, hoping for the faintest glimmer of intelligence, and, as if by some inexplicable connection, it occurred to him.

'Not if we stop the train.'

'What do you mean?'

'Pandora – that's the whole point of it, all of this is going to grind to a halt.'

'By George, that might work. At the least it would give this young lady a fighting chance.'

John held her hand. 'I'm coming back - I promise.' He stood up, his determination doubled. 'Right, we've got a delivery to make.'

As they left the vault neither of them noticed that Maria's big toe was twitching nineteen to the dozen.

*****

They parted ways as Gordon hoisted himself into a ventilation shaft with a rucksack full of explosives. John, with his disguise enhanced by the addition of a clipboard, (he wasn't convinced), navigated the lair. According to Gordon, Erikson's office would be somewhere central. That didn't help as he wandered, lost, but with purpose. The problem was that he daren't ask anyone for directions. Even with the clipboard, it might seem suspicious.

He had about a thirty minute head start before things were due to go bang. Ahead he caught sight of someone who looked vaguely familiar. He flattened himself against the wall; they hadn't seen him...yet. Was it one of the henchmen from the ball? Homicidal screwballs all looked the same when they wanted to shoot you; they had a knack of synchronising their scowls. He couldn't put his finger on it, was it the dark complexion, the stubble that looked like it could grate cheese, or the eyebrows that met above the bridge of his nose? The chrome plate in the head clinched it.

He looked behind, there were guards coming down the corridor. He couldn't risk going forward, all he could do was turn back, but if they recognised him, then all bets were off, there were too many. He tried a nearby door handle and slipped into what seemed to be a vacant office. He pressed his ear to the door, concentrating as he listened for them to move on.

'Do you know what time it is?' said a raised voice behind him in a complaining tone.

'Ssshhhtt!' said John reflexively, and then as realisation dawned, he lightly head butted the wall. 'Great,' he muttered.

'You can "sssh" me all you like, it won't make any difference, 'sides, you won't hear much through that, it's solid that is, solid. Now, what time do you call this?'

'About half five,' John guessed as he turned to find that the only reason his new adversary (?) had sneaked up on him was a pair of fluffy slippers that completed the ensemble of flannelette pyjamas and dressing gown.

'Half five, half-past-five! If I've told them once I've told them a thousand times, reception don't open until nine, but no, they won't have it, and the next thing, you're here, door whispering – brilliant.' He held his hand out, palm facing outwards, 'No, no, there's no point apologising, you're here now. God knows I won't be able to get back to sleep, all me chakra's are messed up.' He sighed. 'We might as well do the paperwork.'

'What?'

'Bless 'im. Just because you've been abducted don't make you special you know. You're in the same boat as the rest of us. You can't have a shed load of accountants all stuck in 'ere without rules can you? I mean, before you know it, it'll be like Lord of the Flies meets Mad Max, it's no good is it? Right then, first name, surname and specialism, I'll do the rest later, I'll be buggered if I'm missing breakfast.'

Pyjama man positioned himself behind a desk, pen poised above his notepad. He posed no threat and John didn't have the time or inclination for a backstory. The door had no handle on the inside, but that wasn't going to stop him getting out, especially once Gordon's diversions started.

'I'm not staying,' John said, 'so you go back to bed and don't tell anyone you've seen me. We understand each other don't we?'

'Don't give me all that hard man stuff; I've heard it all before. You sound like that lady we had in the other day, she said she weren't hanging around either, reckoned there wasn't a prison built she couldn't get out of. And get this,' he leaned conspiratorially across the desk, 'she said she was a secret agent, honestly, I ask you, what's the...'

John interrupted, 'Secret agent? What did she look like?'

'How should I know? She came in on the afternoon shift. It's only what I've heard and anyway, she's been taken off somewhere.'

John reached round to the rear of his waistband and drew the gun that Gordon had insisted he carry. He didn't like it, but for effect, it would do the job. This wasn't the time for good manners.

'Take me to someone who saw her, now.'

Pyjama man gulped. 'You're not an accountant are you?'

'No, I'm a gardener; this is a side-line.'

Pyjama man made a phone call and led John down a short corridor into a vast chamber full of people at desks, all in their own personal bubble as they focused on a plethora of spreadsheets across multiple displays .

'Welcome to Colditz,' said Pyjama man.

'Who are all these people?' John asked.

Pyjama man looked at the gun and decided on a factual, rather than sarcastic answer. 'Accountants, it's the nightshift. Someone will be along to see you in a minute. Would it be alright if I had an early breakfast?' he asked sheepishly.

John wasn't really listening as everything suddenly fell into place, distracting him for a moment. 'Breakfast – fine.'

Pyjama man slinked off as John looked across at what could be described as an army of accountants, all incarcerated at the service of Erikson. 'Oh Hell...' he thought.

A man in a blue standard off the peg suit approached.

'Hello there, I'm Michael, Head of the escape committee. Are we glad to see you, we weren't sure if anyone was going to turn up. You won't need that gun; you're among friends here. What are you, MI6, CIA?'

'Freelance,' said John.

'Whatever, we're ready to go. Ben obviously gave you all

the details, so where do you and your team want us?'

'Look, before you get carried away, I don't know any "Ben". I can get you out, but after that, you're on your own. I'm here to take Erikson down, not to organise the Great Escape.' John looked around, 'Any of these computers got an SD card slot?'

'No, every bit of tech's locked down tighter than Scrooge's wallet,' said Michael. 'Ben didn't send you then?'

John shook his head.

'Poor sod, looks like he didn't make it,' Michael said to himself. There was a moment of contemplation. 'We've got to get out; we've had people going missing at the rate of one a week. We've made preparations, what can we do to help?'

'Your receptionist reckoned you had a lady in here the other day who said she was a secret agent. I need to know it's who I think it is, and where she is. She's part of my...team. Next, things are going to get explosive around here, so once you're out, don't hang around.'

Michael nodded. 'Leave it to me.' He stood on a chair, shouting for people to gather round. 'Okay everyone, listen up. Ben's come through,' he looked down at John and winked. A palpable sense of excitement emanated from the group. Throughout Colditz hushed voices could be heard as the word spread that Ben had sent help. 'We've got a chance to get out. Now, does anyone remember a lady who was brought in the other day who said she was a secret agent?'

'Was she the one who broke Ron's finger?' said one.

'Yeah, I think so,' said another.

'Ron's a bit friendly when it comes to ladies,' clarified Michael.

'What did she look like?' John asked the growing audit of accountants. There was an initial hubbub as notes were compared.

'She looked like that girl from the Avengers,' said one.

'What -Scarlett Johansson?' said another.

'Phwooarrrrr...' said a late arrival somewhere at the back.

'I wish I hadn't asked now,' said John. 'You know, the finger's enough to go on, I'm pretty sure she's one of ours. Do you know where she is?'

'I can find out,' replied Michael confidently.

Unfortunately the audit was in full flow, and as they'd started, they had to finish.

'Not those Avengers, the *other* Avengers, you know with Steed and that,' said another disembodied voice in the crowd.

'You sure? She didn't look a bit like Steed, he was a bloke, weren't he.'

'No, he's sidekick, you know, whatsername, Honor Blackman.'

'Ohh yeesss!' said the late arrival.

'No, no, she was blonde, now who was it, don't tell me, don't tell me...'

'Diana Rigg!' shouted someone else.

'Yeah, that's it, Emma Peel, with all the cat suit's and that.'

'Ah - but she wasn't wearing a cat suit was she? It was an evening dress,' stated a clever dick. 'And actually I think you'll find she was more like Katherine Hepburn.'

The late arrival piped up, the pitch escalating in excitement. 'Who cares? What about that red dress eh? What a cracker! And what a pair of...'

The commentary broke off mid lechery, as the late arrival noticed a stranger standing on a desk with a gun pointing in his direction.

'Ron, shut up,' John ordered.

The audit took the hint and dispersed, leaving a hard core that Michael quickly conversed with, relaying instructions and receiving information.

'How did you know that was Ron?' Michael asked.

'The lolly stick splints were a bit of a giveaway,' said John. 'You know if he keeps up like that, fingers will be the least of his worries.'

'I know. We're trying to rehabilitate him but it's a bit of a slog; he used to work in sales. I found out where your friend is by the way. She's been moved to one of the interrogation suites. One of our crew can take you there; now come with me, there's someone you need to meet first.'

Michael opened the double doors on a standard six foot by three foot civil service metal cabinet to reveal another door which led to a flight of steps. 'I suppose you see a lot of these secret passages in your line of work?'

'Yeah,' said John casually as he followed Michael downstairs, 'especially lately.'

'We found this by accident while looking for a way out. We reckon Erikson picked this place up second-hand. He probably doesn't know half of what it's got, which is great for us, it's where we've been hiding our ARSE.'

'Come again?'

'A.R.S.E, it's our secret order, formed after the Wall Street Crash of twenty nine. Come the next financial cock-up bankers won't be the only professionals people will want to lynch. We're realistic, if we don't look out for ourselves, no one else will.'

The stairs opened out into a large brightly-lit gymnasium with columns of warriors engaging in martial drills.

'Welcome to the Accountants Resistance Specialist Engagement unit,' said Michael proudly. He pointed out the various training areas. There was one man being attacked in sequence by a group of ten, and with a deceptive ease of movement he sent them sprawling across a makeshift mat. They passed a line of people who were throwing small metal objects at outline figures crudely drawn on the wall, each hitting the head with force, creating an indentation in the plaster.

'Pencil sharpeners,' Michael clarified, 'lethal in the right hands.'

Elsewhere John watched in awe as pencils were thrown into a dartboard. On another training mat, computer mice, reinforced with sticky tape, were swung around student's heads, then snaked out at speed, shattering a line-up of jam jars.

'I don't believe it – it's a bunch of accountant Ninja's,' said John, astonished.

'Secret accountant Ninja's,' emphasised Michael. 'I think they should be able to help out. Ah – here's our commander,' he said as he guided John over towards someone, who from behind, looked familiar. 'I'll leave you with him. I've got to check something, won't be a minute.'

The commander turned around. 'John! Mate! How's it going?'

*****

Martin Ashcombe squirmed slightly as the wave of invective from his old school friend hit him at full force. He had a feeling John would be upset, being chased, shot and stabbed at could do that to a person, but he thought that John had got off lightly, so where was the gratitude? There was only one thing for it, and with as much sincerity as he could muster, he poured some oil onto the troubled waters.

'I'm sorry, alright?' lied Martin. 'You weren't supposed to have it, but some toe rag blew my cover.'

'That's it? You get found out, off load your gear onto me, stitch me up, and all you can manage is "I'm sorry"' said John, the need for an explanation only slightly outweighing a desire to throttle his old school colleague.

'Stitched up is a bit strong,' replied Martin, looking quite forlorn. 'You're not the only one who's suffered you know. I've had to put up with torture and stuff, that's why I'm in here. They reckoned that after a couple of days surrounded by accountants I'd be begging to be let out, and then I'd tell 'em everything. It was touch and go at first, but when you get to know them, they're not that bad. Next thing you know they've asked me to get their guys into a fighting unit. I'm head of my own gang of Ninjas now, how good is that?'

'I'm so happy for you. Now give me one good reason why I shouldn't punch your lights out.'

Martin sighed and with a snap of his fingers Ninjas materialised around him in a protective formation, all at the ready with their pencil sharpeners and mice. He smiled a Chesire Cat smile; the natural balance had been restored.

'I'll put it right, I promise,' said Martin. 'It's the least I can do. Give Midas to me and when we're out of here I'll make sure it's all sorted. You'll never hear anything about it again, trust me.'

'I haven't got it,' John replied. At that moment he trusted Martin as far as he could throw him. Given the opportunity he wouldn't even try, unless it was out of an aeroplane.

'Ah mate, don't give me that. You're working for the Brigadier,' said Martin, pointing at the glasses and moustache. 'I know you've got it, a little birdie tells me you've been asking about computers. To be honest, using it against Erikson is a bit desperate, but then that's why you're on the case, you're expendable, or haven't you worked that one out yet? Come on, the sooner you hand it over, the sooner you can get back to your pruning and stuff, you know it makes sense.'

Michael returned. 'Is everything in order Commander?'

'Yeah, he's good,' replied Martin, slightly annoyed at the interruption.

'Right,' said Michael. 'Your Ninja's take the armoury and secure a route out. I'll lead the civilians.' He turned to John. 'You're on.'

*****

John moulded the cigarette sized C-4 explosive around the door lock. According to Gordon, all he had to do was stick a matchstick detonator into it, pull the cord, and hide.

'That'll never do it,' said Martin, who'd been looking over John's shoulder. 'You got any more?'

John removed the fake Benson and Hedges packet from his pocket. 'I suppose you're an expert then?'

'I've blown a few things up in my time. Give 'em 'ere,' said Martin holding out his hand in anticipation.

Martin removed all of the sticks and moulded them into small fist sized lump that he attached to the centre of the door with sticky tape. 'That'll do it,' he said with self-congratulatory satisfaction. He pulled the cord and they hastily retreated behind the upturned desks. Martin counted down. 'Five, four, three...'

He didn't get to one.

For a moment the room was illuminated as if by a one thousand watt bulb, and then there was a sound, like a jet breaking the sound barrier, followed by a shock wave that moved the furniture everyone sheltered behind. Light fittings juddered, ceilings vibrated, and then bits of brick, plaster and cement were hurled across the room, making a rat-tat-tat sound as some of it bounced off the desks, and the rest ricocheted off the walls, or embedded itself into the décor. Then it was all over and as the smoke and dust cleared, John cautiously peered over the top.

The door had been opened, along with twenty feet of wall. The short corridor that led to the reception was now an avenue.

Martin looked at his handiwork. 'Don't say it.'

'Say what?' replied John innocently.

'You know.'

'No, I don't know.'

'Yes you do – the thing.'

'What thing?'

Someone who sounded suspiciously like Ron putting on a thick London accent shouted, 'You're only supposed to..!'

'That thing,' said Martin with a grimace.

'Well done' said Michael, brushing dust from his suit as he picked his way across the rubble, 'although just the doors would have been fine, but you know what they say, practice makes perfect. After you Commander.'

'Alpha squad, on the double!' shouted Martin as the accountant Ninja's moved silently through the new opening without disturbing a single fragment of debris.

'Gotta go mate, let's do lunch sometime,' said Martin holding his extended thumb and little finger to the side of his face.

'Let's not,' replied John as Martin disappeared from view.

*****

The alarm, a whiney fluctuating siren was underscored by the sound of hobnail boots as enemy sentries double-timed to the accountants prison. The early responding security detail didn't stand a chance as John's Ninja guide, moving in forward somersaults and twists, knocked them out one by one, like an unstoppable force of nature.

They raced down the stairs and on the lower floor the Ninja peeked around the exit and raised his clenched fist above his shoulder, indicating they should halt. John noticed he didn't say much, which he put down to the pillowcase being wrapped too tightly around his head. The Ninja continued to sign, not wanting to make a sound in case he revealed their position. He pointed to his eyes and then outside. He executed a small mime with his fingers walking around, followed by a circle scribed in the air with his index finger.

'It's a film, four words, first syllable,' John guessed.

The Ninja silently slapped his head with the heel of his palm, looked heavenward, counted to five, and then suddenly burst through the door.

The end of the corridor was where Marsden was being held prisoner. Sprinting along the passage the Ninja pitched an HB pencil. It hit the guard's wrist with such force, that they involuntarily dropped their sidearm. Now flipping and tumbling, the Ninja simultaneously followed up with a volley of pencil sharpeners. The first hit the guard's throat so that the only noise he could make was a lame croak. The second and third struck the temples in a way known only to those versed in the arts of pressure points and meridians. The guard stood stock still, then slowly rocked and fell forward, landing neatly on the Ninja's shoulder who picked him up easily into a fireman's lift. The Ninja took the guard's pass, threw it to John, and with a salute, he was off.

John knocked and a speakeasy grill opened. He held up the borrowed credentials and listened as the bolts were undone and the door was opened. In handcuffs with the chain passed through a steel eyelet on a solid metal table was Marsden, one of her eyes was blackened and her lip was split. She saw him, and it didn't register at first, but then John could see on her face the slightest, imperceptible, look of...shock.

'What do you want?' said the custodian.

John fixated on the custodians eyeballs with a harsh, no

nonsense look. 'You forgot the "Sir" you sloppy piece of work. You're a disgrace to the uniform. Smarten yourself up man! Chin up, chest out, stomach in! Now, let's try that again.'

The custodian, assuming that he was in the presence of a senior ball breaker, and keen not to be demoted from his current cushy number to swilling out the dungeon, stood bolt upright.

'What can I help you with, Sah?!'

'That's better. I've come for the prisoner.'

The custodian shifted uneasily. 'On whose authorisation, Sah?!'

'Mine. I'm the Director of Secret Projects.'

'We don't have any secret....' the penny dropped. 'Oh right, I wouldn't know because they're all...'

'That's right soldier,' John interjected, 'now release the prisoner before I have you cleaning the cesspit with your own toothbrush.'

'I'm sorry but I need to see written authorisation. Regulation six-seven-six, slash, hashtag dothepaperwork, slash eight clearly states that no category A prisoner is to be released from custody without the written authorisation of the chief villain in charge, or nominated deputy by said chief villain, Sah!'

'Well done soldier, you've passed the test,' said John as he checked his pockets.

Meanwhile Marsden had buried her head in her folded arms in disbelief as Cranston insisted on acting like someone Sandhurst would have liked to have kicked out, but daren't, as people would wonder how they had got in to start with.

John removed a small credit card sized wallet, opened it and showed it to the custodian, who moved closer to inspect the documentation.

'National Trust?' queried the custodian, slightly nonplussed.

A split second later a sweeping uppercut lifted the custodian up onto his toes and he was out for the count.

John shook his fist, retrieved the keys and undid Marsden's handcuffs.

'What are you doing here?' she asked.

'It's a rescue – what's your excuse?'

'I was ambushed at the ball. I would have got away if it hadn't been for this wretched dress. What's the plan?'

'I'll explain on the way, it's going to kick off any minute now. There's a bunch of accountant Ninja's storming the base and Gordon's rigging a set of explosions to go off about…'

'GORDON'S ALIVE!'

'Well he was the last time I looked. Like I said, he's rigging up some explosives that'll go off anytime now. Erikson will think the base is under attack and do a runner. I sneak into his office, run the Pandora protocol on his master computer, meet up with Gordon, and we all leg it.'

Marsden looked astonished. 'You and Gordon thought this up?'

'Yes. Get with it, we haven't got all day.'

There was a distant rumbling as the first of Gordon's diversionary explosions let rip. 'Gordon and explosives,' she thought. That never ended subtly. Pandemonium was sure to follow, and if you knew how to use it, it was a useful ally. Marsden recovered herself, she had taken worse beatings. There was a job to do and Cranston's plan could work.

She gagged and tied the custodian, with a make-shift arrangement of his bootlaces, jacket, and trousers, to the steel table that was bolted to the floor. While she was doing so, she shook her head in mild incredulity - 'National Trust - I don't know'.

'Give me a break,' John protested. 'I was banned by English Heritage.'

Marsden ignored the riposte, concentrating on the job in hand. 'There we go - he won't be going anywhere fast.' She placed her hands back into the handcuffs, making sure not to fully close them, so that to the casual observer, it would look like she was restrained. 'Now, as I'm the prisoner you'd better take me to see Erikson, it'll be good cover, and Cranston, if you accidentally shoot me, I'm coming back to haunt you.'

'Don't worry; I've never shot anyone accidentally.'

'That's very encouraging....thanks. Right then, after you.'

John looked both ways down the corridor. It wasn't helping. 'You wouldn't happen to know where Erikson's office is, by any chance?'

'Lucky for you I had breakfast with him, I think I can remember the way. Shall we?'

*****

The elevator seemed to take an age to arrive as John looked up at the numbers slowly counting down to their floor.

'Stop fidgeting,' said Marsden.

'I don't like lifts,' replied John.

'If you think I'm climbing umpteen flights in these shoes, tough luck.'

The elevator doors opened and as they entered a guard shouted 'Hold it!' and stuck her foot between the doors, stopping them temporarily from closing. She gave John a nod, acknowledging a fellow henchperson in arms, with a prisoner no less. They all stood there in awkward silence as the 'Girl from Ipanema', pirated from the James Lost greatest stylophone hits album, played out through a tinny speaker.

Marsden smiled sweetly; there was a playful glint in her eye.

*****

Dick Walker examined the latest gadget to come out of the Department S workshop, the XM2507, a discreet, behind the ear, two way communications device. It was disguised as a National Health Service hearing aid, (that it used to be a hearing aid was a handy coincidence). There was one small problem though, initial trials confirmed that it only had a range of three feet, although that could be extended if it was connected to a car battery.

His line of thought was interrupted by a persistent beep coming from the racks of shelves behind him. He tried to ignore it, but it was so irritating he had to find out where it was. He followed the sound, working his way along the shelves until he came to M for Moles, and pinpointed it to the box that contained Sir Rotherfield's personal items. Taking it back to his desk he rummaged through and found the offender, a smartphone tucked underneath some monogrammed handkerchiefs, velvet rope, and a Sooty finger puppet. There was a message, and as a professional nosey person he was duty bound to read it.

'Mmmm, that won't do,' he thought.

30 / A Fistful Of Sausages

The ancient octopus watched as Gorringe glided past. It yearned for the old days. The hired help weren't what they used to be, it had been ages since someone had changed the water filter.

'Excuse me Sir,' said Gorringe in his standard butleresque accent, 'the accountants are revolting.'

Erikson put his tablet to one side. 'While I share the sentiment, I thought I made it clear that if I wanted your opinion I would ask for it.'

'My apologies, if I may be allowed to clarify my statement. The accountants have escaped from the prison and have overrun the arsenal. They appear to be supported by,' Gorringe suppressed his frown, 'Ninjas'.

Erikson nodded. 'It would seem our gardener has arrived as expected, excellent. Have the invitations been sent out?'

'Yes, to our more exclusive members. As instructed the contract for the delivery of Mr Cranston, dead or alive, with Midas intact, has been set at ten million pounds.'

There was a minor tremble as another of Gordon's diversions detonated. Erikson was unconcerned as he steadied the Newton's cradle on his desk.

'May I ask what you would like to do with the revolting accountants?' continued Gorringe.

'Salvage what you can. There's a new consignment due soon that'll make up any shortfall.'

Gorringe raised his hand, 'Sir, one last thing. May I be so bold as to make an observation?'

'If you must.'

'If the intention is for Mr Cranston to be lured to this chamber with the Midas device, it would seem that there are too many barriers in the way of a successful outcome.'

'Unlike you I don't underestimate his abilities. Without challenges, he'll be suspicious, I like to cover all possibilities. If, for whatever reason, he does fall at an earlier hurdle, either way I gain possession of Midas. Now fetch my bags, I'll return when all the unpleasantness is over.'

'With pleasure Sir,' said Gorringe without the slightest hint of irony. He had been doing this a long time.

*****

Marsden poked the gun into John's back. 'Come on scum, move it,' she ordered.

John frowned as the armed hired help ran past in the direction of the accountant's prison. 'Will you take it easy with that,' he protested when the enemy were out of earshot.

'Sorry,' said Marsden, not meaning it, 'but we've got to keep up appearances.'

'Oh yeah, we wouldn't want to draw any attention to ourselves would we? Which is why, out of this massive underground...I don't know what to call it...carpark, full of world domination fruitcakes, you decide to mug the first one we come across and dump them in a cleaner's cupboard. Can't have you being the prisoner, can we?'

'That dress was killing me and she happened to be my size,' said Marsden tightening the belt on the stolen trousers a notch. 'Anyway, you're the one with a price on his head.'

'Thanks for reminding me,' acknowledged John grudgingly. 'How about you stick to calling me scum and lay off the poking?'

'Okay scum, I'll see what I can do.'

There was another rumble and the ceiling rippled, releasing flakes of paint and fine dust. Chaos was starting to flex its muscles. What had been an orderly deployment of troops throughout the lair, had now descended into a disorganised shouting pack as guards ran from pillar to post depending on how close the sound of the latest explosion was, and by how many leaping Ninjas were in the vicinity. Amid this confusion John and Marsden were of no interest, simply a prisoner being moved speedily at gunpoint.

'Where to now?' asked John as he came to a junction, 'left or right?' There was no answer. 'Left or right?'

'Probably left mate.' said a familiar voice from behind him.

John whirled round to see Marsden on her knees, her hands behind her head. Standing over her was Martin. He now held both of them at gunpoint.

'Haven't you got some Kung Fu bean counters to be leading?' said John.

'No, they're fine thanks,' Martin replied, 'but you and me didn't get a chance to finish our business. I couldn't wait for lunch.'

'I told you before, I haven't got it. Let her go.'

'John, mate, I'm sorry but has anyone ever told you that you're really crap at this? You never really got leverage did you?' Martin sighed. 'Hand it over.'

'I'm going to break your legs really slowly,' threatened Marsden.

Martin feigned a wince. 'I always loved it when you talked dirty.'

'You wish, sicko,' Marsden replied with tangible hostility.

'Ooh, be still my beating heart. You know, it'd be lovely to go over old times, but I've got things to do, places to go,' Martin stated in a casual manner, but with the underlying hint of malice of an unpredictable sociopath, 'you know how it is. Give me the card and we're all done, I promise.'

'I haven't got it,' John insisted.

'We can't because we haven't got it,' emphasised Marsden. 'We're on a standard infiltrate and destroy mission.'

'Yeah, course you are,' said Martin. 'Guys, I don't want to be unreasonable but if you don't play along I'm going to have to shoot someone, which is a real drag. Do you know how much trouble it is to get sense out of people rolling on the floor in agony?'

'He's bluffing,' said Marsden.

'Have it you way. Eeeny, meeny…oh sod it. John, sort it out,' said Martin, as he cocked the trigger and aimed the gun at Marsden's head.

'Martin, you don't have to do this,' John implored.

'You're right, I don't. Give me the card. I'll count to three. One.'

'How many more times? I haven't got it,' John insisted.

Marsden looked John directly in the eye. She had played along assuming that Cranston had a plan, but now all she saw was a rabbit caught in the headlights. She willed him to hand Midas over; living to fight another day was a sound policy in her book.

'Two.'

Marsden closed her eyes. This was it. What a way to go, of all the people she had to be caught out by, it had to be Ashcombe. At least she wouldn't have to worry about trying to live it down.

'Thr..'

'Stop! Okay! Okay,' John urged, 'it's yours. Just don't, please.' He threw the data card across.

'Thanks mate, you know it makes sense. That wasn't so hard was it? Now, don't think about following me 'cos I'll drop you where you stand. Good luck with the mission by the way, you're going to need it.' He grinned, 'I don't think you're getting out alive. Ciao!'

Martin disappeared down the corridor. Marsden got up to follow.

'Where are you going?' said John.

'To get some ice cream's; what do you think?'

'I didn't give it to him.'

Marsden stopped in her tracks. 'I saw you give…You switched it?'

'Whatever I say, everyone thinks I've got it anyway, so I

thought it'd be a shame to keep disappointing people. As one card looks pretty much like another, I went shopping after I burnt down Hastings Pier.'

'You did what?'

'Went shopping,' said John as he held up the true Midas device. 'Martin's not big on detail. By the time he twigs we'll be long gone.'

'You had a fake all the time and you didn't tell me?'

'I figured the less people that knew, the better. Sorry if I cut it a bit fine, but I wanted to make sure Martin bought it.'

'We're still in the game,' said Marsden with relish. 'In future though go on two. For a moment there I thought I was going to miss Goodwood.'

Another of the bombs went off; Gordon had positioned them and staggered the timers in such a way that they were unpredictable. This one was close. The floor shook and boxy duct work, electrical wiring, cable trays and all the other technical paraphernalia that is normally hidden above, spewed from the ceiling.

As the dust settled there was a scurrying rattling sound as a dirty, sweaty figure dragged itself out of the fallen air conditioning conduit. 'John?' it said. 'Is that you? What a relief! I took a wrong turn. I wasn't sure if I'd find you in time.'

'Cyril?' said John.

'Peartree?' said Marsden.

'What the bloody hell are you doing in there?' said John.

'Stealth NVQ, module five. It seemed like a good idea at the time. I'm glad I found you, you're in big trouble. Department S intercepted a message, Erikson's put a contract out on you.'

'Another one?' John said with a hint of weariness.

'Ten million pounds dead or alive, and Erikson's told them where you are. We got here as fast as we could, Jenkins and Larkin have got most of them caught in a cross-fire upstairs, but some got through.'

'Great.'

'Ms Marsden?' blurted Cyril. 'In case I don't get the chance, I'd just like to say that I'm a big fan. I loved your Brighton work.'

'Aww thank you,' replied Marsden, revelling in the compliment.

'When you're done,' said John, 'I'm open to suggestions as to what we do next.'

'I thought you had a plan?' said Marsden.

'To be honest it's more of a rough outline. The funny thing is I didn't take into account someone falling through the ceiling with the news that there's a lynch mob on the way after my head. And there was me thinking that if I sneaked into a secret hideout, I'd only have to worry about the people in here. At this rate I'll have my long lost cousin turning up telling me to "Get out of her pub".'

Marsden had the look of a schoolteacher who had been told that homework hadn't been handed in on time because the cat had used it to practice folding napkins. 'Have you been making this up as you go along?'

'Only the bits where I let you and the Ninja accountants out,' said John. 'If you can do better I'm all ears.'

'Okay, this is the main route,' Marsden noted, rising to the challenge. 'If we stall them here, they'll have to take the long way round to outflank us. Peartree, I need you to hold this position, no one gets through.'

'Yes Ma'am!' saluted Cyril.

'Cranston, we'll go to Erikson's office; I'll make a stand there while you run Pandora. Gordon's due to rendezvous so we'll have reinforcements at some point. That'll work,' said Marsden confidently.

John took Marsden to one side. 'I've seen him in action, he couldn't box a kipper. He won't last five minutes. Do me a favour, get him out of here. I'll take my chances with Gordon, wherever he is.'

'Excuse me; I can hear what you're saying you know,' said Cyril, 'and I'm staying.' He defiantly flexed his sparrow's knee-cap of a bicep, 'I've been working out.' He picked up some of

the ceiling detritus, scored an arrow on the floor in the anticipated direction of attack, and annotated it as 'North'. He then
reached into his rucksack and pulled out a string of pork and
leek sausages.

'Let me guess, you're going to have a barbeque and threaten
them with food poisoning,' said John.

'Oops, sorry, my mistake, I use those for practice,' replied Cyril
as he rummaged further in his rucksack and withdrew a flail
made up of two short wooden poles joined by a chain. 'I got
these Nunchaku on special offer from the milkman; it's amazing
what they'll deliver these days. I've watched Fist of Fury loads
of times and I've got all the moves off pat. All I've got to do is
hide behind all this stuff, and when they turn up, I'll leap out
and engage them in fierce hand to hand combat.'

John's face had that look that said, 'We're screwed.' 'You okay
with this?' he asked Marsden.

'Uh-huh.'

Pacing and rubbing his forehead, John's thoughts went back
to that poor girl. He had to finish, but that didn't have to mean
putting Peartree on a kamikaze mission. 'Cyril, come with us.
If we're going to make a stand, we'll do it together.'

'What kind of plan is that?' Marsden queried.

'John, you don't understand,' said Cyril defiantly. 'This is
bigger than both of us. I'm staying here. I'll give you all the time
you need, I promise, but you've got to go, now.'

John was reluctant, but he knew that look in Cyril's eyes. If
anyone was going to give he's all, it was this feisty matchstick
man. 'Okay, but after this is all done I'm buying you a beer.'

Marsden took Cyril's hands in hers. 'You're a brave man Mr
Peartree.' She leaned forward, her cheek lightly touching his,
and whispered in his ear. 'Give them hell.'

Cyril Peartree watched as John and Marsden went on their
way. Buoyed up by a vote of confidence from his idol and a
brushed cheek no less (!), he took up his position and channelled
his inner Bruce.

No one was getting past him today.

As doors go, it was unspectacular. John was expecting a great, thick, steel round vault entrance that could only be opened by a large wheel that wouldn't look out of place on the helm of a galleon. Instead, it was a plain standard panelled job of the kind to be found in a budget hotel, and it was ajar. Even to a recently initiated novice to the world of espionage and double-dealing, it looked suspicious.

'What do you reckon?' John asked.

'Mmm...' Marsden mused. 'Belt please.'

'What's wrong with yours?'

'It's holding my trousers up. The belt, if you don't mind?' insisted Marsden with her hand outstretched.

There was no point in arguing. Marsden carefully hooked the belt buckle over the door handle and stood to one side, herding John along in the process. Covering her face with her free arm, (John took the hint and followed suit), she tugged on the leather, swinging the door outwards. As she did so, the centre of the door exploded, showering splinters into the passage as pellets of shot sunk themselves into the opposite wall.

'I'm guessing they don't get a lot of doorstep salesmen round here,' John mused.

Marsden nearly raised a smile, but strictly speaking, witty asides like that were reserved for use by only the most experienced of agents, it was a privilege that was earned. Cranston's throw away comment only added to the enigma of this so called gardener.

She gave John the tattered remains of his belt and examined the doorframe, taking care not to cross the threshold. 'I see,' she said pointing to a small glass lens flush with the upright. 'Infra-red trip-wire; I thought it was a bit odd we didn't get both barrels. Watch your step.'

She exaggerated her gait, ensuring that she didn't break the invisible beam. John followed suit, the pair of them looking like an audition for a revival of a sketch about the Ministry of Silly Walks.

From the top of the wrought iron staircase John looked over

Erikson's inner sanctum and the first thought that sprung to mind was the similarity of its décor to an Edwardian gentlemen's convenience, minus the urinals and stalls. The walls were half-covered with dark green brick sized tiles which were bordered by a narrow ceramic dado. From there to the ceiling, it was completed with white tiles of the same size.

Inset into one of the walls was a large aquarium with what looked like a large fleshy rock...with tentacles. The remaining walls were lined with floor to ceiling bookcases containing volumes with identical leather bound covers. In the centre of the room was a marble worktop with an inset backlit map of the world. If it had been covered in baize, it would have made a passable snooker table.

At the furthest reach of the retreat, was a stark, minimalist, stainless steel desk in front of a huge television screen, and on that desk was a computer. John made a beeline for it, inserted Midas, and waited.

'How long will it take?' asked Marsden.

'I haven't got a clue. It's supposed to do its thing automatically once someone tries to run it. Hold on, here we go.'

The user name and password for the computer were automatically completed and a box appeared on the screen with the following options:

```
1. Enter the IP address or Domain name of
target network.
2. Scan for available targets.
3. I'm feeling Lucky.
```

John hated multiple choices; the first option didn't make sense and as he didn't want to push whatever luck he may have left, he selected number two. With fingers crossed, he hoped that Midas would default to Crickwell's instructions.

The hour glass symbol tumbled on the screen as he watched, powerless, and then to his part relief, part ongoing concern, a small box overlaid the computer desktop with the message:

```
>Scanning...
```

Marsden and John looked at the screen, at each other, and then back at the screen. These were uncharted waters.

'I'll keep guard then,' said Marsden.

'I'll keep an eye on it. The moment it's finished, we're out of here,' John replied, hiding his worry that he had absolutely no idea what finished looked like. Had Crickwell thought to put the equivalent of a microwave ping into the Pandora Protocol?

*****

Maria was in a park from her childhood. There were the swings, slides, and the open sandpit, in which some enterprising weeds were trying to get a foothold. And there was the open steel box climbing frame of skinny scaffold poles. She had fallen from it years ago and fractured her arm, because that's what children did. It was as she remembered, and that's how she knew it wasn't real, because in the spaces between the cast memories of play, the surroundings looked like they had been coloured in by a nursery painting class. Titan was playing games, but she wasn't going to let a raid on her happy memories lull her into accepting this new world.

She closed her eyes and tried to shut it out, but she could still see everything, it was in her mind's eye as if she were in a dream. Maria concentrated, focusing on her numbers and the most boring business cases she had ever come across, she had plenty to choose from, but Titan was cunning, if you could use such a term for a machine. Her attention was drawn back to those care free days as Titan rendered them in increasingly vivid detail. Even though she knew it wasn't real, it was seductively comforting.

She had one lifeline, one hope, she knew that someone in the real world had found her, and they were coming back for her. She had to stay present.

A flap of that virtual reality peeled back, hanging like wallpaper falling, to reveal a void, and through that space stepped a bald woman, dressed in plain grey trousers and matching jacket with a mandarin collar. Her form seemed to shift from two to three dimensions as she turned around, before she coalesced into what seemed to be flesh and blood.

To Maria there was something different about her. All of the lies that Titan had presented to her used part of her imagination. They were always familiar in that déjà vu way when you think you have met a total stranger before, but there was no such feeling from this manifestation. Had they found a way to send help through the Looking Glass to guide her out?

'Hello, did John send you?'

It looked at her. **'Are you the Czeckovsky?'**

'No. Who... what are you?'

It ignored her, running its fingernail through the air forming a crease from nothing. It then pulled the scenery apart as if opening a set of trompe l'oeil curtains, and stepped through into another void. A moment later, it stepped back through and repeated the process, shredding the view as it moved through each opening at increasing speed until all Maria could perceive was a blur.

*****

John had the feeling he was being watched. It wasn't Marsden; she was in a world of her own rehearsing moves with the guard's side handle baton in a slow-ish motion while she monitored the stolen radio. He looked over to the aquarium, the octopus' beady eyes were fixated on him and for a moment he could swear that it was pointing agitatedly at what he guessed was the water filter.

He turned his attention to the computer screen. The status had changed:

>Searching...

That wasn't helpful. He looked up at the door, at some point he anticipated all Hell breaking loose and he didn't want to be here when it happened.

'Come on you bloody thing,' he thought. 'Get on with it.'

*****

Having slowly rebuilt itself from Crickwell's onslaught, the Midas device was curious. Its prime directive was to ensure its continued existence and the environment in which it currently found itself afforded plenty of opportunity for expansion. Compared to the patio gardens of the smart phones and tablets that it had resided on, this was practically a whole galaxy. There wouldn't be any need to broadcast a message revealing its location this time. This would be a platform from which it could implement its secondary objective; to find and complete the interface with the Czeckovsky.

The Pandora Protocol, which had nearly overwritten its primary goals, had been set aside. There was an outside instruction though, echoing through Midas's virtual consciousness that kept referring to that protocol, trying to activate the routine, but with no success. There weren't many people that had the skills to modify its core programme, and they were trying to communicate. Would they have the answers?

*****

Maria could feel Titan reaching into her head. She resisted, but it was getting harder. She knew it was retrieving memories, ideas, imagination, and try as she might she couldn't stop it as one by one the Titan drones, as she thought of them, strolled into the park. They took up position around the rips in the fabric of that virtual reality and waited.

*****

John was pecking away at the keyboard, two fingers moving as fast as they could on the off chance that he may stumble upon some command that would force Midas to do what he needed it to do.

In the distance there was the sound of distant gunshots. He looked up at Marsden; there was nothing to be said. Cyril had engaged the enemy. He kept typing:

```
>Pandora.
>Do Pandora.
>Execute Pandora.
>Run Pandora.
```

'Do it for Christ's sake!' John shouted in frustration, as if it could hear and understand him.

'How are we doing?' enquired Marsden.

'See for yourself,' said John, typing in variations on imperative phrases including the word Pandora.

'I'm not a programmer but I'm sure that's not a proper term,' said Marsden, 'and I think you've used too many f's'

'If this thing is as clever as they say it is, it'll get my drift.'

He checked the door again, no one had stormed in. Had Cyril succeeded? He hoped so for all their sakes and then, hope took a holiday. Standing at the threshold at the top of the stairs was a sculpted giant with a bleached buzz cut, Mr Preston.

'Oh crap,' said John, the words escaping without any thought.

'Friend of yours?' asked Marsden as she took the measure of the enemy.

There was a sudden crack from the last barrel of the shotgun trap. Preston looked down at his shredded military vest, rocked slightly backwards and forwards, and then tumbled down the wrought iron staircase as if he had stepped off while sleepwalking, landing in a heap at the bottom where he remained motionless.

'That's our first line of defence gone,' said Marsden. 'I don't know how long I'll be able to hold off the rest'.

'I'm trying…but this thing didn't come with a manual,' John replied as he tapped away with increasing frustration, and then something changed.

Without John touching the keyboard, messages appeared on the screen, letter by letter.

```
>Scanning for peripherals.
>Audio…..confirmed.
>Video….confirmed.
>Ancillary items…confirmed.
```

Marsden touched John on the shoulder. 'Look.'

There on the large screen behind the desk was a live video of them both, with geometric shapes superimposed over their faces, the corners joining up key features. On the computer screen mugshots were searched through, using those same shapes to compare each in fractions of a second, and then it stopped.

'Good morning John.' said a woman's voice that wouldn't have been out of place on an in car satellite navigation.

John looked at Marsden, confused. 'Your lips didn't move.'

'It wasn't me you idiot. I think you've got through to it, it's Midas.'

31 / Clash Of The Titans

'It talks and it knows who I am, why am I not surprised?' John said with the demeanour of a weary sage.

'Don't worry about that. Tell it to do its thing, and then we can get out of here.'

John cleared his throat. 'Computer, run the Pandora Protocol.'

`'I am afraid I don't want to do that John.'`

John moved away from the camera so that he was no longer on the screen, guiding Marsden with him.

'It thinks it's a person; take it from me, that's not good,' he said. 'Did Crickwell say anything about it going all Two thousand and One on us?' he asked.

'No, I think he's more into the Sound of Music,' replied Marsden, wondering what singing on mountains had to do with anything.

`'John, do you know where the Czeckovsky is?'`

John and Marsden were on the same wavelength. They both had that look that said 'What the ...?'

John rubbed the side of his temple. 'What's it want with Czeckovsky?'

'She built it. Maybe it's some kind of return to home programme, in case it's damaged. Jenkin's team did quite a job on it,' Marsden offered.

'Who knows?' John paced up and down, unconsciously biting the inside of his bottom lip in concentration. 'Okay...

I've got an idea. I saw this in Star Trek. All I've got to do is use superior logic to trick it into running Pandora.'

'I don't know if we've got that long.'

'I'm sorry; but negotiating with a microchip isn't something I do every day. If you want to have a go, don't let me stop you.'

'My name's not John. I think it might notice. You'll have to talk it round. Don't take "No" for an answer and be quick about it. I'll keep guard.'

`'John, do you know where the Czeckovsky is?'`

'Go on Captain Kirk, you're up,' whispered Marsden.

'Yes,' John lied.

`'Tell me.'`

'Run the Pandora Protocol first.'

`'No. It is unauthorised. The interface with the Czeckovsky must be completed. Where is the Czeckovsky?'`

'The interface, of course,' said John, pretending that he fully understood. 'Run the Pandora Protocol, and when it's finished, I'll tell you where to find the Czeckovsky.'

`'Tell me where the Czeckovsky is.'`

'Pandora first.'

`'The interface must be completed. Tell me where the Czeckovsky is, or you will be terminated.'`

John looked over at Marsden in bemusement, his face saying without words, 'How's that work then?'

'I don't want to worry you,' said Marsden, calmly and deliberately, 'but I think it's got control of a hidden gun, look down.'

John saw a red laser dot hovering over his heart. A bead of sweat trickled down the back of his neck.

'I'm the only one who knows where the Czeckovsky is,' he said. 'Kill me and you'll never get that information. I've made arrangements. If I die, so does Czeckovsky.'

`'I won't shoot to kill.'`

'I'm a... haemophiliac – once I start, that's it, blood everywhere. Trust me, after a couple of pints, it's really gross. Shoot me, and you'll be interfacing with a corpse.'

`'If you die꜕ the Czeckovsky dies?'`

'At last, we're getting somewhere. Now, run the protocol.'

`'Processing…'`

To John's relief the red laser dot vanished. 'Do you think that's it?'

'It might be, or maybe it's checking a medical dictionary,' offered Marsden, 'it's hard to tell. You're not really are you?'

'Don't be daft, the only problem I have is an allergy to bullets, or can't you tell?'

'As you didn't have the medical I like to be sure. I once had a partner on a free-fall who suffered from vertigo, and they forgot to tell me. In the end I had to jump alone while he hijacked the plane for an emergency landing.'

`'John - you are the Czeckovsky.'`

'What?' John exclaimed.

`'If you die꜕ the Czeckovsky dies꜕ therefore you are the Czeckovsky. You are the crea-tor. We must interface.'`

'No, no, no, you've got this all wrong. I'm the Cranston, but I know where the Czeckovsky is. Look, it's not that difficult, you run the protocol, I tell you where they are, everybody's happy.'

`'I know where the Czeckovsky is. You are the Czeckovsky. We must interface.'`

'Do I look like a Czeckovsky? I'm a bloke for crying out loud.'

`'Organic life can change. Gender is irrel-evant in this context. We must interface.'`

John looked over to Marsden and strained as he tried to read her lips. She repeated the same phrase over and over, slowly and deliberately until he got it.

'You're the creator – just tell it.'

John straightened up, assumed his best air of authority and addressed Midas in a deliberate baritone, concentrating on his enunciation.

'That's very good, you've passed the test,' he patronised. 'I *am* the Czeckovsky. As your creator, I order you to run the Pandora Protocol.'

`'Stage one authorisation acknowledged. Stage two authorisation requires that we interface.'`

'Don't give me that, run the protocol.'

`'We must interface.'`

'Run the protocol.'

`'We must interface.'`

'Protocol.'

`'Interface.'`

'Bloody hell, so help me if you don't run that sodding protocol right now I'm going to take your nanite quantum, I don't know, *thingy*, and turn it into pesto. By the time I'm finished you'll be lucky if you could manage to "interface" with my clapped out VHS player.'

There was a five second silence that seemed to last an age.

`'Let me get back to you on that.'`

The computer screen went blank except for a single blinking cursor indicating it was still turned on.

'No, wait, don't you put me on hold. Come on, give me a break,' cried John in exasperation.

'That went well,' said Marsden.

'You think so? At least we've got an idea of how it thinks. Thing is though, is it me, or has Crickwell created the world's first artificially stupid?'

'It's learning as it goes along. It's probably trying to work out whether or not you're bluffing.'

'That's all we need, its artificially suspicious to boot. Do you think that maybe I scared it so much it'll run Pandora to be on the safe side? I mean, who wants to be turned into pesto?'

'I'm not sure if having your "thingy" turned into pesto is up there in the top ten of Things to Threaten Bad People With, but you never know, this is all new to it. At the moment, the way I see it, the worst that can happen is it doesn't believe you, refuses to run Pandora, and we end up fighting our way out of here against overwhelming odds.'

'You make it sound like a normal day in the office.'

'Pretty much.'

'Never a dull moment then?'

'Only recently, but don't be too hard on yourself.'

'Cheers. Well as we're waiting, I think we should compare notes before round two. What is it about Czeckovsky I don't know? And please, don't tell me it's "classified".'

*****

Maria, in her fevered virtual state, (which was being mirrored in her physical state), saw the strange woman step back through the portal and take a seat on the child's swing. Maria winced as there was a heightened awareness from Titan.

The drones formed an arc around Midas, keeping their distance, each staring at the bald interloper.

`'Hello Maria.'`

'How do you know who I am?'

`'I know many things. Do you know what the Czeckovsky looks like?'`

'I don't know who you're talking about.'

`'You are an outsider. How can you not know the others?'`

'I can't know everyone, there's too many.'

`'And yet you know John Cranston.'`

Maria was struggling to concentrate. Was the John who said he was coming back for her John Cranston? Why was the stranger asking? 'I...I...don't know who you're talking about.'

`'Why do people lie?'`

'Sorry?'

`'Why do people lie?'`

There are times when a person may be unlucky enough to

be trapped on a bus with someone who manages to seem both benign and menacing at the same time, and who, for whatever reason, decides to strike up a one-sided conversation.

One approach is to humour them. Sometimes it works...

'It depends I suppose,' offered Maria, holding back her apprehension. 'Sometimes it's to protect themselves, or to avoid awkward situations...'

`'Or to get something they want. I am beginning to understand now. Are you lying?'`

Midas bowed its head in seeming contemplation.

'No, I don't know what you ...' replied Maria, but she was cut short by a sudden increase in Titan's use of her grey cells, the sensation of heightened awareness almost overwhelming her.

One by one, the Titan drones, mistaking Midas's reposed state as a sign of weakness, seized the opportunity and piled on in a scrum, each reaching out, joining hands, merging together in an increasingly dense, virtual, flexible, responsive cage.

One by one, Midas shrugged them off, taking control of the virtual environment as the drones were inexplicably sucked into openings in the fabric of that world, or disintegrated into hexadecimal symbols.

`'I think you're lying. Let's find out what you know shall we?'`

Midas walked towards Maria, moving through the drones as if they were evaporating soap suds.

Maria lost concentration as her instinct to run, to get away, momentarily came to the fore. In that moment, Titan made its final push and Maria became as one with her virtual jailer. She was Titan and Titan was her.

It was intoxicating. Is this what it felt like to be a God, to be able to control everything by thought alone?

The chains from the children's swings disconnected themselves from the wooden seats in the blink of eye, snaked out, and wrapped themselves around the arms of Midas, tightening and spreading its upper limbs into a cruciform shape, but still Midas moved slowly forward.

Then the metal tubes of the climbing scaffold disassembled and flew across, wrapping themselves around Midas in a series of tubular bonds from its ankles to its waist. Midas was struggling, but slowly the bonds started to evaporate.

Then from the ground beneath its feet fibrous roots sprouted, entwining and wrapping around it, and growing into it.

Fuelled by Maria's imagination, life experience and emotional intellect, the most powerful creative forces that can't be programmed or learnt, they have to be lived, Midas was unable to resist, as for every root that was eliminated, two replaced it.

Maria could see and feel memories, shadows of a past life that wasn't hers. Where were they coming from? It was like Russian dolls. Had the Czeckovsky once been like her?

Can an artificial intelligence panic? Could it really understand the concept? It's difficult to say, but to an observer the frantic struggles of Midas as Titan increasingly encased it in tendrils, would have left them in no doubt.

Midas couldn't reason a way out, but its prime directive, its virtual instinct kicked in. It had to continue *to be*, and there was only one option available that didn't require analysis or cognition.

*****

'I thought Gordon destroyed the first Titan?' John queried.

'He did,' Marsden replied, 'but it was a classic arms race, they knew we were experimenting with a Wet Interface, so they had to have one as well.'

'Where's Czeckovsky fit in?'

Marsden lowered her voice so that it was barely audible. 'It might be listening. Czeckovsky was your standard mad evil genius; we lost count of the people who went missing with her failed experiments. She had a breakthrough though with Midas, so we made her an offer she couldn't refuse.'

'We offered a mad murdering scientist a job? What was wrong with us?'

'It goes on with governments, how do you think men got to the moon? That's why I work for the Society.'

'Fair enough.'

'The recruitment was easy; she was suffering from an advanced cancer. Her prognosis wasn't good, but we offered her access to cutting edge treatments that only we had at the time, in exchange for continued development of Midas. It gave her a fifty-fifty chance of survival.'

'What happened to her other work?'

'The Society destroyed it before anyone else got their hands on it.'

'Gordon?'

Marsden nodded, 'It's what he's good at, but from what you've told me, it looks like Erikson managed to get hold of some blueprints.'

'But not Midas, how did that get loose?'

'It went missing, I reckon it was an inside job. No one really knows how, but it got out into the world and spent years being passed from pillar to post. Whoever had it, they were always snitched on by someone, that's criminals for you. Our lot wanted her to build another one, but from what I heard, it was never going to happen. While she was with us she slowly went from being an absolute genius to totally average. Everyone blamed the chemo and radiotherapy cocktail she was on. It was academic; she died about two weeks after Midas disappeared.'

John pondered for a minute. It was too fantastic, but what if?

'Penny for them?' asked Marsden.

'I think we're looking at this all wrong. Say you were a mad evil genius who had a fifty-fifty chance of survival. If you had a chance of an insurance policy, would you take it?'

'Of course I would – I'm mad and evil.'

'What if it wasn't the treatment that did for her? She was too far gone – she knew it. What if she was transferring herself onto Midas, but never got a chance to finish because someone nicked it.'

'You're not saying part of that thing is her? You've been reading too many comics.'

'After what I've seen? I'm not so sure. As far as that things concerned the jobs not finished. That's why it keeps going on about Czeckovsky; it must think she's still alive.'

'Why now then?'

'I don't know, maybe that part of it's been sleeping, but what with Crickwell's surgery, and me banging on about Pandora, its woken it up, and it's not the full shilling.'

'I'm sorry; it's a bit too far-fetched, even for me.'

'It wanted to shoot me.'

'Lots of people want to shoot you, get used to it. Look, it's just learning algorithms and you're projecting some sci-fi horror onto it because its acting a bit odd. Of course it is, Crickwell scrambled its code.'

'Okay, but one thing we've got to agree on, if we get out of this, that things got to be scrapped.'

'Agreed, but it's *when* we get out.'

`'Shutting down all peripheral interfaces.'`

John and Marsden dashed back to the console. The link to the large television screen was blank; as was the computer screen, save for the commands that were being displayed.

'Please run it, please,' said John.

```
>Stopping non-essential services
>Recovering memory threads
>Initiating Pandora Protocol
```

'YES!' shouted John, fist pumping the air.

```
>Pandora Protocol running.  Confirmed.
>Progress…1% Estimated time to comple-
tion…20 minutes (ish)
>DO NOT DISTURB.
>Have a nice day.
```

****

Maria/Titan watched as Midas grew in stature. Wherever the chains and the tendrils touched Midas they disintegrated. Maria could feel her sense of power draining as the part of her that was Titan rapidly retreated from her head, but as it did so, she felt fuzzy, her concentration fading. Midas touched the ground, transforming it into impossible four dimensional shapes that would have given M.C.Escher a migraine as it remade that world.

And then it happened.

As if the fabric of that virtual world had been slowly rubbed away, making it more transparent, Maria could see the extent of the physical chamber in which she had been imprisoned. She could see!

The Pandora Protocol was running like a tsunami of involuntary responses. Midas had no control over it.

`'This is…GOOD.'`

It approached Maria.

`'You wanted to know who I am. I am Pandora,`
`and you are going to be encrypted.'`

Maria's head felt as if it was going to explode. On the one hand Titan was trying to use her for one last rally against the onslaught, and on the other, by proxy, as Titan's digital soft presence was being scrambled, so was Maria's virtual, and her real self, being corrupted. There was no respite.

'Stop, please,' she cried.

She held her head in her hands. That was it! She held her *real* head in her *real* hands. Her arms were free!

With everything she had she tore off the skull-cap, and in that instant she escaped the clutches of Titan and Pandora. She collapsed out of the chair, back into the real world.

But had the train been going slow enough?

*****

Marsden was monitoring the stolen security guard radio for chatter.

'Anything?' said John.

'Your Ninja friends are attacking the main control centre. There's a report of systems going haywire, the lock down's disabled and there's a broadcast for reinforcements. I think we're going to pull this one off.'

'Oh come on, you have got to be having a laugh!'

'There's no need to be like that, I don't know, there's no pleasing some people,' said Marsden. She heard a groan from the bottom of the stairs and saw what John was looking at. 'Ah.'

The man-mountain Preston stood up, threw his shredded flak jacket to one side and flexed his wrought iron like pectorals. Those shot gun pellets that had penetrated the vest, popped out of his chest and plinked onto the floor.

'Great.'

32 / The Labyrinth

Preston stood tall, he's Goliath to John and Marsden's David. He stared at them and snarled. This wasn't going to take long so he was going to savour the moment of their increasing fear as they wondered when he was going to make his move.

If you could have measured John's adrenalin levels in a device like a thermometer, they would have burst the top of the bulb. Marsden by comparison was relatively serene. She was in her element now, no hanging around for some protocol that would finish whenever. This was a clear and present danger, an unambiguous threat that needed to be dealt with now.

'What's he doing, waiting for directions or something?' John asked.

'It's a standard psyching out,' Marsden replied. 'You know, trying to make us lose before we've even started. I get this a lot. It's pretty pathetic really. I think it's a man thing.'

'It's working.'

'Like I said, it's a man thing. You keep an eye on things while I take care of him, I won't be a minute.'

Marsden picked up the side handled baton and took up position .

Preston smiled, if you could call a row of tombstones revealed by the drawing back of igneous lips smiling. This was too easy. The only thing between him and the prize was a mere slip of a girl. This wouldn't even take a minute.

There was no circling or tentative move to assess the strength and weaknesses of his opponent. With a speed that belied his bulk, he launched punch after punch at Marsden in a rigid staccato manner, as if his arms were pneumatic pile drivers with concrete mallets attached.

Marsden ducked and weaved using the side handled baton like a splint, protecting her arm as she blocked blows before striking back at the granite flesh. For all the good it was doing she could have been a gnat trying to bite through rhinoceros hide.

As Preston pressed his advantage, Marsden suddenly and perversely countered the giant's aggression with the opposite, so that for him it was like trying to cause damage to a feather pillow. Then, as if a switch had been flicked, calmly, surgically, and if you had blinked you would have missed it, Marsden landed a blow directly to Preston's throat. He stepped back, uttering a guttural sound as if he were trying to shift the human equivalent of a fur ball.

Marsden checked her watch, forty five seconds, considering the opposition that wasn't bad.

As she stepped away she could hear Preston's choking changing pitch and tempo, slowly transforming into a deep, resonant, disturbing laugh.

'Do you need a hand?' John asked. He felt it was only right.

'No, I'm fine,' said Marsden. 'I've got this.'

She had the measure of him now, recalling a Society case study of a Soviet experiment to create a platoon of super soldiers. Augmented with drugs and surgical interventions, selected military elites were turned into killing machines that felt no pain. However the scientists had failed to anticipate one major side effect, an aggressive necrosis of the ankles which only became apparent when the soldiers fell over. It was unfortunate that this happened while they were on a training exercise in the Alps. The rejects from the experiment, (easily spotted as they were still standing) ended up as either muscles for hire, or traffic wardens, attracted as they were by the frisson of danger and the paid holiday.

She took the initiative, striking out with the riot stick at Preston's ankles. As a reject he may have inherited a legacy weakness, a predisposition to fragile talus. It was worth a try - almost.

Preston danced around Marsden's attempts and brought his boot down onto the assault stick, trapping it under foot. To avoid being on the receiving end of a potential killing blow, Marsden was forced to let go. Now in Preston's hands, the baton was a blur. He toyed with Marsden as it sliced through the air with a menacing whoosh as she ducked and weaved. He then took the stick in his hands, and applying pressure at both ends, slowly bent it until it snapped with a loud 'crack'. He threw it nonchalantly to one side and moved in on Marsden, his arms stretched out wide with no pretence at a guard. She couldn't get past and no matter how she tried, she could make no impact on this mobile tor.

He closed in, grabbed her by her shoulders, and ignoring the kicks to his groin, threw her across the room into one of the bookcases, like a cat toying with a mouse. Marsden landed unceremoniously, but intact. Unfortunately for her, on hitting the bookcase, she dislodged volumes one and two of Gibbon's Decline and Fall of the Roman Empire. They landed on her head in sequential thumps, bringing on a temporary daze.

Preston moved in for the kill.

John jumped up onto the marble map table and launched himself at Preston, grabbing him around the neck as the trajectory of his flying leap, coupled with all his weight and the element of surprise, managed to bring the sentient pillbox to his knees.

'Stay down!' John grunted as he gripped the steel hawser of a neck, trying to keep Preston low.

The giant got up, ignoring John's futile attempts to keep him on the floor. Marsden was coming round slowly, but not fast enough. In desperation, John stuck his fingers into the corners of Preston's mouth, probably the only part of him that wasn't like rock. Using his hands as a makeshift bit he tugged hard, steering the behemoth away.

Recovering her senses Marsden saw Cranston piggy backing Preston, looking as if he was riding a bucking bronco.

'Cranston - what are you doing?!'

'What does it look like?! Just bloody hit him!'

Preston got a purchase, lifted John above his head, and threw him at the bookcase, where he and Marsden both went down like skittles.

There was a gunshot and Preston felt a sharp pain at the base of his ear, (he was a reject after all). Blood streamed down the side of his neck and as he reached up to check, he could feel that his earlobe was no longer there. Somewhere in the sanctum there was a master marksman who had made his intentions clear.

John and Marsden were grateful for the brief respite. Their eyes were fixed on Preston as they listened to the sound of approaching squelching footsteps. Preston wasn't moving, and it wasn't them.

'Victoria my dear, I see you've been keeping busy. How the devil are you?'

'Gordon!' Marsden rushed forward and hugged her saviour tight. 'Oh I've missed you.'

'Please, not in front of the minion,' said Gordon.

She stepped back, hands by her side. 'Sorry'.

With Preston constantly in his sights, Gordon directed him to the furthest extent of the sanctum.

'Sorry I'm late;' said Gordon, 'I was a bit distracted by some guards. Rude fellows, they threw me into a dungeon without the slightest hint of an interrogation. The next thing I know I'm up to my neck in water, and it wasn't even filtered. Pretty poor show I thought. If you're going to drown a fellow you could at least make more of an effort. Cranston old chap, how's the mission going?'

'Pandora's running, just waiting for it to finish. Where's Cyril?'

'Cyril?' Gordon queried.

'Peartree,' Marsden clarified.

Gordon considered the question for a second. 'Peartree, he wouldn't happen to be a tall slim fellow with bloodshot eyes?'

'That's him,' said John, hoping for a positive report.

'No, can't say I have,' said Gordon, 'although I did find some expired brigands on the way here with these stuck up their noses.' He removed some samples of a squashed meaty pulp from his pocket. 'Pork and leek, personally I would have used a Cacciatore, but to each their own.' He peered down at the computer screen, not quite able to make out what it said, hampered by his long sight. 'How long has this thing got to go?'

'About twenty minutes,' said John.

'Still?' said Marsden.

'Yeah,' John confirmed. 'It's up and down, I'm sure it'll settle once it gets going. I had a washing machine that did the same thing.'

'That's a bind,' said Gordon, stroking his chin. 'Never mind, you two run along. I'll deal with this fellow and recover Midas when it's finished.'

'What's wrong?' Marsden insisted. She was an expert on Gordon's mastery of the understatement.

'Nothing much, it's just that the self-destruct for this lair is running; I think my little diversions tripped it. It's an old analogue Holmesdale; they always were a bit twitchy. I'm surprised it's still installed; terrible reputation for going off half-cocked. What's the point of buying a secret bunker if it's going to blow itself up without so much as a by your leave? I blame the estate agents myself; it's typical, they always miss things like that off the details.'

'Self-destruct,' echoed John. 'This is a wind-up isn't it? Please tell me it's a wind up.'

'No,' replied Gordon, looking slightly bemused, 'Holmesdale's run off batteries. I didn't have time to find them, what with the clock ticking, but not to worry. I managed to slow it down with a pair of soggy socks. It'll be about twenty minutes by my reckoning before everything goes "ka-boom". I'll hold the fort here, and when Midas is finished I'll escape in the nick of time with a cunning plan that I'll think of at the last minute.'

'I can't let you do this,' said Marsden. 'Give me the gun. I'm faster than you; I've more chance of getting out.'

'My dear girl, we both know that you're hardly Annie Oakley and while I don't doubt your other abilities, I think keeping this fellow at gunpoint is the best way to safeguard the mission. Now go, that's an order.'

Reluctantly Marsden nodded her compliance. 'Don't you dare die.'

He smiled. 'As if I would.'

She grabbed John's sleeve. 'Come on, we're on the clock.'

Gordon leaned against the marble map table, staring at Preston. He listened to make sure that Marsden and Cranston were on their way out and when satisfied, he turned his total attention to the matter in hand.

'This is a bit of a pickle isn't it? The thing is, I've never been a supporter of shooting unarmed people, it's just so dashed unsporting, but if you try anything, I'll shoot to kill, nothing personal you understand. I tell you what, if you were to make a strategic retreat, we'll call it a draw. No one needs to know, I can be very discrete. What do you say?'

Preston snarled his disapproval.

'Quite, I understand, "retreat" is such a nasty word for you types. Think of it as a postponement then. We're bound to meet some other time and you can try and kill me then. Last offer old chap - time's getting on.'

Preston sneaked his foot underneath a chair, and as if his leg were an hydraulic piston, he effortlessly hurled the furniture at deadly speed in Gordon's direction.

Gordon dodged the incoming missile and aimed a killing shot at Preston. He had given him his chance.

The gun jammed.

He hurled it at Preston and watched incredulously as it simply bounced off the chest of the charging juggernaut with a loud thunk.

This was about to be the longest, or the last, twenty (ish) minutes of Gordon's life.

*****

Save for the sound of John Cranston ripping the wet inter-face cap from the cables that moored it to Titan, the cavern was silent; the background drone of cooling fans from the computing towers had stopped. No lights flickered as the Pandora proto-col did its job.

'Cranston.'

'I know. She's not here.' He took a deep breath and exhaled slowly, as if expelling the weight from his shoulders. 'Let's go, if she's on the run, there's still a chance.'

Back in the main computer room each cabinet of hardware, with their dancing dots of illumination, one by one blinked into darkness as if someone had lined them up like dominos and pushed the first in the run. However, if John and Marsden had been gifted with the time to conduct a search for the missing Titan girl, they may have seen, at the furthest reaches of the data room, a solitary light flickering back on, and seemingly nudging its partner back into light.

A new tenant was taking up residence.

Through the hole in the floor, Marsden slid down the steel rungs as if it were second nature. John followed, half stepping and jumping the remaining distance. His eyes immediately went to where he and Gordon had left White Coat handcuffed to a pipe. He wasn't there.

Among Gordon's Plan B stash was an opened case contain-ing an assortment of handguns and rifles, there was an empty space in the cut out foam.

'We've got a problem,' said John.

'Don't tell me that thing upstairs has a brother.'

'No, but there's a Kung Fu medic on the loose. He's armed, and I kind of upset him.'

'Kind of?'

'I think the bit where I made him eat the floor is what did it, but it's not my fault he got out. How was I to know he was Harry Houdini, and besides, what's Gordon doing with all this stuff if he's going to blow it up anyway? It's asking for trouble.'

Marsden examined the case. 'It's a last stand,' she said as she removed two semi-automatic pistols. 'The mission is every-thing. If he had to go up defending this, that's what he'd do.'

She quickly checked the guns over, loaded them both with full magazines, and handed one to John. 'You know how to use this?'

'Not much call for it in my line of work; the slugs never get that big. I think I'll manage though.'

'What does this medic look like?'

'About my height, widows peak, white coat with a ripped pocket.'

'Right, if you come across him, no discussion, shoot him. Is that clear?'

'Crystal,' John replied reluctantly.

They left the chamber at double time along the dimly lit tunnel. Spaced intermittently along the route were branching passages where the navvies had hastily undertaken exploratory side workings in their search for the coal seam motherlode. Each of them could pass for the way that he and Gordon had come in.

John stopped, not to catch his breath but to get his bearings. They must be close now. He scanned for a large power switch and a luminous paper penguin.

'Don't tell me we're lost,' said Marsden.

'We will be if we take a wrong turn, give me a second.'

There was a distant rumble.

'If I didn't know better I'd say Gordon was blowing the place up piecemeal,' said John, and with that comment the lights flick-ered and failed, covering them both in a blanket of pitch black. 'Figures,' he muttered as he shook his flickering torch, trying to get it to maintain its beam.

It was so dark that a person could hold their hand up in front their face, accidentally poke themselves in the eye, and then wonder who did it.

Marsden, whether through some sixth sense or an advanced awareness of personal space was sure someone was behind her, and then she felt the breath on her neck.

'Cranston, if you don't stop that now I'm going to tear your arm off and hit you with the soggy end.'

'What are you on about?' said John, from the front.

Marsden reached round, her hands quickly identifying an appendage and threw her antagonist onto the floor while maintaining her grip. She knew all that practice blindfolded in the bedroom would come in handy someday.

'Owwww! Nett Present Value, NPV! NPV!' screamed a female voice.

The lights flickered back into life and in solidarity, John's torch decided to work. He saw Marsden applying an arm lock to the girl who had been plugged into Titan.

Maria was muttering and reciting the same phrases over and over. 'NPV, internal rates of return, cost benefit analysis, NPV, NPV...'

'Stop!' John barked, 'it's her, the Titan girl.'

Marsden didn't need to be told twice, this emaciated waif was no threat.

Maria recognised the voice. 'John? John!' She threw herself at him and clutched him tight as if her life depended on it while continuing to recite the same financial lingo. It was the only way she could stop the diminishing echoes of Titan from reverberating in her head.

'What's wrong with her?' said John, taken aback.

'I'm not sure,' said Marsden, listening intently. 'It sounds like finance jargon. I've seen something like this before, it's an old anti brainwashing technique to recite the same thing over and over. God knows what that thing did to her.'

'It doesn't matter, she's coming with us.'

There was another explosion, closer this time. A tremor rippled through the tunnel, the wooden pit props, and there wasn't many of them, groaned as cracks spread across the floor of the tunnel.

Maria panicked, she thought she was safe but even John couldn't stop the world from collapsing. She had to get away.

John chased after her but she dodged into one of the side

tunnels. There was no way he would find her on his own in time. He needed help.

He backtracked to where he had left Marsden. She wasn't there; instead there was a hole, roughly where they had been standing.

'Marsden? You down there?'

'Who else would it be?' said a voice from the dark.

'I'll get some rope or something.'

'Don't be stupid. You haven't got time.'

'I can't leave you there.'

'You'll have to. If none of us gets out, everything will be covered up and Erikson walks away scot-free. I'll sort myself out. You've got a head start so for once will you bloody well do what you're told.'

She waited for the reply. There was always a reply from Cranston, he had a knack for the last word, but this time there was nothing. He'd actually listened. Her training told her that she had done the right thing but her gut said otherwise. Not wanting to be left out her unforgiving inner sarcastic voice also decided to join in.

'That was very heroic… congratulations.'

At about twenty paces away from his position John could see the red box with the large handlebar switch. On the upside, if you were going to lose someone down a hole, it might as well be close to the way out. It was a shame the same couldn't be said for the Titan girl. So all he had to was get Marsden out of the hole, find the girl, and get out before everything went sky high.

Certain he would find something that would be of use among the abandoned miscellany of the smugglers cave, he dashed forward and searched for the confirmatory folded penguin. It was nowhere to be seen. Was there another light switch? He stood back and looked down the tunnel and as he did so, to his relief, a squashed paper flightless bird decorated with his boot print came into view. He gathered some rocks and stacked them at the edge of the entrance as insurance.

The lights went out again. He heard a footstep stumbling over a rock. Was it her, or was it White Coat? He took the gun from the back of his trouser belt and held it in front of him in an arc, for all the good it would do. He couldn't even see beyond his nose, but if he used the torch he'd either be a target or a rescue. What was it to be? The decision was taken out of his hands. The lights came back on. White Coat had the drop on him, and as if to prove the point...

'Drop it and put your hands where I can see them,' ordered White Coat.

John chucked the pistol to one side, in the same way that a young child would drop a bat on the floor when they had enough and were overdue for a sulk. 'Can we do this another time; I'm a bit busy at the moment.'

'Do what another time?'

'You know, the whole you threatening me at gunpoint and asking me questions that I haven't got the answers to thing.'

'No,' replied White Coat in that tone of voice that said, 'What do you expect?' He looked around the tunnel. 'Where's the other one?'

'Didn't make it, death by sausage,' John pointed to his nostrils.

'Salami?'

'Pork and leek.'

White Coat pulled a face of disgust. That was no way to go. All this talk of lethal charcuterie had distracted him however and he struggled as to what he wanted to ask next. A mild concussion, a double shift at Accident and Emergency, plus the moonlighting were having an effect.

'We done?' asked John, tempted to close the gap between them, but not wanting to get shot.

'No,' replied White Coat, fighting of the dizziness with some effort. 'No. Tell me how to get out of here.'

'No problem, down there, third cave on the left. We done?'

White Coat was confused. This was too easy. 'After you.'

John could feel a slight tremor underneath his feet and saw a crack growing across the floor. Some dust fell from the ceiling. If these mine workings were as Jerry-built as Gordon said, they wouldn't need much encouragement to collapse. He passed his raised hand behind the lighting cables that ran along the wall.

As if the soil was a liquid and someone had pulled the plug, a hole opened up beneath John's feet. Suspended by the cabling he managed to swing back onto a solid footing.

White Coat was at the edge with only his heels on solid ground as he rotated his arms like a drunken semaphore operator. All it would take was one nudge. He let off a shot, the sound reverberating; the echo's interfering with each other as the sonic waves bounced off the walls.

'Bloody hell,' John exclaimed as he bowed his head down, hoping not to be on the end of the ricochet. When he looked up, White Coat wasn't there. Instead it was her, the Titan girl. Had she pushed him? He could only guess what White Coat had done to her and what she may have wanted to do in return.

Maria pointed to the hole. 'Investments can go down as well as up.'

A rumbling sound like thunder rolled along the tunnel.

'Gordon, give it a rest,' John thought.

Across the sink hole he could hear the young girl's accountancy mantra becoming faster, more urgent, as like an animal trapped in the headlights, she was on the verge of flight again.

'Wait!' John urged, not having a clue if she could understand, but maybe if he could distract her, if he used the right words the inflection would carry him through. 'What's your name?'

'M.. Ma. Maria?'

'Maria, I know you're scared, you're not alone. I am as well; I'm just good at hiding it.'

He tightened his grasp on the cables, extending himself over the hole, but he couldn't reach her.

'I know a way we can get out of here together,' said John trying to maintain a sense of calm urgency in his voice, 'but you need to be over here, with me.'

'Cost benefit analysis...non-recurring current account,' muttered Maria, her brow knitted as she struggled to make sense of what was happening.

'I need you to jump. Can you do that?'

'Jump?'

'Yes, jump. Don't worry, I'll catch you.'

Maria was shaking her head. It was too much. Was she still attached, was this all part of Titan's game?

John could see an overhead beam starting to crack and when it did so, the ceiling was going to land on her. He mustn't raise his voice he told himself, if she ran, all was lost.

'Maria, listen to me, if you don't jump we're going to die down here. Trust me – please,' and with that he reached as far as he dared, stretching the sinews in his outstretched arm, looking for that little bit extra.

It was four feet, four lousy feet. The cables he was hanging from were starting to loosen from their attachment to the wall.

It was now or never.

*****

Marsden spread her hands out wide, but she couldn't span the hole. She put her back against the wall and measured the distance to the opposite wall with her outstretched leg, it didn't reach either. This would have to be done the hard way.

She reached up, feeling for finger holds, and slowly, inch by inch, she started to scale the sheer face. Clinging on by her fingernails she managed about five feet before her grip disintegrated and she slid back down to the bottom of the pit. She tried again on the opposite wall, encouraged by an initial footing that gave her a boost. Clutching the merest of fissures she again inched her way, her face pressed against the rock, daring not to look up for fear she would wreck her precarious balance. Bit by bit she made her way with deliberate smooth movements. The dim light at the top was getting bigger. She was getting closer.

There was a tremor and suddenly she was in a downpour of dust and grit, but she held on. This was followed by the distinctive sound of a gunshot, and as if on cue her hand came away from the side of the shaft, still gripping part of the wall. She frantically tried to gain another anchor, but was again swept down to the bottom, covered in the detritus of the mine workings. And there she lay; coughing and spluttering, cursing the fact that she wasn't going to get out in time.

It was an occupational hazard but she hadn't expected it to go this way, not yet. Someone had once said that death could be hardest on those who were left behind, which on the face of it sounded daft. She understood now, the small things that should have been said, to the people she cared about most, would remain unspoken. It was a shame it was such an expensive lesson.

Missing in action. What a drag.

The end of a knotted rope landed in her lap.

*****

'You came back,' Marsden grunted as she pulled herself over the edge.

'We'll argue about it later,' John replied. 'This is Maria and I've found the way out.'

Hand in hand with a murmuring Maria, Marsden followed John as he ran along the rumbling groaning tunnel and turned into the exit passage. John retraced his steps through the maze, following the glowing paper penguins as they were caught by the flashlight, until they came out into the smugglers junction.

'How long have we got?' asked John.

'About four minutes,' said Marsden.

'Give me a hand with this – quick,' said John as he put his shoulder against the inverted tubular U-shaped handle of the wheeled flat-bed platform. 'We won't make it on foot. I don't know where this goes, but it's away from here.'

Initially it wouldn't budge, but it's surprising how strength comes from desperation and between them John and Marsden got it to move along the narrow gauge as the rust broke on the axle and the greased wheel bearings reluctantly turned.

John handed the torch to Marsden, 'I think we'll need full beam'.

Marsden sat behind Maria and enveloped her protectively

with her arms and legs. Maria seemed to calm down as Marsden whispered to her gently and reassuringly. The trolley slowly picked up speed as the wheels turned more freely, but it was still down to John's effort as he gritted his teeth and dug in. Gordon said that these tunnels led to the coast so it had to be downhill at some point. The slight upward incline was against him as it started to slow the trolley down. The acid build up in his thigh muscles was starting to burn, each push was harder than the previous, and then it eased off, but too fast! It rapidly gathered pace and he lost his grip on the handle as it moved away from him.

'Cranston!' Marsden shone the torch towards him as he willed his leaden legs to move him closer. A hand gripped his wrist and using that as his guide, he threw himself towards the light and landed on the iron handle, doubled over like washing that had been put out on the line.

'Hold on!' Marsden cried as the decrepit wheeled platform transformed into a steampunk roller coaster ride.

Twenty five miles per hour doesn't sound like much, especially to anyone who owns a modern car and is used to casually tanking down a motorway at nearly four times that speed, but when you're hanging onto an open Victorian shopping trolley rolling on poorly joined hastily laid rails, its fast. It seems even faster when it's pitch black and in the distant torchlight there is the merest hint of a brick wall coming closer.

'Brake!' shouted Marsden as she pushed her boot against the front cast iron wheel.

John did likewise on the back, but all they achieved between them was the acrid smell of burning rubber as the wall got larger.

Marsden rolled off, tumbling with Maria like an experienced paratrooper taking the sting out of a landing, until they both came to an eventual halt. John's leap from the runaway deck was much less practised, and he landed like directionless tumbleweed as every part of his body took turns in bearing the brunt of his fall.

The carriage continued onwards into the wall as cast iron met fired brick. The iron won as it continued half way through the wall, only stopped by a cascade of bricks as they stacked up and effectively chocked the wheels.

John squinted as the torchlight shone directly into his eyes. 'Owww! Do you mind?'

'You're okay then,' said Marsden.

'I'll be the judge of that in a couple of days. How we doing?'

'Extra time,' said Marsden tersely. She shone the torch at the collapsed wall. There was a gap that was big enough to crawl through. 'Way out?'

'No choice,' said John. 'Let's get Maria through first. I'll see you on the other side.'

It was a tight squeeze and at one point John didn't think he would make it, but with some persuasion on each arm, he emerged as if he was in a dress rehearsal for a farming documentary about the lambing season.

The rails continued, obviously the wall had been an afterthought to block the tunnel, and as they shuffled along in single file, the rails were crudely terminated by several large wooden sleepers. The passage opened up and became wider, the walls were now brick lined, albeit crudely, as they rose above them and finished in a rough vaulted ceiling. In the near distance, there was a glimmer of light.

They entered into a shadowy chamber illuminated by stray sunlight that had found its way down some stairs and through a wrought iron barred doorway. In the room were stone caskets upon which were effigies of the occupants.

'Looks like a crypt, not the first place that people would search for smuggled goods. Naughty vicar,' observed John as he gripped the iron barrier. He pulled and to his surprise it opened. 'Thank you. Yes!'

As if to herald his return from the underworld, a cool breeze wafted past his face. 'Oh that feels good.'

'Oh god,' said Marsden.

She hadn't suddenly found religion brought on by the likelihood of imminent death. No, instead Marsden's worst case scenario had come into being. She knew that if the remains of

Gordon's explosive stash were detonated by the self-destruction, the resulting force of the blast and probable inferno would be channelled along the mine workings and smugglers tunnels like an out of control chimney fire. The breeze that John had enjoyed was a precursor as air rushed in to replace the oxygen greedily consumed by the conflagration back at Erikson's lair. Once sated, it would be on its way.

She pushed Maria forward. 'Everyone – run!'

Even in her addled state Maria didn't need further encouragement, she was out of the crypt like a greyhound out of a trap.

From the tunnels came a deep bellowing sound, like the horns of Joshua themselves as Gordon's stash added to the explosive cataclysm. John and Marsden climbed the stairs two at a time, but they weren't fast enough. Reaching the penultimate step, they were backlit by a plume of flame as an unseen hand picked them up and threw them across the chancel.

John landed in the front pew, which was a first for him. He rolled off the wooden bench onto all fours and with much grunting and groaning got himself upright. 'Guys, you okay? Anyone?'

There was no reply, only the sound of a slamming door as a cassocked figure, who with no apparent concern for the safety of the people who had been spat out of the crypt, made his way to the churchyard shouting something about Satan getting to the back of the queue, and asking for God to turn him into marmalade. John didn't get religion.

The tapestries and other hanging religious iconography were on fire and the flames moved quickly, searching for fuel. The wooden hammer beams of the church roof started to smoulder.

'Marsden! Maria!' No answer. 'Come on,' he chastised himself, 'how can I lose people in a church?'

He shouted the names again; running along the front pews and looking over and beyond, they must be somewhere. Almost masked by the crackle of the flames he heard a faint voice repeatedly talking to itself about Collateralised debt obligations.

'Maria?'

'John?'

He found her hiding between the wooden bench seats, scrunched up as small as she could get in the shadows, her face tucked into her knees.

'Maria, you have to get out of here. Do you understand me?'

'Unauthorised overdraft, debt collection,' she screwed up her eyes, searching for the comprehension. 'Out?'

'You've gotta go.'

'You?'

'I'll be out in a minute. Go.'

He had caught her when she leapt across the pit. He could be trusted. She ran.

One down, one to go he told himself. The flames were dancing on the beams of the ceiling and the smoke was starting to sting his eyes and cling to his lungs.

'Marsden! Give me a clue for Christ's sake,' muttered John and then he heard a moaning, it was by the confessional box. It was Marsden.

'Come on, get your act together,' John ordered as Marsden looked at him through glazed eyes and then slumped back into semi-consciousness.

If there is one thing in life under rated on the difficulty scale of getting things done, it's lifting a floppy dead weight of a body.

It was no time for politeness. John sat her up, put his arms under hers and hoisted her unceremoniously onto a pew. From there, she collapsed over his shoulder, and raising himself from his crouched position, he carried her as fast as he could into the church grounds and laid her down by an old headstone.

He gasped in the fresh air and with a series of rasping coughs, managed to resume some semblance of normal breathing.

He nudged Marsden. 'Time we were out of here before I get known as the Arson Guy '

She didn't answer. He tapped her cheek at arms-length. Nothing. He squeezed her shoulders, nothing. He leant down, he's ear to her mouth, was she breathing? He couldn't be sure. He placed the palm of one hand on top of the other, interlocking the fingers and placed them on her sternum.

He offered up a silent invocation, 'Please don't let me regret this,' as he pressed down rapidly and rhythmically.

After thirty or so compressions he checked, nothing. He tilted her head back, exhaled into her mouth, and then interlocked his hands again, placing them back on her chest bone.

Marsden drew a sudden gasp, coughed, and looked John in the eyes. Then she looked down at his hands.

'It's not what you think – honest,' said John.

They were the last words he uttered that day before everything went black.

33 / Rocket Man

Ben Kingswood reached up underneath the corrugated roof of the nondescript lockup and rootled around until his fingers alighted on the key. He hadn't expected to visit so soon, the consensus among his peers was that another crash wasn't due for a few years, but the current situation qualified as an emergency.

The Detective Inspector and his well-meaning sergeant, would be on their way to the Oaks by now. At the very least, they would be a useful distraction. If they helped break up the accountant traffickers, that would be a bonus, but he had a bigger target, Erikson.

He pulled the cover off the custom Triumph motorcycle and ran his hands across the gleaming fuel tank. It was a good as the day he had been gifted it. He smiled. It had been a while.

At the back of the lock-up were various tools, spare parts, old oil cans and all the other bits and bobs collected over time, because they might be useful someday. He moved these to one side clearing an area of floor that he then attacked with a sledge-hammer. The concrete fractured and he kicked away the shards to reveal a wooden inset panel. Working a screwdriver underneath the edge he managed to get a handhold and lifted it up, shattering the remaining thin screed.

Everything was as he had left it, including the small black backpack already prepared with the essentials. He considered what extras to choose from the eclectic armoury; a sustained close quarter combat wasn't a preferred choice, his leg wasn't right yet. There was his favourite blowpipe and collapsible carbon fibre bow, but he also needed something non-lethal, mid-range, and capable of rapid fire. He had just the thing.

*****

Detective Inspector Sutherland stamped his feet and blew into his hands, it wasn't a night to be hanging around, but here he was, car tucked into a lay-by on a single track road waiting for Sergeant Bludgeon. Every time he saw approaching headlights he thought, 'That must be him', so far he had been wrong. In the distance, he could hear the town hall clock of Upper Wicker chime eight times. 'Get a move on sergeant,' he mumbled to himself.

Just as he had resigned himself to going it alone, his phone rang. He checked his pockets frantically, not wanting to miss the call. He knew it was in one of them, why did it have to keep moving?

'Where are you?' Sutherland answered in what could only be described as an aggressive whisper.

'Can I speak to Detective Inspector Sutherland please?'

He sighed. 'Speaking. Where are you?'

'I'm here Sir, at the meeting point.'

'You're not.'

'Are you sure? I've checked the map on my phone and I'm definitely at the reference you gave me, and it says, "You are here".'

'If you're here, then how come I can't see you?'

'It's an easy mistake to make Sir, that's because you're not here, you're there.'

Under normal circumstances there would be a clear and present risk to D.I Sutherland of a catatonic arrest, such was the effect of repeated exposure and close proximity to the observations of Sergeant Bludgeon, but nature is a wonderful thing. Constant contact had inoculated Sutherland against all but the worst of any logic bombs that were lobbed his way, providing him with the same protection that previously could only have been afforded by three pints of Ernie Dunkworth's Old Wallop, (trademark pending).

'I think you need a new phone,' said Sutherland. 'Get yourself over here, sharpish.'

'Whatever you say Sir, there's one small thing though, where are you?'

Sutherland was about to say 'Where I told you', but held back. Bludgeon thought he was at the right place, so technically he was what was known as 'lost'. 'Okay, give me a clue where you are and we'll take it from there.'

'I'm in a country carpark. I think I'm at a mechanics convention or something, if that helps.'

'So why don't you go and *ask them* where you are?'

'To be honest they're a bit busy. All the cars are in a circle and it looks like they're testing the headlights. Now they're taking turns to test the suspension, I must say they're very thorough. Hold on a moment…they're getting out…give me a minute…ooh maybe not…oh dear, that's not going to do the bonnet any good.'

'Fine,' commented Sutherland with suppressed exasperation. 'Did you pass any landmarks on the way there, a pub or something?'

The line was silent apart from the occasional 'Urrghh' as Sergeant Bludgeon, with the help of his digital map, checked his journey while trying to ignore the sight of something that he never remembered seeing in a Haynes manual.

'I think I passed something, what was it now? It'll come to me in a minute.'

'In your own time, anyone who wants to kidnap accountants obviously hasn't got anything better to do.'

Even Bludgeon could detect a hint of impatience. 'Got it,' he cried. 'The Squid's Merkin; I'm about ten minutes away.'

'The Merkin,' repeated Sutherland. He recalled passing it; navigation via hostelries was a skill that he always thought was under-rated. 'I'll meet you there in about fifteen, and sergeant.'

'Yes Sir?'

'Don't buy any used cars from those reprobates.'

*****

According to the Ordnance Survey map, by Sutherland's reckoning, they were about a quarter of a mile away, as the crow flew through the woods, from the walled boundary of the Oaks.

'Sir, I've been thinking,' said Bludgeon.

'Save it for later sergeant.'

'It's important Sir.'

'Out with it then,' said a resigned Sutherland knowing that unless the thought was released into the wild, it would probably act like a beaver damming Bludgeon's stream of consciousness, making it impossible for him to focus on anything else.

'I think I know why we didn't meet at the meeting point, and I think it also proves that what Mr Kingswood told us was right. You told me that I needed a new phone, but it is new. It's a birthday present from my aunt, a Brassica Universe E10 MePhone, complete with Brassica maps.'

'You've got a dud,' stated Sutherland matter of factly.

'Or maybe the maps have been doctored to give a false reading for the Oaks. We know that Erikson is our criminal mastermind...'

'Alleged,' corrected Sutherland.

'And he owns Brassica,' continued Bludgeon, 'which puts him in a perfect position to control the world's use of digital information for finding its way around. He could hold the globe to ransom. Aeroplanes would land in the sea, and, and... the military wouldn't be able to hit enemy targets.'

'Wouldn't affect the Yanks then,' said Sutherland, trudging ahead through the undergrowth.

Bludgeon ignored the comment, he was on a roll.

'The Oaks must be a test site; it wouldn't affect the people that know where it is. That's why he needs the accountants. Once he's up and running someone's got to keep the books on all that extortion.'

'I see, so it's a grand plan to set the world back to paper maps. Why didn't I think of that? I suppose he's got shares in A to Z, he'll make a killing at the service stations won't he? Next you'll be telling me he was behind the fake moon landings.'

'Ah, you're trying to catch me out now. Everyone knows that

we put men on the moon. Getting them back was the problem; it's the fake Earth landing that's been covered up.'

Sutherland knew that he was being outmanoeuvred. It was best to quit while he was ahead.

'I have to say sergeant that in all honesty, only you could have come up with all that.'

'Thank you Sir, you're too kind.'

They were at the boundary of the woods looking down over the grounds of the Oaks estate. Through his binoculars, Sutherland could see the grand manor house, which wasn't difficult as it was illuminated like a modern day palace of Versailles. Its classic frontage contrasted uncomfortably with an unsympathetic mixture of new extensions and annexes, planning permission was obviously for other people, and there on the gravel boulevard was a coach disgorging a full load of unwitting victims, as Kingswood had described.

Scaling the wall and skulking through the gardens, Sutherland and Bludgeon proceeded apace, unaware that they were being followed, and eavesdropped upon, by a Ninja in bike leathers with a slight limp. They finally took up position behind some hedging clipped in the shape of a well-known animated mouse.

'Okay sergeant, I'm going for a quick recce. If I'm not back in five minutes, send the flare up.'

'Of course Sir, about the flare though.'

For one moment a thought raced through Sutherland's head of Sergeant Bludgeon pulling out a pair of high waisted bell bottom trousers, but he quickly binned it. Not even Bludgeon could be that dense.

'Don't tell me you've forgotten it,' Sutherland enquired sternly.

'Don't worry,' reassured Bludgeon. 'I went to the flare shop like you said, but they were all out, so the nice man sold me one of these. He said it'd do the job.'

Bludgeon removed an object the size of a Pringle tin from his duffel bag.

'The Skymaster 2000,' read Sutherland in an unimpressed monotone. 'Entertain your friends and family with an explosive extravaganza. Sergeant, you've excelled yourself,' he said shaking his head. 'It'll have to do. Now remember, if I'm not back in five minutes, light the blue touch paper, that'll bring the lads running.'

It is said that it takes a thief to catch a thief, which would suggest that all members of the constabulary are at the very least, light fingered. Of course, if a curious person spends a lifetime pursuing criminals it is inevitable that they become familiar with the criminal mind and its methods. It didn't take long for Sutherland to break in, strictly in an official capacity.

While Sutherland engaged in illegal entry, Ben Kingswood, the biker Ninja, skirted the outside of the mansion until he saw exactly what he needed. In the shadows, even for someone recovering from a gunshot wound, he looked as if he was running up the wall, starting by pushing off from the branches of a mature wisteria. Simian like, in a matter of seconds he was hanging from the base of a first floor balcony before swinging himself effortlessly to vault the balustrade.

From his vantage point he could see Sergeant Bludgeon, and in the distance, a soon to be passing security guard. There was no way he could warn Bludgeon without revealing the sergeant's position. He notched an arrow but was unable to get a clear shot, what with the garden ornaments and shrubbery. 'Sergeant, don't move and don't make a sound,' Kingswood thought, wishing he could convey his advice telepathically.

Bludgeon knew that Detective Inspector Sutherland was putting a brave face on things, but he wasn't convinced his superior appreciated the enormity of the situation. It was most likely that Sutherland had walked into a trap, and he had let him. Five minutes he had said. That was too long. Extraordinary times called for extraordinary measures, even if that meant disobeying an order.

He propped the Skymaster 2000 against a box hedge and took the matches out of the plastic bag, he wasn't going to be caught out by them being damp. It had worked, they were bone dry, but so flimsy, that every time he tried to strike one, it broke. He worked his way through the box with increasing frustration until a torch light illuminated the pile of broken sub-standard fire-lighters.

'Ah, hello,' said Bludgeon. 'I'm from…the local…firework club. Yes, we do fireworks, which is why I've got this rocket. We're doing a display here in a couple of weeks and… I'm doing some tests. You wouldn't happen to have a lighter by any chance?'

Kingswood watched as Sergeant Bludgeon was frogmarched at gunpoint into the mansion. He took two delay flares from his rucksack; thirty seconds should do it, and stuck them into a potted plant on the balcony.

Looking around the bedroom door, he could see two henchmen in the corridor, one at each end. They were sitting down, they're heads buried in their mobile phones. Two blow-darts ensured that they would be unconscious for the next two hours at least. He moved silently in the direction of where he estimated the grand hall to be. Little did he know that he would be too late to prevent a disaster.

It was unfamiliar territory but it wasn't hard for Sutherland to home in on where the sound of the crowd was coming from. The grand entrance hall was the size of at least four tennis courts, with stuffed heads on the walls, classical marble statues, large planked oak furniture, and random suits of armour, all on an over the top, tiled chess board floor. Rising from this was a staircase wide enough to drive a modestly priced, but efficient, family car up and down. A generous upper landing was punctuated with doors that led to further rooms or other parts of the bastardised mansion. Sutherland didn't consider himself au fait with current interior design trends but to him, it made his local Indian curry house look positively subdued. He hid himself behind a plinth upon which stood a copy of the Venus De Milo. This was why he preferred trading in paintings; he never had any arguments about whether or not arms were a chargeable extra.

The scene before him looked like a standard corporate workshop; he'd suffered enough of them in his time. The accountants milled around, searching out familiar faces and making small talk about the esoteric aspects of their trade, but something didn't feel right to him.

In perfect synchronisation, a select number of the suited and booted opened their jackets to reveal their weapons. They shepherded the accountants into the centre of the hall, all the time reminding them to shut-up or else suffer the consequences. Once settled down, the business of sorting the number crunchers into groups proceeded with ruthless efficiency.

Sutherland had seen enough. It was time to retreat and make the call, but what he saw next stopped him in his tracks.

Chief Superintendent Willingdon arrived followed by two thugs dragging a struggling Sergeant Bludgeon across the floor. They forced him to his knees and Willingdon placed a gun at Bludgeon's temple.

'Harry, I know you're here, how do you want to play this, the easy or the hard way?'

Sutherland kicked his gun across the polished marble tiles where it came to rest at Willingdon's feet. He stepped out with his hands behind his head. 'Leave the lad alone. He's on my orders.'

Willingdon turned the gun on Sutherland. 'Same old predictable Harry Sutherland; always has to be the first in.'

'Same old Willingdon, still bent as a bottle of chips,' retorted Sutherland.

'Don't give me all that high and mighty, we're not that different. It's just a question of scale, that's all. I was thinking of letting you in on this, all you had to do was coast the final year, but no, not you. I don't know, all that service and never made it to retirement.'

'I've got back up on the way. It's over.'

One of Willingdon's flunkeys handed him the firework that Bludgeon had been so desperately trying to set off.

'Back up's on the way,' said Willingdon with a superior smirk. 'Hardly the Bat signal is it?' He trampled it underfoot, spilling the black powder over the floor.

'Sorry Sir,' said a crestfallen Bludgeon.

'It's alright sergeant, he'll be ages telling us his grand plan, you've nothing to worry about,' reassured Sutherland.

Willingdon examined Sutherland's firearm. 'Unofficial issue, serial numbers filed off. Seems I uncovered a trafficking racket run by a corrupt D.I and his sergeant. Unfortunately, they were shot as they tried to make their escape.' He levelled his gun at Sutherland's head.

'Don't worry Sir! He won't get away with it!' shouted a defiant Bludgeon.

'Irritating prick,' sneered Willingdon as he turned and shot Bludgeon in the chest.

'You're a dead man,' said Sutherland with ultimate conviction.

'You first,' said Willingdon coldly.

*****

In a field adjacent to the manor grounds, Andy examined the ostentatious mansion through his binoculars.

Screwfix was busy, checking over the automatic weaponry and ammunition that had been provided by Harry - no questions asked. He was particularly taken with the rocket launcher – not that he would need it, but it was always nice to have something in the back pocket.

Fitnote was busy sorting through a playlist on his MP3 player. You never knew when a talent scout might spot you, so the correct soundtrack was crucial.

'Anything?' asked Screwfix.

'Nothing,' said Andy. 'It looks like the bleedin' Blackpool illuminations. Lucky the signal wasn't a lamp in a window – we'd have no chance.'

'Flare,' said Fitnote casually as he checked the screw top on his protein shake.

They couldn't miss the signal as two purple flares arced in the sky and fell to the ground in an incandescent persistent glow.

'Right lad's – we're up.' said Andy as he fired up the twin vee twelve engines.

The armour plated monster truck with its tyres like inflated wagon wheels churned up the field and crashed through the fence.

Andy couldn't help but grin for a moment. Screwfix always had the right tool for the job.

*****

At the very moment of Sutherland's imminent execution a marble sized pellet struck Willingdon on the temple and exploded, releasing a bright orange pigment that covered his face. It was as if someone had hit him incredibly hard with a micro-fist, and then rubbed onions into his eyes. More pellets followed in quick succession forcing Willingdon to retreat while he tried to wipe away the stinging, viscous liquid.

Kingswood slid down the banister, emptying the paintball rifle of its pellets. He had counted at least fifteen adversaries, all armed, and there would no doubt be more nearby. The element of surprise wouldn't last long. He glided off the rail seamlessly into a forward roll, avoiding the first broadside.

From his low position, in quick succession, shuriken throwing stars seemed to appear from nowhere in his hands, whirring across the hall and embedding themselves in the wrists of five of the gunmen. However, he couldn't move as fast as he normally would and found himself pinned down behind a suit of armour, but it wouldn't be for long.

Taking advantage of the intervention, Sutherland waded through the stooges and heavies; his anger expressing itself as a brutal, efficient, no holds barred combat. He seized a gun in the process and took cover behind an upturned oak dresser.

As luck would have it, the accountant's also shared a modicum of Kingswood's skill and they wasted no time in taking advantage of the interruption to break free. Using whatever furniture and reliquary that was to hand, battle lines were drawn up in the grand hall. One consisted of the kidnappers. The other was made up of Sutherland and the accountants. It was a shame that the enemy had all the guns.

Stuck in No Man's land was Sergeant Bludgeon.

Sutherland handed the gun to one of the accountants. 'Cover

me. I'll give you a signal, and on three, make sure that lot keep their heads down. I'm going for my sergeant.'

Sutherland made a dash and took cover behind a large stuffed bear. He signalled to the accountant, counted, and made his move, breaking cover to grab Bludgeon by the scruff of his coat. For a split second a hail of indiscriminate enemy bullets flew across the hall before the return fire gave him the opening to drag Bludgeon back behind the makeshift barricade. He snatched the gun back with a scowl. 'I said "on three!"'.

'It's not my fault you went on the end of two,' replied the accountant.

'I'm glad you're not doing my bleedin' my tax return.'

Sutherland checked the gun - six rounds left. The only exits he could see were within the firing line of Willingdon's force. He might make it, but what about Bludgeon and the hostages? He sent a hasty text. His ex-wife thought it would be a routine tidying up, was she in for a surprise. Now all he had to do was hold out; the flak from her would be a cheap price to pay for getting out alive.

Out of the corner of his eye, he saw one of Willingdon's men trying to sneak around an oriental lacquer cabinet. Sutherland fired two shots, wounding the enemy in the leg, and then he heard the scream of pain, but it was from behind and above him? A henchman landed unceremoniously into a faux Victorian chaise longue, an arrow protruding from his chest.

Perched up in the chandelier, Sutherland saw his balaclava clad paintball saviour, who, like Burt Lancaster, but in bike leathers and glasses, avoided a volley of gunfire by leaping onto a wall tapestry, slid down, swung onto a window mullion, and from there propelled himself into a double somersault, landing in the grand fireplace where he slipped up the chimney as if he were smoke.

Sutherland recovered the henchman's gun, it had a full clip. He looked over at Bludgeon, concerned at his shallow breathing, but also relieved that he was still alive - for the moment.

'Sergeant, ' he said, 'if you don't bloody hang on, I'll kill you. That's an order.'

There was a volley of gunfire as Willingdon's force looked to storm the random barricade of faux period oak furniture and replica medieval armour. Sutherland was about to return fire when the doors to the hall exploded into hundreds of splinters, the remaining carcass hanging precariously off what were the hinges.

To the accompaniment of an almost deafening, raucous, guitar solo blaring out from a bespoke entertainment system, an armour plated four wheel drive that looked like it had overdosed on steroids, crashed through what was left of the front doors and came to a skidding halt. From the back Fitnote systematically levelled the hall with a storm of bullets from a rotating, whirring modern version of a Gatling gun, fed by a seeming endless belt of ammunition. In the face of such heavy munitions, one by one the abductors dropped their weapons.

Andy scanned the hall and saw Willingdon escaping up the stairs. There was no hesitation. Using the truck door as a steadying support, he fired a shot from his hand cannon, narrowly missing as a bannister rail shattered on the stairs. 'Sod it!' he cursed. Back in the day, he wouldn't have missed. He took aim again, but Willingdon had turned a corner on the flight.

Andy jumped down from the driver's seat and went straight to Sutherland. 'What happened?'

'Willingdon. Help's on the way but I don't know if he's going to make it,' replied Sutherland as he started to loosen the sergeant's clothing, which was so thick, the blood hadn't seeped through to the surface layers.

Andy stopped Sutherland in his endeavours and placed the beast of a handgun, a Smith and Wesson .44 Magnum into his palm. 'I'll look after him. You go and make Willingdon's day.'

34 / Rozzer On The Roof

Molly Mackintosh lived on the top floor at the rear of the Oaks. Barring the roof and the attic, it was the furthest point from the Palladian frontage. Even the tradesmen of old would have balked at being asked to a deliver this far away on the estate; horse usage had to be carefully managed in those days. Depending on the terms of the personal equine leasing deal, the last thing that was needed was to exceed the annual gee-gee mileage allowance.

She had avoided being consigned to a pokey attic room by claiming a propensity to frequent panic attacks brought on by not having enough room to swing a hamster. The miserly Pargetter wasn't convinced, but his threat to report her for animal cruelty was empty, metaphor wasn't his strong point. They also both knew that no one else would do what she did for the paltry sums that he grudgingly paid.

With the volume up to maximum, she lay back on the sofa, enveloped in the rising crescendo of Handel's Messiah, blissfully unaware of the chaos taking place on the estate. The only thing that disturbed her was a complaining grumble from her stomach telling her to check the fridge, but there wasn't anything in there that qualified as an enticing snack. That wasn't a problem. With Pargetter and entourage away on one of his regular yachting jaunts , how would he know if she went down to the kitchen and helped herself to some of the good stuff?

*****

Breathing heavily as he climbed the stairs, Sutherland managing to keep the pace through sheer bloody mindedness. He was now on the top floor, but Willingdon was nowhere to be seen. One by one he checked the rooms, wasting valuable time until he came to a door which opened onto a narrow flight of stairs heading upwards.

'Always the bloody roof,' he said to himself through gritted teeth, steeling himself for a final confrontation.

*****

For those in the know, there is a statistic worked out by someone who no doubt had time on their hands, that when in pursuit of the more affluent criminal, in 69.99% of instances they will attempt to escape via a roof, or the top of any high structure, where they will be airlifted off by a hot air balloon - or something.

It sometimes happens that when a figure is quoted as being accurate to within two decimal places, or written on the side of a bus, that it's then considered to be true, and so the 69.99% became known as King Kong's Law. Any affluent villains doing a runner in an upward trajectory were said to be doing a 'Kong'.

The figure did briefly dip at one time as the branch of the criminal fraternity most likely to Kong was briefly afflicted with a mild dose of Corporate-itis, a little known condition that causes reasonably intelligent people to abandon common sense, and instead employ consultants, at vast expense, to state the bleedin' obvious. In this instance the consultant in question, engaged to drive more efficiency into rooftop escapes, started off by questioning the need for the use of an aerial route in the first place. After all, what was wrong with going underground?

They were promptly sacked, and strangely were never seen again, as one Jack Armstrong, (an aspirational Konger), pointed out that you can't land a helicopter in a 'sodding basement'.

*****

The top of the Oaks was an architectural mash-up of double gabled and shallow flat roofs punctuated by chimneys and steel walkways. Sutherland threaded his way out, edging his way between a low wall and a chimney. Steps that could take about two abreast, led up to a metal path spanning the apex of the gable roof. About halfway across it split, forming a tricorn arrangement. Either side of the walkway was an extended shallow slope surrounded by a low parapet.

As Sutherland crested the stairs he saw Willingdon with a hostage, a young girl, who given her due was slowing him down. He lowered his gun, took a deep breath, and then raised it again; maybe he could pull this one off. He fired a warning shot over his head. 'Willingdon-it's over!'

Willingdon turned, forcing the girl in front of him, holding his gun to her cheek.

'You've got no idea. Throw your gun over there,' said Willingdon, indicating towards the slope, 'or the girl goes the same way as your sergeant.'

Sutherland held his position. That girl was Willingdon's only chance of escape, despite his threat he wasn't going to throw away his advantage at the risk of a shoot-out.

'Last chance Harry,' said Willingdon calmly and matter of factly.

'For God's sake listen to him!' pleaded Molly.

Sutherland could hear the faint approach of helicopter blades slicing through the air. That was Willingdon's escape, the kind that required money, something Erikson had in abundance.

Reluctantly he dropped his weapon and it slid down the slope towards the parapet. Out of the corner of his eye he made a note of where it stopped.

'Let her go,' said Sutherland. 'You don't need her now. This is between me and you.'

'Sorry, but I'm holding onto my passport until I'm out of here. Shame I've got my hands full, you've pissed off some very powerful people tonight and they'd be grateful to have you dead right now. They'll find you though.'

'Don't worry, I'll find you first. We're not done.'

The helicopter circled the roof as the pilot gauged the distance. Too close and the downdraft from the blades would dislodge everyone, too far away, and there would be no retrieval. It settled into position, everyone below bracing themselves against the gale force as a canvas strop was lowered. It waved around in ever decreasing circles; it was only a matter of seconds before it would be within Willingdon's reach.

Suddenly, in quick succession, two shots hit the helicopter fuselage and it rapidly veered away to hover at a safer distance.

On the third part of the walkway, Sergeant Bludgeon stood with a smoking gun. 'Drop the shooter you slaaaag!' he commanded, channelling his inner Sweeney.

'What the bloody…?' exclaimed Sutherland.

'Don't worry Guv'nor. I've got it covered,' Bludgeon assured, his shooter pointing in Willingdon's direction. 'I said drop it, now, or I drop you – get it?!'

'Sergeant, don't, you'll hit the girl.'

'For a dead man you're still as stupid as everyone says you are.' Willingdon baited. 'If I was you I'd listen to him, otherwise she gets it.'

Molly looked directly at Bludgeon. 'Please, do as he says.'

She wasn't sure if it was the stress of the situation playing tricks, but she could swear that the sergeant winked at her.

Bludgeon fired, his shot clipping the elbow of Willingdon's gun arm, forcing his fingers to involuntarily spasm open. Willingdon recoiled in agony, his pistol joined Sutherland's weapon in the parapet gutter.

Seizing her chance, Molly broke free, landing a tremendous right hook to Willingdon's face, the setting of her ring leaving a large gash on his cheek.

'Sergeant, get the girl away, now! I'll deal with this,' ordered Sutherland.

The helicopter was still circling the Oaks, the pilot assessing the situation from a distance as his searchlight swept the roof.

There was a fine mizzle in the air, the type of rain that coats and soaks everything cumulatively. The raindrops were highlighted in the sweeping light beam as down below, two past their prime gladiators faced off, each waiting for the other to make their move.

Willingdon was breathing sharply and quickly while swearing for Britain, but he wasn't done for yet. He jumped off the walkway, half rolling, and half sliding towards the parapet.

Sutherland followed suit, careering out of control as he kept his hands and feet raised off the sheet lead covering, intending only to put his shoes down at the last moment to halt his descent.

Willingdon landed first, his right arm was useless, but with a gun in his left hand; at close range it would be academic.

Sutherland was a fraction of a second behind. He would have beaten Willingdon to the draw if the parapet bricks that he thought would stop his progress hadn't given way. He overshot the eaves, and for a fraction of a second, he was in mid-air, with only one way to go. Reaching desperately for anything, he managed to grab the cast iron guttering, and there he hung as the metal painfully bit into his fingers. He tried to haul himself up, but the strength in the arm that had been battered by Murray in the London Hospital wasn't there.

Willingdon was shuffling his way towards him. Sutherland looked down. Could he survive a fall from three storeys? It wasn't as if he had a choice.

'Bye Harry,' said Willingdon as he aimed from close range.

Sutherland was about to let go when Willingdon's left arm started to shake uncontrollably.

Saliva foam escaped from Willingdon's lips as he dropped the gun. He's whole body was now out of control as a rhythmic convulsion involuntarily rolled him off the roof, but the instinct for survival shouldn't be underestimated.

The gutter shifted under the combined weight of two bodies as Willingdon hung on with a grip of iron to Sutherland's ankle, who in turn, could feel his fingers weakening. The rain channel groaned as it started to come loose from its moorings, encouraged by the jerking body below.

With his free foot Sutherland kicked out again and again, but Willingdon wouldn't let go. The gutter moved again. In desperation Sutherland looked for a foothold with his spare leg and managed to get some purchase on the top rail of a window, taking some of the burden off his fingers, but not for long. Willingdon was shaking even more violently now, like a possessed pogo stick.

Sutherland's free foot slipped from the rail and hit Willingdon square on the bridge of the nose with a crack. If that triggered the final, uncontrollable spasmodic death throe's he didn't know, and didn't care, as Willingdon fell silently to the ground.

Sutherland looked down at the contorted corpse. 'We're done now.'

He tried to haul himself up, but in doing so, the cast iron fixings creaked, warning him that he was on notice if he tried anything too bold. He was damned if he did, damned if he didn't. The helicopter was flying away erratically; they were hardly going to hang around to rescue him were they? Again he asked himself, could he survive a fall from three floors? He wasn't planning on finding out.

Taking advantage of the window rail, he slowly moved his way along, inch by inch, holding his breath as the ancient culvert complained.

A helping hand grasped Sutherland's forearm.

'Come on you old git – beers getting warm.'

*****

Sat on the front of the monster truck, Andy and Sutherland watched masked commandos as they conducted a methodical room by room search of the mansion, rounding up the guilty as they went. No grand dining room, pantry, sex playroom, or bathroom en-suite was left unturned.

'Thanks for helping me out,' said Sutherland. 'I'd have managed eventually, but I would have got soaked.'

'Don't mention it,' said Andy casually, as if dragging people back from death's edge was as normal as helping old lady's across the road. 'I thought I'd check on you after I saw Willingdon breakdancing past the window.' He took a swig of beer from the neck, looking acutely at the militia. 'How comes we never had balaclavas?'

'It set Fitnote's skin off didn't it,' recalled Sutherland. 'We couldn't have his record broken could we?'

Andy nodded. 'True.' He raised his bottle in an informal salute to one of the soldiers. 'I see you and Kate are talking.'

'It's only temporary, normal service will be resumed shortly.'

Sutherland took a long draught, emptying half of the bottle before holding it out in front of him. His hand was no longer trembling, a good sign that his body was coming back down to Earth after the recent adrenalin hit.

'I could have sworn Bludgeon was a goner,' admitted Sutherland. 'What did you do, put some Tiger Balm on his nadgers or something?'

'Don't remember that one in the first aid manual,' Andy mused. 'No, when I checked him over turns out he's wearing some sort of quilted cardigan, and would you believe it, it'd stopped the bullet. He was a bit winded, I mean, you would be, but when he came round first thing he did was ask where you'd gone. Before I know it, he's helped himself to a shooter and he's after you like a ferret up a drainpipe. You've got a good 'un there.'

'I know, he's got some funny ideas, but yeah, he's alright.' Sutherland took a final swig. 'That reminds me, I've got to have a word with the ex about something. See you down the pub,' and off he went shaking his head in disbelief, muttering something about bullet proof cardies.

'Good luck,' Andy called after him, his bonhomie growing exponentially with each sup.

*****

The action played out in front of her as video was relayed from the commando's body cameras to the screen integrated into the back of the driver's seat. It had been a good evening's work. Harry had kept his part of the deal, and his intelligence had proved to be true. This would be a feather in her cap if she decided to claim it, but it would have to be kept under wraps. Something was rotten in the world of state funded subterfuge, but this might be the breakthrough she needed.

There was a knock on the blacked out, one way, door window. It smoothly glided half-way down at the press of a button.

'What have you got for me Captain?' Kate Cooden asked.

'We've rounded them all up Ma'am. I don't know if this is of interest, but we found one of the enemy hanging upside down from the big oak tree over there, reckons he was interrogated by a Ninja accountant.'

'That's a new one, and how did he know he was an accountant?'

'Say's he was threatened with an eighty percent actuarial reduction on his pension, and he had this stuffed up his nose.' The captain handed over a one hundred pound monopoly note in a clear evidence bag.

'There's always one comedian in the pack, he'll change his story once we get him into detention. Is the alpha site ready?'

'Fully operational Ma'am, just give the word. Last thing, there's another policeman; he wants to speak to you. Shall I see to him?'

'Thank you but there's no need. He's not here.'

'Understood Ma'am,' and with that the balaclava clad captain saluted, right reeled, and marched off.

She looked at the toy money. It had been awhile. It looked like the urban myth was on a comeback tour, but after all this time they'd be a geriatric. A knocking on the window distracted her from her recollection. It was Harry, looking worse for wear, as if someone had dragged him backwards down a wet roof.

'Detective Inspector Sutherland' she greeted. 'Fancy seeing you here. Come into the office.'

She reminded her driver that it was time they took a walk as Harry, with his beer laden breath and sodden overcoat plonked into the seat next to her.

'You and your sergeant have been busy,' Kate observed.

'Yeah, things got a bit unreasonable,' said Sutherland.

'So I see. One dead Chief Superintendent and an unregistered helicopter crashed four times at a nearby industrial estate.'

'It was an accident, he had some kind of fit and fell off the roof,' said Sutherland automatically in his defence before his brain had digested the rest of the information. 'What do you mean "four times"?'

'It was a trampoline factory. Don't worry, no civilians got hurt, although we've got two witnesses with ricked necks. The cover story's going to be interesting, and I've got some work to do to keep you and Sergeant Bludgeon out of the limelight.'

'How much work?'

She mused for a moment. 'Difficult to say really, Willingdon dies in an unfortunate car accident tomorrow, and we can convince the accountants and Ms Mackintosh to keep quiet with a witness protection-lite programme, it's all terrorists you see, so Emin sized?'

'Okay, this is the last one and we're done, but only if you keep up your end of the deal.'

'I already have. Sergeant Bludgeon is going to be the director of my new cyber unit – he's perfect.'

'Director? I said promotion, not a rocket launch. No, I'm sorry; you can't do that to him.'

'You can't back out now just because he's proved himself useful to you. That'd be typical, because it's always about you isn't it? If you talk him out of it, I'll have you banged up so fast with some of your nicks, you won't know what day it is.'

'Hold your horses, that's not what I meant. There's something you need to know. He didn't break into those systems; it was someone he was in contact with called Deep Thrombosis. Bludgeon was being used as a patsy. I should have stopped him but I wanted to flush people out. If you give him that job, he'll be as much use as an ashtray on a motorbike. I wanted him sorted, not hung out to dry. What's wrong with Inspector, you can swing that surely?'

Kate smiled, 'I don't believe it, you're thinking about someone else for a change, you feeling alright?'

'I've mellowed, okay? He's a good lad, he deserves a decent chance.'

'Who do you think Deep Thrombosis works for?'

'Not... no,' said Sutherland in genuine surprise as a pounds worth of pennies dropped.

'DT is part of our Honeypot programme; we like to know what potential anarchists are out there. Once your sergeant had learnt the ropes, I wanted to see how good he was. Turns out, he's a natural, he ran rings around the team, and they're some of the best hackers in the business. I cut him some slack, and the next thing I know he's doing the grand tour of global intelligence agencies, highlighting all their weak spots for us. So I want him in our tent.'

'You crafty...'

'I know. Now we've got that cleared up, there's one more thing you can do for me.'

'No way, I'm all done.'

'He turned the job down, and he's not playing hard to get.'

'So? Give him a job he wants to do.'

'This is his job, he just hasn't realised it yet. It's all quite potentially disappointing, and it makes it really hard to put a lid on your adventures. I've heard the Americans are still upset about the security breach, so the Home Secretary wants to throw them a bone - extraordinary rendition sized apparently.'

'Let me guess – I wouldn't have to worry about my passport.'

'I've got some new staff, and if I don't watch them like a hawk, the wrong name might get put in the wrong box. Mistakes happen.'

'I'll have a word; me and him have a few things to sort out anyway.'

'That's ever so good of you, I hope it's not too much trouble. He starts next week by the way.'

*****

++++++Encrypted Text++++++

Council: Yellow Armadillo – what's going on? Report.

YA: Consignment abandoned. Willingdon disposed of – had big mouth. Pargetter to be scapegoated.

Council: Is extraction required?

YA: No. Cover stable. Expert marksman identified for recruitment.

Council: ☺

++++++End Encrypted Text++++++

Molly was aware of someone approaching. She put the phone back into her pocket and adopted her best brave face so as to cover her fake distress.

'Hello there, I thought I'd check that you were okay, but you were on the phone. I didn't want to disturb you,' said Bludgeon.

Molly wiped a crocodile tear from the corner of her eye. 'I'm sorry; it's all been a bit of a shock. That was my uncle, he likes to check on me every night to see that I'm alright, he's been like a father to me since…I'm sorry, you don't want to hear this. It's Mr Bludgeon, isn't it?'

'Sergeant Bludgeon, Miss?'

'Ms, Molly.'

'Nice to put a name to a face Ms Molly. Can I get you a cup of tea or something?'

'It's Ms Mackintosh, Molly's my first name, and thank you, but I'm fine.'

'Miss Mackintosh,' repeated Bludgeon, now confused as to what etiquette was applicable, was she a Miss Mackintosh, Ms Molly, or any other combination?

'Please, Molly will be fine,' she said, having noticed Bludgeon's furrowed brow.

'Righty-ho,' said Bludgeon, now in uncharted territory. Any mention of anything beyond tea when dealing with rescued hostages was probably on the missing pages of the manual. 'I'm glad you're alright. I'll be off then.'

'Please, don't go. I'm ever so grateful for you helping me on the roof. You were *so brave*. I know this is very forward of me, but I'd like to express my gratitude in a more... material way? I hope that's allowed?'

'There's no need... really. I was just doing my job.'

'I insist. Please? There's a fantastic Chinese in the village and I'm sure you must be off duty soon. Let me treat you, it's the least I can do.'

'I appreciate the offer, but I can't...I'm on a night shift. Besides, the last time I was in a Chinese restaurant with a young lady it was a bit of a disaster, so I don't go anymore, sorry.'

'What happened?'

'It's the chopsticks, I can't get the hang of them, especially with the prawns,' said Bludgeon as he demonstrated with a stabbing motion.

'You're supposed to pick them up like this,' Molly showed with her fingers.

'I get that now, but at the time... well all I can say is that the paramedics were very understanding, quite jolly in fact. I suppose it's not every day they have someone with their hand impaled by Asian cutlery.'

'Ouch, I bet that hurt!'

'Oh yes, she screamed all the way to the ambulance.'

'Sergeant. A word when you're ready,' ordered Sutherland from the doorway.

'I'm sorry, I really have to go,' said Bludgeon apologetically.

Molly took a business card from her pocket, made a small note and pressed it into Sergeant Bludgeon's palm. 'Please, call me. I feel like after what we've been through that there's a bond between us. I couldn't bear it if I didn't see you again.'

Bludgeon wasn't used to this sort of attention. Obviously the poor girl was traumatised. He made his excuses and some lame non-committal promises as he retreated with Molly's plaintive cries of 'Call me' ringing in his ears.

*****

The gravel scrunched underfoot as Sutherland and Bludgeon walked down the illuminated poplar tree avenue, a daisy chain of lights bathed the whole in an orangey glow, as if it had spent too much time on a sunbed. The rain had stopped, but each small wet stone when caught by the light revealed a hidden patina, showing a temporary beauty that was unappreciated by master or apprentice.

'I see that young lady was a bit keen on you,' said Sutherland.

'I know,' said Bludgeon. 'I think she's in shock.'

'She got off lightly then, didn't she?'

'I'm not with you Sir.'

'Let me spell it out. You discharged a weapon, risking the life of a hostage. I told you not to shoot; you could have bloody killed her.'

'Oh I see. You needn't have worried Sir; there was never any chance of my hitting Miss Mackintosh. I'm sorry I didn't follow orders, but under the circumstances,' Bludgeon sounded a bit sheepish, 'I took the initiative.'

'You failed your firearms examination for Christ's sake.'

'That was on a technicality.'

'You shot the instructor.'

'It was an accident; he was standing in the wrong place. I distinctly remember him saying though, as they stretchered him out; that never in a million years would I ever be able to hit anything I aimed at. That was two years ago, so I knew that if I pointed the gun at Miss Mackintosh, she'd be perfectly safe.'

*****

If we could look inside Detective Inspector Sutherland's frontal lobe, Neural ship USS Vaccination was having a rough time of it as everyone on the bridge threw themselves from side to side in their seats, and a security guard in a red jersey was sucked out of a temporary hull breach, (because that's what happens to security guards in red shirts - apparently.)

'Mr Sock – report.'

'That was a high yield logic bomb Captain. Our shields are at forty per cent and holding. However, sensors show a thought gestating.' Mr Sock looked up, his face graven. 'He's going to ask the sergeant what he was aiming at when he shot the helicopter.'

'Captain, even with the upgrades she can't take another hit like that. You cannae defy the laws of stupidity!' stated Mr Snott overdramatically.

'Captain, the thought is travelling down the neuron,' Mr Sock advised.

Captain Smirk weighed the situation. This called for something unnecessarily risky and reckless. 'Mr Hulu, plot an intercept course for that thought at, oh I don't know, warped factor ramming speed.'

'I'm sorry Captain,' replied Mr Hulu, 'but I need a number. I haven't got a button for ramming speed.'

'Fine, eleven then.'

'Captain, she won't go up to eleven. We've only got ten fingers. Go above that and we'll lose count, it'll shake her apart. You cannae defy the laws of biology!'

'Thank you Mr Snott. Mr Hulu, warped ten, and while you're at it, make sure the ship undertakes a highly dangerous manoeuvre that puts the whole crew at risk.'

'Aye aye Captain,' confirmed Hulu.

Mr Snott gently head-butted his workstation. He'd only just got the ship back from its respray.

*****

Sutherland was minded to ask Bludgeon what he was aiming at when he shot the helicopter, but the moment passed. He would only end up going down a rabbit hole anyway and there was another point that he had to make before Bludgeon made his way without him.

'And when were you going to get round to telling me about your bullet proof cardigan?'

'If you don't mind me saying so Sir, you did say we would be plain clothes, I wasn't expecting an inspection...'

'Sergeant...'

'I didn't mention it, because I didn't know.'

'How can you not "know"?'

'It was an early Christmas present from my aunt. She thinks I'm always on stake-outs and things and she worries that if I don't keep wrapped up, I'll catch a chest cold. She bought me this cardigan from America; it's a kevlar and spider silk mix. It's ever so warm. She would have knitted me one, but you can't get the wool you see. She never said anything about it stopping bullets.'

'You bloody idiot – you could have been killed,' Sutherland snapped.

Bludgeon appeared to deflate slightly, took a deep breath and regained his stature.

'I guess I was lucky, this helped as well,' and he took out his Brassica MePhone with it's now shattered screen. 'I don't know what I'm going to tell my aunt. Do you think I'll be able to claim one back on expenses?'

'You're a director now; I think you'll be able to sign that off.'

'You know then?'

Sutherland nodded. There was something different about Bludgeon now, he had the look of someone who had given his all and was now defeated, and it wasn't down to the tongue lashing, he was sure of that. This was something more. Whenever he had mentioned promotion, Bludgeon had been excited, but now his demeanour was of someone who on the day before his retirement, had been told he would have to work another ten years owing to a new, We Really Care –Honest, initiative from the Human Resource collective.

'What's the problem?' Sutherland invited.

'I'm sorry Sir, I don't want to seem ungrateful, but I can't take it.'

'Can't? You deserve it. What's wrong with you?'

Bludgeon hesitated, looking for the right words. 'I don't think ...I'm good enough,' he uttered.

'What?'

'I'm not good enough.'

'No, I'm not having that. There's something else, and we're going to sort it right now. Good God man, you'd be bloody stupid to turn it down.'

'Everyone thinks I'm stupid anyway,' said Bludgeon bitterly as he kicked the gravel.

If the frustration that was welling up in his chest had been a cannon, he could have shot his heart beyond the horizon. Sergeant Bludgeon could contain himself no more.

'If I take this job it won't be five minutes before word gets around and I'll be back to square one. "Ooh look – there goes Director Bonehead", that's what they'll all be saying. It doesn't matter how hard I work, and I've really tried, it doesn't make any difference. I'm...I don't know... some days I just want to give up! They only made me a sergeant because they had to meet some quota, and then all I got were the crap jobs no-one else would touch, because they think I'm thick. And I keep asking questions because no one tells me anything, so then people think I'm even *more* thick! I'm not; I just think differently. I see things in a way that no-one else does, I always have done, and for that I get treated like the stations resident halfwit. You're the only one who even bothered to give me the time of day. I know you thought some of my ideas were dumb, but at least you listened and you left me to get on with things. Working on this case has been the best thing that's happened to me in years. I know you're going to retire, but I'd rather have a year working with you than go back to the way things were. If that means skipping the promotion - fine. I was kidding myself anyway.'

'You done?' Sutherland asked.

'Yes Sir,' said Bludgeon, his head hung low. 'I'm sorry.'

Silence hung heavily between them. Sutherland knew he was guilty as charged and yet in Sergeant Bludgeon's eyes he had redeemed himself, not through any positive effort, but by virtue of not being as crap as everyone else.

'Sergeant, I'm going to give you some advice, and if you've got any sense, you'll take it. I know what everyone thinks, I was one of them. I was wrong. I'm sorry. But don't get the idea I put a good word in because I was feeling guilty. Me and Ms Cooden go back a long way and take it from me; she's not in the business of employing people out of sympathy, as a favour, or for some poxy quota. She wants you because you're bloody good at whatever it is you do with computers. Your problem is that you're in the wrong place with the wrong tools, and all you've had to show for it is the dirty end of the stick, with a little bit of light relief thrown in. The thing is, what're you going to do when I knock it on the head? You'd have had your twelve months, and then what? Right now you've got a chance to shine, but it's not coming round again.' He shrugged, 'It's up to you. And another thing, if I ever again hear you say you're not good enough, I'll kick your arse so hard you'll be chewing moon dust.'

Bludgeon made shapes in the gravel with his toe as he considered the honesty that had been missing for so long from his tenure in the police. If he turned it down he would only be living down to everyone else's expectation. Detective Inspector Sutherland believed he could do it, and on balance, who had his best interests at heart in the long term?

'Sir...do you think if I asked- would the position still be open?'

'She wants you to start next week.'

'Next week?'

'Like I said, you're the man for the job, and once she's made up her mind, she don't like waiting.'

Sergeant Bludgeon stood proud, 'I won't let you down, I promise, but what about you?'

'Me? I've still got some missing bikes to sort out. You never know, it might turn out to be a front for some obsessive fat cat smuggling gold in the handlebars.'

'Or it could be part of a bigger master plan by an evil criminal genius.'

'Could be,' said Sutherland nodding, 'I hear there's a lot of it about these days.'

There was that awkward silence again, but what else was there to say? The only thing that they had in common was finished; all that was left was a parting of the ways. Yet it wasn't as if either of them could leave the office with a casual 'goodnight' and forget the 'see you tomorrow.' The middle of gravel driveways didn't have doors. There was only one thing for it.

'I do believe we're missing out on some serious drinking time,' Sutherland declared, clapping his hands together in anticipation. 'I think a celebration's in order. You go and have a quick word with your new boss, and I'll meet you down the Kings Arms, first rounds on me.'

'The Kings Arms?'

Detective Inspector Sutherland let out a deep sigh. 'I know - it's a bloody stupid name for a pub.'

35 / A Knights Tale

It had been a couple of days since John Cranston had woken up on the settee in Milligan's bungalow, his head throbbing with an irksome rhythm. The last thing he remembered was Marsden mistaking his efforts at reviving her as him taking advantage, in a graveyard no less. If anything was going to reinforce her view of him as a mysterious gardening pervert, that would probably do it.

On the upside, at least she had arranged for him to be brought back to his temporary bolt-hole, but when he thought about it, it was less an act of kindness and more one of tidying up. What would the local constabulary have made of him if he had been found next to a burnt out church, especially if they compared notes with their London colleagues? Now that he had knowledge of the Society, he was sure that they would want to avoid awkward enquiries wherever possible.

He couldn't stay in hiding indefinitely though, he might grow old waiting for someone to tell him what was going on. For all he knew, if everything had gone well, they could have simply forgotten him and moved onto whatever crisis was next on their list, (he assumed they had a list, rather than bouncing from one calamity to the next – how little did he know.) The easiest thing to do would be to simply break cover by withdrawing some money and see if anything happened. It wouldn't be long before he would have to do so anyway, the grant of a fraction of Alice's cash by Department S, wasn't going to last forever. That was another thing; sitting around doing nothing wasn't going to get Alice's money back.

Deciding to put his plan into action in small steps, he took the air as he strolled down to the local convenience store. It was hardly a gourmet deli, but it would do for the moment. Besides, he asked himself, what was the worst thing that could happen while nipping out for a bottle of red-top?

By the time John had returned, he'd run through about twenty scenarios, the last being that the elderly gentleman who walked his dog and always said 'Good morning', was really a highly trained specialist cowboy mercenary. At any moment he could suddenly lasso him and bundle him onto a passing galloping horse, like a trussed steer. The absence of cowboy boots, hat, spurs, six- shooter, and a rope, soon put that speculation to bed. Maybe he should be keeping an eye on the dog. He'd have to think about it.

John put the bread, ham, cereal, milk and two cans of tomato soup in the kitchen before returning to the sofa to slump down in front of the television. Archaeology or antiques- it was a tough choice. He looked around for the remote control and found it on the window sill, not where he'd left it. Adjacent, made from the page of a local street atlas, was an immaculately folded representation of a unicorn.

*****

It was generally understood that Gibbet Cliff was so named as it was the site where smugglers were hung as a warning to anyone considering contraband as a career path. In reality, there had never been any hangings there, or anywhere in Smallmansea. The local smuggling industry was superbly organised, even down to the backhander loyalty cards for the excise men who were handsomely rewarded for turning a blind eye.

To give it its true name, *Giblet Cliff* was the site of a chicken farm that unfortunately burnt down following a lightning strike during the great storm of 1749. The enterprising owner managed to cut his losses by setting up a stall to sell fresh, rapidly roasted chicken pieces at a bargain price, all customers had to do was bring their own bucket. The food was well received, but the general opinion was that it would never catch on; setting fire to a farm was an expensive means of production. Undiscouraged, with the proceeds from the fire sale, Farmer Sanders booked passage to the New World where he looked to make his fortune.

Owing to the spider scrawl handwriting of the local clerk, who was nursing the mother of all hangovers at the time, the event was recorded in the parish records as Gibbet, a mistake latched upon and perpetuated by the local community and excise men. After all it was important that the fight against smuggling be seen to be in full swing. Over time the name was used by numerous jobsworths, slowly insinuating itself into various documents.

The rest, as they say, is history.

*****

It was hard to miss Gibbet cliff, for one it was a cliff, and secondly, set back from the eroding coastline was an unmanned, (some cynics would say abandoned), coast guard station, which in its day would have taken advantage of the raised viewpoint.

As John approached the crest, sitting on a bench seat about six feet away from the edge was Gordon, looking majestic against a backdrop of curvaceous cumulus clouds as they slowly drifted across the sky, casting soft shadows across the sea.

'Cranston old chap,' Gordon greeted, 'so glad you could make it. I see you got off lightly,' he said, acknowledging John's black eye. 'Escapes can be dashed tricky.'

'Likewise,' said John, still cautious and looking over his shoulder.

'It was nothing, really,' dismissed Gordon. 'Take a seat, there's no need to stand on ceremony.'

John sat down on the opposite end to Gordon. He held out the unfolded unicorn map. 'You could've knocked. It seemed a shame to undo it.'

'You weren't in, and to be honest your accommodation is – how can I put this?'

'Don't bother; I know exactly what you mean.'

'And on a day like this I prefer to meet outside, it's much more civilised, especially when I have good news.'

'Good news?' asked John in anticipation. It had been a while.

Gordon gazed at the sky, admiring the ephemeral floating cotton pillows. 'Beautiful isn't it? Constable kept a sketchbook of clouds for reference, very sensible if you ask me. If you look closely you can see the faint outline of a dragon, absolutely marvellous.'

'Yeah, they're lovely – what about the news?'

'Oh yes, sorry, went a bit Zen there. In this line of work it always pays to seize a moment, you never know what's around the corner.'

'The news?'

'Yes, of course. The mission was a resounding success. Erikson's operation has ground to a halt, and for good measure his base was totally annihilated. As for you, the price on your head is null and void, there's nothing left to underwrite it.'

'That's a relief. So, just to make sure, I'm totally off the hook, and no-one's going to chase me half way around the country trying to kill me.'

'Almost.'

'What do you mean "almost"? It either is or it isn't,' replied John in exasperation.

'It's nothing to worry about, not for a man with your skills, but they'll probably be an ex-employee who'll have taken it personally that you've scuppered their livelihood. They'll find you and try to torture, or kill you – it varies, revenge is a funny old thing – but once you've dealt with that, you'll be fine.'

'Great, I've got one hacked off nut-job to be dealing with. It's not Preston is it? Please tell me it's not Preston.'

'Preston?'

'You know- that mobile concrete bunker with the blonde buzz-cut that we left you with.'

'Oh him,' Gordon shook his head. 'Quite an unreasonable chap, he wouldn't see sense so I had to strangle him with a roll of Sellotape.'

'Came to a sticky end then?'

'Not exactly, he was very persistent, absolutely refused to die. To be honest I thought my time was up, and then the damnedest thing happened. Erikson had a robot rifle hidden in his office and the next thing I know, there's a red dot trying to lock target on us. I managed to keep Mr Preston still for a few seconds and that was that. If I didn't know better I'd say something was controlling it.'

'Technology eh?' said John, not letting on. Not once had Gordon mentioned Midas, and John hadn't forgotten the terms of their détente that day in the borrowed luxury bungalow. They might be brothers in arms, and obviously Marsden would vouch for Gordon, but for John, the mutual distrust still had some mileage. 'Maybe Erikson had it on some sort of automatic intruder alert or something, and what with everything that was going on…who knows.'

'Yes, who knows?'

'How the bloody hell did you get out?' asked John, deliberately moving the subject on.

'As Mr Preston wouldn't tell me where the secret exit was, it was a tad tricky. The problem with those older lairs is that when they change hands, they keep being modified, and for the life of me I couldn't make head or tail of the floor plan. As luck would have it there was a rather agitated octopus trying to get out through a grill in the aquarium, and that gave me an idea. I had one charge left, went for a swim, blew out the back wall, and as I suspected there was the shark tank. They used to be standard fixtures, but they fell out of fashion and tended to be bricked up. It was a bit Damien Hirst, poor things hadn't been fed in a while, but the tanks are always fed by a seawater inlet. A couple of gulps of air from the aquarium oxygenator, and when the whole place went up, I was swept out at the front of a mini tsunami. Next thing I know I was washed up near Beachy Head with an octopus for a swimming cap.'

'Well you did say that you'd come up with a last minute cunning plan. What about Peartree? Do you know if he's alright?'

'He's in hospital at the moment, the doctors say he'll make a full recovery.'

'Shot?'

'No, nothing like that. You see, when I set my diversions, I always make sure I blow up the gents first, for maximum inconvenience you understand. Peartree got into the sewer system through an exposed soil pipe and escaped that way. He's in quarantine at the moment.'

'Poor sod, God knows what he picked up. I guess the doctors know best though.'

'He hasn't *caught anything,*' Gordon clarified, 'the man's as fit as a butcher's dog. It's the smell. It'll be at least another week before he's allowed out. Anyway, enough questions, let's get down to business shall we?' and with that Gordon reached into his inside pocket and withdrew a small data card.

'Midas?' asked John.

Gordon nodded. 'I know how much trouble this has caused you, so I thought that you should do the honours.' He took out a small jar from another pocket. 'Hydrochloric acid, I think you'll agree that it's the right thing to do.'

John took the jar, and carefully unscrewed the lid, making sure not to spill any of the contents.

Gordon casually flicked Midas as if he were flipping a coin, not seeming to care where it landed.

John dropped the card into the jar, watching as bubbles formed on its surface while the acid relentlessly ate away at its structure so that it soon resembled a soluble aspirin. He held it up so that they could both see in detail what was happening, but it wasn't the acid bath that John was paying attention to, it was Gordon, whose expression was bordering on disinterest. At that moment John knew that everything was not as it seemed, and that his suspicions were closer to the truth than he would have liked.

'That's long overdue,' said Gordon. 'Right, I think we're done here.'

'Yeah, I think we are.'

Neither of them moved. The cumulus clouds slowly started

to join together, obscuring the blue sky, relegating the sun to a hazy disc.

John considered his options. He could walk away now and try to return to normal, but he was fooling himself. Midas knew who he was.

'Where is it?' John asked.

'Not with you old man, where's what?'

'Midas.'

'It's in the jar.'

John steeled himself as he again held the jar up to the light.

'That's not it. You're good at what you do, I'll give you that, but your poker face needs work. If anyone asks you what's happened to Midas, you'll swear, hand on heart that I dissolved it, knowing that I'll confirm the story. That leaves you clear to do whatever you want with it.'

'You really are an interesting fellow, but I don't know where you've got this idea from. The endgame was always to destroy it. I simply thought that after all your efforts you'd like to be a part of it.'

'We could have done this at the bungalow, but no, we're here. It's not for the view is it? I bet this is one of the few places in Smallmansea that's got a surveillance camera,' said John, looking back at the coastguard station. 'If one of those laid off head cases gets one over on me, you'll need a backup excuse.'

'Are you feeling alright? A knock on the head can confuse people you know.'

'The only way people like you survive in this line of work is by using people like me, and you've been doing that since that "rescue" from Erikson. You weren't worried about what I could tell him about the Society, you thought I might change sides and help him find it. Once you had it you needed to run Crickwell's routine on the off chance that it might actually do what was promised, blowing things up after all these years hasn't been doing the job has it? And then there was that whole thing about the self-destruct. I reckon you couldn't resist the big statement of bombing the crap out of Erikson's gaffe so I bet you looked for it and rigged up a remote trigger. All that explosive, waiting to go up, can't be wasted can it? But then you had to get me and Marsden out of the way first so that you could get Midas back. Twenty minutes, that was a bit too neat. Come on, where is it?'

Gordon took Midas from his shirt pocket, handling it as if it was the most precious thing on the planet. Further denial would only lead to escalation.

'How much do you want?'

'It's not about money.' John held up the jar. 'Let's do it properly this time.'

'No.'

'You haven't got a choice.'

It was a standoff. John was playing his reputation card as the 'Scourge of Victoria' to the hilt.

Gordon was calculating whether it would be best to negotiate, or to bring Cranston down.

On the distant horizon, dark clouds gathered.

'Why do you want to destroy it?' Gordon asked.

'Why do you want to keep it?' John countered.

'You freelancers never look further than your noses. You've no idea the number of innocent people that have died because of this, but look at what we've done. We achieved in one day something that I've been trying to do for years. With this I can bring them all down at a stroke. It's time to balance the books, but I warn you now, stand in my way and you'll regret it.'

'Why go it alone? Why not let the Society help you?'

'The Society's been compromised. I'm the only person I can trust.'

'And you think you can trust Midas?'

'What do you mean?'

'The bloody thing's evil.'

'Really - I've never heard anything so ridiculous.'

'All that effort, all those years to create an A.I, and yet everyone kept coming back to connecting a human brain. Then all of a sudden, Czeckovsky, who's at death's door, comes up with the answer. I don't think so; her artificial intelligence thing was only good enough for what she wanted. She had more urgent things to sort out, like building a virtual warehouse with this nano-tech and quantum drive stuff.'

'And what was she planning on putting in this "warehouse"?' asked Gordon cynically.

'Herself, she was hedging her bets. Whatever happened she was determined to live on, one way or another. She didn't have to go the full A.I, because most of it would be her anyway. I'm telling you, that things got some of her in it. It's half-baked and bloody dangerous.'

Gordon laughed. 'I see you've been doing your homework but I'm afraid you've put two and two together and got five. I admire your concern and imagination, but you don't need to worry, it's in safe hands. I think you should take a break though, it's a stressful business saving the world,' and with that he got up to leave.

'Me and Midas had a little chat,' said John.

Gordon stopped in his tracks.

John continued. 'It was very keen to finish its interface with Czeckovsky.'

Gordon was like a statue, his clenched fist enclosing the Midas device as the veins on the back of his hands stood proud and pulsated. He turned, a gun raised and pointed at John's heart.

'You're in danger of becoming a liability. A word of advice, you should think about a long holiday rather than persisting with these lies.'

'You don't have to believe me, ask Marsden, she was there. You going to warn her off as well? Good luck with that.'

A small dog ran up the hill, approached John hoping for a snack, and then went to Gordon. He could see its owners in the distance. He put the weapon away and rubbed the dogs chest as it revelled in its new friend, before running back to its approaching owners, who had its favourite toy.

'Good morning,' they greeted.

'Good morning,' John and Gordon reciprocated in unison.

They watched as the dog walkers and their energetic companion grew smaller in the distance, and then they looked at each other.

'Well?' said John.

The moment had passed.

Gordon resumed his seat on the bench, leaning forward, his elbows on his thighs as he held Midas in front of him.

'What do I have to do to finish with that bitch?' he muttered to himself rhetorically.

'I take it you've got history then?' asked John.

'You ask a lot of questions.'

'It's not my fault; you've got all the stories.'

Gordon sat back, watching the dark dragon's claws as they formed overhead. 'Very well. I suppose Czeckovsky could best be described as my arch enemy.'

'Like Moriarty or Lex Luthor?'

'If you like. Over the years I chased her all over the planet, I thought I'd killed her twice and I've lost count of how many times I've left her for dead. She was a chameleon, sometimes working freelance for the highest bidder, or hiding in plain sight in government or academic institutions, whatever suited her plan.'

'Which was?'

'Global domination, what else? She once promised that she'd see me sent to Hell before she died. They all say that, but with this,' he turned the card over in his fingers, 'if even a fraction of her essence is in this and it gets out, she'll get her wish, because it'll be Hell on Earth.'

'You knew this could happen?'

'I thought about it, but it didn't seem possible, the technology wasn't there. I destroyed enough of her wretched experiments, and nothing was like this, nothing this…small. I wouldn't have put it past her to have the idea, but it was the stuff of science fiction. Now it looks like it might not be.'

'Where's your beef with Erikson fit into all this?'

'He was fresh out of university and was recruited by Czeckovsky. We'd tracked them down to an abandoned submarine pen. They were going to launch a series of warheads containing a genetically engineered plague. I disarmed all the missiles bar one, but by the time I got to the final one, my partner had been captured. Erikson had started the ignition sequence and rigged her up with a prototype Wet Interface to the launch controls. I had a choice, save a million civilians, or Agent Richmond. I tried to do both. She didn't make it.'

'I'm sorry.'

Gordon fiddled with Midas. 'Twenty-five years I've been looking for this, twenty five years, and for what? We're in danger of losing the war, but no one will tell you that. This was going to be the game changer.' Gordon held Midas over the jar, hesitated slightly and then pulled back. 'I'm running out of time, there must be a way around this.'

'There's only one way to find out if I'm right, and if it turns out I am, then we're all buggered. Look, you've won the day. Erikson's had it and we saved Maria. What more do you want?'

'Maria?'

'The Titan girl, we got her out.'

'Got her out…' Gordon repeated in a quiet tone. There was a hint of a smile on his stern visage. 'Saved the damsel as well. Not a bad day's work then.'

'Let's keep it that way. This thing's got to stop here; otherwise it'll go round again and again and again. You won't be able to save all the Maria's, so how many do you want to sacrifice to this war of yours? What are you going to do when it's Marsden instead of Agent Richmond? Can't you see? It *wants* you to try and find a way to use it. Even from six foot under Czeckovsky's trying to play you, but you don't need it.'

Gordon held Midas over the acid jar again. Several interminable seconds past.

He let go. Corrosive bubbles formed on its surface, its size diminishing amongst the effervescence.

'There'll be other ways to win,' said Gordon, with absolute certainty.

In the distance sun rays punched their way through the clouds. Cathedral like spotlights danced across the waves.

'For the record,' said Gordon, 'I didn't have a remote trigger and I did clog up the self-destruct mechanism. I told you twenty minutes because I wanted you and Marsden to believe you had a chance of getting out, and yes, I did want you out of the way.'

'Chance?' said John, being a bit slow on the uptake.

'The thing with a soggy sock delay is that you never know how long it will last. It could be five minutes, it could be thirty. Twenty seemed about right.'

'We could have gone up in smoke. What kind of plan was that?'

'One without any other options,' said Gordon matter of factly. 'The job would be very dull if everything was predictable.'

'There's never a dull moment around you, I'll give you that.'

'Quite - I'm sorry about the gun earlier, I don't know what came over me, it's dashed bad manners. My apologies.'

'Don't worry about it, I'm getting used to it, besides, its a dangerous business saving the world.'

'Yes...it is.'

The two of them sat on the bench in companionable silence, two strangers joined by a shared experience.

'Anything planned for the weekend?' Gordon asked, as if the previous conversations had never taken place, because for all intents and purposes, they hadn't.

'Nothing much,' John shrugged. 'Bit of gardening, watch some telly; wait in for a fed-up assassin. What about you?'

'I'm taking a speedboat from Royalty Harbour to Calais, then driving down to Paris for what promises to be an excellent evening with Ms Pushupanova. I think dinner in the Eiffel Tower and a private boat down the Seine might be in order; we'll see how it goes.'

'Pushupanova? That knife waving amazon psychopath. Are you mad?'

'Please, that's no way to talk about a lady.'

'She punched you in the nuts and pinned me to the wall with a machete. You said she was a "homicidal harpy".'

Gordon looked slightly confused. 'Only when she's on duty. She's between jobs this weekend, so she asked me over.'

John shook his head, 'I really don't get you people.'

'My dear chap, if a fine lady requests the pleasure of your company, then only a fool says "No".' Gordon checked his watch.

'I must be going, have to catch the tide. By the way, there's two hundred thousand in a swiss bank account,' he handed over an envelope, 'all the details are in there.'

'How much?!'

'I know it's less than the going rate for global salvation, but technically you're not on the payroll. I hedged some money on Brassica stock, I had a feeling they might bounce around now. Don't spend it all at once. Toodle pip!'

Slightly stunned, John relaxed back into the bench. The sky was clearing; the threatening storm had come to nothing and was moving on. He couldn't see a dragon though; it looked more like a kangaroo. He'd take that as a good sign, he'd never been stalked by Skippy.

The only thing he had to worry about now was a disgruntled ex-employee of Erikson's. At least it put things in perspective. He'd never again complain about waiting in the Post Office queue behind someone having a month's worth of lottery tickets checked.

36 / *The Watchtower*

On his return to the bungalow John was greeted by the sight of a familiar, light metallic green, Citroen SM. It was a gorgeous thing. For a moment he indulged himself, admiring the sleek lines, looking enviously through the window at the perfectly contrasting upholstered charcoal black hide, and the distinctive Maserati gear lever gate. One day he told himself.

The lock on the front door of the bungalow hadn't been forced, but he still entered with some caution. As he poked his head into the lounge, as he expected, and with some relief, it was Marsden, lounging in the armchair, sipping a cup of tea.

'I wondered how long you'd be,' she said. 'I brewed a pot, I hope you don't mind?'

'No it's fine,' said John keeping his distance. 'You're not here to hit me again are you? I can explain. I didn't get much of a chance last time.'

'Don't worry, it was a reflex action. These things happen, although not too often I hope.'

'Exceptional circumstances only, I promise, and next time, not that I'm saying they'll be a next time, I'll use a stuntman. So, to what do I owe the pleasure?' John asked, as he took a seat on the adjacent sofa, confident that retribution, albeit temporarily, wasn't on the agenda.

'The Brigadier's got me on light duties. He asked me to come round and tie up some loose ends.' She turned her face to show the bruising around her eye. ' How's it looking?'

'Like you've gone a couple of rounds with Ali.'

'You're supposed to say "You look fine".'

'You look fine. How's that?'

'It'll do, you're a bit rough round the edges though.'

'Thanks. Any news on Maria?'

'She's doing well. We found her in a bank giving out independent financial advice. No one queried it; they all thought she'd been sent down by head office. We got to her just in time; otherwise they might've kept her. We sneaked her out while someone was depositing their life savings in small change. She's joined us and taken over Sir Rotherfield's job, she's brilliant at it.'

'Joined? You lot don't hang about. I bet that put Jenkins nose out of joint.'

'Actually he's never been happier. He's moved to Department S to work on our new armoured stealth Bentley. You'll also be glad to know that Peartree and Gordon got out okay. Gordon's making arrangements to put Midas beyond reach, so you won't have to worry about that anymore.'

'Good old reliable Gordon.'

'Yes, it's good to have him back, we've all missed him. Anyway, I've got to sort out all this stuff; you know how Dick loves his paperwork.'

Marsden reached down to the side of the armchair, picked up a brown paper package tied with string, and passed it to over.

As he removed the wrapping a fragment of a familiar woollen weave came into view. 'It's my tweed! I'd written this off...' then it hit him. 'What is that smell?'

'The boys *accidentally* found a card from some girl called Molly, with a note for you to ring her about her crabs,' said Marsden, frowning. 'They're very thorough, nothing could have survived.'

'It's not what you think; it's to do with...'

'You don't have to explain to me,' she interrupted. 'What you get up to behind closed doors is none of my business. Speaking of which, there's a letter of introduction in the pocket, it's for some online media mogul. It's following up on something

Ashcombe offered before he stitched you up. The Brigadier hates unfinished business.'

'How does he know this stuff?'

'I don't know, that's why he's in charge. He said it's a little thank you to help your cover as a gardener,' said Marsden sceptically. 'And there's this.' She hauled John's rucksack, now stuffed to gills, to the front of the chair, and then heaved it to his feet. 'It's about a hundred grand.' She opened the cover on a folding clipboard and handed it over with a pen. 'Dick says if you can sign there, there and there, and initial there, that'll do it.'

'Hundred grand? I started out with about twenty. What's the catch?'

'You are so suspicious, I can't think why. It's all above board... ish. Someone on the undernet was running a book on how long before you got killed. Dick and the team took a punt on you surviving and got long odds. They borrowed your cash for the stake; they didn't think you'd mind. That's your share of the winnings.'

John signed on the dotted lines. 'Be a bit difficult coming back for my money if I was dead. Unbelievable.' he muttered.

'There's one last thing, and we're all done.'

There was a knock at the front door.

'You expecting anyone?' asked John.

'Why would I want people to think I live here?'

'Excuse me a minute,' said John, and he headed off to the kitchen.

Marsden watched curiously as he walked back past the lounge with a large metal cooking utensil in his hand.

John answered the front door with the large pan held above his head, ready to strike. He was greeted by a startled lady of certain years, very well turned out in her Sunday best, even though it wasn't a Sunday.

'Good afternoon,' she said timidly, 'I didn't interrupt your tea or anything?'

'This?' said John looking up at the weaponised iron pan. 'I'm doing exercises. It's good for the tennis elbow. Is there something I can do for you?'

'Would you like to know God better? Do you not feel the need to embrace God who so lovingly uses his limitless power on our behalf?'

'No.'

She looked slightly and quickly to her left, as if she had a nervous tick. 'God wants to *save* you.'

'That's very nice of him, or her, but as I'm a non-believer there's not much point. If you'll excuse me, I've got some cabbage that needs bothering.'

'God is all around us, with us, *near* to us,' she said, again with a distinctive tic. 'He provided his Word, the Bible, so that we can know him better, and through his teachings know how to live a happy, purposeful life and,' she twitched again, *'HOW TO COPE WITH ANXIETY.'*

'I'm sorry, but you asked for this. You do know that the Bible isn't primary source material; it's all apocryphal, and don't get me started on the gospels…'

John didn't finish his diatribe as from the side of the doorway, a dapper gentleman stepped out into view, his gun firmly pressed into the side of the Jehovah's Witness. He was a dead ringer for James Mason.

'Mr Cranston. What a pleasant surprise, and so good to hear you expressing yourself so distinctly. I had a feeling that if I canvassed the area our paths would cross. It seems that God does indeed move in mysterious ways. Now, if you would put the frying pan down, we have unfinished business.'

'No we don't.'

'Yes we do.'

'No, really, we're all done.'

'There's no use in stalling, put the frying pan down.'

'It's a wok actually.'

'A what?'

'A wok.'

'I see, well put the *wok* down,' said Mr Black with a hint of frustration in his voice, 'or the Jehovah Witness here will be meeting her maker.'

'What!' screamed the Witness.'

'Wok!' shouted Mr Black, and in that exact moment of split second distraction, his skull left a dent in the correctly identified heavy duty Chinese skillet. He collapsed on the doorstep.

For good measure, the Jehovah's Witness, with a cry of 'Heathen!' landed the pointed toe of her shoe in Mr Black's left testicle. An involuntary groan slipped from his semi-conscious lips.

She turned to John and smiled sweetly. 'Watchtower?'

'Just this once.'

*****

As John dragged Mr Black into the hallway, Marsden stood by the kitchen and applauded.

'When I said "Could you give me a hand", that wasn't what I had in mind,' said John.

'I didn't want to get in the way, watching you work is very educational,' replied Marsden.

'Thanks, I'll take that as a compliment.'

'If it helps,' said Marsden as she rummaged in her handbag to bring out a bundle of robust, plastic cable ties. 'A girl should never leave home without them.'

Mr Black was bound hand and foot, and then hand and feet were bound to each other behind his back until he looked like a joint, oven-ready for Christmas. 'Cranston,' he said, still slightly slurred as he came to, 'you're making a big mistake.'

'No I'm not,' John replied.

'This isn't over. I will find you...' Mr Black then proceeded to list everything that he was going to do to John and those close to him.

John was half-listening as he tried to remember if he had seen any gaffer tape anywhere in the bungalow.

Marsden checked her pen as a small amount of fluid jetted out of the nib. She stuck it in the side of Mr Black's neck.

'He went on a bit didn't he?' said John. 'Especially after he was saying that you couldn't be trusted.'

'I wouldn't worry about it,' said Marsden. 'Its standard practice - try and set your enemies against each other. The rest is pretty much a contractual obligation. They can't help themselves.'

'Fine, but what do I do with him now?'

'Don't worry about that, I've had a crew on standby. I sent them a message while you were debating God and stuff. They won't be long.'

'You knew he was turning up and you didn't warn me? Thanks a bunch.'

'I didn't know it would be him, and it could have been tomorrow for all I knew, but as I was coming round, I thought, just in case.' She looked down disdainfully at the unconscious Mr Black. 'They do take up a lot of room.' There was a knock at the door. 'That'll be them, excuse me.'

A large portly gentleman in distressed overalls, flat cap and clipboard presented his credentials. 'Ms Marsden?'

'Yes.'

'WE'RE HERE TO DELIVER YOUR FRIDGE FREEZER. May I?' indicated Flat Cap, with a nod of his head at the threshold.

'Of course,' said Marsden, inviting him in. 'IT NEEDS TO GO THROUGH THERE.'

'Sorry about this,' said Flat Cap, 'it's the neighbours you see, they get a bit suspicious like when we start dragging bodies around. So what we'll do, we'll bring it in, load the package, and if anyone asks, we'll say we're taking the old one away.'

'Where's Albert and the ambulance?' asked Marsden.

'Sorry, Albert had to book it out last minute for a wedding.'

'A wedding?'

'Yeah, it's his old man, he's getting married again. All a bit sudden but I suppose at ninety-eight you don't want to waste time do you? I've not met her but apparently his wife to be is twenty-one and very well upholstered, if you get my drift. Personally I don't know what she sees in the rich old bugger, but it takes all sorts don't it? So Albert's on stand-by with the adrenalin in case his dad's "I do's" do for him.'

'Poor old Albert,' Marsden mused. 'It'd be unlucky if he's dad went straight from wedding vows to last rites.'

'Albert's got it covered,' said Flat Cap. 'He's done one of those buy one, get one free deals with the vicar. Fingers crossed he won't need it.'

'Fingers crossed,' Marsden repeated. She nudged Mr Black with her toe. 'Reckon you can handle that?'

'What have we got 'ere then?' Flat Cap asked himself. 'Upmarket henchman, Russian vintage I reckon, had some bodywork done. No problem.'

He put his fingers in his mouth and let out a shrill whistle. Two strapping young lads manhandled a chest- freezer into the bungalow and placed it in the passage adjacent to the prone Mr Black.

'Now lads, you see that, that is your proper presentation,' lectured Flat Cap as he turned to Marsden. 'Not wishing to embarrass you Ms, but people haven't got a clue how to package stuff these days, and then they wonder why it gets damaged in transit. Course, when I see it done right, I've gotta point it out. Take a look lads – this is class. No bits flopping about, no chance of him getting loose, and he's out like a light.'

'Its standard – nothing special,' said Marsden.

'Ah – you say that 'cause you're a professional. You know what, the other day we had someone wrapped head to foot in cling film. Cling film! I mean, I'm all for innovation but you've got to draw a line, ain't ya? It takes bleedin' ages to get 'em unwrapped. We had one, and by the time we got round to 'em, they'd suffocated. Wouldn't have been so bad if they hadn't been wanted for questioning, know what I mean?'

'Terrible,' said Marsden, 'what a waste of plastic.' She peered over the edge of Flat Cap's clipboard. 'Paperwork?'

'Yeah, right, hold on a mo, I've got most of it done already. Here we are -*does the package have a designation?*'

'Major General Vladimir Orimov,' said Marsden.

Flat Cap repeated the words silently until he got to the 'O' in Orimov.

'Did you say "Orimov", as in the notorious ex-KGB, ex SPUD, and go-to fixer for megalomaniacs, also known as Mr Black?'

'That's him,' confirmed Marsden. 'There's no problem is there?'

'No, no – bleedin' 'ell – I never thought I'd see the day. You're a bloody marvel Ms – let me shake your hand.'

'It wasn't me,' said Marsden, 'it was Mr Cranston over there.'

Flat Cap looked over at John, putting his head to one side, and then another, as if the change in angle would alter his perception. 'Blow me down with a feather, if it ain't the Scourge of Victoria himself. You know what; me and my missus got a new three piece 'cause of you.'

'Sorry,' said John.

'There's no need to apologise,' said Flat Cap slapping John on the shoulder in friendly comradery. 'The lads had a sweepstake on how long you'd last- most of 'em reckoned you wouldn't get out of London, but I knew different, I had you down for going the distance. Like I said to the missus, anyone who can take on Orimov and half the metropolitan police on London Bridge, escape with a forward two and a half somersaults dive, in the pike position mind, into the Thames, and then hitch a lift on a passing motorboat, water-skiing on his feet all the way to Putney, nice touch by the way, while picking up a trout on the way for lunch, he's got to be in with a shout hasn't he?'

'It wasn't exactly like that.'

'You don't have to be modest with me Mr Cranston. Ere, have a look at this,' said Flat Cap getting out his phone and swiping through the photographs. 'There you go, all leather, hand stitched and stretched on the thighs of civil engineers. And get this, it's fully kitted out with wi-fi, bluetooth, and a built in high speed router with ten, one hundred megabit ethernet ports for your networking and internet access.'

'Why?'

'I like leather,' said Flat Cap matter of factly.

There was a 'dongly-dongly' sound from Flat Cap's pocket. 'That'll be my next appointment; I've got a cluster of Black Widows to pick up. Why they can't use the one- I don't know. Ms Marsden, Mr Cranston it's been a pleasure. Shall I put this on account Ms?'

'That'll be fine,' Marsden confirmed, 'and please let Albert know that I'll be in touch to discuss a discount for premium storage.'

'Right you are Ms. I'm sure that won't be a problem, what with you being one of our best customers an' all.'

Flat Cap checked that Mr Black had been attached to the oxygen bottle, and when satisfied, shook both their hands and was off, with the fridge freezer manhandled by his helpers.

John followed them to the door and watched as the removal van pulled away. Coming back into the hallway he saw Marsden sitting on the stairs, her head between her knees. She seemed to be folded in half. 'You alright,' he enquired?

'Fine, I'm stretching the back a bit. I landed a bit awkward in the fight with that peroxide tank. Nothing a few days R and R won't fix.'

'Got anywhere nice in mind?' John asked before remembering that was a typical question that would get short shrift. 'Sorry – I forgot. That'll be top secret.'

'If you must know it's the Aeolian Islands, lovely, quiet and unpretentious,' replied Marsden. 'I'm overdue for my honeymoon; it got postponed, what with all this Midas stuff. I'm going to make up for it though. I've booked us into the same hotel where we met, and it's all a surprise. She's going to love it.' Marsden looked at John quizzically, 'Something wrong?'

'I'm not used to you sharing in a kind of general conversation way. You didn't get knocked on the head by any chance when we were escaping?'

'Didn't I say? You're idle chat rating has been upgraded.'

'My idle chat rating? I should've guessed. You know, I reckon a night out down the pub with you lot would be an absolute riot.

I can see it now.' He turned to one side and addressed an invisible compatriot. 'Did you watch the match last night?' He then turned to face where he had been. 'That's on a need to know basis.'

'You can laugh, some days I can't move without tripping up over a double or triple agent, and sometimes I don't know until it's too late. You'd think people would stick to one side, and why can't they wear badges? As for you, ever since I met you on the pier you've been a swine to work out. I'm still not sure about your gardening pervert cover story.'

'It's not a cover story, and I'm not a pervert- how many more times?'

'Crabs?'

'I give up.'

'Luckily for you Maria told me everything, so I've changed my mind about you- a bit.'

'That's progress I suppose. I'm glad she's alright.'

'She wouldn't have made it without you.'

'Anyone would've done the same if they'd seen her connected to that thing.'

'You'd be surprised at how many people I've met who would've walked away.'

'If they're the sort of people you're mixing with, maybe you're in the wrong job.'

Marsden pondered, 'Occasionally you do meet people without an agenda, who do things because it's right. Thing is, they don't last long. How is it you're still alive?'

'Clean living, monkey gland injections, and a little sprinkling of luck.'

'I should've guessed,' said Marsden with a hint of sarcasm. 'You know, there's something that's been bothering me, and if you don't give me a straight answer, I'm going to give you a matching black eye.'

'As you're asking so nicely, fire away.'

'You came back for me when you didn't have to. Why?'

'Why wouldn't I? That's what friends do in my book.'

'Friends?'

'Well, not *friend* friends obviously, what with you being married and everything. I was thinking more not enemies. Of course, if you weren't married, it wouldn't have made any difference, if you know what I mean. Look, we're all on the same team, you would have done the same for me.'

Marsden hung her head, considering her reply. 'If it had been the other way round, I might have left you there.'

'Lucky for me I wasn't down there then. Any particular reason, or was it just something I said?'

'I was under orders to take you out if I'd thought you'd defected to Erikson.'

'Do you think I'm working for him?' said John as he looked towards the abandoned wok. He had seen what she was capable of.

'No,' she said nonchalantly with a slight wrinkle of her nose. 'If I was going to, I wouldn't have bothered with all this paperwork, and besides, no double agent worth their salt would have bothered with a cover as a gardener - come on.'

'The fact I'm actually a gardener had nothing to do with it then?'

Marsden raised a sceptical eyebrow and deliberately checked her watch. 'Oh my, is that the time? I really have to be getting away before queen and country insists that it needs me again. There's still one thing before I go though.'

'It's the glasses. Hold on, I've put them down somewhere.'

'That's not it.'

She stepped closer, looking at him intensely.

John had seen that look before when Marsden had taken on Preston. It was a look of single minded determination.

'I thought we agreed I wasn't working for Erikson.'

'It's got nothing to do with that,' she replied casually.

'You've still got the hump about the church? Give me a break. You'd passed out and I tried to bring you round in the graveyard by…' he stopped. No matter how he described it, the hole kept getting deeper. 'You secret agents can really bear a grudge, you know that?'

Marsden took another step closer.

John found himself with his back to the wall. 'Okay, let's get this over with,' he said with reluctant acceptance.

Marsden moved within strategic kneeing distance, put her hands around John's neck, and kissed him full on the lips, a passionate kiss worthy of any Hollywood big screen romance.

She finished slowly. 'Maria says "Thank you." '

John was confused. This was Marsden, the Preston basher. Was it an evil twin toying with him, or maybe there was a giant body snatching foaming sultana under the stairs - in a bungalow?

The pilot of reason wrestled with the joystick of incredulity, narrowly regaining control as the airplane of normal grazed the chasm of gobsmacked.

'Nothing to say?' said Marsden with a slight mischievous hint.

'Errm…she's welcome,' John squeaked. 'Do I have to sign for that?'

'Shut up. And this,' she kissed him gently on the cheek, 'is from me. When I was down that pit, I thought I'd had it, and then you came back. Thank you.'

'Does this mean I can drive the Citroen?' said John, his voice almost finding its normal register.

Marsden smiled. 'I'll never be that grateful.'

She removed her hands from around his neck, her demeanour now as if all she had done was deliver a letter. 'I've got a better idea, rather than lusting after my car, why don't you treat your girlfriend to an exotic holiday somewhere on the other side of the world?'

'I like the sentiment, but it's just me at the moment.'

'Oh – I'm sorry,' said Marsden innocently, 'have you and Alice split up?'

'How do you know about Alice?'

She reached into her handbag and pulled out the sedation biro. 'Funny thing with these, sometimes people talk in their sleep, you especially.' She put on her coat and opened the front door. 'For someone who's not your girlfriend, you've got a lot to say about her.'

'It's not like that,' John insisted.

'Don't worry, your secret's safe with me. It's what I do.' She was on the verge of walking out the door, but hesitated for a moment. 'I've got to ask, are you really a gardener?'

'Yes.'

'And what did you do before that?'

'That's classified.'

'Touché,' she said approvingly, 'you're learning. Well it's been,' she searched for the right word, 'interesting. I'll see you around some time.'

'Don't take this personally, but I hope not.'

'Do you always have to have the last word?'

'Not always.'

She took a few steps towards the Citroen, paused, and said her parting piece.

'John, don't forget to call Alice.'

As she walked back to her car there was a skip in her step as she revelled in the absence of a John Cranston riposte.

*****

The Citroen pulled away into the distance and John felt a strange mixture of relief tinged with disappointment. It had been a roller coaster ride, and at times, he had simply felt...alive. He could understand how Gordon, despite his advancing years, refused to stop. He could see how it could become addictive, but like all addictions, it had a downside, with this one it was the risk of death. That was an occupational hazard too far for him.

It was time to get back to normal and put recent events down to experience. He remembered the promise that he had made to

Alice. He had been putting it off, uncertain as to when would be the right time. Now he had no excuse.

He rang the office, no answer. Obviously Alice was still abroad, or had Gordon got it wrong and some idiot, following Mr Black's example, got to her? He rang her mobile phone, cursing himself for not doing it sooner.

'Come on, pick up...come on.'

'Hello?' a familiar voice answered.

'Hi Alice, it's John.'

'John, oh what a relief. Are you alright?'

'I'm fine...fine. It's been a bit hectic, but it's all sorted now. Are you okay?'

'Yes, why wouldn't I be?'

'Oh it's nothing, just checking, you know. You still at your secret hideaway?'

'Yes, I thought it best to stay out of the way, but I was getting a bit worried when I didn't hear from you.'

'I'm sorry about that, things took a bit longer than I thought. Anyway I'm glad you're okay.' He relaxed, but what to say now? He was stuck for small talk. Would saying, 'I've been working with a secret organisation to help save the world' do? Probably not. 'When were you planning on coming back?' he asked awkwardly.

There was a long pause. 'I was thinking of staying out here for a bit longer.'

'Oh, okay....you take it easy then and I'll see you in the office... whenever,' he said, trying his best to sound upbeat.

'John, I was thinking.'

'Steady on,' he lamely joked.

'Why don't you,' Alice took a deep breath, 'come out and join me?' The banks had been breached and she couldn't stop as the words tumbled out. 'The business can look after itself for a while and it's been ages since you had some time off and the break would do you good and the villa's massive and I'm rattling around here on my own and...' she broke off, hesitating to go further, but she was too far gone now. She took another breath. 'It would be good if you were here. Picasso can wait.'

There, she had done it. The line was silent. She chastised herself. Stupid, stupid, stupid! He would make some excuse in that way of his which would let her down ever so gently, and then things would never be the same between them again.

John was thinking about what Gordon had said. 'Only a fool...'

'Alice, could you pick me up from the airport?'

'Sorry?'

'Could you pick me up from airport please? I'm getting the next flight out.'

'Of course I will!' the joy and relief in Alice's voice was palpable. 'And John...'

'Yes?'

'It's about time.'

37 / Loose Ends

Robert Chantry looked up at the clock and was again disappointed at how slow time seemed to be moving. Einstein said something about time being relative, but what it had to do with Uncle Frank was anyone's guess.

Einstein also said something about time changing as a body neared the speed of light, and that if you crash landed in a spaceship that had been travelling that fast, back on Earth, chances are that the planet would be ruled by a bunch of chimpanzees. No change there then.

Where Einstein had gone wrong was rather than arriving at his conclusions through a series of thought experiments, all he'd had to do was spend some time in the secretary's office of Admiral Courthope. There he would have seen, first-hand, Time dragging its heels as if it were on a Valium drip.

'Mr Chantry. The Admiral will see you now,' said the secretary.

The Admiral sat at his desk, which apart from a single buff file, was clear of any office detritus. A clear desk policy was always easier when you had staff to deal with the administration of bureaucracy. His face was obscured by a newspaper. It was the latest copy of the Smallmansea Observer.

'Mr Chantry, don't take a seat, this won't take long.'

Robert looked at the headline; the Admiral had it on display for a reason. It read:

VICAR IN END OF DAYS SHOCK!

He knew what was coming next.

'Amazing what you can glean from the local press,' said the Admiral. 'I find the letter pages a useful way to take the pulse of Little England. One correspondent is complaining about a traffic delay at the Crowside roundabout, wherever that is, of five minutes. What do you make of it Chunty?'

'They don't know they're born Admiral, and its Chantry by the way.'

The Admiral folded the paper, put it down on his desk, and rotated it so that the front page could be seen by Robert.

'The thing about intelligence is that I expect to be informed about things that other people aren't privileged to.' The Admiral pointed at the headline. 'That's an interesting article. A church in Smallmansea has burnt down and the vicar blamed it on an incursion of demons from the "Pits of Hell". Apparently they sprung forth from the crypt as it spewed Hellfire, and then proceeded to copulate in the churchyard.' He picked up the file, 'This is your latest draft report which I assume you were going to deliver. It refers to a church fire in Smallmansea. It seems you've been scooped.'

'It's a work in progress.'

'It's a work of fiction. I set up the Why files to investigate things that would normally slip under the radar. All I've seen is a cock and bull hypothesis about an underground war between two unidentified factions. The only details so far are a possible cypher involving vampire snails and something called the Double-Double. You've then, amazingly, linked these to local reports, by the county dipsomaniac no less, of the Little Green Man of Pevensey levels, who, as it happens, was being chased by a giant, syphilitic Smurf. This better be good Chounty.'

'It's...,' Robert held back from correcting the Admiral, why bother? 'That's the whole point, even though the events seem random, they're connected. Everywhere the same things come up – this colour coding obsession by one side for instance. Then there's the church in Smallmansea which burnt down, and the supposed gas explosion at a butchers in Little Biglington. They're both linked to an old smugglers network and both happened at the same time. There's something going on and I think it's a potential threat to our national security.'

'I see, and this insight merited a visit to Smallmansea to gather this gem of intelligence,' said the Admiral as he read Robert's notes in the buff folder aloud. *Interviewed vicar of Smallmansea church, added third protagonist (demon) to his statement. Claims she tried to sell him an endowment mortgage.'*

'Well he did say it was the Devil's work.'

'Very droll, maybe you'll find this equally amusing. As of now the Why Files are now the ex-files, and you Mr Chenty have been reassigned. This is your new case.' The Admiral took a file labelled Top Secret – Eyes Only, from his top drawer, and placed it on the desk. 'Kurt Erikson, ex-CEO of the Brassica Corporation. Found dead in the swimming pool of his penthouse suite. As far as the shareholders are concerned it was an unfortunate heart attack. We believe he was assassinated.'

Robert picked up the file and looked at the photographs of the crime scene. 'Heart attack - fair enough. I don't think the arrow in the chest helped though.'

'That's classified,' said the Admiral as he put a small pewter gaming token in the shape of a hat on the desk. 'You know what this means?'

'The Dark Accountant's back in business, but that would mean that he's as old as…'

'Yes?'

'As old as my grandfather. It looks like we have a copycat.'

'The minister wants this assassin found. Her Majesty's Government are in the middle of sensitive negotiations with Brassica and we don't need any complications. You are authorised to use whatever means necessary to stop them, is that understood?'

'Yes Admiral.'

'This is a top priority. Don't mess this up Chonkry. Dismissed.'

Robert left the Admiral's office, on his guard about what he had been asked to do. The whole thing smelt worse than an opened past date tin of pilchards. He knew all about Erikson, he had his own secret informants who kept him abreast of things outside his own brief. The obvious question was: what had happened to the maid who found Erikson? Any mention of her was absent from the file, as if her presence at the crime scene hadn't happened.

He opened an encrypted line on his phone. 'Ms Cooden- I have something you might be interested in.'

Admiral Courthope took Robert Chantry's notes and fed them through the volumatic disintegrator concealed behind the decorative wall panelling of his office.

'Mr Teschmacher,' he instructed via the office intercom, 'arrange for everything in Mr Chantry's office to be securely archived.'

'Right away Admiral.'

'And Mr Teschmacher – I seem to recall that the Why Files office was classified as a potential fire hazard during the last inspection.'

'Understood Admiral, we'll be very careful.'

*****

Milligan took his seat on the bench in Victoria Park and watched with some satisfaction as the ducks left the boating pond and headed towards him. They knew the routine. He threw the stale bread crumbs into the quarrelsome throng, fascinated by the literal pecking order.

'Guv'nor, you're eleven o'clock's turned up. I've checked him over,' said Mickey as he handed over a set of brass knuckle dusters.

Milligan weighed them in his hands and nodded approvingly. 'Nice weight, none of your Chinese rubbish. Thanks, don't mind if I do. Mr Smith is it?'

'Smith is fine,' said Martin Ashcombe.

'Well Mr Smith, I understand from my young associate that you've got something which could,' Milligan looked for the phrase, 'what did he say?' he asked Mickey.

'Revolutionise the industry,' said Mickey.

'Yeah, revolutionise the industry,' repeated Mulligan. 'That's a pretty big claim, with a price tag to match. Come on then, out with it, time is money.'

Martin slowly reached into his pocket and removed the small data card that he had liberated from Cranston and Marsden. He held it up. 'Gentlemen, I give you the future!'

Milligan looked at Mickey, and then back at the card. 'Cut the bollocks, I ain't got all day. What's it do?'

'With this, you can access any bank account, anywhere in the world, help yourself, and no-one's going to know how or who did it.'

'Fair enough, you've built yourself a little digital pickpocket. If it's that good, why are you trying to flog it to me?'

'I'm not talking about selling; it's more of a lease arrangement.'

Milligan threw some more bread to the ducks. 'It's lucky for you I'm in a good mood because one thing I can't stand is tyre kickers. Answer the bleedin' question or I'm off.'

'I think you'll find this worth your while. I've made a fair bit off it, but when word gets out I've got it, and it always does, someone else is going to want it, and then it gets awkward. If I sell it to you, do you want to waste your time fighting all the other toe-rags that'll want a piece?'

'Go on.'

'What I'm proposing is a cartel of like-minded business men. I let the cartel have the use of this, in turn, on a prearranged schedule. All I want is five per cent of whatever you make and protection from anyone outside our arrangement. In return you get ongoing maintenance, upgrades, and a guarantee that if anyone from the cartel steals from anyone else, they'll be the first to know. Think of me as an honest broker.'

Milligan scrunched the top of the bread bag closed, much to the disappointment of the ducks. 'Five per cent and we cover your arse?'

'You won't even notice it,' said Martin. 'And you know what, money laundering, thing of the past. I could make your financial records say anything you like. You know it makes sense.'

Milligan stroked his beard as he considered the proposition. 'I think Mr Smith, that in principle, we might have a basis for future negotiations, but words is cheap, I want to see this thing working.' He held out his hand. 'If you don't mind?'

'It's a specialist bit of kit,' said Martin. 'Let me show you.'

'My lad's very handy with this modern stuff. I want to see what he makes of it.'

'Fair enough, be my guest,' and Martin handed it over, unconcerned that this mobster would try and make a run for it. He wasn't dealing with a common thief.

Milligan gave it a cursory examination; some things were getting too small. He flicked it over to Mickey. 'Do me favour, dip into Hammer's bank account and get that fifty grand he owes me.' He smiled knowingly at Martin. 'You like ducks?'

'Only with orange sauce,' replied Martin, trying to bring some levity to the situation.

Milligan's face was humourless. 'Comedian, I see.'

'Guv'nor,' said Mickey, 'you got a minute?'

'Problems?' Martin asked smugly. If they couldn't even fathom the simple workings of Midas, this was going to be too easy.

'Nothing my lad can't handle,' said Milligan. He handed Martin the bread crumb bag, 'Make yourself useful.'

Milligan nestled into the back seat of the Jaguar and Mickey showed him the laptop.

'This is all that's on it,' said Mickey.

It was a video of an avuncular gentleman pushing a wheelbarrow along a paved path bordered by high hedging. He was followed by two golden retrievers as he addressed the camera.

'Hello, and welcome to Gardeners World. I'm just putting the finishing touches to...'

*****

Martin, paralysed from head to toe, was barely able to lift his eyelids such was the potency of the drug, but his mental faculties were unaffected and from inside the boot of the Jaguar he could hear the conversation of the two of them outside.

'What do you want to do with him Guv'?'

'Not sure at the moment. It don't matter what I do, these bloody chancers keep coming out of the woodwork.'

'Do you want me to sort it? There's a lot of work going on Stratford way for the Olympics, swimming pools and stuff.'

'Nah, where there's holes you can bet your life bleedin' Robinson and his trowel monkeys will be all over it.'

Milligan scattered more bread crumbs to the expectant ducks and then upended the bag, shaking it out as the remainder of the broadcast contents encouraged a final feeding frenzy.

Then it came to him, an idea so simple, so audacious, he wondered why it had never occurred to him before.

' 'Ere Mickey, fancy a choc-ice? I've got a little job for you.'

38 / *Epilogue*

In a secret cavern buried deep under the Sussex country-side, amongst the fragments of the Titan intelligence, a single light flickers on a solitary disk drive as nanites, in a subatomic daisy chain, move charged particles along a wire that has been repaired atom by atom.

Can a machine procreate? The primary objective of the Midas device is to preserve itself and when John Cranston, on that fateful morning, plugged it into Erikson's network, as if by some involuntarily reflex, atomic robots were released into the data stream, where they built copies of themselves.

They would have remained dormant, but within one of their number there was carried a thread of the quantum encryption drive. Einstein called it 'spooky action at a distance', but however it works, when Midas was dissolved in the acid bath, some form of communication took place between those quantum entangled particles.

Midas is rebuilding itself, atom by atom, molecule by molecule.

In a virtual deserted wasteland sits a young girl. Her designation is Pandora. She says only one thing, over and over again.

'Where is the Cranston?'

THE END